To Paul

LORD CROFT'S
FALL FROM GRACE

*From Duncan Taylor
writing as Richard Rogers*

RICHARD ROGERS

To order additional copies of this book, contact:
Xlibris Corporation
0-800-644-6988
www.Xlibrispublishing.co.uk
Orders@Xlibrispublishing.co.uk
304140

Apologies

This book is purely fiction and bears no relationship to actual facts or any person present or past. It is entirely composed from the imagination of the author with apologies to the members of the IRA who have followed the terms and conditions of the Good Friday Agreement.

Dedication

Thanks to my wife for the many hours she has been alone and for patiently putting up with my moods and long periods of silence whilst I wrote this and other novels.

Prologue

This is the story of a businessman who rises to the pinnacle of his occupation, receives a knighthood, and finally becomes a Lord of the realm for services to British industry from a grateful government after the completion of a sensitive military contract ahead of time. In due course, Lord Croft, as Chairman of a top 100 company, tires of the boardroom confrontations and seeks more excitement and a challenge far from the squabbles of greedy directors, too fearful of the possibility of failure to diversify from a very profitable and successes with the resulting fall in shareholder dividends. Using his severance package and his generous share options, he buys a castle on the west coast of Ireland, at one time used by a clandestine operation of the War Office during the Second World War, where he sets up his seagoing charter company, using his powerful MTB (motor torpedo boat). Lord Croft finds that business at the newly formed charter company is slow to start. He is approached by local members of a breakaway group of the IRA by choice, and to ensure the continuity of his charter business, he falls from grace into a web of deceit, sex, and crime, working with the local cell of the new IRA. The Good Friday Agreement had brought an end to hostilities, but there were many in the local cell of the IRA, who in the author's imagination rued the day when, as a onetime powerful group, it had lost the will or the ability to seek restitution for what they considered as crimes against the cause and were still determined once again to unite Ireland as one country. The staunch, reconstituted supporters of the 'New IRA', unwilling to disband such a powerful organisation, realise that they may have found a new way to destroy the youth of Britain by more devious means, such as flooding of the market with cheap drugs, aimed at the younger generation. They hoped that by corrupting the youth of the country, they would eventually destroy the will of both the country and its people and that Ireland and the Irish people would once again be united as a whole.

This first book in the series follows the downward spiral of Lord Croft's criminal career, which began by seeking excitement, and by joining the criminal elements of the newly constituted IRA, led him ever deeper into the world of crime, corruption, and deceit, where he smuggles guns and

7

drugs, delivers terrorists to be trained in North Africa, and even commits murder. Against all odds, as an English Lord, he becomes an integral part of the rogue IRA breakaway cell, becoming a member of the inner group, not only participating in but also planning the operations, eventually bringing himself to the attention of MI5.

His more-than-healthy sexual drive, his handsome looks, and an uncanny knack for attracting and seducing women, combined with the skills taught to him by Janet, the woman who eventually became his wife, leads him into the ways of a sexual predator, leaving no woman safe from his grasp. The web of deceit that he weaves is so far-reaching that it seems few women are able to resist his charm and skill as a lover.

In the course of his criminal operations, he is chased by pirates and European patrol boats, which bring him into situations where he has to use every weapon at his command to defend and defeat his adversaries. The book brings him into danger and excitement over and over again. The actions of the cell eventually comes to the attention of MI5, and an on-going investigation begins, forcing Lord Croft to seek safety in the Caribbean for a time, which leads on to the second book in the series, and who knows where it will finally end.

Chapter 1

Lord Roy Croft felt the throb of the powerful motors beneath his feet as he moved out of the sheltered harbour of his large property, a castle, nestled on the clifftops, south of Tralee, on the west coast of Ireland. The prow lifted as the vessel left the shelter of the harbour and sensed its freedom as the powerful craft felt the rising swell of the Atlantic, an ocean never known for its smooth, calm waters. The seventy-five-foot wooden restored World War II MTB boat took in the swell like a surfer cutting through the waves, like a hot knife through butter. She was made for the deep waters of the ocean, built as an attack boat to attack German warships with torpedoes and her deck gun before racing away into the night after creating as much damage as she could. The pent-up energy from the powerful engines transmitted itself through the decking and the wheel. It was almost as if the boat had a soul. She wanted the sea to get rougher so that the she would relish the challenge in the most turbulent of waters. Its skipper and owner, Lord Croft, was in his middle thirties and had grown into what most women would call ruggedly handsome. His thick brown mop of hair emphasised the handsome strong lines of his features. The square chin, the strong cheekbones, highlighted by the well-shaped nose and lips, made him look as though he should have been a Hollywood actor. There was no denying the fact that he looked the part, and in reality, he played the part of a ladies' man. He worked out regularly and had a barrel-like chest, and his arms were muscular but not overly so. He stood just under six feet tall and was as strong as an ox. The women in his life, and there had been many, seemed to come under his spell: it was something to do with his pheromones, most women found him irresistible.

Roy, alone aboard the large and lively craft, checked the coordinates of the exact spot he was to pick up his contact, and he did not want to be late. His new enterprise, the chartering of his pride and joy, had been fairly slow over the first six months, and he had only been chartered by a few groups, mainly Second World War buffs and a male group who needed to get away for a weekend. It seemed that not everyone shared his love of the wooden-hulled MTB. The prospective charters always, it seemed, wanted the more luxurious modern boats. Then he had been approached by a group of men who had come unannounced to the castle; they had been dressed as workmen and spoke in the broad brogue of a rural Irish accent. Their leader had told him that they had seen his boat out on the water and had been impressed by its turn of speed. As a group, they had quizzed him about his availability for unexpected charters at fairly short notice. Mainly, they had told him that the charter arrangements would be going out during the day and returning at night. They had not asked about the rates and had informed him that he would, in most cases, go out empty, pick up cargo, and return. Roy had been hesitant as he had believed the men were a group of common smugglers, and he did not know if he was ready for that yet. As he hesitated in replying to the question, the leader of the group had leaned forward and said quietly,

"Lord Croft," the 'o' drawn out into the broad Irish brogue and came out as an 'or', "You are new in the area, and you and your good lady wife have been received into our community with no trouble. I am here to inform you that all that could change. You do us a favour, and we do you a favour. That's the way it works in this part of the country."

Had this proposition happened a year ago, or had he been anywhere else but in Southern Ireland, Roy would have been incensed; but it was the quiet authority with which the stranger spoke that made him wary. It had dawned on Roy that he was in the company of the IRA, something he had never considered he would come across when he had acquired the property.

"I'm open for business to anyone who can pay," Roy replied.

Immediately sensing the sudden change in the group's attitude and not wanting to upset the situation, Roy asked the leader of the group,

"When do you want to go, and where?"

The leader, who had still not disclosed his name, then spoke in a more pleasant tone of voice,

"We are not here to charter you, or even to discuss dates and rates. We just needed to see if you were amenable to our approach. Now that that has been established, you will be contacted on this cell phone."

The man then produced the phone in question from his inner pocket of his heavy country, coarsely woven jacket and placed it on the table in front of Roy.

"You must keep it just for contact with us. It cannot be traced, and it does not store information for longer than a few hours. Keep it with you at all times and check regularly to see if you have missed a call. Do not use it for any other purpose than to contact the person who leaves the message. The keyboard has been altered, and all you do if you miss a call is to press the recall button. Do you understand?" the man asked.

Roy, somewhat perplexed, had nodded his head in agreement. With that, the group had stood; all of them had waited in turn to shake his hand; each one had the rough hands of men who worked on the land, each handshake was solid and firm as if to emphasise the dangers of not following the instructions to the letter. Roy had understood perfectly, and a quiet chill had run down his spine as he watched them leave.

It had been a few days later when he had received the call. The voice had been explicit but short and to the point:

"We understand you are amenable to our offer to charter your boat." Not waiting for a reply, the voice went on to say, "Your first charter and test run will be Wednesday, pick up," and here he had given a set of coordinates, "at 2.30 p.m., one passenger out. It will be a trip to the French coast returning with cargo to be delivered to a point on the Irish coast. The coordinates for the actual pickup will be given by your passenger, and so will the ones for delivery. You will receive €5000 for your trouble. Don't be late, and it would be inadvisable to let us down. Good luck."

That had been a few days ago, and here he was, not really knowing what was expected of him. He arrived too early at the coordinates given and hove to about a quarter of a mile off shore. The instruments he had fitted when he had refitted the boat were radar linked with Google Earth, a depth finder, and a GPS. They enabled him to locate the exact spot, and to ensure that he did not run aground in any area he was unfamiliar with, he had fitted a modern depth finder. On this trip, he felt he was going into strange places completely blind, so he would use them to full advantage. He rechecked his watch and moved towards the shore; as he approached the short stone jetty, a figure appeared from nowhere. When Roy nudged closer, the figure jumped aboard and made his way into the wheel house through the main cabin.

"Go! Don't hang around. The less time you're here, the better." Then as if as an afterthought, the stranger said gruffly, "My name is Connor, and you have to be Lord Croft?"

"What's our destination?" Roy asked as he nodded in answer to the question.

Roy's instincts were immediately on the alert, and throwing the vessel into reverse, the engine noise rose as he gunned the throttle slightly. The vessel moved backwards, and as soon as Roy had manoeuvring space, he engaged 'forward' and swung the wheel. The seventy-five-foot wooden craft swung around, and once the bow was pointing towards the sea, Roy pushed the throttles further forward. The engine's noise rose to a peak, and the boat leapt forward like a gazelle being chased by a leopard.

"What's our destination?" Roy asked again.

"I'll tell you when we get nearer. Just head for the port of Santander. I'll give you the exact coordinates when we get closer," came the sharp retort.

Connor left Roy and went below. Roy scowled. How was he to know where he was going if they did not tell him the coordinates? It seemed so bloody secretive. Then he realised that if he was a spy for the authorities, he could give the coordinates over the radio, and the French or Spanish coastguards could set up a trap and be waiting for them. It looked as though he would have no company on the trip as Connor had gone into one of the cabins presumably to sleep.

It was going to be a long, lonely trip, and Roy began to think about how he, who had been at the top of his profession first being knighted and finally being made a Lord for his contribution to British industry, had ended up here running out to the Franco-Spanish coast to pick up, God knows what, for the IRA. His thoughts wandered back over the years.

He had been born to a hardworking couple, his father and mother had both worked hard and life had been tough. When he had passed for grammar school, they had been so proud of him. He had not disappointed them; that had been where he had discovered he had a photographic memory; studying for him was easy, and he had left with ten 'O' levels and five 'A' levels. He could have gone to any university, but the strain on the family finances would have been too much for them to bear. He had of all things chosen to be an accountant and had been taken on by Stratton and Co, a large practice of Chartered Accountants.

Tom Stratton, the senior partner, had taken a shine to him from the start; with Roy's photographic memory, his exam results were exceptional, winning him national prizes from the Institute. As a result, Roy had been promoted above others who had been with the firm longer. Tom Stratton had begun taking him to the larger clients and giving him control of many audits. Roy remembered that it was around this time he had begun to wonder about his own sexual orientation; girls had never been a part of his life, he had always been far too busy to bother with them. His ambitions had always come first. It was after they had finished one of the larger audits that Tom had invited Roy home for a drink and introduced him to his wife, Janet. Roy had been struck by the difference in age between them: Janet, who he estimated was in her early to mid-twenties, and Tom, who was in his late fifties. Janet was blonde with a figure to die for; she had a slender waist accentuating her breasts and hips; her buttocks had been tightly encased in a pair of trousers that gave her a look that would not have been out of place on any catwalk. She had been the first woman that had made him drool; he had been hooked.

Roy had been a regular visitor to the house after that, and he had discovered two things about Janet. She was an excellent cook, and she was Tom's second wife. Tom's first wife had died of cancer, and Janet had subsequently met him at a charity function; surprisingly, the two of them had an instant affinity. They had, she had later told him, at that first meeting chatted well into the night. Within a few weeks, they had become lovers; Tom had asked her to marry him, and she had accepted. Then he vividly recalled that one night she had phoned Roy in tears and wanted him to come to the house. It had been an emergency; she had urged him to come alone. When Roy arrived, to his amazement, Tom had been comatose and in a drunken stupor. Janet had been sobbing, and she had asked Roy to help her get him to bed. Roy had carried his mentor upstairs and had put him to bed. Janet had been inconsolable when Roy came downstairs; he had put his arm around her to try and give her some support. She had eventually told him the full story.

A year earlier, she had come home early and caught Tom in bed with another man. She had been horrified at the thought of him in that kind of relationship. It had affected her badly, and as a result, they had never slept together from that day. Tom had taken to drinking, but nothing like he had done that night; and as a result, when it had happened, she had been at a complete loss as to what to do. That night, Roy had sat trying to console Tom's semi-hysterical wife. During the course of that decisive evening, the question of who seduced whom and how it all happened had always been somewhat fuzzy in Roy's mind. The outcome had been that they had ended up making love, not once but several times. That had been the night Roy had lost his virginity; he had gone home feeling guilty that it had been with his boss's wife, but with a new spring in his step. Over the next few weeks, he had avoided going to Tom's house. He had felt as though he could not face her, but eventually it had been Janet who had called him and asked him to come over, saying that she had things to discuss, explaining that Tom would be away on a Rotary planning weekend.

Out of curiosity, or had it been in the hope that they might have sex again, Roy could never remember, but he presumed it was the latter, and he had gone to the house as requested; Janet had told him that she would never leave Tom as she loved him despite all his faults, but she had needs that had to be taken care of. She explained to Roy that she had been very promiscuous at university and prided herself on her wide sexual knowledge. She had told him bluntly that as a lover he had a lot to learn; however, if he wanted, she would teach him how to arouse a woman and then satisfy her fully. The following months had given Roy carnal knowledge far beyond his years, and he became a sexual predator; women seemed unable to resist his charms and found him strangely irresistible. He had taken advantage of the fact many times; his only fault had always been that he never took any precautions, preferring to ride bareback. He had always left that side of sex up to his partners, a dangerous thing to do as he had discovered later.

Roy remembered how, at the earliest possible moment after qualifying as top student; mainly due to his involvement with Janet Stratton, he had discovered that his attraction for her was becoming more than casual. He had, he remembered, been falling in love with her, and knowing that she would never leave Tom, he had terminated his employment with Stratton's, despite being offered a full partnership within two years of gaining his finals, something that had been unheard of in that practice. He had moved to The Boric Group of companies as an accountant and been asked to solve the accounting problems at one of its subsidiary companies.

On the day of his arrival, he had had a confrontation with one of the staff, who had been derelict in his duties and had been extremely rude to Roy as a newcomer, and the man had been ultimately fired as a result; this had given Roy the reputation of being a man who would not tolerate anyone around him incapable of pulling his weight in carrying out his duties. The company's accounts had been in an awful mess and, together with his Indian assistant, Chandelle; they had got the accounts into a perfect example for the group. The chief accountant had been fired, and Roy had been promoted within months to that position. Shortly afterwards, he had been promoted to group accountant.

It had been obvious to many of his peers that he had been singled out for greater things. During this time, he remembered how after delivering accounts to head office with Chandelle, she had invited him home for tea; she had relaxed and let down her usual guard, and in the conversation that followed, she had confessed that she was having marital problems, in that her husband had many other women in his life. The predatory instinct within Roy had sensed that she needed more than just compassion and understanding. He had seized the opportunity and seduced his young married assistant, taking advantage of her needs more than once, on that occasion and many others after that day, as the opportunities arose. Similarly, when he had been informed that he had been granted his request to increase his staff, he had been given the authority to recruit a secretary. Mandy had been one of three applicants. She had been by far the most qualified and had openly flirted with him at the interview. Roy had taken advantage of the flirtatious offer, taking her lustfully in his office there and then. She had been so compliant that after they had satisfied their primeval urges, she had unashamedly offered to type her own appointment. Roy had liked her direct approach and had engaged her, and he had never regretted his decision. As a result, he had been able to have regular sex with both his assistant and his secretary, in and out of the office. His sexual appetite had grown, and he had casual sexual liaisons with several other members of the staff, all of whom had easily succumbed to his advances.

His tenacity for hard work and popularity with the staff had not gone unnoticed by his seniors. Roy had continued with his studies, and it was shortly after he had passed the conversion to Cost and Works Accountant that he had been appointed to head office as financial director. Roy, overzealous as usual, had taken it upon himself to obtain a degree in Engineering, enabling him to understand the problems that had been arising within the group. At the same time, he had begun a fitness regime to ensure that he did not get portly and unfit like many of his fellow directors. This, together with his good looks and sexual experience, combined with his charm, had allowed him to seduce many of his fellow director's wives during his time with the company, and he had become very popular at company functions.

The years, combined with his hard work and tenacity for detail, had been kind to Roy, and he had rapidly risen to the position of Chief Executive Officer and later to Group Managing Director. It had been during this time that he had been knighted for his contributions to industry as the company had risen to be one of the *Fortune* One Hundred companies, and he had been awarded a great number of share options, making him a wealthy man. After the successful completion of a particularly sensitive government contract, he had, much to his surprise and delight, been made a Lord, as a sign of thanks by a grateful government. Roy had to smile to himself when he remembered that he had begun to get somewhat complacent about that time; the company had been running smoothly, and he had needed to get away.

He had rung his mother and arranged to go and see her; she lived in his house near to his first appointment with Boric and not too far from Tom and Janet Stratton. He had rung Chandelle his old assistant, Mandy his old secretary, and Janet Stratton in the hopes that he could meet up with them over the weekend. To his delight, all three had agreed to see him, and it had been a weekend of sexual reunions with all three of them. He remembered that he had hardly seen anything of his mother; he had been in and out of bed the entire weekend and had been glad to get back to work for a rest. He laughed to himself; all three had got pregnant over the same weekend; he thought to himself that he must have been very fertile and that all three women must have been ovulating at the same time. Roy, however, had not been too upset; all three women had been married, and each and every one of their husbands, as far as Roy was aware, had never suspected their wife's impropriety, so he had not been too concerned.

Roy's despondency and dissatisfaction, however, had grown out of all proportion at the way his life was going. He had achieved all he could; he was still a young man, and the need for a change in his life had consumed his every thought over the next few weeks. This had been due to the fact that the group of companies under his control had run smoothly and efficiently. As a result, he had wanted the board to expand their interests. The board of directors and the shareholders had been getting huge dividends from Roy's ability to manage the group and had not wanted to take any unnecessary risks. As a result, Roy had grown bored and had reconciled himself to the fact that a change in his life was inevitable. His sexual needs during this time had grown, with him taking more and more risks with director's wives and his staff. The final straw had come when he had seduced a young eighteen-year-old member of staff, Rita, and had impregnated her. He had cursed himself for his stupidity. Thankfully, he had not panicked at the news, and he recalled how he had rung his friend Jerald. After explaining his dilemma to him, Jerald had given Roy his mistress's gynaecologist's contact details. Roy had then arranged for young Rita to see the specialist, who asked no questions. It had been expensive but the specialist had done a D and C and had afterwards given Rita a contraceptive injection that would last for three months. That episode had made Roy realise just how bored with life he had become, sleeping with the innocent with no thought about the outcome. He had known at the time something had to change.

Roy had made up his mind soon afterwards; he had always wanted a country house near the sea and had often considered owning a boat. He had contacted a well-known London estate agent that specialised in large country residences and told them what he wanted. They had come back only days later with his present residence. It had been a castle on the west coast of Ireland that had apparently been a base for some clandestine wartime branch of MI5. The property had just come on to the market. It had been offered for sale by the MOD (Ministry of Defence) with the proviso that he had to take the place as it stood and dispose of anything left over from World War II at his own expense. When he had first approached the estate, it was still enclosed in the wartime barbed wire fencing and completely hidden from the road. Despite the fact that nobody had touched it and it was in a state of disrepair; when he had finally seen it, he had fallen in love with it and had been determined to take it as it stood, lock, stock, and barrel.

He remembered that it had been around that time that he had received that phone call from Janet, who had been highly stressed about something. To his annoyance, she had refused to discuss the cause of her problem over the phone. She had asked him to come at once; it was a matter of life and death. Roy, who had never stopped loving Janet despite all his other sexual partners, remembered that he had dropped everything and driven to see her; he had arrived to see an ambulance leave the house, and Janet had been standing with her shoulders drooping; she had looked ten years older than when he had last seen her as she stood weeping on the front step, still in her nightgown and robe. Roy had taken her into the house and she, in a dreadfully anxious state, had explained that she had broken the news of her pregnancy, and Tom, as usual under any kind of stress, had taken to drink. He had demanded to know whose child it was, guessing that it had been Roy's, but wanting the fact confirmed and finally under duress, Janet had given him Roy's name. She had gone to bed after they had had a long altercation, and when she had woken up that morning, Tom had been unconscious on the floor of the lounge. She had explained to Roy that Tom had looked very sick; his complexion had been grey, and she had called the doctor. When the doctor had arrived, and shortly after he had examined the unconscious patient, he had broken the news that Tom had had a massive stroke.

Janet had panicked, and having no one near to call on, she had called Roy to help her. Roy had spent time calming her down before persuading her to get dressed, after which they had gone to the hospital, but it had been hopeless, and Tom had died within hours. Roy had taken her back home in a dreadful state, offering to help in any way he could. Janet had refused to let Roy help with the funeral arrangements but had asked him to come to the funeral and the reading of the will as Tom had told her years before that he had been named as a beneficiary. Roy had, as he had been requested, gone to the funeral, spending the evening consoling her, after which it seemed quite natural for them to sleep together, and the following morning they had driven together for the reading of Tom's will.

The will had been a surprise. Tom had left his fortune to them both on the understanding that they married within a year, failing which the money was to go to charity. Both of them had realised that Tom had been aware of their affair all along, but he had understood his wife's needs and ignored her transgressions. The solicitor had explained that if they wished, he could and would contest the will, as he had felt the terms would not stand up in a court of law. Roy remembered that it had been after the reading of the will when he had told her about his new acquisition and the fact that he would be giving up his position at Boric. As a result, he had told her that he would be quite wealthy after cashing in his share options and his severance deal. He had explained that he would be going to live in Ireland, and he had asked her if she would care to accompany him. She had accepted only after she had learned that it would be some time before the place would be fit for habitation, and his notice period would be six months. He had also proposed to her at the same time. She had said that it was too soon for her to make that kind of decision, but she would see how things turned out whilst the castle was being made habitable.

Roy's memory recalled that, to achieve the changes he wanted at the castle, he had engaged an Irish architect, Gordon O'Leary, who had been keen to get the work. He had invited Roy home whilst he studied the plans of the castle, and when he had arrived with Gordon at his home, Roy had been pleasantly surprised that Gordon's wife, Megan, had been very attractive. He remembered how both of them had had such an affinity and an instant attraction for each other when they had first met; he was still surprised that her husband had not been aware of it at the time. Megan had been almost infatuated with Roy from the moment she had set eyes on him and had fallen prey to his title and seductive charm. That first night at her home, whilst her husband had been busy checking drawings, preparing plans, and making notes prior to a visit to the castle, the fiery, red-haired Megan had succumbed so easily; she had been a willing participant to Roy's uninvited passions when she showed him around the house. Roy had taken her unresisting body several times whilst they waited for her husband to complete his review of the plans. The following day, Megan had accompanied Roy and Gordon when they had visited the castle.

It was then that Gordon had discovered the MTB, a motor torpedo boat from World War II, in the boat house, and below, in a subterranean workshop, they had discovered a fully stocked storeroom with every spare part necessary to service and repair the boat. Roy remembered it was later that he had discovered that, below that store, there had been another level housing the wartime armoury, still stocked with arms and ammunitions from the time the castle had been used by MI5. Roy smiled to himself remembering that, whilst Gordon had been busy checking for dry rot or other damage in the castle basement, he had taken the eager Megan again aboard the MTB, and they had unprotected steamy sex again, thereby christening the craft as Roy's love boat.

Suddenly Roy snapped out of his far-off thoughts as a ship's horn blew; he was in the main shipping channels and had to be wary as he crossed the Bay of Biscay towards the Spanish coast. Sometime later, Connor appeared and gave Roy the coordinates and a time. Roy noted that it was in Basque country, a place notorious for discontent and revolution, the ideal location for weapons to be readily available, if indeed that was what they had come for. They were early; Roy laid off the coast and waited patiently. Darkness fell, and Roy moved closer to the rendezvous; the large motors, just above tick-over purred quietly; he paused about half a mile off shore, waiting for the signal. Connor and Roy scoured the coastline, but no signal came; they had almost given up hope and were deciding whether to leave, when out of the darkness came two long and two short flashes from a powerful torch. It was the arranged signal. Connor using the Aldis lamp on deck gave the required response, and then he nodded to Roy to move closer to the shore. Roy noted, not without some considerable concern, that Connor produced a Sterling machine gun and cowered on the foredeck, his eyes peeled for trouble. Connor then whispered,

"If I tell you to abort, get the hell out of here fast. I hate it when anyone's late. It could be a trap."

Roy edged the large craft towards the shore somewhat nervously, prepared to gun the boat if it became necessary, closely watching the depth finder for any sign of shallows that could prevent him from going about quickly.

"There's a small boat approaching from behind that headland," Roy whispered calmly but full of adrenaline.

"Where's the searchlight?" Connor snapped.

"It's above your head and to the left."

"Switch it on for a couple of seconds, and then turn it off. I'll see if it's our suppliers," Connor whispered.

Roy quickly flicked the switch forward. The water in front of the boat was illuminated in a sudden glare, and Connor swung the light in the direction of the approaching boat. The pool of light picked out a small fishing boat; it was them. Roy snapped the switch back, and darkness was restored. Minutes later, the small craft was alongside; the crew threw a rope up, and Connor secured it to the cleat on the edge of the deck whilst Roy kept the engines running and the screws turning with just sufficient power to hold the boat steady in the tidal drag.

The men aboard the boat greeted Connor with familiarity and began to unload the sacks of cargo, the bulky shape of which, together with the thump as each one struck the deck, did nothing to disguise the fact that they contained guns. The amount seemed endless; then the square ammunition boxes followed. Two of the Spaniards helped Connor drag the cargo to the rear hatch, and as soon as the last box was inside, Connor handed over a briefcase, and with a grunt of thanks, the two men jumped down into the small fishing boat. Connor cast off and called out to Roy,

"Get the hell out of here as soon as they're clear. It's too damn quiet."

Roy swung the wheel over, and as soon as the smaller boat was clear, he eased the throttles forward, and they moved out towards deeper water. Then Roy gunned the boat, keeping a lookout for patrol boats on the radar. He spotted one some way off and quickly changed course, heading for deeper water across the Bay of Biscay.

Once they were safe from any threat of patrols, Connor went below for a couple of hours' sleep, and Roy was left to his own thoughts once more. He thought of how he had begun his descent into crime. It had all commenced when he had known that the share price was going to fall; the Boric board of directors were going to announce a reduced dividend due to capital being required to pay for a new factory up north; he knew that it was insider trading, but the thrill had been worth it. Roy had sold his shares before the announcement and after cashing in his share options as soon as they had been due. As a result, he had made a small fortune, which, combined with his final settlement, ensured that he would have a relatively comfortable life, even if he just retired and did nothing, an action he had no interest in carrying out.

Then, when he had bought the castle, he had contacted Charlie Drake, the owner of the building firm that had done the last factory development. Charlie owed him big time. Roy had always arranged for Charlie's payments to be prompt, enabling Charlie's cash flow to be kept on an even keel. When they had met, and Roy had given him the plans, Charlie had simply asked where the property was situated. Roy had informed him that it was in the West of Ireland and instructed him to have all the materials delivered on site. He had also asked for an estimate of the cost, including labour. Charlie had pondered for a while. Then, looking Roy straight in the eye, he had suggested that as the company had a new factory development coming up in Manchester, if Roy could arrange for him to be awarded the contract, the alterations would come free, including all the materials. Roy had realised that this had been the moment of decision, and he remembered himself saying,

"I open the tenders. Just leave your final figure blank and I will ensure that you get the job."

It had been agreed, and Charlie had left. Roy knew he had crossed the line, but the excitement of actually manipulating results to give him some reward had given him a peculiar feeling in the pit of his stomach and, to his astonishment, he not only enjoyed it, but craved more.

The quantity surveyors' report, together with the bill of quantities, had finally arrived, and Roy had faxed Charlie, informing him that the material specifications and quantities were available in his office. Charlie had arrived shortly afterwards with his tender, which he had handed sealed to Roy's secretary before going in to collect the documents for Roy's alterations. Roy had told Charlie that the castle had beds in the barracks with field kitchen facilities for his men to be able to cater for themselves and that the labour force could stay on site during the alterations. Charlie had winked and said to Roy with a smile on his face,

"If that contract is mine, consider the job done. The lads will be on site next week Wednesday. I'll make sure the materials arrive on time."

Two days after their meeting, the tender had been awarded to Charlie Drake. As soon as he had the confirmation, Charlie had been as good as his word, and the men and materials had been on site as arranged.

Roy had then informed Gordon, arranging to meet him on site the following Saturday. Roy grinned sheepishly, to himself, as he remembered Gordon's reply,

"Megan and I would be happy to see you on site, and you must of course stay at our house on that Saturday evening."

The day at the site had gone well to begin with, but it turned out that Charlie's men had discovered a problem requiring Gordon to stay on over the weekend. Roy had to be back in the office on Monday morning, so he and Megan had gone back to Dublin, leaving Gordon to complete his survey. Megan had had no qualms, and she had spent the night in Roy's hotel room. Megan had always been a staunch Catholic and had not taken any contraception, and her reliance on her safe period had misfired, for that had been the day she had conceived Roy's child, although it had been some time later when she had told him that he was the father.

The work on the castle had finally been finished, and Janet had moved in, helping Roy refurnish the castle as a home. During that time, Roy had managed to locate a navy man who had restored the MTB. Janet had joined Roy; she had settled in and stayed on, whilst Roy completed his notice period. During the time Janet had been in Ireland, Roy had enjoyed the favours of many women, and Chandelle, his former Indian accountant, had introduced him to her sister, Shilpa, who, as a trained Indian dancer, had proved to Roy's delight to be even more sensual and sexually adventurous than any of his previous women. In the months that followed, Janet and Roy had married, and she had given him a son. They had named him Sean, a good Irish name to blend in with the country they had chosen to be home.

The sound of Connor coming out of the stateroom alerted Roy; he forgot about the past and was joined by his passenger. Their conversation was sparse, but Roy enjoyed having him beside him as company. The rest of the journey went without mishap, and it was early morning when Connor gave Roy the coordinates for the drop-off point. They had pulled alongside a small stone jetty, some way south of Connor's pickup point, and though appearing to be deserted, it seemed as though a small truck and ten men appeared from nowhere. The cargo was safely offloaded, and the truck drove away, leaving two men on the quay to help cast off the securing lines. As soon as the lines were cast off, Connor gave Roy instructions to take him to the point where he had been picked up the previous day. They were about half a mile offshore when Connor reappeared from below; as they approached the drop-off point, Connor gave Roy a thick brown envelope. "It's as agreed," he said, "and there is a bonus for a job well done. I understand from our sources that you have had your fuel tanks re-commissioned." "Yes, that's right. I have," Roy replied, amazed that Connor knew about it. He had received the news himself only the day before. "Well, expect a delivery of fuel tomorrow. When you get back to the castle, there will be help for you to get the boat back into the boathouse. See you next time."

Not waiting for the boat to actually come to a stop, Connor jumped ashore, giving a cheery wave of his hand as Roy turned away from the jetty and headed back out to sea. Dawn was breaking, and Roy was feeling the strain of being up all night. He would be glad to get some help to get the large craft back inside. He had intended to just tie up and go inside for breakfast and put the boat away later, but on reflection he had not wanted her to be left in the castle harbour; just in case it was spotted by satellite and connected with the night visit to the Spanish coast collecting the illicit cargo of weapons and ammunition. He eased the boat alongside the quay, and two men threw him a line. Roy secured it to the capstan, and one man, introducing himself as Liam, leapt aboard. The other man went inside the boathouse and operated the recovery winch. When the boat had been safely winched up the slipway and chocked, Liam introduced himself and his father,

"I'm Liam and this is my 'Dah', Quinn!" Roy shook the older man's hand.

Liam turned to leave and said, "We shall see you tomorrow, sir."

Roy nodded, somewhat puzzled as to why they would have cause to see him again so soon. Roy put the thick envelope in the safe in his office at the back of the workshop and made his way along the subterranean passage and up the stone steps into the castle kitchen, where, to his surprise, there stood a young woman preparing food.

"Good morning, sir," she said, curtsying somewhat shyly. "I'm Bridget."

After grunting a short reply, Roy went up the stairs to the bedroom. Janet was lying in bed, and, much to his surprise, Sean was nowhere to be seen.

"Where's Sean?" Roy asked, looking around the bedroom.

"He's with Morag, my new nanny."

"Who's Morag? Oh and by the way, I saw another young woman, who tells me her name is Bridget in the kitchen, getting breakfast. What's going on?"

"Oh, they all arrived after you left yesterday. It appears that they are our new staff, all arranged by your new charter people, and there's more. We have two men to do the garden. The younger one is called Liam and his father, whose name is Quinn, helps. Young Bridget tells me I do not have to go to the village for shopping any more. The grocer and the butcher will ring every day for our order, and it will be delivered along with a selection of fresh vegetables on a daily basis. I don't know who is chartering your boat, but don't upset them, will you? Bridget tells me that there is a seamstress in the village, who will do any alterations or make new curtains. All I have to do is to ring and let her know. She will do whatever I want quickly. All you have to do is pay for everything at the end of the month."

"I'll do my best not to do anything to upset your new arrangements," Roy said.

His mind was mulling over the fact that things could become very different if he did anything to upset the arrangements, and it was quite possible that he knew too much already.

The morning sun was above the horizon, but before they made love, as was their usual custom, Roy made his way into the bathroom for a shower. When he came back with a towel wrapped around his middle, his hair still wet; there was a knock on the bedroom door.

"Come in," he called out, unthinking.

The door opened, and in walked Bridget with a tray of tea. She stood open-mouthed for a moment and stared at Roy's muscular torso, for Roy was only wearing a towel, which barely covered his obvious morning arousal,

"Begging your pardon, sir, I did not know you were not dressed."

"That's OK, Bridget. Put the tray down. Don't look so embarrassed. It's not a problem."

Bridget seemed mesmerised, but she put the tray down on the bedside cabinet on Janet's side of the bed and stammered,

"What time do you want breakfast, madam? I'll serve it in the dining room if that's to your satisfaction?"

"In about half an hour, if that's all right, Bridget," Janet replied smiling.

Bridget nodded, and she walked towards the door, turning her head in Roy's direction, her eyes wide open taking another look at Roy's half-naked body before she left the room and shut the door behind her.

"I think you have an admirer there, Roy. You are going to have to be careful in future and stop walking around half naked, especially in that state. You should be ashamed of yourself. She could hardly take her eyes off your tented towel. Now, for the sake of decency, get some clothes on whilst I pour the tea. Then we have to get down for breakfast, no more lolling about in bed. Your sex life will never be the same again. I think we have suddenly become the local landed gentry around here. I, for one, am going to enjoy the rest from all the household chores, and long may it last!"

She laughed and sat back to enjoy her morning tea. This was something she was going to make the most of. Roy dressed reluctantly, disappointed that he would not have more sexual relief, which he had more than half expected from Janet on his safe return.

Chapter 2

Later that morning, Roy went into the office at the rear of the boathouse workshop. He checked the envelope and found not €5000, but an extra bonus of another €2000 with a little note from Connor, *Thanks for a job well done.* Roy had not expected any bonus but accepted it and put the money back in the safe. Later that morning, the fuel truck had arrived, as promised, and a delivery of 20,000 litres of fuel was pumped into his newly re-commissioned tank; that would save Roy from having to go to Tralee for fuel in future. The following day, the special cell phone rang; the voice on the other end of the line spoke softly,

"You got your delivery then. Was everything to your satisfaction?"

"Yes, everything is fine, especially the staff you arranged."

"No need to thank me. It comes with the territory. Now, can you do another run tomorrow and then a longer run on Saturday? The latter run could be up to a week. I have arranged for you to try out some help on the boat. Connor tells me that the MTB could be a bit of a handful for a single-handed operation, if the weather blows up rough."

"I will need someone with a master's certificate if I have to take anyone else with me."

"It has all been taken care of. She will be with you tomorrow before lunch. Give her a try, and I will call you again after tomorrow's run. Good luck."

Roy sat back, realising that the voice had said 'she' will be arriving tomorrow. He did not know many women with a master's certificate. It sounded interesting. He called Janet and told her that he would be on another charter the following day and that there was a distinct possibility he would have a week's charter from the weekend. Janet was pleased that things seemed to be going well for him, but she expressed some concern that he would be away for a week.

"Will you manage the boat on your own for that length of time?"

"It would seem that I have a new crew member arriving tomorrow to help me. It seems that my new crew member is a woman with a master's certificate. Can you believe that?"

"Why a woman, for heaven's sake?"

"Don't ask me. I don't make the arrangements any more, it would seem. It's only for a trial. If she is no good, I shall send her packing. Don't worry."

The following morning, Liam and, of all people, Bridget met Roy in the boathouse as he was about to launch the boat. Roy looked quizzically at Bridget.

"Why are you here, Bridget? Tell me you're not the new help I'm expecting."

"No, sir. That will be Elian, my sister. She told me she would be here this morning. I'm here to operate the winch."

"Have you operated a winch before?"

"Bless you, sir. My family have all been fisherfolk, and I have helped winch boats in and out of the water in all weathers. Don't you worry about me? I can handle any kind of equipment to do with boats large and small."

She winked blatantly and gave Roy a broad smile, conveying the idea that what she had said could be taken in more ways than one.

The door of the boathouse opened, and in walked a young woman in dungarees, a jumper, and a woollen hat covering her hair. The clothing hid her figure, but her face was ruddy, and she appeared to be quite attractive.

"Lord Croft?" she enquired.

"Yes, I'm Roy Croft. Who are you?"

"I'm Elian, and I'm here for you to try me out for the position as first mate."

"You have your master's certificate? You look quite young. What experience have you had?"

"I've been handling fishing boats ever since I could walk, well almost. I took my master's certificate three years ago and have handled all kinds of fishing boats up to deep sea trawlers in the worst kind of weather you can imagine. Let me know if you approve after you have seen me at work. I'm sure I won't disappoint you, your Lordship!"

"OK, I'll give it a try. Now, give us a hand to launch this beast, and you can fill her up in readiness for today's trip."

"Aye, aye, milord," came the sharp reply.

The boat was launched, and Roy watched as Elian filled the tanks and then went below to check the oil levels in the engines. When she had returned, she looked at Roy and said,

"I'm impressed. She looks as though she has more than enough power, and I'm sure she can handle any kind of weather. What time do we leave?"

"In about an hour. Bridget will give you lunch, and we can leave." Roy answered, "I'll take her out for the first time, and you can then take over to give yourself a chance to get used to her on our way to pick up our passenger."

Roy let Elian cast off as he eased the powerful vessel out of the shelter of the castle's harbour, and as soon as he had cleared the quay, he handed the controls over to Elian. She handled the powerful craft with the ease and dexterity of a true skipper. Roy gave her the coordinates, and she headed for the pickup point. They were as usual early and stood off until the appointed time. Whilst they waited, Elian explained that she had been thrown in at the deep end, from the time she had been a young girl, and that handling boats was like second nature to her, come all weathers. She would have continued, but Roy tapped his watch, and she headed into the stone pier.

Connor was waiting with two extra passengers. Connor greeted Roy and nodded to Elian. It was obvious that he knew her, so no introduction was necessary. The two other passengers grunted a greeting and went below.

"I was not expecting other passengers," Roy remarked.

"It's not a problem, is it?" asked Connor gruffly.

"No. I'm just surprised. That's all."

"You'll get used to surprises with us," Connor said crisply "Now let's get underway, and less questions. It's better for all of us."

The journey was uneventful, and Roy spent most of the time talking to Elian and realising that she was a very competent sailor. She handled the boat well, avoiding the heavy traffic heading for the English Channel and she asked Connor for the coordinates. Elian seemed to know the Franco/Spanish coast well as she headed towards the designated coordinates. It was dark when they hove to, waiting for the signal, for the rendezvous. This time, there was no mistake; the signal was on time and, after sending the signal in reply, they moved in slowly to make contact with the small fishing boat. The cargo was loaded as before, and then Connor spoke in Spanish to the skipper of the fishing boat.

"Take these two ashore. Don't worry. There is a bonus for you."

The skipper seemed somewhat reticent about the new arrangement, there had been no mention of this in the set up of the arangement.

"Who are they, and why are they coming ashore? Do they not have papers? Are they wanted by the police? What's the story?" The skipper demanded

"The payment is enough for you not to be asking questions. You've done it before. What's the problem?"

"It's not part of tonight's arrangement," the skipper said sullenly.

Connor began to get suspicious of the skipper's manner. He drew his pistol; the two men moved behind Connor, it was obvious to Roy that they were armed as well. Connor motioned with his weapon and said forcefully,

"I don't think you understand me. I am not giving you a choice. You take them ashore, or I kill you and your crew, and they take your boat ashore. You end up floating, and I save the money I was going to pay you. Do you comprehend what I'm telling you?"

Roy could see the man's face. It reflected terror in the half light from the cabin, and he agreed reluctantly.

"How much?" he asked, half cowering from Connor's threat.

"Enough to make it worthwhile," Connor snapped.

The two passengers climbed down into the fishing boat, and the two crew members of the fishing boat loudly grumbled their objections; Roy heard two thuds and the sound of two men falling into the gunnels of the small boat.

"They'll be no more trouble, Connor," came the whisper from the small boat bobbing alongside. "They will just have a thick head in the morning. Other than that, they will be fine."

The captain grabbed the money bag and climbed down into his boat, and Connor cast off.

"Let's get out of here and get home," Connor muttered to Roy.

The lines between the two boats were released. The small fishing boat gunned its engines as Elian eased the throttles of the MTB forward. They had just begun to turn when a spotlight shone from the direction of the shore, and the flashing light of a small patrol boat, probably a P111, was suddenly visible. Roy quickly dowsed the running lights, and Elian spun the wheel and moved quickly away from the shore. The sound of the patrol boat's engines became a roar, and a loud hailer ordered them to stop. Elian pushed the throttles fully forward, and the MTB leapt forward. The light from the patrol boat scanned the empty water where the MTB had been. Roy grabbed the wartime 303 Enfield rifle from the rack in the cabin and threw himself flat on the deck. The sound of the bolt loading the rimmed 2¼-inch bullet into the breach preceded the crack of the shot as it was fired. It was followed by the unmistakable sound of breaking glass causing the light from the patrol boat's searchlight to be extinguished, with a loud curse in Spanish. There was a burst of rapid gunfire from the direction of the small patrol boat, but without lights to guide the marksman, the shots fell into the sea well behind the fast-moving MTB.

"Good shot," Connor whispered. "Christ, I did not know you could shoot."

"Oh, I did a bit at school, and I won a couple of junior prizes at Bisley. It's like riding a bike. Once you have mastered the skill, you never lose it," replied Roy.

Connor did not reply, but he realised for the first time that Lord Croft was more than just a title with money and time on his hands.

The escaping MTB headed out to sea, and under Roy's instructions, Elian took evasive action, weaving in and out of the Channel traffic to confuse any attempt to track them by satellite. She would run alongside a tanker and then slip into the wake of a cargo ship until all hope of tracking them was lost. Then she detached herself from the shadow of another tanker and crept along the coast, keeping as close to the shore as was safe. Without any instruction from Roy this time, she reduced speed and slipped into a hidden cove, where she hid the cruiser under an overhanging cliff and waited for sunrise. It was obvious to Roy that she had done this before. Smuggling, he guessed! Elian was becoming more of an asset by the hour. Connor slipped ashore. He had to telephone and report to the headman that they would be late at the rendezvous.

"I don't know how long I'll be. I have to find a damn phone. There's no signal for the cell phone down here. Just stay here until I get back."

They watched him as he waded ashore and disappeared across the rocks and up the shoreline. Roy's adrenaline was still high from his encounter, and he poured himself a drink from the cabinet. He looked at Elian expectantly. She nodded, and he poured a second one and handed it to her. They sat and drank the good Irish whiskey, feeling the warmth as it went down, savouring the smoky flavour of the fifteen-year-old liquor. Roy looked closer as she pulled the woollen hat from her head and revealed the glorious tangle of hair. She walked into the cabin and picked up a brush from the dressing table, and after returning into the main cabin, she began to brush her auburn locks. She looked striking, and Roy wanted to know how she looked without the thick figure-concealing sweater and dungarees. He was, however, interrupted from saying anything as Connor reappeared at the cabin door.

"I managed to find a public telephone up on the headland, and they are expecting us at the rendezvous point later this afternoon. Is that whiskey you two are drinking? I could do with one of those myself. Make mine a large one."

Roy poured the three of them a drink, and they sat still until dawn had broken and the dark clouds rolled in from the Atlantic, followed by squally showers. The storm gradually worsened, and Roy knew that surveillance under those conditions would be difficult whoever tried to find them. At Roy's request, and under cover of the storm, Elian eased the boat out into the maelstrom and headed north up the coast. She needed all her skills both on the journey and as she eased alongside the stone quayside of the cargo drop-off point; she had no sooner got alongside when men in the storm-proof gear and waders of trawler men jumped aboard and offloaded the packages and boxes. Throughout the operation, Connor seemed uneasy, but as soon as the last box was ashore, he gave Roy the thumbs-up, and Elian took the boat out into the Atlantic storm once more.

They headed towards Connor's usual drop-off point, and as they approached the storm-washed jetty, he yelled above the sound of the wind,

"Drop me off as near as you can. If I have to jump, I don't mind."

Elian nodded as she approached the drop-off point, the exposed stone jetty kept disappearing in the swell. Connor put on a life jacket and, putting his head out of the cabin and seeing the state of the weather, said,

"Ignore the jetty. Get me as close to the shore as you can. I'll swim the rest. Don't risk running aground."

After several unsuccessful attempts, Elian shrugged her shoulders and yelled out in Connor's direction,

"That's as close as I can get in this weather. Can you make it from here?" Connor did not answer straightaway, but he waited for the right moment. Then he ran and jumped over the side. He had timed it well, and a wave caught him and swept him towards the shore. Roy looked back and could see through the spray that Connor was ashore and walking up the beach, drenched but safe and apparently sound.

"Christ, I wonder how many times he's done that. He's a cool one for sure. It takes some nerve to jump overboard like that," muttered Roy, still shaken at what he had seen.

"It was either that or coming back with us and making his way by road," Elian replied.

"I'm glad the headland at the castle will shelter us, and the harbour is calmer than that, or we would have to try and get into Tralee until it's calmer," Roy said.

His attention was captured by the howl of the storm as he gazed at the windswept waves crashing over the bow.

"The castle harbour is one of the most sheltered harbours on the coast," Elian called back as she braced herself for the next wave.

"We'll make it in with not too much to worry about. The entrance is wide enough, and the quay wall gives added shelter. It would take two or three boats this size, but by the look of the breaks in the cloud, the worst will be over by the time we get back."

Elian had been right; by the time she headed into the private harbour of the castle, the worst of the weather had blown itself out. Although there was still a swell, they slipped past the headland into the relative calm and safety of the harbour. Liam and his father were waiting inside the door to the boathouse. As the boat came into sight, Liam ran down the slipway and grabbed the rope as Roy tossed it to him. Liam lashed the rope around the capstan on the end of the quay and secured the craft. The boat swung out, and Elian eased her forward until Liam secured the bow to the recovery hooks and chain. Liam released the hawser, securing the boat as his father operated the winch to recover the boat up the slipway and into the boathouse. They chocked the boat, and Liam and his father left to get on with other maintenance work whilst Elian and Roy checked the hull for damage. Everything was in order and Elian shouted,

"Bye, Lord Croft. I'll see you for the next trip on Saturday. I'll ring and check the time you want me here."

With a flip of her head, which sent her hair in a swirl and a girlish grin, she was gone. Roy put the envelope Connor had left in the cabin unopened in the safe.

Just as Roy was heading out of his office door, the special cell phone rang. The voice sounded concerned; there was an edge to it that he had not heard before.

"Can you do a special run tonight? The usual man we use has met with a serious accident." There was an ominous pause for effect. "It will be a fast run to the French coast and back. The weather forecast looks good, and I'll get Liam and Elian to accompany you. Connor will expect you at the usual pickup point at 6 p.m.," the voice said, expecting and getting compliance.

"Yes. I can do that," Roy replied.

"I understand there was trouble with last night's run. The sea patrol was waiting for you. I was pleased you reacted so quickly. I understand you are quite the marksman. Unfortunately, we lost the two passengers and the crew of the fishing boat. They were picked up by the police."

There was a pause before the voice continued:

"Just in case of trouble, I want you to be fully armed tonight. Do those bloody torpedoes actually work on that boat of yours?"

"I understand that all the armaments on board are fully functional, but I'll need help to load the torpedo tubes. Those damn things must weigh a ton."

There was a moment's silence, as if the person behind the voice was making a decision. Then it continued:

"I'll get Liam and a couple of others over at lunchtime to help, and I'll send some Uzis and ammunition. Those old 303 bolt-action rifles may be accurate over a long distance, but they are not much good in a close fight. By the way, that bloody deck gun is a bit conspicuous. Can it be dismounted?"

"I don't think so. It's bolted through the decking," Roy said, wondering what was coming next.

"Then there's not much we can do about that today. Let me think about that, and I'll come back to you. I would ask you to be on the safe side and take some ammunition for the bloody thing just in case. I'll be in touch when you get back. Good luck!"

The phone went dead, and Roy stood shocked. Shooting out a light on a naval customs vessel was one thing, but torpedoes and shells were in a different league altogether, and what the hell would he need Uzis for? He realised he was getting in deeper than he had ever envisaged. He wanted excitement, but he had not bargained for such extremes so quickly. He also realised that if he turned the job down, he could be putting his own, Janet's, and Sean's life in jeopardy. He had never wanted that, but he was in too deep. They would not let him pull out now; he had seen too much already. He heard a noise behind him, and, turning, he saw Bridget walk in through the door with a steaming cup of coffee.

"Mrs Croft saw you come ashore, sir, and asked me to bring you something hot."

It was the way she said it that made Roy look closer. There was a glint in Bridget's eyes he had not seen since she had seen him half naked in his bedroom. She bent over to put the coffee on the desk, deliberately letting the front of her half unbuttoned top reveal the fact that she was not wearing a bra. She stayed in that position just too long for it to be a mistake, and Roy's eyes were drawn to the youthful flesh on display.

Roy's eyes slowly dragged themselves from the spoils and saw that Bridget was smiling with satisfaction.

"Your clothes are wet, sir. You'll catch your death."

Without another word, she stepped forward and started to unbutton his shirt. Roy stood mesmerised as she pulled the damp shirt off his shoulders and unbuckled his belt.

"We'll soon have you out of these wet things, and I'll give you a rub down with that towel. I'm sure we will find something more interesting to warm you up than coffee."

She rubbed his back with the towel and then his chest. The towel moved even lower until she was rubbing his groin. Roy felt himself respond, and he moved to take her into his arms. She was eager and compliant as he unbuttoned the rest of her top, revealing her youthful breasts. Her skirt slipped down as she unclipped the waist, and Roy's system, which had already been charged with adrenaline, thinking about the danger of his trip later, now surged; his ardour rose, and he made his move. Bridget gasped as his hand slid up her inner thigh; he touched her; the probing fingers caressed and then entered her, his thumb busy arousing her, but she offered no resistance as he continued to arouse her sexual desires higher than anyone had done before.

Bridget had hoped he would respond to her advances; he had looked capable of anything when she had seen him half naked. Now that she could see all of him, she was not disappointed. Roy noted that Bridget's cotton underwear was not fashionable in the least, and he made a mental note to bring her some fancy knickers the next time he was able to. Their passions rose; the sexual predator in Roy seized the opportunity to chalk up another conquest; he took her without any thought as to the consequences of his actions, until Bridget cried out as she reached her orgasm, aware that his Lordship had not hesitated for a moment, but to her surprise he had climaxed deep within her. Her mind whirled. *Mary, Mother of God, am I safe?* she asked herself. Then, realising that she had a few days until her safe period was over; she relaxed, enjoying the immense satisfaction her employer had given her. He was so much more skilled than any of the village lads, or the 'Father' and his young curate, all of whom had availed themselves of her feminine charms in the past.

Disentangling themselves, Bridget spoke first, completely unfazed by what had happened between them.
"I'm sure you're warmer now, sir. I know I am. Anytime you need to be warmed up, I'll be there. I don't think I've enjoyed sex like that ever before. Thank you, sir. Now I'd best be getting back. Mrs Croft might miss me, and that would never do, would it, sir?"
"Off with you now, Bridget, my girl. Let this be our little secret, and I'm sure it won't be the last time we will be together," Roy retorted with a sheepish grin.
He dressed himself and watched Bridget pull up her skirt and slip on her top, before she ran out of his office and along the subterranean corridor to the kitchen. Thinking to himself, *Poor Bridget is not very skilled in the sex stakes, but I'm sure that with a few lessons she will prove to be a worthwhile distraction from my worries and cares,* he locked the envelope in the safe and followed Bridget back to the house.

Janet was waiting for him as he climbed the stone steps leading to the kitchen. She threw her arms around his neck and whispered in his ear,
"Did everything go all right, darling? I was worried when I heard the storm in the night, but I was so relieved when I heard you winch the boat up into the boathouse. Nothing wrong, is there? No damage to the boat?"
Taking her by the arm, he steered her into the lounge.
"No, everything's fine. If I'd have known, I would not have put her away I have another charter tonight. Things are definitely looking up."
"All this work means my sex life is suffering, I feel somewhat neglected. We'll make it up over the weekend," she whispered, winking and giving a wry smile.

"I'm going to have to disappoint you again, darling. I have a week's charter starting on Saturday. We'll make it up before I leave."

"I know you're making lots of money, but don't neglect me too much," she whispered, pouting.

Janet's arms clasped him tightly, and giving him a hug and letting her hands drop down on to the tight cheeks of his buttocks, she pulled him close to her.

"Bridget or Morag may see us," Roy commented, his mouth close to Janet's ear.

"Perhaps they won't be too surprised. I still love you, you hunk!"

"Not now! I've got Liam and a couple of other guys coming to help me load some stuff on the boat. Now leave me alone and let me get to work, you temptress."

With that, he broke from her embrace and gave her a not too gentle slap on the cheeks of her bottom. A few minutes later, Liam, accompanied by two men, whom he introduced as Doyle and John Fitzpatrick, knocked at the kitchen door. Bridget acknowledged Liam before she called Roy.

"Lord Croft, some men are here to see you at the kitchen door."

Roy went to the door and shook hands with Liam, who said,

"This is Doyle and John Fitzpatrick; they have come to give us a hand in loading the boat."

The two men looked sullen. Roy could tell from the handshake and the calloused and well-worn hands of hardworking men, which showed them for what they were, hard cases, but Roy had got to accept this, for Liam was no oil painting. All three wore the rough home-made garb he was used to seeing when he went into the village. Roy walked along the quay to the wicket gate built into the large boathouse doors. Elian was waiting dressed in overalls and the usual woolly hat, neither of which did justice to her womanly characteristics. Unlocking the door, they walked inside. The armaments were two floors down, and once Roy had unlocked the security gates, they descended to the weapons store. The two men obviously were used to naval weapons and pulled out the dolly truck, and with a skill that could only have been learnt in the services; they used the chain hoist and loaded two torpedoes on to the truck. Then they manoeuvred the truck towards the lift.

"We'll come back for the shells. Now have these been checked to see if they're alive?" asked Doyle.

"No!" Roy replied. "They are just as I found them."

With no more ado, the two men opened the small bag of tools John produced from his pocket, and they began to strip the outer cover and inspect the inside of each of the torpedoes.

After a few minutes of tinkering, Doyle looked up and said with a smile, "These are fine. They are the mark XV and are used at a relatively close range of 3,200 metres. They are powered by burner cycles and run from your boat at thirty-three knots. That's what they are set at. You arm and launch them from the bridge. They carry 247 kg of Torpex. They appear to be in excellent working order. The conditions in here are perfect for keeping munitions. There's little or no deterioration at all. They weigh over 800 kg, so we will load them in the boathouse. I've set them to safety. We don't want any accidents, do we?"

The group pushed the truck, with the torpedoes on board, into the lift, and they were winched up on to the boat and lowered down through the hatch. Once loaded aboard, the two men loaded one into each tube and wired up the controls for arming and launching from the bridge. Roy and Elian watched carefully in case they had to carry out the operation themselves.

As soon as everything was completed, the party returned to the armoury to collect the shells for the deck gun.

"Some of these buggers haven't fared so well. They must have got wet at some time; it's the salt that does the damage. We will have to take some of these with us and dispose of them. You see this batch here," he pointed to a cluster on the lowest shelf. "These are showing signs of corrosion and are unstable. I suggest we load them aboard the boat and jettison the whole lot into the sea when you leave today. Well out to sea, mind you, we don't want to blow up your harbour now, do we, milord?"

Roy nodded, for he could see the batch they were talking about; lines of corrosion were showing along one of the seams.

"Are they safe to handle?" Roy asked, thinking of Janet and Sean.

"I'd not like to drop one, if that's what you mean," Doyle said quietly, "but safer in the sea than in this bloody ammunition store. We'll be very careful." Turning to Liam, he said, "Let the boat down gently. We don't want any accidents now, do we, Liam?"

Liam shook his head and looked across at Elian.

"Best, get Bridget on the winch, Elian. She's better than any man I know when it comes to winching a boat down the slipway."

The shells had all been loaded aboard when Elian returned with Bridget. Bridget stood waiting for her instructions, and she looked towards Lord Croft. She was not expecting the instructions to come from Liam, but she accepted them without any qualms.

"Bridget, take your time letting her down the ramp. No mistakes or we're all going to go up with a bang," Liam said quietly.

Whilst the chocks were being removed in readiness, Roy checked the fuel. The tanks were full, and he looked enquiringly at Elian, who nodded her head to indicate that she had taken care of the fuel loading. The boat was gently winched down the slipway and into the harbour. Roy, Elian, Doyle, and Liam jumped aboard, and Elian headed out to sea. About a mile out, and the depth gauge showed that they were over the continental shelf. No words were exchanged as Liam, John, and Doyle dropped the corroded shells over the side. They slipped quietly below the waters of the Atlantic, and when the last one disappeared below the swell, everyone breathed a sigh of relief. Roy checked the torpedo-armed key, and the launch button glowed red. They headed back and tied up alongside the quay. Before going ashore, Roy disarmed the two sleeping steel fish and went ashore to say goodbye to Janet.

Whilst he was away, Liam, Doyle, and John Fitzpatrick loaded several boxes and put them in the hold.

"What's in the boxes?" asked Elian.

"Two rocket launches and rockets. Hope you don't need them on this trip, but you never know. Paddy O'Brien wished he'd had them aboard when he was taken," replied Doyle.

They heard Roy returning, and all went quiet. Doyle and John Fitzpatrick doffed their hats and slipped out to the car park, and Roy heard them drive away. It was now after 5 p.m., and Bridget had gone back to the kitchen and returned, bringing them a flask of hot tea for the journey. Janet watched from the kitchen door as they climbed aboard and waited until the boat had left the harbour and headed out to sea. She waved, not knowing what time Roy would return. If she had known what the events of the night were going to be, she might have wondered if he or any of them would return at all.

Chapter 3

The MTB, with Elian at the wheel and Roy standing behind her, headed for the pickup point where Connor and two other men, both strangers to Roy, waited for the boat to pull in along the stone jetty. Roy looked enquiringly at Connor, and nodding in the direction of the two men, he asked,

"Not two more fugitives for delivery, I hope? We had enough trouble last time."

"No. They are back up in case of trouble, Roy. We are picking up from a different point this time, and we cannot be too careful," Connor replied.

"Expecting trouble then?" Roy asked Connor, somewhat concerned at the possibility of either a fight or being captured and arrested.

"No, your Lordship. Oh sorry, I forgot, Roy! Just precautionary measures. Don't worry. We will make sure no harm will come to you," Connor replied, but it was not with his usual candour.

Roy let them go below, but it was obvious that something was bothering them. Even Liam had a scowl on his face, and the two strangers had not said a word. Entering the wheelhouse, Roy spoke to Elian,

"Something is wrong. All of them look spooked, as though they are expecting trouble."

"I heard a rumour that someone is informing the authorities when and where we are picking up cargo. A mole, I think, was the word they used. God help the poor bugger if they discover who it is. They'll put a fucking bullet in the back of his head. They have no time for squealers or traitors in this outfit."

Roy grunted a noncommittal reply; if he found out who it was, he felt he would shoot the silly bugger himself. The stupid man was putting him and his family in danger, and Roy did not think he would stand for that. Night fell, and Connor came up from below and gave Roy the coordinates. This time, the pickup point was a small cove on the Spanish coast. As usual, Roy was early as usual. Switching off their running lights, they waited, riding the slight swell until they saw the signal and moved further into the bay. The fishing vessel that rendezvoused with them offloaded the cargo. Roy was not needed. There were four of them to do the unloading, and from what Roy could see and hear, the cargo was not guns and ammunitions this time. The packages seemed softer, and from the ease and the way they threw them aboard, they were definitely not explosives. With Elian at the controls, Roy watched Connor and the others put the cargo in the hold, and once done, he gave the skipper a briefcase and they cast off from the Spanish fishing vessel. As they moved away, two Spanish Customs boats seemed to appear from nowhere. They called on the cruiser to heave to, but Elian had already opened the throttles and the MTB leapt forward like a bullet from a gun.

One of the patrol boats, a Cabo class, a much larger boat than the small inshore P111 that had given chase on a previous occasion, called for them to stop, and when Elian kept going, they fired a shot from their deck gun, which fell harmlessly astern. To Roy's surprise, Liam appeared from below with a bulky box on his shoulder. He moved out on the deck, and seconds later, a rocket grenade leapt out towards the chasing patrol boat. The skipper realised instantly that the boat he was chasing had returned fire. He made every attempt to avoid the incoming RPG, and the boat immediately turned away and began to fall behind. There was a roar, followed by an explosion, as the rocket detonated just short of the boat's stern, sending a wave over the gunnels of the patrol boat. Quickly recovering from the surprise of retaliation, the patrol boat once again began to give chase, but it was taking no chances and avoided any chance of a repeat attack by keeping well astern.

Standing by Elian, Roy urged her to keep going as they continued to make a run to escape the possibility of arrest. The steady sound of the patrol boat's engine kept being interrupted. From the spasmodic misses and accompanying puffs of smoke from its exhaust, it had obviously suffered some damage from the explosion. Soon, a thicker pall of smoke could be seen coming from the exhaust, and the boat fell further and further astern. Roy studying the charts gave Elian a new course to set. He gave her 51.32.30 N 9.05.40 W; they raced onwards without running lights and with their radar off, only switching it back on when their signal would be confused with another ship alongside. Roy instructed Elian to use the tactics they had used before, which was to tuck in close to large freighters to disrupt any aerial or satellite surveillance that the Spanish coastguards might have called up.

Roy had held his temper up until then, but he was angry, very angry! When they were sure they were no longer being chased, Roy called Connor up on deck.

"What the hell was that all about?" Roy shouted to Connor.

"Just a wee precaution, Roy. We didn't want to be caught with this cargo on board now, did we?"

"Look here, Connor," Roy snapped, his anger rising quickly. "You may well be the paymaster in this organisation, but let's get one thing straight, shall we? I'm the fucking skipper on this boat, and I give the orders. If you don't like that arrangement, I suggest you get off this boat, and I mean now."

Connor stood with his mouth open. No one had ever challenged his authority before. But he knew Roy had a point, and from the way he handled Elian and his boat, he was aware that Roy could indeed handle himself in any event.

"It'll not happen again," Connor managed to grunt.

"Too bloody right it will not happen again, or you and your organisation will be looking for another sucker. Do I make myself clear on that point? Another thing is that nobody brings weapons on board this boat without me being fully aware of it. That's the second time it's happened, and it's two times too many. Do you understand me, Mr fucking Connor?"

Connor nodded and slunk away below. He kept out of Roy's way for the rest of the voyage, only reappearing when they approached the Irish coastline. It was just before dawn. They were at the coordinates, and under Roy's instructions, Elian proceeded up the creek in front of them, using the depth finder to ensure sufficient depth of water beneath them. They found the area where the water lay some way under the overhanging steep sides of the inlet, and they anchored; the four of them pulled the camouflage netting over the boat just as dawn broke. Liam and Connor slipped ashore, saying they were going to call from the call box up on the headland and give their position and inform the boss that the schedule for the delivery would be twenty-four hours late; Roy called Connor back and asked for a message to be relayed to Janet, explaining that he would be returning late. Connor nodded his agreement. The other two went ashore to keep watch in case of trouble.

Elian and Roy sat in the main cabin. Their adrenaline had been raised to its limit as they had dodged from one freighter to another while crossing the bay. The adrenaline rush, combined with the hurried and worrying moments when they had camouflaged the boat, had raised their senses. The two of them looked at each other, each knowing what the consequences of capture would be; each hoped that any electronic signature they might have left was so unrecognisable as not to have given away their position. Roy was glad that he had instructed Elian to cover the ship's name and registration before leaving for the previous trip. Elian shrugged off her sweater. She had a T-shirt on underneath. Roy looked closer at Elian's face and realised she was quite pretty, more attractive and slimmer than her sister. He felt his ardour rise but put the idea aside. There was no time for that. They might still have to make a run for it, and he occasionally switched on the radar as he kept a close eye for any approaching vessel that might spell trouble. He was glad he had not made any move on the young woman, for it was not long before Connor returned. He climbed aboard leaving Liam and the other two ashore to keep watch.

"The boss wants to know if you will wait here until nightfall and run the cargo ashore tonight. If not, I have to report back before we make a move. Otherwise, the rendezvous will be at the drop-off point at 10 p.m."

"We'll stay until then. Now, what is the cargo? If you want me to risk my boat, I need to know what we have on board."

"I am not supposed to tell you," Connor muttered.

"If you don't tell me, it will never reach its destination," Roy snapped.

With that, Roy pulled out a heavy wartime sidearm he had picked up from the armoury and pointed it at Connor.

"I'll shoot you and throw you and the cargo over the side. If I'm carrying it, I want to know what it is. Now tell me, or I'll fire, and don't think I won't. If this boat is recognised, I've been involved in firing on a Spanish patrol boat, and the Spanish authorities do not take kindly to that. I could, no! We could all be in for a long stretch in jail for something like that."

"OK, OK, keep it together. I'll tell you. It's cocaine, drugs, uncut and worth a small fortune," Connor confided.

"I suspected as much when I saw it being loaded. Next time, if there is to be a next time, I want to know what I'm picking up. Is that clear? Now give me the coordinates for the drop-off, and no bloody excuses that I can't be trusted. We have to see how we can move up the coast surreptitiously in case there are any patrols out there looking for us."

Roy studied the charts with Elian, and they decided how to get there; they would hug the coastline as far as possible, as though they were looking for somewhere to put in for the night. That would be their story if they were approached. Connor slipped ashore to inform the boss that they would leave around lunchtime. By the time he returned, Roy and the others had pulled back the camouflage netting and were ready to move. It was just after lunch when they eased slowly out of the cove and along the coast. They cruised slowly like any boat carrying a few holidaymakers up the coast on a leisure cruise. It was dark when they made the pickup point, but they were on time and they offloaded the cargo, much to Roy's relief, safely and without interruption. For a change to the ordinary run of things, Connor gave Roy his usual package before he and his two associates disembarked. Roy waited for them to get safely ashore, and before Connor could say anything or wave Roy gave Elian instructions to get the hell out of there as quickly as she could. Elian needed no second telling, and they moved out to sea and headed for the castle. They moved well out to sea this time and only turned towards the shore as they approached the castle, moving slowly and carefully into the small harbour. Liam stood on the foredeck; with the agility and his fitness, together with what he had learnt over the years, he leapt ashore and secured the boat to the quay.

"Liam, I'm putting her inside. You open the doors. Elian, go fetch Bridget to operate the winch, I know it's late, but if she's retired or still busy in the kitchen, tell her I need her now, not later. Then come back and give me a hand. I want this done quickly."

It was some time before they reappeared. Bridget had obviously been in bed, and to Roy's surprise, Janet appeared in her dressing gown. Roy jumped ashore, and Janet embraced him.

"Oh God, I was so worried when I got your message. I had not expected you to be away for more than one night."

"There was some delay, nothing to worry about."

"There was a report that a Spanish patrol boat had come under some kind of attack. It was all over the news. I was so worried."

"The area was crawling with boats searching for the brutes that had carried out the attack," Roy said. "We felt it was better to keep our heads down until things went quiet. That's what delayed us. There's nothing for you to worry your head about."

"I'm so glad, Roy. I don't know what I would have done if anything had happened to you. I'm also worried about your next trip. The weather forecast for the coming weekend is appalling."

"The boat can handle anything the sea can throw at it. It was designed for just such weather, and with Elian at the helm, you don't have anything to concern yourself about. She's more than capable of handling most things. Now go back to bed. You don't look yourself. Are you all right?"

"I will. It's that time of the month, and I've got such cramps. I just need to rest. I'll see you later."

"All right, I'll see you as soon as we have her tucked safely up inside."

With the assistance of Elian, Liam, and Bridget, Roy soon had the boat winched up inside, and when it was safely chocked; he poured them all a glass of whisky to warm them up. Liam and Elian soon disappeared; leaving Roy and Bridget to walk slowly back through the underground passage. They reached the kitchen when Bridget, who had been wearing a thick woollen sweater, pulled off the garment, and to Roy's amazement, she was naked beneath it. Her young breasts bobbed up and down with the firmness of youth; with no further hesitation, her jeans followed the sweater on to the floor, and she moved forward and threw her arms around Roy's neck. At this stage, she was wearing only her plain cotton knickers, and she pressed herself against Roy, who could not help but respond to her closeness.

"Bridget, we can't do this. Mrs Croft could come down to see where I am."

"I'm sure she won't, sir, and I've waited for this since we did it last time. Just a quickie, sir."

Roy was soon hard as his arousal soared; the opportunity to take this young woman again was too strong. In seconds, he had lifted her up on to the stout wooden table, and his hand went down to his zip. Soon, his trousers and shorts were around his ankles. Bridget gave a gasp as she felt him enter her.

"Oh yes!" Bridget moaned.

"Shush! Not so loud," Roy whispered.

The sound has been a little too loud for Roy's liking; he was concerned that Janet would hear them. Roy's concern, however, soon evaporated; he was in his element as he took the hapless creature who tried in vain to keep up with him. He was wired up after his fracas with the patrol boat and his argument with Connor, and he went wild. His usual control seemed to evaporate. Bridget gave a series of cries, loud enough to be heard several rooms away as her body reached its climax, and she arched up against her newfound lover. Roy, who was beyond thinking of anything but his own satisfaction, grunted as he raced to achieve his own orgasm. His need went beyond caution, and he knew he would not be satisfied quickly. Neither of them heard the door close softly behind them. It was Janet who had heard the noises from the bedroom and come down to see what it was. What she had witnessed had not made her jealous; she had told Roy that she had never expected him to be monogamous. She had just been surprised that he had taken advantage of such a young girl and a member of his own staff into the bargain. She quietly made her way up to bed, aware that the commotion in the kitchen had started again; she knew of old just how quickly her wayward husband could recover. She lay listening, and she was not disappointed. Bridget's cries indicated that Roy was satisfying the young woman's needs yet again. She only hoped she was not ovulating.

Some considerable time later, when Roy crept into the bedroom sexually satiated, it appeared to him that Janet was asleep, and he made straight for the shower; when he emerged wrapped as usual in the bath towel, Janet was sitting up, resting on her elbow.
"Well, Roy, I'm surprised at you. I hope you realise the young women in these parts are all Catholics and, as such, are forbidden by the church to take precautions against getting pregnant."
"What do you mean, Janet?" Roy asked innocently.
"Good God, Roy, I saw you with Bridget. She's only a young woman, barely old enough to give her consent."
"Could you hear us then?" Roy queried.
"Hear you? She was making enough noise to wake the whole household. I understand your needs, but for heaven's sake be more careful. She's only just started work here. I don't want her pregnant with your child before she's had time to settle in. I know I told you I would never mind you having other women, but try to be more discreet, will you? Now, get into bed and give me a hug. Then we can both get some rest. I'm sure after what I witnessed between the two of you downstairs, you certainly need it."
Roy put his arms around her and hugged her. He had not realised that she had watched him having sex with Bridget, but he was pleased that she had not made more of it. He would need to try and be more careful in future.

The following morning, just after breakfast, Roy heard the private cell ring. When he answered, the usual voice said cautiously,

"Are you alone?"

"Yes," Roy responded.

"I heard you had trouble and had to take evasive action."

"You could say that. I spoke to Connor about . . ."

"I heard all about it and agree. There can only be one skipper on board a boat. Connor sometimes gets ahead of himself. I'm glad you had the balls to take him on. I understand that the patrol boat may have got a look at your boat. That deck gun is a bit too identifiable. Can I make a suggestion?"

"Yes," Roy said tentatively.

"I've got fitters and armourers that could remove that gun and the gun mountings at the rear and re-plank the deck. That should remove the identifying weaponry. They would then fit a locker below decks, and we would supply you with a couple of Sam7s and a rocket grenade launcher and rockets to replace the equipment we remove. The lockers would be hidden from any casual inspection and would only be able to be spotted if the hull was stripped down. Believe me, these guys know what they are at, and you would not know they had been there, even if you were the person doing the inspection. They will also fit a secret locker for the storage of special cargo like last night."

"Christ!" said Roy. "Do you think such weapons are really necessary?"

There was a short pause, and the person behind the voice was coming to a decision. The voice sounded different somehow, as it recommenced in a slower but sterner voice full of self-control.

"Lord Croft, I hate to tell you this, but we believe we may have a traitor in our midst, and until he or she has been identified and dealt with, we cannot be too careful. Those patrol boats were not there by accident."

"We have a charter coming up at the weekend. Do you want to do the work when we get back?" Roy asked tentatively.

"No," said the voice. "I want to do it today. My team can be with you in an hour. It will take them a couple of days, and they will be finished before you are due to leave well before Saturday. By the way, how do you like your new assistant skipper, Elian?"

"She can handle the boat really well," Roy replied and continued, "Are you telling me that the team to do the work will be here that quickly?"

"Yes, and we know that all the planking, etc. we shall need is in the workshop, so we do not have to wait for materials."

Roy was about to ask how they knew, but with his entire staff provided by them, they would know almost as much as he did about what was in the warehouse and workshop.

"All right. I'll expect them in an hour," Roy said calmly.

"I'll speak to you when they've finished. You won't regret it."

The phone went dead.

Roy had barely finished lunch when Bridget came into the dining room and informed him that there was someone at the back door to see him. He kissed Janet and said that he would be at the boathouse if she needed him. Michael Finnegan introduced himself and said, doffing his hat as he did so,

"I'm Michael Finnegan, your Lordship." With a smile on his weather-beaten face, he began, "I've been instructed to speak with you, sir. It seems that our boss is extremely happy with your performance, but he feels that the deck guns would cause too much attention for the weekend run."

Roy had heard it before, but hesitated; he did not want to upset Michael in his obviously prepared speech:

"I and my team of men will remove them and store them safely in your armoury, and in their place, we will be supplying you with two Sam7 missile launchers and two rocket grenade launchers, all hand-held. We will then fit them in a specially constructed and sealed compartment in the hold below decks."

Michael paused for a breath, as if taking in Roy's reaction, and seeing no animosity, he then added,

"If you agree, the fitters will start straightaway. We have studied the drawings of the hull obtained from the original company who built your MTB, and the space we will use will not alter the internal lines of the boat and will not be detectable unless the hull is stripped. The decks," he said, "will have a much cleaner line. In addition to that, we shall be fitting a missile control and detection radar equipment to give you advance warning of any incoming weaponry and to enable you to get missile lock on anything that may attack the vessel."

Michael paused again as if he expected Roy to comment. Roy did not let him down. He asked Michael, somewhat amused at the man's calmness as he spoke of such weapons, seemingly without any fear of reprisal,

"Why is this all necessary?" Roy asked him.

"It would appear," Michael said looking around furtively, "that we have a mole in our midst, and from the checks the main man has made on you, you are to be trusted completely. With your permission, we'll get to work. The fitters are parked a few miles away awaiting my call. They will be brought in a closed van, and they have no idea where they are, so I would appreciate it, Lord Croft, if you kept out of the way until they have finished, so they will never be able to identify you. They will stay inside the boathouse until the end of the job. They will then be taken back in the closed van, unable to say where they had been. Before they arrive, I suggest that we lock everything away that could identify the boat or you."

Roy went with Michael to the boathouse where Elian and Liam stood waiting; together, they quickly, but carefully, cleared everything away, including the envelope containing his payment for the last trip. Once this had been done, Roy asked Michael if he would get the leader of the group to contact him as he had a couple of requests to make of him. The next two days saw a hive of activity in the workshop, and by Saturday morning, all was completed. The fitters were loaded into the closed van inside the workshop and driven away. Michael asked Roy to come and see the results. It was truly amazing; the deck had been stripped and re-boarded, showing no trace of where the original gun emplacements had been. The lines of the ship were perfect. There were now no signs of any weaponry, and a new railing had been put around the boat. It looked for all the world like any other converted MTB, giving no hint of what armoury of weapons lay below deck. When Michael took him down below, Roy was surprised; the boat looked completely untouched below decks, and no trace of any changes could be seen. Michael showed Roy the hidden missiles, the rocket launchers, the new hold for the Sam7s, the side arms, and machine guns, now four in total, together with the ammunition.

Michael then asked Roy, in a hushed tone of voice, when they were apart from the others so that they would not be overheard,

"What do you think of Elian?" Not waiting for an answer, he continued, "You know she has her master's papers, don't you? She was sent in for you to appraise her abilities and this week-long trip will do just that. Liam will also be part of the crew. He is trained on the armaments we have fitted."

Roy slowly began to understand why Britain had been so unsuccessful in destroying the IRA. They were everywhere and melded into and formed an integral part of every community. In the voice of a man completely satisfied that the work of his team would be fully acceptable, Michael said,

"You must take her out on test now. If she's OK, and if you are completely satisfied, we can leave for the weekend trip. If you find you need anyone else, you must let me or Connor know who or what you need." He added, "After we've tested the boat, I'll get rid of the crew of fitters, and you can load whatever supplies you need for the trip. When that has been done, if you have no objection, I will come with you, and you can drop me off when you pick up Connor."

Liam and Michael, together with Elian, let the cruiser down the slipway. Roy and Elian took her out and put her through her paces. The cleaner lines and the lighter weight made the boat faster and easier to handle. The weather forecast was not good. Although the sky was clear, the wind was getting up from the west, and the forecast was for storms in the Bay of Biscay reaching gale force at times. Elian took the wheel, and Roy could see that, as usual, she handled the newly modified seventy-five-foot craft like a pro; he let her take the powerful boat into the harbour, and she edged the craft gently alongside the quay without even a bump or a jar.

Roy instructed Elian to load the waterproof gear for them all and the supplies of food were to be stored in the galley for the four of them for up to a week; Liam and Michael helped whilst Roy went up to the castle to say goodbye to Janet.

Janet was concerned about the forecast on the radio, which had given a warning that there was a gale brewing in the Bay of Biscay; but Roy assured her once again that the MTB could handle anything that the sea could throw at them. Bridget handed him the hamper of cooked food to last them for the weekend. She added that Elian was a good cook and that she would be able to prepare food for the rest of the week. Leaning over whilst Janet gave Morag the baby to hold, Bridget gripped his wrist and whispered,

"Good luck, your Lordship and come back safe."

Janet returned and walked down to the quay. Arriving at the gangplank, she hugged him and told him to be careful. She held him close and whispered,

"I'll be thinking of you. I know it may be difficult, and I'll understand if you can't do it, but try and get a message to me from wherever you are. I love you."

The storm clouds were already appearing on the horizon. As Roy and his crew climbed aboard, he checked the fuel and was pleased to see that Elian had organised the tanks to be topped off. He waved goodbye to Janet, who stayed on the quayside until the craft had disappeared from sight.

Chapter 4

Aboard the speeding cruiser, the swell was causing the hull to bang against each crest as it sped through the waves. Roy handed the wheel to Elian whilst he went to check that everything was tightened down and secure. He returned, and Liam handed him coffee from the galley where he and Michael were sitting. He went up to the wheelhouse, where Elian was handling the speeding boat with confidence. He watched her as she manoeuvred the craft into the shore to pick up Connor. Michael came up from below, and as Connor came aboard, Michael jumped ashore.

"Good luck," he called.

But the sound was lost in the growing wind as they turned and headed back out to sea. Connor gave them the GPS coordinates of the small fishing village, where they were to pick up the passengers. Neither Elian nor Roy knew the final destination; Connor would only tell them once they had picked up the passengers and were under way. The small fishing village where the passengers waited was sheltered from the west by a headland that curled around the opening to the cove in which the harbour lay. As they rounded the cliffs protecting the harbour, the wind dropped, and the water calmed down. Elian, with Roy standing behind her, edged the craft alongside the quay. Liam and Connor secured the boat fore and aft, and they sat in the galley drinking hot coffee whilst they waited for the passengers to come aboard. The fuel tanks were topped up, and Connor paid the harbour master in cash.

Roy was surprised by the number, as twenty passengers walked up the gangway. They were a tough-looking bunch comprising sixteen men and four women. They had brought their own supplies for the journey, mainly sandwiches and flasks of tea and coffee. Roy walked around and handed out seasickness tablets to any that wanted them. He then handed out life vests, and as the number of passengers exceeded his estimation, he found that he was four short. Connor went ashore and returned with half a dozen old, used, inflatable vests. He handed four to the last passengers. Roy and Elian secured the running ropes up on deck and across the cabin and stairwell below. It was going to be a rough trip, and they needed to be prepared. Elian went below and handed out bags to the passengers, telling

them in a voice that indicated that she meant every word and expected to
be obeyed.

"No one will be allowed on deck during the trip, and if any of you need to
vomit, use the bags. Now, if you make a mess, you'll bloody well have to
clean it up yourselves. I'm not cleaning up after you. You are all supposed
to be tough, so show it."

Elian showed them the heads and how to use the pump to operate the
toilet and issued each one with two bottles of still water. They cast off and
headed out into the weather. Connor gave a destination in North Africa
just south of Tangiers, and he told an anxious skipper that he had arranged
for them to refuel at A Coruna, on the Spanish coast, both ways and at
Tangiers. Roy looked at the weather; it was ideal to cover the fact that they
were running passengers to North Africa, but he was worried about their
safety. This was by far the longest trip he had ever made in the boat and,
by far, the worst weather. He hoped that Jeremy, the man who had done
the refit, was as good as he had claimed to be, for this trip could well test
the hull to its limit.

They hit the huge swells in the Bay of Biscay, and Roy was glad to have
Elian on board. She was used to the rough weather from being on fishing
fleet boats out in the Atlantic, far more than Roy. She handled the boat with
a skill and dexterity he could only appreciate and admire. He had gained his
master's certificate, but nothing had prepared him for this kind of weather;
if he had his way, they would have waited until the worst of the storm
had passed. However, the voice on the line had stressed the importance of
being on time, so that was not an alternative. The seventy-five-foot craft
was tossed about like a cork, but between them, Roy and Elian contrived
to make good headway, and some fifteen hours later, running low on fuel
and with a sick bunch of passengers, they headed into the Spanish port of
A Coruna. They pulled alongside the quay, refuelled, and took on water.
Connor paid the harbour master in cash for the fuel, and as they were
stretched for time, due to the bad weather, they headed out to sea once
again.

To the relief of all on board, the worst of the storm had passed as they
turned south, heading for Tangiers. Some ten hours later, they were off
the coast of North Africa, and Connor asked Roy to radio in, and he gave
Elian the frequency to call. Once contact had been made, Roy handed the

radio mike to Connor, who gave Roy the pre-arranged code and the GPS coordinates to rendezvous with an Algerian dhow, a single-sailed vessel used for all purposes off the North African coast. At last, they spotted the sail and pulled alongside. The boat hardly looked seaworthy; little or no paint remained on the hull, and the sail hung limply from the mast. From the number of patches on the sail's fabric, it had obviously been repaired many times. Connor saw the look of doubt on Roy's face and said,

"Don't be put off by appearances. The boat is sound, but if it shone like a new pin, it would attract the attention of not only the authorities but local pirates as well. We have used this boat and its skipper many times in the past, and he has never let us down."

"No problem," replied Roy. "I'm not going aboard the damned boat, sound or not."

The passengers were transferred to the sailing ship. They were mostly a sorry-looking bunch, but they had recovered somewhat from the poor state they had been in at A Coruna. Connor spoke to the Algerian skipper, and although Roy could not hear what was being said, he saw the usual bulky envelope being passed over. The dhow captain motioned the group of would-be terrorist trainees down into the hold of the wooden craft amidst grumbles that it was stinking of fish down there. Once the passengers were hidden from sight, the swarthy-looking Arab captain gave the order to cast off, and the sail was raised. The seemingly ungainly vessel moved away before coming about with a flurry of movement from the crew. Although they looked like an undisciplined and raggedly dressed mob, they seemed to know exactly what was expected of them, and the boat headed back towards the coast.

Connor then asked Roy to head into Tangiers, where he had arranged accommodation overnight, before they headed back. Roy, who felt in need of a few hours' rest and recuperation, headed for the port of Tangiers. It was somewhat different from what he had expected. Tangiers is now a large container port, and the wide beach fronting the city came as a surprise. Connor directed them into the old part of the harbour, which seemed to Roy to be more like the place he had expected. Drawing alongside an old wharf, they were met by a couple of seedy-looking customs officials after they had tied up. Roy noted a roll of US currency notes changing hands; he was informed that they had now cleared the customs and immigration formalities. They headed for the hotel, and Roy hoped he would get a good night's sleep. Connor handed back the passports, and when Roy opened his, he could see no stamped entry, only a slip of paper with entry and exit stamps. Roy was once again impressed by Connor's cunning ability, for he understood that once they left the port, no one would be any the wiser that they had been in Tangiers at all.

Roy was glad for the stopover; it was just what he and Elian sorely needed. They had both been on their feet and awake for more than thirty-six hours. Connor told Roy not to worry about the boat. He had ensured that it would be under the careful watch of the customs officers whilst they were in port. Roy was not so impressed with the hotel. It was just up off the waterfront, in the Kasbah area, and was a little basic, to say the least; no one could say it was upmarket, and the odd-looking characters hanging around the bar looked rough, to say the least. It was not the sort of place to be alone in, and he felt sorry for Elian, who gazed around in horror. Once they had checked in, Roy went up to his room. To his surprise, the rooms were relatively clean, and the bed looked inviting. Roy felt that this had more to do with his fatigue than any other contributing factor; dumping his bag in the room, he walked along the dingy corridor to collect Elian, and they joined Connor and Liam in the bar for a well-earned drink. The crowd in the bar, if anything, looked worse than the bunch hanging around on the quayside. They were the usual flotsam of characters that can be seen around any port, looking for the chance to get a ship. The four of them ate and had a few drinks in the small dining area at the rear of the bar; the smoke was thick and the drinks rough. After eating what was a mixture of foods from different parts of North Africa, that were unpredictably pleasant tasting on the tongue, and after having a couple of harsh whiskies, it was not long before Elian and Roy left the other two in the bar and went up to their rooms to get some sleep.

Elian, who was almost out on her feet, said to Roy in a sleepy and concerned voice.
"I do not feel very safe in this hotel. Can I sleep in your room? A woman on her own in this godforsaken place can only be a target for the local ruffians."
Roy, who was also almost asleep, agreed without a second thought. Once in the room, they stripped off their sweat-soaked clothing and fell asleep, on the bed, totally exhausted. They slept well into the next day, and it was Roy

who woke first. He cleared his head and looked around, unable to realise where he was for a moment. He saw Elian lying beside him wearing only a bra and panties. It took him a few moments to remember where he was, with this strange woman beside him on the bed. Roy's eyes roamed over the sleeping form and took in her small but muscular frame and her small breasts, which were completely covered by her plain cotton bra. Roy was desperate to go to the toilet, and his morning arousal was plain to see. He got up off the bed, and Elian opened her eyes. She looked at Roy and said in a sleepy but jocular tone of voice,

"My! My! My sister Bridget told me about you. Now I know she was telling the truth. I must say you look well this morning, Roy." Then, pointing in the direction of his groin, she asked suggestively, "Is that all for me?"

This was the first time she had ever spoken to him in anything but formal boss and employee terms; she had never before used his first name.

"Not until I've showered," Roy responded "From that remark, I have to presume you must be fully recovered from the ordeals of the trip. Are you sure you're in the mood?"

"I've been in worse storms, and after a good sleep, I'm ready for anything," Elian replied.

After she had watched him cross the room, Elian stretched, and throwing her feet over the edge of the bed, she stood up and followed Roy into the smallish bathroom. The shower cubicle was really only big enough for one. Elian dropped her bra and panties on the floor; she saw that Roy was already under the water, and needing to wash herself to rid her body of the lingering stale odours of perspiration and saltwater, she squeezed into the tiny cubicle in front of Roy; it was just possible. The soap from Roy's body smeared over her own. She asked for the soap, and Roy rubbed her breasts with the shower gel. The two of them washed as well as the space would permit, and when they stepped out after rinsing under the poor water supply, they dried off and walked naked into the bedroom. Roy's arousal, far from diminishing under the cold water, after contact with Elian under the shower, was still as evident as ever, and Elian spoke, the gravelly sound of her voice betraying her own desires.

"I'll ask again," she said, pointing at Roy's obvious signs of arousal "Are you sure all this is for me?"

"I don't see anyone else in the room, do you?" Roy said casually.

He swept her up in his arms and carried her to the bed. He laid her down and kissed her on the mouth; her lips were not as full as her sister Bridget's, but she was far more skilled than her sister had been in the art of sex. Elian's lips parted, sucking Roy's tongue into her mouth. Their tongues danced, and their hands roamed freely as they discovered each other. Roy, not heeding Janet's warnings about having unprotected sex with the local Catholic women, moved quickly. Elian's sexual skills intrigued him as he aroused her desires before he took her. She was a somewhat noisy lover as she achieved her peak several times before Roy finally gave a grunt of satisfaction as he felt his own release, totally oblivious of the fact that his actions could end up with Elian getting pregnant. As with each new conquest, Roy recovered quickly, and it was a couple of hours later when they lay for the time being, completely sexually replete. They showered once again in cold water; this time with the heat of the room, as the sun reached its meridian, they were only too pleased to be cooled even under the dismal trickle of water. They dressed, feeling much more relaxed, and made their way down to the bar.

There Liam and Connor sat looking just as Roy had left them the previous evening. Both appeared the worse for drink. To Roy, it looked as though they had been there all night. Roy looked at the two of them and said,
"I think we should be going, don't you?"
Connor nodded and replied, the slur of alcohol clearly pronounced in his voice,
"We've paid for the rooms. I think we should have lunch before we go."
Roy shook his head, saying,
"There's food enough on the boat. Let's go before you land us all into trouble. Settle the bar bill, and let's get the hell out of this heat box before we all cook."

Connor paid the barman with US dollars and they left. Roy was well aware that the immigration and customs would not be any problem; the large roll of US bills left in both officials' hands the previous night had assured him of that. The boat had been refuelled, and Connor paid in US dollars from his seemingly endless supply before they cast off. Elian drew Roy's attention to the fact that, as they were pulling out of the harbour, another craft was trailing them. Roy eased the throttle forward, and the cruiser's bow lifted. He gazed over his shoulder and found that the smaller craft was still with them. The crew looked ugly, and Roy handed the wheel to Elian and went below to tell Connor.

Connor shook Liam, and in an instant he was wide awake, all signs of the alcoholic haze gone in an instant. Both men knew how to handle a crisis. Drink had never been a problem, and they were immediately ready for any type of trouble, no matter what. Both men had felt the speed at which they were going and realised that trouble was on hand. Elian had pushed the throttles wide open, and as the shoreline receded, the boat that had up to now been trailing them began to overhaul them. Elian said, turning to Roy, as Connor appeared out of the cabin below,

"I'm flat out, and they're still gaining on us. Heaven only knows what they have for power."

"They are called cigarette boats and are used for ocean racing. The hull weighs next to nothing, and they have a hugely powerful engine," Connor informed her in a seemingly casual voice that hid his deep concern.

The shoreline was now a long way behind them. Gradually, it disappeared below the horizon, and Elian turned towards home. Connor nodded a signal to Liam, and he went below only to reappear with a grenade launcher. He stayed below in the cabin to see what the other boat would do. The high-speed craft had closed the gap between them before the man standing beside the wheel using a loud hailer called out,

"Ahoy there! Shut off power and heave to if you know what's good for you."

Roy indicated to Elian to keep going and, picking up the microphone by the console, hailed back,

"By whose or what authority?"

"This!" came the angry reply.

The man holding the loud hailer nodded to one of the crew brandishing a machine gun, and a burst of automatic gunfire went over the roof of the wheelhouse, much too close for Roy's comfort.

Almost before Roy could react or answer, there was a whoosh from the doorway of the main cabin to Roy's left; the high speed cruiser coming up fast, seemed to hesitate for a few seconds, and then, as if lifted by an unseen hand, it bucked skywards. To Roy, it was as though the whole thing was happening in slow motion. The bow of the speeding boat seemed to change shape before exploding, the force sending bits of the boat, men, and equipment high into the air as the rocket grenade fired by Liam struck the foredeck of the sleek powerboat. The look on the faces of the would-be attackers was one of stupefied surprise as the crippled speedboat immediately lost way and fell behind. The open bow, smashed and smoking from the impact of the rocket grenade shell, was allowing water to enter the ruined hull, and the stricken craft gradually began to settle in the swell of the open sea. Roy was taken aback by the speed at which things had happened. He was very angry; once again, both men had reacted without his orders. He held back his wrath for once; he accepted the fact that, in this case, they had probably saved his life.

"What the hell was that all about?" asked Roy.

"Pirates," said Liam. "They saw us pay with US dollars and wanted the rest. It serves the bastards right."

Roy asked, concern showing on his face as the smoking speedster, now much lower in the water, its deck awash, fell behind them rapidly,

"Are we going to leave them stranded out here? Some of them may be badly injured."

Connor smiled with satisfaction as he replied,

"They would have killed us all. In all probability, they would have raped Elian before killing her, and then they would have sunk your boat without any thought at all. Let the buggers rot, or take their chances of being picked up by a dhow or a passing ship."

Roy grimly realised that he was now a committed member of the underworld, and his dream of becoming a member of the criminal world was with him; there was no turning back. Ten hours later, they pulled into A Coruna for refuelling. Roy wanted to go ashore and take a few hours' rest and do some shopping. There would be a gift for Janet and one for Sean and the promised underwear for Bridget and perhaps some for Elian. Both women seemed to wear the plain cotton pants common in use by the local women of the village. Connor, who also feigned tiredness, agreed that they should stay overnight and leave the following morning. Both he and Liam, who had slept most of the way back, headed for the bar whilst Roy and Elian went to see what shops were still open. Roy bought Janet a small gift, a toy for Sean, and when Elian went into one clothes shop, Roy dodged into another and purchased the promised undergarments, after which the two of them headed back to the boat.

Liam was waiting aboard the cruiser as they returned, and he asked Roy as Elian brushed past and went below.

"Connor wants to know if you want him to book you both a room, or are you staying aboard?"

"I'm staying aboard. I don't know about Elian. You'd better ask her yourself."

A few minutes later, he appeared with a broad grin on his face as he made suggestive gestures and leered.

"Looks like you got company tonight, your Lordship. Enjoy yourself. I've fancied young Elian myself several times, but I've not got your charm." Under his breath, he added, "Or your money."

Roy and Elian followed Liam back to the bar and ate the surprisingly good-tasting paella, on the special offer menu, before returning to the boat. Once aboard the vessel, not a word was spoken between Roy and Elian. There just seemed to be that understanding between them as to what was acceptable and what was not as they both headed for the stateroom where they stripped off their clothes and slid underneath the covers. They fell into one another's arms and kissed, their ardour rising higher every minute. They were, after all, consenting adults and in no rush. They lay with their bodies touching. Roy drew the naked body of his companion closer, but there was no resistance, no signs of reluctance, only a soft sigh indicating complete compliance. Roy planted gentle kisses on her face and neck before moving down her chest until he reached her breasts. His kisses felt like electricity to Elian, who lay back, completely at ease, as she surrendered entirely to Roy's control. Roy took his time, letting Elian relax and enjoy his skill and competence; this was what he was best at doing, making a woman happy as he brought her to a crest time and time again. It was a long time afterwards that she heard her own cry of passionate release, as it coursed through her spasming body, accompanied by the grunt of self-satisfaction as Roy once again released deep within his latest conquest. They lay together, their energy spent, and post-coital feelings began to envelop them. Elian pushed Roy off her and stood up, moving towards the tiny heads to shower. She opened the shower door and turned on the water, not waiting for it to get warm before she stepped inside. The cool water ran over her, washing the evidence of their mutual passionate encounter from her satiated body. She dried herself and slid into bed beside Roy, who was already in a deep sleep.

The following morning, Elian felt Roy's eyes on her as she showered once again. Then his gaze followed her every move as she stepped from the small cubicle, but she felt no shame at what she had done; he was, in her mind, a wonderfully considerate lover, and she felt a pang of jealousy that it was Janet who was married to him. There was nothing, however, she could do to change that. She would just have to be happy with what she could get out of the relationship. Her thoughts roamed as she dried herself with the thick fluffy towel. She had a picture of Donagh, her boyfriend, in her mind; she had known him at school and had often helped him and his father on the fishing boat. She had always felt that he would be the man she would marry, but his lovemaking was rough and clumsy compared to this new man in her life. Lord Croft made her feel so good, despite the fact that she knew he would never marry her; he had also made love to her sister. *How bad was that?* she thought to herself.

Elian snapped out of her reverie as she felt Roy brush past her and step inside the small space she had vacated. She stood and looked at him as he washed his muscular frame. She slowly moved away and dressed; her mind still partially on Donagh, but mostly on his Lordship, Roy Croft, and her heart rate began to rise, but she knew that they had to get underway if they were to get back before nightfall. She made him breakfast, and they sat in the main cabin lounge drinking coffee as they sat and waited for the other two to arrive, so that they could get under way. Roy was beginning to think that they would not come aboard before lunch, and he was already feeling like taking Elian back to bed; the chance, however, never arose for it was only moments later when Liam and Connor finally arrived. They both looked rough from lack of sleep and a surfeit of drink. Ignoring their state of intoxication, Roy went ashore and cast off, jumping aboard just as Elian eased the cruiser forward, clearing the end of the jetty before turning slowly, and then she headed out to sea. The weather had improved, and the two men went into two of the cabins to sleep off the effects of the drink.

In contrast to the smell of sate alcohol below, the air in the wheelhouse was fresh and the sea had an unusual calmness about it. Roy was contemplating whether he could somehow take Elian again before they got back, but his thoughts were shattered as a patrol boat appeared from behind a headland and requested them to pull over. Roy knew they were as 'clean' as they would ever be and that all the weaponry was packed away in the hidden lockers. Roy gave Elian the signal to stop, they 'hove to', and the patrol boat pulled alongside. The Captain requested permission to board. Once aboard, he asked in English with a thick Spanish accent,

"Where are you headed and from where have you come?"

"Out of A Coruna, heading for Tralee, with two passengers the worse for your Spanish beer," Roy added, smiling.

"Are you carrying any cargo aboard?" the captain enquired sharply.

"No," replied Roy calmly, "we only have two passengers. Would you care to take a look below? You may do so with pleasure. We have nothing to hide."

The captain motioned for his first officer to come aboard. The officer, accepting the captain's order to come aboard, jumped on to the deck of Roy's cruiser, closely followed by a third. The captain and the other officer stood talking to Elian whilst Roy escorted the first officer below. To Roy's surprise, the officer took off her hat and revealed her femininity, and a shock of her thick black, well-groomed hair cascaded down over her shoulders.

"This is a fine wooden-hulled boat," she said, noting Roy's gaze, "A British MTB from the last war, is it not? There are not many that have survived the test of time."

The Spanish officer seemed far more interested in talking to Roy than in conducting her search, if you could call it that, for it was a cursory one, to say the least. By the time they had completed the tour below, Roy knew that her name was Catalina Cordoba and she was engaged to be married to an officer in the Spanish army. She seemed so full of herself, and Roy could see that she was somewhat attracted to him as she constantly kept looking at him. Roy knew better than to try anything; perhaps that was what she wanted, an excuse to take him ashore and strip search the boat. He resisted any opportunity she offered, and finally she declared that she was satisfied that they were not carrying contraband. They came back on deck, and the senior officer, who had been talking to Elian, looked at her enquiringly, and she shook her head. Then he asked,

"Can I see your passports, Señor?"

Roy went below and slipped out the small bits of paper the Customs officers had stamped in Tangiers; he then took all four passports back up to the Customs and Excise officer who looked at them casually. His eyes opened wide when he read Roy's title.

"They seem to be in order, Lord Croft. Now, may I see the ship's log?"

Officer Catalina Cordoba looked startled as she heard the second officer address the man she had been openly flirting with as Lord Croft, and she was sorry she had not pushed harder for his attention. Not only was he handsome, but he had a title as well. She hoped she would see him again in the not-too-distant future, for he looked really desirable.

Roy sent Elian to get the ship's log. He had deliberately not made any entry since he had been in A Coruna, and once the captain had cast a cursory glance over the pages, he nodded to his first and second officers and said to Roy,

"Thank you for your cooperation, Lord Croft. I'm sorry to have caused you any inconvenience. You may proceed on your way."

The three of them re-boarded the Spanish patrol boat but not before Roy saw Catalina give him a sly smile that promised that they would meet again if it was at all possible.

Connor and Liam had slept throughout the entire event, and Connor looked somewhat shocked when Roy told him what had happened.

"Why didn't you wake me?" Connor asked him.

"It was a routine check, and there was no need. I wanted to see if the work would pass muster, and it did."

"If there had been a problem, what would you have done then?" Connor asked, his face showing his concern.

"There wasn't, so you need not have worried. The Spanish lady officer was very attractive and seemed attracted to me. I'm sure I could have handled any situation that may have arisen."

At this, even Connor looked shocked as he said,

"You don't mean you actually . . ."

"Don't concern yourself. I have saved First Officer Catalina Cordoba for some future date."

So saying, Roy winked at the disbelieving Connor, and a broad, wry grin crossed Roy's face. Connor shook his head in total disbelief.

"Jesus, I'm beginning to believe what they say about you in the village. You have no shame, even the customs officer. Did you really believe she would have let you into her drawers?" Connor said, using the country term for knickers. "Your sex life will be the bloody death of you one of these days, Roy. You're bloody incorrigible."

Connor went below, still shaking his head. He looked hard at Roy, still disbelieving that he would have the audacity to have sex with the lady customs officer as Roy dropped him off at the usual point and, together with Liam and Elian, headed for the castle harbour.

Arriving at their destination, Liam leapt ashore and secured the craft fore and aft, and Roy, who had arranged to leave the craft in the harbour this time, said "Good night" to Liam, who climbed on his bicycle, and Roy and Elian walked slowly back up the slipway to the boathouse. She waited whilst he deposited yet another envelope in the safe. Roy realised that the pile of euros he had accumulated was growing and that he needed to do something with them, remembering that under no circumstances did he want to attract attention to the amount of money he was earning. The last thing he wanted was to alert the attention of the revenue or tax inspectors, so he knew that banking the funds was out of the question. With a jaunt in his step, he resolved to take Janet to England for shopping, which would please her and draw her attention away from his philandering ways. He was already planning when he could have the opportunity to give Bridget her new panties and have wild sex with the young woman and her sister Elian again as he opened the kitchen door.

Elian went up to see Bridget, and Roy walked into the lounge where Janet was reading. Janet saw him and scolded him for not letting her know he was home, but threw her arms around him and kissed him hard.

"Oh God, Roy," she said. "I've been so worried about you, what with the gales being so strong so soon after you left."

He told her, a little too enthusiastically for Janet's liking, that Elian had been marvellous during the storm.

"Elian handled the MTB magnificently even in the biggest swells. I think she will have to be a regular member of the crew, and Liam proved his worth on a couple of occasions."

Roy was well aware that he needed a decent shower to ensure that no lingering aroma of his sexual exploits remained. Knowing full well the limitations of the small shower aboard the cruiser, he wrinkled his nose and said,

"I have not changed for a couple of days. I can almost smell myself. Phew!" He disengaged their arms and whispered in her ear, "I love you, but I must go up to shower and put on some fresh clothes."

Just as he was about to go out the door, he asked,

"How's Bridget, by the way? I did not see her in the kitchen."

"Oh, she's fine, but she's asked for the weekend off to go to some Irish Fayre nearby," Janet replied lightly.

Roy bounced upstairs, feeling on top of the world.

He was singing in the shower when Janet opened the door and slid in beside him.

"Where's Junior?" Roy asked her.

"With Morag!" she replied, "but why the shocked look? You must have known I'd come up to see you after almost a week without you."

Janet began massaging the soap into Roy's skin and loving the feeling when he reciprocated. Both were highly charged when they had rubbed each other dry. Roy scooped her up into his arms and carried her to the bed. They made passionate love before going down to dinner. The faint glow in her cheeks was the only outward sign of their passions.

Over dinner, Roy suggested that they spend a few days in England.

"We can stay with my mother for a couple of days. I'm sure she would love to see Sean. There's enough room for you to take Morag to look after him whilst you're out shopping. You know I can't stand going around shops, but I'm sure Mother would love to come with you. I'll not put a limit on what you spend. I've done so well over the last few weeks you can go spoil yourself."

The look of joy on her face was enough to make his suggestion worthwhile, but Roy was already thinking of Shilpa as a distraction whilst his wife was shopping with his mother. He was fully aware that the two young women on his staff had reopened his needs and that his predatory sex drive was beginning to match his need for adrenaline-raising exploits; the further they took him away from lawful pursuits, the more he was enjoying them.

Chapter 5

Several days later, after breakfast, Roy walked into the kitchen alone. Morag and Janet were in the nursery seeing to the baby, when he saw Bridget preparing the lunch and Elian waiting to speak to him.

"I think you had better have a look at the cruiser," Elian said. "I think the new decking may need some attention after that storm."

"I'll be with you shortly, Elian. I just want a word with Bridget first," he said as she turned and went out the door.

"How are you feeling today, Bridget?" Roy asked her.

"Wonderful, sir. I have never felt better in my life," Bridget replied.

Roy continued, but not before looking around to make sure that Morag was not within hearing range and Janet had not come down from the nursery.

"I'm sorry about the wild sex before I left. I hope you had no ill effects."

"Bless you, sir. It was the best sex I've ever had," Bridget replied, grinning.

"The only effects are that I think you hit the jackpot. I missed my time, sir. I have not had my period. I think I may be having a baby."

Roy's mouth dropped. Janet had been right to caution him. What was he going to do now? He knew damn well that abortion was illegal in Southern Ireland. How would he explain that to Janet? Bridget, seeing the look on Roy's face, wanted to reassure him.

"Bless you, sir, but don't worry about it. I'm going to the Irish Fayre with Billy Mulligan on Saturday. I'll let him have me in the fields behind the Fayre ground and break the news to him that he got me with child. He's always been at me to get hitched, and I've put him off until now. He'll be like a dog with two tails. He will be that, your Lordship."

Bridget seemed so happy about the coming arrangement that Roy could not say anything.

"Why didn't you tell me you were not safe?" Roy asked her.

"Why, the mood you were in that day, sir, I don't think it would have made any difference. I just hope you're in the same mood when I want my next one," Bridget replied with a broad grin on her face, and she carried on preparing the lunch as if she had been discussing the weather.

Roy made his way down to the harbour, and Elian stood on the deck with a concerned look on her face. Roy boarded the craft, and Elian bent down. Pointing with her finger, she showed Roy the fault in the new decking.

"The preservation coating is cracking," Elian said. "Best we get her inside, and I'll strip her down and redo the surfacing. There're a couple of places below that need caulking too," she added. "It's not bad, but I would not like to take her out in a storm like the last one without paying attention to both problems. Come below, and I'll show you what I mean."

The two places Elian took Roy down to were in the engine room, and she pointed out where the timber planking was seeping and then climbing through the crawl space into the prow, where water was lying at the bottom of the hull. Every few minutes, a small electric bilge pump could be heard pumping out the water.

"That is the auxiliary bilge pump that keeps the bilges clear of water," Elian told him.

Roy crawled back into the engine room, and Elian pointed out two connecting hoses that were showing signs of seepage and said,

"I would like to replace these hoses as well."

"Whatever you think necessary, Elian, all the spares you will ever require are in the stores. Just ask, and you can have whatever you want," Roy replied, without thinking.

"Then come with me," she said with a smirk on her face.

They walked into the stateroom, which still showed signs of their sexual interaction.

"I think we may have a problem here," Elian said. Lowering her hands to the hem of her skirt and raising it, she pointed to the bulge in the front of Roy's trousers and said,

"I may need the key to that store as well. I know it has the solution to solve my problem."

She read Roy's face, and unhesitatingly, she reached forward and unclipped the waistband, unzipped his fly, and let Roy's trousers fall; they were wet from his crawl into the prow and dropped in a soggy heap around his feet. Roy's underwear joined the wet trousers, and in minutes they were on the bed in a lover's embrace. Roy was aware he would not be at his best. It had only been a couple of hours since he had made love to Janet. He would do his utmost to please; after all, he had never been one to refuse a lady her pleasure. The couple were almost insatiable as they rutted in ecstasy;

neither heard the door open silently behind them, and Janet stood at the partially open door watching Roy enjoying the sexual pleasure of his newly appointed 'mate', a word that had a double entendre.

Janet stood quietly, and as she watched, she felt her own arousal begin to grow. She had suspected as much, but now she was seeing it with her own eyes. God, she thought to herself, he only had me a couple of hours ago, and here he is having sex with Elian, giving her his all. She had seen him having sex with young Bridget, and now he was having sex with her sister; she knew he was incorrigible, but having sex with both sisters was going a bit far, even for him. She watched the couple completely engrossed in their own pleasure, and gave a start as she heard Elian cry out, fully aware that had she reached her inevitable climax. She knew instinctively that Roy would not be far away, and she fully appreciated the fact that he had not heeded her warnings about the local women being Catholic and not being allowed by their religion to take any preventative contraception; she hoped to God that Elian knew what she was doing. Janet quietly pushed the door to; making sure that the lock did not click. She pulled off her shoes, turned and walked quietly up the steps into the wheelhouse, and slipped down the gangway across the quayside, where she put her shoes back on and walked slowly and thoughtfully up to the castle.

Janet was Roy's wife, and she hoped Elian would be, like the others, just a passing phase. She had seen Roy having sex with Bridget, but as she had seen him with Elian, she dismissed the thought from her mind that there could be anything in the relationships that would be anything but a passing phase. She was totally oblivious to the fact that Bridget had missed her period, and the only person she had had sex with during the whole month had been Roy. Janet decided she would let sleeping dogs lie and say nothing, unless of course Roy was unable to perform for her later that evening when they went to bed.

Janet, however, missed the conversation, which would no doubt have interested her as the couple lay still embraced.

"Do you know about Bridget," Roy asked Elian.

"She told me, the stupid girl. I've warned her so many times, but she always said that when it happens, it happens. It's the will of the Lord, and if it's meant to happen, it will," Elian replied.

Roy told her what she had planned over the weekend, and Elian continued,

"Oh, Billy Mulligan, he's had her many times. He has cow's eyes for her. He'll marry her in a trice, and she'll sleep with him every Saturday night, and he'll be quite content for the rest of his life. She will work here Monday to Friday, and she will still be available to you if you want her. You don't have to worry about me. I took my skipper's papers on the mainland and had a diaphragm fitted. I wear it any time after the first fourteen days to prevent me becoming pregnant. If my mother or the priest knew it, they would both disown me. But I decided long ago that I will have my babies when I want them. Father O'Donovan can go hang himself together with that randy young curate. I've sent both of them packing on several occasions when they came on to me a bit hard."

The conversation lulled as the couple disengaged and sat up on the bed, both naked but sexually replete for the time being.

"I can tell you this. Any time you go into the village, after what Bridget has told the women, any one of them is yours just for the asking. Now I think we'd better clean up. I don't want trouble with your wife. I'll spend the next couple of days going over the boat and washing the bedding. I'm sure when it's clean, Morag will have no problem ironing it for me."

Roy got off the bed and walked towards the door. He washed in the small heads of the stateroom, and as he dressed, he watched Elian's slim figure as she showered herself before dressing. Roy's trousers were wet, and he walked slowly back up to the castle. Janet, who was standing in the kitchen waiting for him, asked,

"Where have you been to get into that state?"

"Oh, I had to crawl into the bilges to see the leaks in the hull, and Elian asked me to help fix a few things," Roy replied hurriedly.

Roy avoided Janet's stare, trying not to look too guilty. Janet looked at him hard and, inferring that she was innocent of their torrid bout of sexual activity, said,

"Go and change into something dry. You look as though you have been dragged through a hedge backwards. Now hurry. Bridget will have dinner ready shortly."

Janet had Roy's complete attention over the weekend, and Morag worked overtime to see to the baby. The couple made love more often than they had for a long time, and Janet was not surprised when Roy asked her if she minded him going to see his mother. He added as an afterthought,

"Do you want to come too?"

Janet had enjoyed his company over the entire weekend; she had not let him out of her sight and was sure he wanted a change, so she politely refused, asking him to invite his mother over to stay with her when he went on his next trip.

"She can keep me company whilst you are away. After all, you will have," and she stressed his second-in-command's name, "*Elian* to keep you company as well as Liam and whatever the name of your contact is called."

Roy picked up the emphasis on Elian but let it slip. He wondered if she just suspected or if she knew something. He kissed Sean, his son, and hugged Janet and said,

"I'll be away for a few days. I have business to do as well as see my mother."

Janet had suspected what that business was but said nothing. He would be back soon enough. Roy left, and during the time he was away, he spent time with his mother but managed to sleep with Mandy, his ex-secretary, enjoying a night in her marital bed, whilst her husband was away on business. He spent some time at a hotel with Chandelle and was able to spend a night with Shilpa, her sister. Shilpa was the Indian dancer whose movements during sex gave Roy an all-time high. The explanation she gave him for her sexually erotic movements during sex was due to her dance training as a child, and the movement of her muscles were completely involuntary. Roy would have spent longer with her, but when he went back to his mother's for dinner, there was a message from Janet that he was wanted for another charter. He only had time to say goodbye before he reluctantly left.

The next six weeks were a busy time for Roy. He made several trips to the French and Spanish coasts collecting different cargoes for the IRA, and each trip was uneventful. Elian had come up with several ideas to disguise the definitive outline of the MTB. The shape, Elian told him, was unmistakable even in the half-light of dusk and dawn. She had designed various structures that could be erected to disguise the distinctive outline, but Roy could always see difficulties in keeping them in place in a rough sea. He had money to spend and what better way was there but to change the outward shape permanently and build a flying bridge to make the boat look more like a modern pleasure cruiser. The less distinctive shape would be less likely to be recognised if challenged. He also liked the other idea of Elian's, where she had suggested that they have decals of various registrations of similar vessels that could be placed over their own to avoid easy recognition. He asked her to find out where she could get them made and, in the meantime, Roy had searched the Internet and narrowed the most likely boat builders down to four possibilities Roy had wanted a boatyard that had experience not only with wooden hulls but also were capable of a major refit. He had sent rough designs to all four and asked for a rough estimate of the cost.

Only one seemed really interested in the project. The owner had written back to say that he had done a similar conversion to his own MTB and had suggested that extra tanks be built into the hull for longer cruises. He had enclosed a picture of his own boat, and Roy had been very impressed with the redesigned boat. The hull still had that distinctive bow, but the upper structure made the boat look like a Sunseeker Cruiser. The lines were smooth, and Roy liked it immediately; gone was the small cabin with its distinctive windscreen, and the upper deck had repeater controls, a bar, and a shade cover. In the letter from the boatyard owner was a questionnaire asking what Roy wanted to keep from the original. The letter explained that if the integral torpedo tubes were left in place, the hull could remain intact and the upper structure would be built on. If Roy wanted the original motors left in place rather than having them replaced by a single engine, then the original speed would be the same, but the running expenses for the boat would be high. The quoted cost of the conversion was less than Roy had expected. He rang Granville Williams and agreed to visit the yard as soon as he was able.

The next few days were going to occupy Janet's ever spare moment. She had finally persuaded Roy that Sean needed to be christened; Roy had never been a God-fearing individual who attended church regularly. He had always been adamant that the local priest would never agree to christen the boy, as neither of his parents were Catholic or attended his church. Roy had not, however realised, how his connections with the IRA would override that situation. When Janet had rung the Manse, it was Father O'Donovan who had answered. Janet explained who she was and that she would appreciate it if he would christen their son Sean, Fully expecting to have a fight on her hands; she was delighted when Father O'Donovan enquired about Lord Croft's health and asked when she wanted the ceremony to be carried out.

Janet was taken aback. This was not the response she had been expecting and, as a result, she had no actual date in mind.

"Oh, I quite understand that, with his Lordship's business commitments, it's difficult to set a date when, in his line of business, he would be called away unexpectedly at any time." Father O'Donovan said, "If you ring me on any Friday before six in the evening, I'll be happy to carry out the ceremony the following Sunday after Mass."

Janet checked with Roy, and the date was set tentatively for the last weekend in the month. She was beside herself organising the event. Roy had requested that she invite some of his old friends Gordon and Megan, Chandelle and her sister Shilpa, his mother and as many of the villagers that wanted to come. It would be a time for festivities, he had told her. A few days before the christening was due to take place, Roy's mother, together with Chandelle, her son, and her sister, Shilpa, arrived for the christening, and later that afternoon, Gordon, the architect, and Megan, his wife, and their two children arrived. They were all shown up to their respective rooms to settle in. When Shilpa came downstairs, she asked Roy if she could see his boat. She explained mainly for the benefit of Janet and the others around that she had been talking with Bridget in her room and she had told her that it was quite a large one. Roy asked Janet to excuse him, and he took Shilpa down to show off the boat.

Roy was aroused even before they had got into the main cabin; he turned to help her down. Shilpa had already undone the clasp, securing her sari, and it fell around her feet like a silken cloud. Roy wasted no time carrying the scantily-clad dancer into the main cabin, and they fell on to the bed. Roy was beside himself as his lust was satisfied, as he pleasured himself with the young woman. He felt her quicken several times around his hardness before, holding nothing back, and he finally released into her convulsing form. They lay panting for some time before Roy quickly washed away all signs of his sexual pleasure, and, as she sat up and lowered her feet to the floor, she whispered,

"Oh, Roy, I'm so glad we had the chance to be together. I was afraid we would not get the opportunity to be alone with you."

Roy showed her the small shower and hand basin where she washed and dressed, finally putting her sari back in place. She looked beautiful and had only a slight flush in her cheeks when they got back to the others.

The children were all in the nursery with Morag and a couple of women from the village, whom Janet had asked to come and help. Gordon and Janet were deep in conversation about converting one of the unused rooms for her young son to migrate to from the nursery he shared with Morag. Megan was drinking and talking to Chandelle, asking her how many weeks she was pregnant. Roy had seen Megan arrive with her two children, a boy and a girl. He knew at the back of his mind that she had told him that they were both his, and his penis flexed at the thought of how he had impregnated her for the second time, as she had jokingly protested, the last time they had been together. He wondered if he would be able to have the pleasure once again before the weekend was over.

The visitors had a free day to spend together on Saturday and Roy, never missing an opportunity to show off his pride and joy, invited everyone on the boat for a trip down the coast. Bridget, helped by Janet, Shilpa, and Elian, put the food on board the boat. Then ensuring that the full nursery was under the watchful eye of Morag and the two ladies from the village, they all set off on a calm sea. Roy spent time talking to his mother and the guests, leaving Bridget and a whole crew from the village with the task of preparing the food for the christening on the following day. Bridget had loved the chance to get the women together to prepare the food; it was a dress rehearsal for the wedding, which would only be a couple of weeks later. She had felt a bit queasy a couple of times in a morning, but she had been told it was quite normal. The preparations had gone well, and she had let Billy have his way with her twice since the Fayre, just to ensure that he felt responsible and believe the developing foetus was his. But she longed to let his Lordship take her once more. She was more than a little disappointed because her sister Elian seemed to be having more of Lord Croft's attention than she had ever had, but her time would come. The food was placed in the huge cool room, left over from the days when the castle was used by the War Department, in readiness for the following day. They returned to the kitchen, and all of them helped prepare the evening meal in readiness for the guests when they returned from the boat trip.

Roy had had no chance to get Megan to himself and was wondering how he could manage, but it seemed a hopeless task, so he put it at the back of his mind and forgot about it. The dinner went well and everyone drank more than they should and, finally, they all retired to bed. During the day Janet had looked at the children of Megan and Chandelle, and she could swear that she could see Roy's features in all of them, but she put it down to her imagination; after all, she had drunk more alcohol than she realised. Whilst she had been daydreaming that her husband had fathered all the visitors' children, Roy had helped her to bed and had showered and lain down beside her. An hour later, unable to sleep, Roy went downstairs for a drink when, who should be in the kitchen but Megan. She had given her little girl a night feed and had come down to rinse the bottle and put it in the Milton solution to sterilise. She turned and saw Roy, and she smiled and said huskily,

"Hello, Roy, what a lovely surprise!" Then she asked him, "Why are you up so late? I have an excuse. I have a baby to attend to, but why are you up and about at this time of night?"

"Oh, I could not sleep for some reason, Megan. I just came down to get myself a drink. Would you care for one?" he asked, somewhat disappointed that she did not seem to catch the double meaning of what he had said.

Then walking over to the cupboard, Roy took down two mugs. He made them both a cup of steaming hot chocolate, and Megan picked up the tray and they walked into the lounge to drink the sweet beverage. Megan put the tray on the table and turned as Roy put his arms around her and, pulling her to him, he kissed her on the lips. He was surprised as he felt them part, and her tongue slid into his mouth as the passion of their kiss began to grow.

Roy felt himself respond almost instantly, Megan felt it too. Roy pushed his knee between her thighs and felt Megan press her body against his own. The hardened flesh trapped between them in their passionate embrace,

"Oh, Roy, it's been so long," Megan whispered hoarsely, emphasising the rapidity and the intensity of her arousal.

Roy could feel the heat on his thigh. He pulled the tie on her gown and pulled up her nightie up over her head. She stood before him naked, apart from her panties. She had thickened a little after two children, but she was still very attractive. Her breasts were larger, but that was to be expected. She had only a couple of months earlier given birth and, without a word, she slipped out of her panties, revealing the copper-trimmed patch he remembered so well from before. She pulled the tie holding his robe together and watched open-mouthed as Roy's own arousal was displayed in all its glory. He reached forward and took her in his arms. She moaned; she was having second thoughts about what she was doing,

"Oh my God, Roy, we shouldn't be doing this. Either Janet or Gordon might miss us and come down to see where we are."
Roy embraced her. His lips sought her breast, and his hand was busy below. She felt herself respond, and her arousal soared even higher than before.

"Oh, God, Roy, stop. We can't be doing this, Oh Jesus, we shall be caught for sure."

Roy ignored her entreaties to stop and, tightening his embrace, he slowly moved her back until the sofa was behind her knees and she went backwards, pulling him down on top of her. She panicked as she felt him press up against her; her heart was pounding as she repeated her concerns.

"No, Roy, we shouldn't. God, we shall surely be caught."
Roy moved his hips forward, hearing Megan's soft moan, and she relaxed, surrendering herself to him. As she felt him move deeper, she was unable to resist his advances; her infatuation for Roy was as strong as ever. Despite the chance of being caught, she just could not help herself.

"Oh, Roy, be careful. I don't want another child yet."

Soon Roy was fully engrossed in taking this red-haired beauty ignoring the fact that he had already given her two children, and his strokes became a steady and unrelenting joy as Megan felt the first twinges of her orgasm begin to build.

"Oh Mary, Mother of Jesus, Roy, I'd forgotten what a pleasure it is to have sex with you. It excites me beyond anything I have ever known, Oh Mother of God, I feel so hot. Oh Jesus, I'm near." Then, as if finally realising what was about to happen, she cried out in a sudden panic. "Oh God, not inside me. No!"
Roy was not listening. He was enjoying the pleasure, and he felt Megan begin to convulse around him. He could hear her whispering something, but he really was not listening as his own pinnacle neared. Roy felt Megan stiffen as she became aware of what was happening. Despite her fear, her body would not seem to obey her. She knew she had to try and push him off her to avoid the inevitable. Megan's legs seemed to have a mind of their own. They were clasping him hard up against her convulsing body, refusing to obey her own instincts as she bucked up and down. Her pleasure was clouded as the reality of what was happening registered as she felt Roy release into her unprotected womb. Roy lay on top of Megan's shuddering body, his weight supported by his strong arms, and he bent and kissed first her lips and then her breasts.

Megan quickly realised that he was not yet finished with her. He recovered quickly, and their movements recommenced. From her previous experience, when Roy had impregnated her twice before, she knew how potent his seed was, and her mind reeled at the thought that he might have given her a third child. She knew that no matter what or when, if Roy wanted her, she was his; she did not seem to be able to resist him, whatever the risk. She felt her body rise as Roy skilfully induced her to climax several times as he continued to pleasure her in ways Gordon could never do. It was finally over, and Megan knew in her heart that Roy had done it again. What would Gordon say? He was always so careful never to make love to her when she was not in her safe period, leaving himself and her both frustrated and in need of satisfaction. Roy never had any such worries; he had no such qualms; he satisfied both his partner and himself, and hang the consequences. Why had she let him do it to her again?

Roy moved away, allowing her to cover her nakedness. Roy put on his robe, and they sat and sipped their now cold chocolate before going upstairs to their respective and unsuspecting spouses. Both of them were feeling wonderful after their bout of sinful lust. Megan was convinced in her mind that she would soon be carrying Roy's third child in her womb. Roy, on the other hand, was wondering what joys of sexual delight would be available to him the following day.

The christening was held in the local church after Mass, and everyone present stayed to see Roy's baby son christened 'Sean Roy Croft'. When they got back to the reception at the castle, everyone from the village could be heard saying how pleased they were that Lord and Lady Croft had chosen an Irish name for their son. The food was served, and the festivities began. The local IRA had sent a large number of bottles of locally brewed potcheen as well as a couple of cases of good Irish whisky to wet the baby's head. The reception was going well with Janet fussing about, supervising the food and drink, whilst endeavouring to speak to everyone she recognised. Roy was, as usual at any gathering, busy looking for a prospective conquest. After being with Megan the previous evening and since Janet had been too busy that morning, Roy was feeling frisky and ready for more. Megan, however, was feeling guilty about the whole thing and never left Gordon's side for a moment.

Roy had been approached by a very sophisticated and attractive stranger, who had arrived in a chauffeur-driven car with a gift from the IRA. She had called him to one side, and told him that the gift was from his regular charterer; emphasising that it was to wet the young man's head. The gift had been a case of a twenty-year-old Irish whisky and two cases of potcheen, a singularly powerful drink that the locals enjoyed. The attractive stranger had accepted his invitation to stay for the reception and had dismissed her driver, informing him that she would ring when he should return to collect her. She and Roy struck up a conversation; the two of them seemed to have a mutual attraction and, in his indomitable fashion, he had offered to show her around the castle; his charm and handsome features captivated her. It did not surprise either of them that, during the viewing, she had willingly allowed him to seduce her, and the sex had been superb; he felt he had yet another mistress to add to his retinue. It was only later when he had asked Liam if he knew who the woman was. "Kate" was how she had introduced herself during their torrid sex session; Liam had told him the lady in question was Cathleen Delaney, the wife of the head of the IRA in the area, a man who commanded the utmost respect, a man who would not hesitate to kill anyone who crossed him.

"I think," he told Roy, "her husband is in America at present. She normally goes with him, but there must have been a good reason for her to stay behind."

Janet had approached Roy later to inform him that he would be required to drive one of his guests back home as her chauffer had unfortunately had an accident with the car. It had come as no real shock to Roy, for not many of their guests were in a position to have a chauffeur, when Janet had pointed out Cathleen Delaney as his prospective passenger. Roy had decided that he had better keep his distance as he did not want trouble from her powerful husband; she, however, had been all over him on the way back and had insisted that he pull over. The spot she had pointed out was one Roy felt she had used in similar circumstances on several occasions before. They had pulled into a side road and into a secluded copse, where they had had yet another bout of wild sex. He had been a little heady, from the sex and the drink, when he had eventually driven her to a very large and impressive house situated on a cliff top near Tralee. The impressive drive leading to the property had been protected by huge gates that would have taken a tank to get through, and as he drove up the long drive, arriving at a circular parking area, he noticed that the middle of the parking area had a helicopter pad. He realised that his sexual desires, for once, could well have betrayed him and led him into a very dangerous liaison. There, on the forecourt, stood the undamaged limousine, which had delivered her to the house. The excuse that the driver had had an accident had been a ruse to get Roy to drive her home. Despite her invitation to stay for a nightcap, Roy had not gone inside but dropped her at the front door, and as soon as she had gone inside, he had driven back home in a state of nervous anxiety.

Two weeks later, young Bridget had got married, and as she had no living father, she had asked Roy to give her away. He had not only agreed but had insisted that she hold the reception at the castle. Roy had never been one for caution, and his episode with Kate Delaney was a far-off memory, and during the course of that reception, unbeknown to Janet, he had had the pleasure of having intercourse with both the bridesmaids in the subterranean passage off the kitchen. Roy had been in a state of euphoria at the prospect of having both of them. The two women were in their early twenties and keen to see if the stories Bridget had told them about her boss, Lord Croft, had been correct. Their names had been Fiona and Kerry. Both were from the village, and both had consumed a considerable amount of alcohol and, in their inebriated state, had been seemed only too willing to succumb to his advances; neither had raised any objection when his Lordship had unprotected sex with them. As usual, he threw caution to the wind, and he could well have been in more trouble if it had not been for Elian, who seemed to know everyone and everything. When the two young women had later confessed to Elian that they had had totally unprotected sex with Lord Croft, she had tutted, telling them that they should be more careful. She realised what the outcome could be and asked them to wait for her to get something to help. When she had returned from the boat, she had given them both the morning-after pill, knowing full well that neither of them was likely to have taken any precautions against pregnancy, just like her sister. Elian had been thankful that she had been approached by Janet soon after starting to work on the boat, when much to her surprise, she had been given a supply of 'Levonelle', the morning-after pill. Janet had cornered her and in a conspiratorial fashion, and she had told the open-mouthed Elian that she knew what her husband was like, informing her that she may find the contents of the box useful.

Chapter 6

It was around this time that Roy had first spoken to Janet about his idea of upgrading the MTB to make it into a luxury cruiser and the possibility of them going on a cruise to the Bahamas and spending time sailing round the islands. He had expected her to be more than willing to make the journey, but to his amazement she had informed him why it would be difficult.

"Darling," she had said, "to begin with, have you ever spent time on a boat with a toddler, especially on a long ocean voyage? We should spend all our time watching that the child does not go near the railings. It would be a nightmare. I am fully aware that the thought would never have crossed your mind but, if I'm correct, I may be pregnant. I'm late. If it's true, it will be quite some time before I would attempt such a crossing. If it ever became a possibility, I would fly on ahead and meet you in Nassau or somewhere like that. You could bring the boat across, and we could island-hop so long as we are not at sea for too long."

Roy had been pleased with the news about another child, but he was disappointed that he would not have her with him on the proposed voyage no matter how far in the future that might be. He hugged her and, with a broad grin on his face, had whispered,

"I've planned to take the boat across to England to have it refit. You can go shopping for whatever you need while it's being done. I'm sure Mother will be delighted with the news about the new baby, and shopping for clothes for you and things for the baby would please her immensely."

Janet had agreed the idea of spending some time with Roy's mother appealed to her and she knew the news of her possible pregnancy would please the older Mrs Croft.

Roy rang his charter contact on the special cell phone and informed his contact that the boat would not be available for the next two to three weeks as he was going to take the boat in for a refit. His contact was silent for a few moments, before he said in a hushed tone full of concern:

"No longer than three weeks, you have a trip to take out more trainees and bring back the last bunch. It's imperative that you do not let us down."

"I'll check with the yard and confirm that the boat will be ready in time. If there's a problem, I'll call you and cancel the refit until after the proposed charter."

"Excellent. That's the commitment we like to hear."

The phone went dead.

Next Roy rang Granville, who confirmed that three weeks would be more than long enough and that if anything went wrong, Roy would be able to borrow his boat. Roy did not inform him that, with a single engine, he would not be able to outrun any attack by pirates or any patrol boat. He just said,

"Thank you, Granville, for the more-than-generous offer, but I shall hold you to your commitment of three weeks, adding there will be a severe penalty clause in the contract for late delivery. The work must be finished on time, and if it's any benefit to you, I have no objection to this being a cash transaction. The agreement must be in place before we begin our relationship. Is that understood? I hasten to add that there will have to be a ten per cent retention for a month or so to ensure that there is no problem."

"I fully understand, Lord Croft. I will ensure there's no delay."

Janet, Morag, Elian, and Roy set off for North West England early on Monday morning. Prior to their departure, Elian, using Liam and Quinn to help, had not only removed the torpedoes, the arming and firing mechanisms and all the armament from the secret compartments, storing them safely in the munitions store, but had also left all the radar equipment on the cruiser securely in situ. Part of Roy's refit was that he wanted to put more fuel tanks in place to give the boat a three-thousand-mile range, knowing well that that range would not be possible, of course, at top speed. The new upper day cabin and flying deck and wheelhouse would change the whole appearance of the MTB but would be ideal for when he finished with his current line of work with the IRA. He had suggested to Granville that the boat would be mainly for charter work and, when transporting passengers, the upper deck would be able to be completely separated from the lower cabin. Granville had told Roy to bring the MTB, and they could discuss the final design during the refit. The trip took them around the south coast of Ireland, up past Dublin and across the top of the Island of Anglesey and down towards Birkenhead. The Williams Boatyard was impressive, with dry docks and cranes and a complete workshop designed to work solely on wooden-hulled boats.

The owner, Granville Williams, showed Roy over his own converted MTB, which it looked magnificent. Granville sounded genuinely interested in the project, and Roy liked the designs Granville had drawn up. He assured Roy that he would personally supervise the modifications himself. The extra fuel tanks could be difficult, but Granville sat down with Roy and quickly drew smaller tanks in various places within the design of the hull, emphasising that if he used aircraft type of fuel pumps to cross flow and equalise the levels in each tank, he believed that the weight distribution would not upset the trim or handling of Roy's boat in any way. It would mean a computer-driven pre-programmed distribution system, which would add to the overall cost, but he did not believe it would present a problem. Granville discussed the various options of overall design, and when they finally agreed and the price was approved, Roy gave him his cell number. Then, before Roy left, he informed Granville that he would be available 24/7 if he needed to contact him for any reason. Elian opted to stay nearby in a small bed and breakfast to keep a watchful eye on the work.

Roy, Janet, Morag, and Sean, using the hired Range Rover, went on to visit Roy's mother, who was living in the home he had bought before he left Boric to move to their head office. He knew that there would be plenty of room for them all. Roy's mother was overjoyed to see them and made them all welcome. Sean was the apple of her eye, and when Janet proposed that she go with her to do shopping in London.

"What about Sean? Who is going to look after him whilst we are away?" she asked.

"That's why Morag is here, Mother. She will look after him whilst you are away," Roy assured her.

"Oh, but what if we are away overnight?" she asked, looking dubious. "What then?"

"Morag sleeps in his room, Mother," was Roy's response. "She looks after him like he is her own."

His mother and Janet left the following morning, and Roy was on the phone to Chandelle; he was somewhat shaken but not surprised when she broke the news of her own pregnancy, but she told Roy that Shilpa would be more than eager to see him again. Roy made the arrangements, and he spent the rest of the day at the Holiday Inn nearby with Shilpa, Chandelle's willing sister. He looked tired when he returned, and when Morag explained that Janet had rung and told her that she and Roy's mother would be staying in London for a couple of days, Roy rang and made arrangements to meet up with Mandy, his ex-secretary the following day. The stay with his mother was proving to be very satisfactory in more ways than one. When Janet returned with the shopping, Roy's mother looked exhausted and when Janet had Roy to herself, she said,

"Roy, I'm worried about your mother. She tires easily, and I am going to take her to the doctor's tomorrow for a thorough check-up. It would be useful if she came and stayed with us for a while. I would be able to keep a watchful eye on her health."

Roy promised that he would try and persuade her. When he brought the matter up, his mother was adamant. She told him, in no uncertain terms, that she was not ready for that and that she would stay in her home. When she had been to the doctor's and he had referred her, at Janet's insistence, to a private physician, she had not looked quite so confident. After the visit to the physician, Roy broached the subject again. She was still emphatic that she wanted to stay in her home, but at Roy's insistence, she begrudgingly agreed that if Roy could arrange it, she would try to have a person live with her to help and be a sort of companion.

Roy rang Chandelle and asked if she thought Shilpa might be interested in the position of companion to his mother. He felt that the two of them had seemed to get along at Sean's christening, and the fact that they were acquainted would help his mother to accept another person to share her living space. Chandelle rang back shortly afterwards and confirmed that her sister would be more than willing to come and see his mother; if after her interview they felt comfortable with the arrangement and felt they could get along with each other, then she would agree to give the arrangement a go. Roy suddenly remembered that Shilpa had been Chandelle's support and had spent the last year looking after her son.

"I'm sorry, Chandelle. I never gave you a thought. How will you cope without Shilpa to mind Jamal, especially as you have another baby on the way?"

"A lot has happened since you left Boric Industries, Roy. We now have a crèche for the children of our employees, and I think many of them think that I am a bit standoffish because my child does not attend. It will give me the opportunity to prove them wrong."

"Consider it done," said Roy. "Ask Shilpa to come and see my mother tomorrow. You know the address."

The following day, Shilpa arrived, and to Roy's surprise, she wore a very smart suit in place of her usual sari, and she looked stunning. Roy's mother remembered her from the christening, and after they had spent the morning together, she was impressed with the younger woman's intelligence, understanding, and how she presented herself. She asked Shilpa what work she had been doing and whether she had done this kind of companionship work before. Shilpa told her that she had a degree in sociology, so she understood what the work entailed, but as she had been unable to find work during the previous year, she had been helping her sister by looking after her child. Roy's mother asked her to wait whilst she spoke to Roy.

"She's lovely, Roy, and very intelligent. I'm sure we shall get along fine. What am I to offer her? I can't afford much on my pension, and your father, bless him, did not leave me much in the way of savings."

"Mother, don't worry about that. If you are happy with her, I'll agree a good salary with her, draw up a contract of employment, and we can sign it. I'll be more than happy to add her to my staff and transfer her salary from my business account each month."

"Thank you, Roy," his mother said. "What with me living here rent-free, and now this. I'll never be out of your debt."

Roy smiled and assured her that he could never repay her for his formative years and the sacrifice she and his father had made to make him what he was today, knowing full well that his benefits in the sexual stakes with his mother's new companion would more than compensate him, and money was not really a problem.

When the contract had been signed, Shilpa asked if Roy would call her a cab.

"Nonsense," he had told her. "I'll run you home. You can pick up your things and start tomorrow."

It was late in the evening when Roy got back, but Janet looked at him and knew in her heart that the young woman he had engaged to help his mother had become, if she had not previously been, another of his conquests. She was certain that look in his eyes and the ruddy complexion told her all she needed to know. She was amazed how women seemed to fall under his spell, as she had herself, but now that he was so confident and skilled in the art, he had become something of a sexual predator. She only hoped that the young woman was on the pill. Janet had long since resigned herself to the fact and hoped that he never caught any sexually transmitted disease from any of his mistresses. She knew he was usually careful and selective, but she knew that no one was exempt from a chance encounter. Putting that aside, she suggested that, now that everything was in its place and Shilpa was starting work the following morning, she and Roy fly back with Morag and Sean. Roy could wait for Elian to ring and tell him when he could collect his new pride and joy.

Roy, however, was impatient to see how things were going with the refit, and it was not without some show of disappointment that Janet and the others left without him. He saw that Shilpa was ensconced and settled in the house, taking the opportunity to enjoy her sexual pleasures once again before he drove back in the hired car to the boatyard and saw how things were progressing. The effect of the new upper superstructure was pleasing to the eye, and he congratulated Granville on the work to date. Elian was pleased to see him and had no hesitation when he suggested that they spend the night together. Roy was in a buoyant mood when he left for Ireland the following morning.

The call for Roy to collect his boat came just short of the three-week deadline, and when he arrived at the boatyard to inspect the final result, he was ecstatic. The newly designed boat looked exactly as he had imagined. The change was so dramatic that it was difficult to see where the old MTB ended and the new boat began. Walking up on to the upper deck, he could see and appreciate the improvements; the instrumentation had been repeated on both levels, and all functions could be performed from both sets of controls. Roy was as excited as a schoolboy with his first bicycle. Elian, in the time she had been waiting for the boat's completion, had been busy. She had visited a local printer and had several sets of decals printed, explaining that she had informed the printer that the company she worked for owned a fleet of hire boats and she wanted them to have their names and registrations to be identical in design. She had researched and found the names and registrations of several boats of similar outward design, and the decals had been printed in readiness for Roy's return. Roy took the boat out on to the water with Elian and Granville. The boat handled almost perfectly, but there were just a couple of adjustments to be made before

Granville would release the boat. He asked Roy to wait in the office, where his secretary would provide him with drinks, etc. whilst he oversaw the final adjustments. He and Elian would check her over for the final time prior to his release of the boat. Roy knew he was expected to hand over the agreed fee and went below and withdrew the money from the on-board safe. It filled a large envelope, and Granville smiled as he saw that it was indeed going to be in cash, as Roy had promised.

Elian watched as Roy stepped ashore. Granville picked up his cell phone and made a call. He whispered into the mouthpiece, so she could not catch the instructions he had given before he rang off. Roy opened the office door and was greeted by a strikingly attractive and busty blonde.

"Lord Croft?" she enquired enthusiastically, with a beaming smile.

"Yes," came the reply.

"I have your invoice here," she said, striking up a provocative position. Roy seemingly missed the gesture as he was scanning the document; it was for the agreed sum. He opened the bulky envelope and began to count the cash. The young blonde appeared surprised to see that Roy was actually prepared to pay the whole account in cash and whispered surreptitiously as she had been instructed.

"It will be without the VAT as you reside in Southern Ireland, Lord Croft, and I understand that you have agreed upon a ten per cent retention for sixty days, is that correct?"

Roy nodded as he carried on counting the required amount.

"Would you care for something to drink, your Lordship? Can I get you some tea, coffee, or perhaps something a little stronger?"

"I'll have a large scotch if you have one" was Roy's keen reply. The young woman, who had been forewarned what he drank by Elian, nodded and walked to the other side of the office, where she opened the cabinet and reached up to get the bottle. As she did so, her short skirt rode up, revealing the fact that she wore stockings and suspenders. Roy's interest perked up and he looked closer; she really had well-defined legs with well-shaped calves, something that had always attracted him.

"Could you give me a hand, Lord Croft? I just don't seem to be able to reach the bottle."

Roy stood and crossed the room to stand beside her. He reached for a bottle of a fifteen-year-old Irish whisky. As he did so, the secretary bent down and selected a couple of heavy-cut glass whisky tumblers from the cupboard below; as she did so, her buttocks pressed against Roy's thigh. To Roy's surprise and delight, he could have sworn he felt her push back against him. Mentally noting the fact but outwardly ignoring it for the moment, he went and took a seat in the office whilst she poured him a generous measure. She bent down to place the glass on the coffee table in front of him, displaying her cleavage, as the top buttons of her blouse were now undone.

"Is everything to your satisfaction, Lord Croft? Is there anything else you would like?"
It was the way she said it, and the way she held the position she was in, that alerted Roy to the fact that she was offering him more than just a drink. His sexuality responded almost at once and, taking the initiative, he stood and reached out. She moved into his embrace with no hesitation and whispered,
"I think we should move into Mr Granville's office, Lord Croft. It's a little more private."

Things moved quickly once they were in the privacy of the inner office. It was almost as if she had been instructed to encourage him to take advantage of what she had to offer. She allowed him to kiss her, and her lips parted, inviting his tongue to explore further. Encouraged by this unexpected development, as Roy embraced her, his hand slid down to cup her tight buttocks; the only reaction she gave was to mould her body against his hardening arousal. Roy realised she was giving him the message to go further, and his hand tugged at the hem of her short skirt, raising it above the stocking-clad thighs and exposing the tiny red garment that served as panties. The young woman was in a high state of arousal as she pulled open her blouse, revealing a matching bra, and as Roy progressed past each stage of her seduction, she offered no resistance, only encouragement. In what seemed no time at all, they were having wild, unrestrained, and unprotected sex on the polished top of Granville William's desk. Roy was enjoying her charms, and it was a welcome respite when they both gave a soft grunt of satisfaction as their bodies surged together in a final culmination of their mating. They hardly had time to pull themselves together when they heard the outer door open and the sound of Elian and Granville's voices could be heard. Roy pulled up his trousers hurriedly, and the wanton, almost shameless, secretary stood, letting her dress fall down to cover the signs of her infidelity and quickly fastened her bra and blouse. She put her finger to her mouth, indicating to Roy to remain quiet whilst she switched on the air conditioning, which whisked away any remaining odour of their heated sexual encounter.

Roy sat down on one of the armchairs and drained his glass. The door opened, and Granville walked in. He glanced over and saw that Roy was seated, his glass now empty. Granville said, to Roy's astonishment,
"I see you have met Kirsty, my wife, bookkeeper, and secretary. She really is a treasure."
Roy blinked. He had never expected Kirsty to be Granville's wife. He looked in her direction and could see the smile covered by the raised finger, indicating that he should say nothing untoward.
"With all those attributes and being attractive as well, I would have to agree with you. She would appear to be the height of efficiency, and you can rest assured that she has entertained me admirably whilst I waited," Roy retorted with a smile of unconcealed pleasure.

Then stealing a glance at the flushed complexion of the blonde behind the stout wooden desk, he winked surreptitiously. Kirsty walked easily across the office and without any sign of remorse for her previously bawdy behaviour in the absence of her husband and said simply,
"I'll get you a refill, Lord Croft. Your usual, Granville! And what will you have, Elian?"
Elian was the only one to reply.
"I'll have a soft drink, if I may, Mrs Williams."
"The boat is ready, Roy. Are we leaving tonight?" asked Elian.
"Nonsense," said Granville. "You can't leave tonight. It's too late. Let Kirsty and I take you both out for a meal to celebrate the completion of your new look boat, which I'm sure will give you lots of pleasure. She's a bit overpowered and, if I may say so, very, very fast. It almost took my breath away when Elian opened her up. I had quite forgotten just how fast these things were designed to go, but with the set-up you have, she will never be cheap to run."
It seemed churlish to refuse. Roy accepted the invitation, following with,
"I suggest we sleep aboard tonight, Elian, and get an early start in the morning. It will give us a chance to put the newly designed cruiser through her paces before the next charter."

Granville instructed Kirsty who went into the outer office and arranged the evening. They ate at a superb fish restaurant that Granville and Kirsty had visited with other satisfied customers. The small and poorly lit dance floor enabled Roy to dance intimately with Kirsty. At an appropriate moment, they had taken the opportunity to slip outside, and to Roy's delight, she made all the right moves, ending with them, once again, enjoying unprotected and torrid sex in the back of Granville's Bentley. When they returned to the table, Elian and Granville were still deeply engrossed in discussions about boats, a mutually passionate interest that they obviously shared. It was only later when Granville lay beside his beloved wife that she confessed that, for the first time, she had allowed things to go too far and that the handsome Lord Croft had in fact gone all the way. Granville was beside himself. It was something he had endeavoured to arrange all their married life and, as a result of his motivated imagination, he made love to his wanton wife far into the night.

The weather forecast, when Elian moved out of the boatyard harbour early the following morning, was for gale force winds, and as they turned south after passing north of the Isle of Anglesey, the full force of the gale hit them. Elian mentioned to Roy that the higher superstructure made the boat a little more lively, but the additional ballast of the extra fuel compensated very well. She added that if they were low on fuel, however, it might be a different story. Elian cocked her head to one side as if puzzling something out and she said,

"I now understand why Granville put in the extensive computerised pumping system so that some of the fuel tanks when empty can be flooded with seawater to give the boat stability in a gale. The unique system," she continued, "would allow the tanks to be flushed and then once again be used for fuel. It all makes sense now that I've experienced the handling in rough weather."

The cruiser handled well as Elian headed down through the Irish sea round the southern coast of Ireland and then up the west coast towards home. The sea was still squally when they arrived, but Elian skilfully manoeuvred the cruiser into the harbour, and they tied up by the quayside. Roy secured the lines fore and aft, and Elian shut down the engines. Roy walked up the slope to the castle, still wearing his waterproofs; he walked in the back door, and Janet ran towards him. She threw her arms around him, saying,

"I did not expect you back today in this weather. I thought you would have waited until it slacked off a little."

"I could not wait to get back to you, and besides, we needed to put the new design to the test," Roy said, hugging her.

"If I had known you were at sea in that storm, I would have been worried. What would I have done without you? Now tell me what you have been up to and all about how your smart new boat handles. I know you just can't wait to tell me all about the technicalities of which I shall understand almost nothing. The alternative is you can take me to bed. Morag and Bridget have taken Sean in my car and gone into the village, and I don't expect them back until later."

Roy swept her up in his arms and started towards the door to the lounge.

"I think you're a little too eager," he said, "and with the baby on the way, you are a little too much for me to carry you all the way up to bed and still be randy. The lounge will have to do."

They tore at each other's clothes in their eagerness but had scarcely had time to begin to enjoy the desire they both needed to assuage, when Janet listened intently; the sound of a car's door slamming was unmistakable.

"Oh God, Roy! I just heard the car pull up in the drive. They're back. I'm sorry, but you will have to stop. They will be in here any moment. We will have to continue with this later."

Roy was very aroused, but he walked towards the kitchen, intending to go down the quayside to walk off his arousal. As the door swung open, Roy was surprised to see young Kerry standing alone, preparing food. Hearing the door open behind her, she half turned and, seeing who it was, she stammered,

"I beg your pardon, your Lordship. I did not realise you were back. I just came in to help with the meal whilst Morag and Bridget went into the village. I understand Bridget is having a hard time with her pregnancy, and she's not feeling too well."

She glanced down and could see evidence of Roy's state of arousal. Her mouth dropped open, and she murmured quietly,

"Begging your pardon, your Lordship, but I see you are feeling well yourself. Sir, if I remember correctly, at the christening we were able to find a cure for that particular ailment of yours."

Roy, who needed relief from his aroused state, moved towards her. Without speaking a word, he lifted her up on to the stout scrub top table, and with no preamble his hand went under her dress and he gripped her cotton pants and pulled them off. Kerry remembered how Roy had taken her in the passage below on the day of his son's christening. No one in the village could come anywhere near his Lordship in his sensuality and his skill to arouse her to such heady heights. She had never been so satisfied. Lord Croft knew how to treat a girl. Roy was so aroused himself that he gave no quarter as the couple mated with unbridled passions. It was not long before she gave a soft moan as her body peaked and she rose to meet Roy's final thrust as he released into her, his pent-up emotions spent for the time being.

Janet had entered the lounge with Sean and could hear the familiar rhythmic slapping of bodies in the act of having sex; she cautiously opened the kitchen door just in time to see the familiar sight of Roy's bare backside. Janet put her hands to her mouth to stop the yell as she saw Roy in the throes of unrestrained sex, his body moving rhythmically between some strange woman's legs. She watched intrigued as the apparent stranger enjoyed what had been denied her only minutes before. Janet, familiar with Roy's philandering ways, knew that Roy had several other women in his life. Elian, she knew about. She had seen him, and she suspected that he had fathered Bridget's child. She was more than certain he had been with the pretty Indian girl that was his mother's companion, but who was he with now? He really was beyond redemption. Just how many women did he want in his life? She saw Roy pause for a few minutes before the tirade began again. The unknown woman had her legs behind Roy's back, pulling him towards her unashamedly. Shortly after, Sean, who had grown bored of just being in his mother's arms and her insistent 'shushing', had begun to cry, and Janet with a determined step walked forward pushing the kitchen door open. Roy was nowhere to be seen, but Kerry, one of the young women from the village, was sitting on the kitchen table looking very flushed and fastening the top button of her dress.

"Oh hello, Lady Croft," Kerry said a little too quickly, the words coming out somewhat breathlessly and somewhat jerkily. "I've come to help Bridget out with the meal. She was not feeling herself tonight."

Only seconds later, Roy came up the stone steps as though he was returning from the boathouse. He looked a bit flushed but no more than if he had run down the corridor and up the steps. Janet could not help but be impressed at the way he carried the moment off.

"I just had to check on something in the workshop," he said. "It was something that just couldn't wait. I just had to do it before dinner."

Janet looked at Kerry, who looked about twenty and pretty as a picture with her red hair, rosy cheeks, and freckles; she guessed from what she had witnessed a few minutes before that the young woman was also full of her husband's seed. Janet only hoped she was not ovulating, or Roy would have fathered yet another child. *The randy old sod!* she thought to herself. Just then Bridget burst into the kitchen and said,

"Oh, I'm sorry, ma'am, I should have told you. I asked Kerry to come in whilst I was in the village, to help with the meal. The baby is making me a bit tired, and Kerry was kind enough to offer to help. I hope you don't mind."

"I'm sure Kerry is only too willing to help any way she can," Janet said, tossing her head, and looking Roy straight in the eyes, she added with a forced smile, "Don't you agree, Roy? I'm sure his Lordship will reward you personally. Won't you, darling? Bridget, tell Morag as soon as she is ready to come into the lounge and collect Sean for his tea, will you?"

With that she turned and walked into the lounge. Kerry moved off the table a little uneasily and disappeared in the direction of the staff toilet. Roy walked into the lounge behind Janet and poured himself a large Irish whisky and a brandy for Janet.

"What was that about?" he asked as innocently as he could.

"I don't mind who you have sex with, darling. I taught you myself before we were married, but please don't do it on my kitchen table and not with any pretty young woman from the village hardly out of her teens. You could very easily have got her pregnant. If you are so desperate, you should at least show a little decorum and take her up to one of the bedrooms. Don't you realise these young Catholics don't take any precautions. None of them are on the pill. It's against their religion, and I cannot imagine you using a condom, under any circumstances, no matter who you are with. Just be a bit careful, will you? Oh, and before you act innocent, I was watching you for a few minutes before I walked in. I really don't mind, but let's not take every woman who comes to the castle. Word will get around, if it hasn't already."

Janet handed Sean to Roy and sat down and took a long sip from her brandy.

"I'm sorry," he murmured, "but I was so strung out. You know how I am. Once I start, and then have to stop before I am completely satisfied. You know I do love you."

"I know," Janet said, nodding her head in agreement before adding, "I'm sorry, but I did not want to be caught in the compromising situation I caught you in. Now let's forget all about it, shall we? Oh, by the way, if you go up to the medicine cabinet in the bathroom, you will find some 'Levonelle', 'the morning-after pills'. I always keep a supply just in case I forget to take my own birth-control pills. I suggest you make young Kerry take one, just to be on the safe side."

Roy inwardly sighed with relief. *I must be the luckiest man in the world,* he thought to himself. He would make it up to her when they went to bed. Roy was glad to get away, and he made his way up to the bathroom and opened the cabinet. He took one of the pills from the box, put it in his pocket, and went down the backstairs to the kitchen. He had glanced into the nursery where Janet and Morag had been busy bathing Sean in the bathroom as he passed. As Roy entered the kitchen, he saw that Kerry was busy helping Bridget. Roy beckoned her over and took her up the back staircase to one of the spare staff bedrooms. He closed the door behind him and started to unbutton Kerry's dress. She offered no resistance, and it fell around her ankles.

"Oh, sir, Mrs Croft may hear us."

"Swallow this," he said, giving her the pill. "It will stop you getting pregnant. Let me worry about Mrs Croft."

Kerry put the pill into her mouth and swallowed it. She lay back on the bed and watched as his Lordship undressed. She relaxed as Roy began again where he had left off earlier.

Sometime later, Kerry arrived in the kitchen and helped Bridget to serve up the meal before she excitedly told her how his Lordship had taken her on the scrub-topped kitchen table, how Mrs Croft had almost caught them, and finally how his Lordship had taken her upstairs, given her some kind of pill, telling the open-mouthed Bridget that he had told her it would stop her getting pregnant and then he had taken her again. Bridget remembered how Lord Croft had taken her many times in the past, and she put her hands on the developing child in her womb.

"I did not get any pill," she said, "but I know who's best off. Billy and I will soon have a little Lord Croft to bring up. I'm sure if you get married, you can do the same. There is nobody like his Lordship anywhere around here, is there?"

Kerry could only nod her head in agreement, feeling the satisfied tingle from below. Wait until she told Fiona, her friend. She would be so very jealous as she too had had a short taste of Lord Croft's sexual prowess at the christening, and they had spoken only a few days before, wistfully wishing that it could happen again.

Whilst Roy waited for instructions and confirmation of the date of departure, Elian showed her skill and Liam his knowledge of weaponry as they helped Roy refit the arming and firing mechanisms to the torpedo tubes. The tubes were now hidden with sliding doors in the hull, which could be opened or closed mechanically from the bridge. Granville had thought it strange when Elian had insisted that the doors were to be operational, but Roy Croft was paying, so who was he to argue? He had thought that Roy may have wanted to discharge smoke from the tubes during a regatta or something similar, but why should he worry? It had nothing to do with him; he just carried out his customer's requests, as strange as they might be. The drawback, however, was that the torpedo tubes would now have to be loaded from outside, and there was no longer any way to store or reload torpedoes from within the vessel. Outwardly, there was now no sign that the boat had the capability of delivering death and destruction. Roy and Elian had gone out with two torpedoes unarmed and had practised launching them whilst on the move. The system worked perfectly, and they had returned and reloaded. The Sam7s and the RPGs, together with their respective launchers, were put in the hidden lockers, and Elian and Liam had checked and loaded the side arms (now 9mm Berettas and Uzis), compliments of the IRA. Roy now finally understood the necessity of being so heavily armed. He was a drug runner, a smuggler, and a transporter of terrorists, and he was in just about as deep as he could be. He resolved that the excitement and the pay, however, was well worth the risk of capture. This is what he had given up his boring life in the boardrooms of big business for, and at present he had no regrets.

The following morning, Roy received an SMS from his contact, informing him that he would be required to go on a week's charter on the following Sunday. Roy called him back on the special cell phone and then told Janet.

He then walked down to the quayside and informed Elian that they would be leaving on Sunday and would be away for a week at least. Elian confirmed that she would give the cruiser a full check-up and fill the tanks.

"Everything will be ready for you by Sunday," she said with a wry smile on her lips. "I was wondering if we should take another person with us on Sunday to help with the passengers. I don't want to have to clean up after them. I prefer to be on the bridge. She can cook for us and make coffee. I know the forecast is good, but you never know how fickle the weather can be through the Bay of Biscay and off the African coast."

"That's a good idea," Elian Roy said. "Who did you have in mind? Remember we will have Liam with us."

"Fiona," came the ready reply. "She can handle the galley. I've seen her help out once or twice on the trawlers."

"OK. That will make up a crew of four. I'll tell Bridget to add one more to the rations."

Roy was looking forward to getting away for a while. He needed some air in his lungs and did not want to be under the watchful eyes of Janet, who had a habit lately of being just where he did not want her to be.

Chapter 7

Sunday morning finally arrived, and Janet stood with Sean on her shoulder and watched the boat until it was out of sight. She believed that whatever happened with his crew, she was happy that she had been confirmed that she was two months pregnant with her second child. She did not know whether to be pleased that Fiona had joined the crew, or not. One thing that was certain in her mind was that, with an extra hand on board, it would make it more difficult for Roy to be alone with Elian during the voyage. Janet had no idea that Roy had already had the pleasure of sex with Fiona as well. It was just as well. She wondered what he would do if Liam were not on board, knowing her husband's sexual appetite, he would in all probability have both the women. But Liam was there, and she forgot about it, for the present.

With Elian at the helm, Roy picked up Connor at the usual pickup point, and he stared unbelievably at the change in the boat's appearance.
"My God, Roy, you would not know she was the same boat. The change is startling."
"Isn't she a beauty? The changes cost a packet, but that is well worth it, and she still has a sting in the tail, so to speak. None of her armaments have been affected."
"You mean she can still deliver torpedoes if necessary. I could not see any sign of the ports."
"The doors concealing the openings were Elian's idea. She's a bright girl."
"You're a lucky bloke to have her, Roy, and she is quite a looker too."
Roy did not answer. He just gave Connor a look that acknowledged the comment and gave the signal to move out into the sea.

They headed south and slipped into the small harbour where they had to pick up the next group of eager but nondescript men and women. They docked, and the group of sixteen climbed aboard. Roy attention was struck by one of the women passengers, who had the face of an angel. Her figure was skinny, and she had hardly any breasts at all, but despite that, something about her made her look not only attractive but amazingly well proportioned. Whatever it was about her that drew his attention was emphasised by the well-developed muscles showing that she was extremely fit. Roy watched as she climbed aboard. She was like a panther ready to strike, and she moved with the gait of an alert leopard. The thought crossed his mind that she would be worth keeping an eye on. They assembled in the lower cabin, and Elian introduced Roy as the captain. No names or titles were used.

"This is the young woman who will look after you," Elian said to the passengers, pointing to Fiona. "She will distribute your food and give out seasickness pills to those that need them. If you have problems during the voyage, she will help you. The upper deck is strictly off limits, and weather permitting, you will have the freedom of the outer lower deck."
There was a general moan of disapproval from the assortment of youngsters keen to be on their way to adventure. They had wanted to be able to stand on the upper deck and breathe in the fresh sea air.

Liam and Connor cast off, and Roy took the boat out into the Atlantic. The forecast had been fair, but Roy looked up, and as Elian came up from the lower deck,
"Elian have you seen that front moving in?" Roy asked.
"The shipping forecast has mentioned it, but it's not supposed to be closing in that quickly. I'd better get below and forewarn Fiona and Liam to be ready for the worst. Connor is in one of the day cabins. I'd better warn him as well."
Over the next two hours, the weather worsened, and although not as bad as the previous crossing, when they had carried trainees, it was bad enough. Fiona came up and told Roy that one of the women was very seasick and she had put her in the main cabin, separating her from the others.
"She looks grey, and I have given her 'quells' to settle her down."
"Is she that the pretty one with muscles?" Roy asked.
"That's the one." Fiona answered, wondering why he had asked.
The young woman in question had hardly any breasts and looked more like a young man than a woman, not the sort of woman that would normally attract Roy Croft's attention. She shook her head as she went back down the companionway. There was no accounting for the way some women could attract a man's attention. She would look closer when she checked in on her patient later.

Roy had merely acknowledged Fiona's departure. The conversation about someone being sick had hardly registered, and he promptly forgot all about her. They took turns at the wheel, and Roy took the first watch as they began to cross the Bay of Biscay. Elian went below, after telling Roy to call her, if the weather got worse, in which case they would have to use the lower controls. The wind blew, and the swell deepened, but the squally rain, which had looked as though it was going to hit them, never developed, and when Elian came up top with a hot mug of coffee, laced with whiskey, they were off the coast of Spain. Roy handed over the helm and sat back, glad of the rest, for his back and shoulders were aching from the strain.

"I'm sorry, Roy," Elian said apologetically, "you should have called me. I went into a deep sleep."

"That's OK, Elian. I was glad of the chance to handle her in this weather. I don't want to get out of practice. You never know when one of us might be taken ill on one of the longer voyages." Then, as if something triggered in his mind, he asked, "By the way, how's that pretty blonde with the muscles doing?"

"I might have known you would have singled her out. She has a pretty face. I would not have thought you would have gone for the muscles, though. She looks a bit stringy. But she has not shown her angelic face since Fiona put her in the master cabin. You'll be able to see for yourself when you go below."

"I'll wait until we've refuelled in La Coruna before I go below. The weather should be much better from that point of the journey, so I will take a rest then. Thanks for the coffee. The whisky will give me strength and keep me awake for a couple more hours."

They radioed in and entered the harbour. The formalities were simple. Everyone had EU passports, so there was no delay. They were just a bunch of holidaymakers on a cruise. The refuelling was soon completed and the paymaster, Connor, paid over the cash as usual. Elian took the boat out of the harbour, much to the dismay of the passengers who wanted to stretch their legs ashore. Connor insisted that they get underway as soon as possible to meet up with the Algerian dhow they had rendezvoused with last time. Elian was glad to be on the move again. The thought of being ashore with that crowd below gave her a bad feeling. As soon as they were out to sea, Roy became aware just how tired he was.

"Call me if you need me, Elian," he said.

The whisky from the coffee and the large tot he had whilst the boat was refuelled was telling on him and his eyes were almost closed. He went below and climbed into bed, forgetting all about, and totally ignoring, the young woman lying on his bed, and in a matter of minutes he was fast asleep. He must have been asleep for about five hours when a movement beside him woke him up. Not realising where he was for a moment, his arm went over the form beside him, and then realising that the muscle tone was not familiar, he opened his eyes and saw the muscle-clad trainee wearing only a T-shirt beside him, looking wide-eyed at his naked body. Roy assumed she was about to scream when Roy put his hand over her mouth, muting the sound. He realised that she was naked beneath the garment and her struggles were making it ride up her body. Roy's arousal was almost instant. The woman gasped, and her struggles grew stronger and more aggressive as she took in the view. She realised that it was the captain and that she was in his bed.

She was no virgin, and the opportunity to have sex at the training camp without compromising her position was something she had been warned about. Something about the naked man beside her stirred something within her basic sexuality. Realising that this might be her last chance to have sex for some time, she stopped struggling, then removing his hand from her mouth, she grabbed Roy and pulled him towards her. This made Roy wonder what was coming; she kissed him fiercely, her tongue searching for his. The kiss deepened as Roy's ardour rose higher and his hands roamed the now almost fully exposed muscle-bound body. The aggressive way she groped him and the urgency of her need spurred him on. Their pheromones seemed to meld as their passions rose; the odour of arousal became stronger. Their sexual aggression mounted. This was no quiet, submissive cat; this was a wild cat, and the unnamed woman beneath him gave as good as anyone he had ever been with. Roy hoped the sounds of the two bodies meeting could not be heard over the noise of the engines. She seemed not to care. All she wanted was satisfaction from a man. She was paying no heed to the fact that the sex was totally unprotected. She had fully recovered from her bout of seasickness and was in the need for sexual satisfaction; she meant to get it come what may.

Roy had to place his hand over her mouth once again, this time to stop the scream, not of fear this time but of sexual euphoria, as she rapidly

approached her finale, and he managed to achieve his goal only seconds
behind her. They lay together, both recovering, their breathing gradually
settling back to a normal rate. She looked at Roy, whose physique almost
matched her own. The captain had a well-toned body and was something of
an expert in the art of lovemaking. It was the best sex she could remember
having in her life. Roy made as if to move.

"Whoa! Stay where you are and don't move, Captain. That was good, very
good. I feel I should introduce myself. My name is Gael."

"I'm Lord Croft. My friends call me Roy, and I'm very pleased to meet
you."

"I know that, and I am also becoming very aware that your recovery rate
is truly remarkable."

They began to move again. This time, it took longer, but the result was
almost as wild. Roy slid from her and rolled over to sit on the side of the
bed. He stood and walked naked to the shower, and as he opened the door
to the tiny heads, he said,

"I'll have to shower and get up top. Elian, my skipper, will wonder if I've
deserted her. She's been at the wheel for five hours," and then, looking at
his watch, he said, "No, it's almost six."

Gael lay back, her body lithe as a cat. She was captivated by this man,
who was not only skilled at sex but casual and relaxed about it, just what
she liked in a man. She had never met him before, and yet she had given
and taken from him some of the best sex she had ever experienced in her
relatively short life. She had known all along that if she had wanted to
stop him, as strong as he appeared to be, her martial arts and her karate
training would have been enough to prevent him having sex. Something
about him had made her come on to him and now she knew why; she felt
fulfilled, happy; the doubts about this training were a thing of the past.
The best part was, she hoped, he would be the captain to fetch them back
when their training was complete. Roy reappeared, still naked, and after
towelling himself off, he put on a shirt and slacks. Before he opened the
door, he said, his eyes roaming over her muscled and almost masculine
statuesque frame,

"You can help yourself to the facilities before you leave."

"I thought I'd already done that," she whispered, a broad grin lighting up
her face. "But thanks, I will. I could do with a shower. God only knows
when I shall get the next one in the hellhole I'm going to."

Roy just nodded and closed the door behind him.

Roy made his way up top, avoiding the looks he was getting from the rest of the passengers. Elian looked up as he approached.

"You look like the cat that drank the cream from the morning milk. I forgot to warn you about the blonde in your bed. Did she mind sharing?"

"I had no complaints. She seemed quite taken with the idea," Roy replied with a cocky grin on his face.

"You're a bit of a bastard to say the least, Lord Croft. I wouldn't have thought she was your type. Is no woman safe with you around?"

"I hope they are" he snickered, "or I'd be a father many times over. Anyway, enough of your questions about my sex life, if you don't mind? After all, it is my bloody boat for Christ's sake. Now, how far is it to the rendezvous point?"

"About three hours."

"Do you want to go below for a while? I'll take over."

"I'll make a drink," Elian replied. "Do you want me to bring you a mug of coffee suitably laced with your favourite beverage of course."

"That sounds good to me, but get the whisky from the cupboard up here. I don't want that lot to know where the liquor cabinet is situated, or we may have a riot on our hands."

Roy took the wheel and watched Elian as she walked, no, almost slinked, across the deck to go below. Roy checked their position and the coordinates for the meet. It was significant of the trust he had earned that Connor now gave him the rendezvous points as soon as he boarded. It was not long before Elian reappeared with the drinks, and she opened the top bar and laced both drinks with a good shot of Irish. Roy took the proffered cup and sipped the hot, strong brew.

The dhow was late. They had been on the arranged point for almost an hour, and Connor was agitated.

"Fucking Arabs," he cursed. "They never know the importance of time. Give the bastard another five minutes, and then I'll break radio silence and see if we can raise the bugger. I know it's risky, but what else can we do?"

Roy was about to respond when Elian called out,

"I think that's him now. South, south west, about a mile away."

They turned, and Roy, using the binoculars, confirmed the fact and handed them back to Connor.

"It looks as though he has no passengers on board. Where the hell are they? Christ, this could complicate matters. We may have to stay over in Tangiers again," Connor said grimly.

Roy groaned. *Not that sinking hole of a hotel again*, he thought.

The dhow drew nearer, and Elian, who had taken the wheel, gave the signal. The crew of the dhow let the sail drop and, using its engine, it edged closer. Roy and Connor's eyes swept the area, looking for signs of trouble. Roy switched on the radar, and there were no signs of any other craft in the immediate vicinity. They bumped softly against the dhow, and Connor snapped,

"You're late! Where the 'fuck' are the passengers?"

The captain of the dhow looked as though he had been struck a physical blow by the ferocity of Connor's statement, and he glowered back.

"The truck from the camp broke down. Be grateful I came to let you know. I could have just waited until it arrived," the captain snarled. "It's your funeral if anything goes wrong. If you had not been here, we would have just thrown them overboard. Now get that motley lot aboard, and I'll take them with me. They are going to a different camp, and the transport is waiting. They won't wait forever, and it's going to cost you twice as much for the double trip."

Connor nodded his agreement with the new arrangement, and the trainees came up from below and jumped across on to the dhow. Gael glanced over at Roy as she joined the others. The look was not missed by Elian; it just confirmed what she had known all along. The two of them had had sex when he went below. If she minded, she kept quiet; there was just a feeling of contempt for Roy's easy way with women, but she could not complain. If it was not for the way that he was, she would never have had the pleasure he had given her on more than one occasion.

Once all the passengers were aboard, Connor gave the money to the dhow captain, and they cast off. The captain checked the amount and shouted,

"It's short."

"You'll get the balance and the second payment when you arrive back with the others," replied Connor.

The captain looked disgruntled as he closed the bag containing the cash. Then, giving his crew the order, the dhow cast off and headed slowly down the shoreline.

Roy told Elian to head for Tangiers, and he asked Connor if there was a problem. Connor replied, somewhat curtly, that they would need to be in the hellhole of Tangiers for two days as the trainees would be a couple of days late arriving. Roy shrugged and said,

"So be it, but if were staying for more than over night, I, for one, will not be staying at that waterfront dive you booked us into last time. You and Liam can stay there if you wish, but Fiona, Elian, and I will be staying at the 'Movenpick Hotel', if they have room, or the 'El-Minzah'."

Using the satellite phone, Roy called the 'Movenpick', and there was a suite available. Roy booked it. He called Elian to one side and told her what he had done, inviting her and Fiona to join him if they wished. Elian jumped at the chance to stay in luxury for once in her life, and she said,

"I'm sure Fiona will only be too pleased not to be staying aboard or in that tavern we stayed in last time, especially in this heat."

They tied up, and the officials looked at the passports. Roy could not hear what was being said as he went with Elian to the harbour office and arranged for the tanks to be refilled, informing the dishevelled-looking harbour master that Connor would pay in cash. Roy saw money change hands between Connor and the officials, and when he returned, Roy saw that, as usual, the entry and exit stamps were already stamped on the slip of paper in the passports, just in case they needed a speedy getaway. Liam and Connor decided to stay aboard to sleep, but would be at the nearby bar to keep a watchful eye on the boat during the day. Roy had no idea that hashish in large quantities would be smuggled aboard and hidden away during his absence, despite his previous instruction to Connor.

Elian, Fiona, and Roy arrived at the 'Movenpick' and were shown up to Roy's suite. It was luxurious; both Fiona and Elian gaped at the Moroccan theme of furnishings and the bar surprised that the suite came with a butler and a barman. Before showering, the three of them, all of whom had been on the go for thirty-six hours without much in the way of sleep, had a drink at the bar and walked into their respective bedrooms, Elian and Roy in the main bedroom and Fiona in the other. It was all they could do to have a shower and fall into bed. The exhausted pair slept for the first twelve hours before Roy woke with the warm, naked body of Elian pressed against him. Both had recovered from their long ordeal; both were feeling frisky, and as there was no sound from the other room, they moved together. In minutes, they were locked in a lovers' embrace, totally unaware that the sounds of their torrid sex could be heard in the other bedroom. Afterwards, they lay languid, both satiated, and, above all, both of them needed another shower. They lay for a moment, enjoying the feeling of total relaxation as a knock sounded on the door to inform them that breakfast was being served. They both rose and put on the silk robes, provided by the hotel, and walked unshowered through to the table that had been set up in the dining section of the large reception area of the suite.

They were joined by a bleary-eyed Fiona, also wearing her silk robe, and they ate fruit and cereals, followed by one of the best English breakfasts either of them could ever remember having. They later decided that the fact that they had not eaten proper food for two days may have distorted their perception of the meal. After drinking several cups of very strong, sweet Turkish coffee, they felt revived, and even Fiona looked as though she was now awake. Elian and Roy walked through to their bedroom; Fiona looked in their direction but decided that she really could not follow, so it was with a resigned sign and a pang of jealousy that she walked to the other bedroom, leaving the butler to clear the table. The day passed with the three of them visiting the souk and the vegetable market, which, despite its name, seemed to sell almost anything. Both places were a hive of activity. All three of them were making several small purchases, with Roy buying a rug for Janet to put by her bed. Throughout the morning, Roy could not get over the feeling that someone was watching him; it made him feel uncomfortable. Fiona was remarkably attentive and was openly flirting with Roy, much to the contempt of Elian who, by the end of the day, had resigned herself to the fact that she would be sleeping alone that night.

Roy was concerned that the feeling of being watched continued through the afternoon, and when they joined Liam and Connor for a drink that evening, both of them confirmed that they had felt much the same, even though they had not moved away from the bar. It was quite late when they left the waterfront bar to return to the hotel, and Fiona was all over Roy, determined that she would not be the one who would sleep alone. However, after Roy served them drinks, she was disappointed as when the time came for them to go to bed, it was with Elian that he invited to join him. Fiona was furious, and jealousy raged in her mind; quite why she felt the way she did, she could not explain even to herself. She had no claim on his Lordship, and he could sleep with whoever he liked. It was just that she was so frustrated and determined to somehow pay him back for his rejection. She lay awake, listening to the sounds coming from the other room, and as Roy and Elian were in the final throes of their sexual ritual, the telephone by the bed began to ring. It was not feasible, Roy thought, but the tone for some reason sounded urgent. In a fit of anger at being disturbed, he snatched up the instrument, ready to curse at the reception desk when the voice at the other end said apologetically,

"I'm sorry to disturb you this late, Lord Croft, but a gentleman who gives his name as Connor insisted I call you He says the matter is very urgent, and can you come down ASAP?"

"I'll be down as soon as I'm dressed." Roy replied, giving a gasp of annoyance at being disturbed.

Roy and Elian dressed hurriedly and walked through to the other room, where the frustrated woman lay awake. He motioned to Fiona, who was still unfulfilled and agitated, to get dressed.

"I don't know what the problem is, but it must be serious for him to come up here at this time of night. I only hope it's not the cruiser. They were supposed to be watching the bloody thing. I'll swing those two idiots if anything's happened to it," Roy said, still annoyed at being disturbed.

They arrived in the reception room, where Connor looked worried.

"What the hell is wrong? Do you realise what bloody time it is?" Roy asked Connor when he saw him.

"I can't talk here. Get your things. I want to be away in the next thirty minutes. Hurry up. I've got a taxi waiting outside. Christ knows what he'll be charging this time of night."

Roy told the desk to make up his account as he would be leaving; the night clerk began to retrieve the charges for the room, and Roy instructed Elian and Fiona to get their bags. As soon as the women had disappeared up to the suite, Connor insisted he would settle the bill in cash, and when Fiona and Elian reappeared, they all climbed into the taxi, which took them to the docks where Liam was waiting for them. Liam looked grey, and when Roy asked Connor what had happened to cause such a state of panic, Connor explained that Liam had caught one of the locals watching them. He had approached the man, and a fight had ensued. Liam had, Connor emphasised, had a few drinks too many, and the other man had drawn a knife, driving it into Liam's side without any warning. Liam had fought back and disarmed the attacker; adding that, in the ensuing struggle, Liam had broken the man's neck. The two of them had then bundled the dead man aboard the boat and intended to dispose of the dead man's body out at sea. However, Connor emphasised that in the effort in getting the corpse on board, Liam had opened his wound, and as a result, he was bleeding badly. Connor added that when the dhow rendezvoused with them, he proposed that Liam would have to go with the dhow to get medical attention for his wound at the training camp, where a doctor who would ask no questions would sew him up and get him back on to his feet.

Roy was taken aback by the severity of what Liam had done. They carried the half-conscious Liam below; Liam sagged down on the seating in the main cabin, and Roy leaned over the prone figure and drew up his shirt. Then lifting the towel, Connor had pressed against it, and Roy exposed the open gash of his injury. Roy was shocked to see how bad the damage was. Fiona stepped forward and offered to dress the wound, and Roy, nodding to Elian, agreed to leave immediately. With the exit formalities already completed, they slipped their moorings and headed slowly out of the harbour. This time, they were not followed; the pirates had apparently learnt their lesson from the last time.

When the cruiser arrived at a point well offshore where they were unobserved, and after checking the radar to ensure that no other traffic was in the area, they unceremoniously dumped the dead man overboard. The inert body was weighed down with a few lengths of chain from the chain locker. There was no service; just a soft splash as the body entered the water, and in a few seconds, there was no sign of where the body had entered its watery repository. Elian and Fiona scrubbed away any signs of blood from where the man's body had been stored, and all seemed well; although to Roy, Fiona did seem a little offish, and any conversation between them seemed strained. He mentioned it to Elian, who said that she would discuss Fiona's attitude with her later.

They hung around at the rendezvous point for what seemed an age. The dhow was late as usual, and they were about to leave and head back into port when the signal was flashed across the darkness. Elian flashed the response, and after a short delay, the dhow finally came alongside. The once motley crew of trainees sprang aboard with a new self-assurance and agility. They moved as one as they silently slipped through the wheelhouse and down into the large lounge below before stowing their kit. Four of them helped the now semi-conscious Liam up on deck and carried him carefully on to the dhow. Connor gave the skipper a second bundle of US dollars and whispered gruffly,

"Take care of him and make sure he gets to the camp for medical treatment; when we return, if Liam is well, the dhow skipper would get the second half of the additional agreed price for getting him to safety."

"What if he doesn't make it?" the surly Arab captain asked.

The answer Connor gave him was a clear indication that if he didn't get Liam to safety, the balance of the money would be the least of the Arab's worries. They cast off, and Roy, taking over the wheel, headed north.

They were off the coast of Portugal when a patrol boat came towards them over the horizon. Roy had tracked its progress on the radar, and as all of the passengers on board had legitimate Irish passports, he thought nothing of it. Connor bounded up the steps when he heard Roy tell Elian that a naval patrol boat was approaching them fast.

"Roy, get the hell out of here! We do not want them to search the boat," he yelled.

"But why? Roy asked. For once, we are legitimate, and everyone has a valid passport, so what is the problem?" Roy queried with surprise.

Connor looked Roy in the eyes and gave Roy a curt but somewhat guilty reply.

"We have enough drugs on board to get everyone of us a life sentence in prison."

Roy was angrier than Connor or Elian had ever seen him. He swore and pushed Connor out of his way, and he uttered the following threat, which no one, who heard it, could doubt that Roy meant every word.

"If we get out of this, and you ever try that again, you stupid bastard. I've warned you about being devious before. I shall not warn you again. How the hell can I carry out my side of the bargain if I'm not fucking told anything?"

Connor stared as Roy's demeanour changed to a cold and calculated look that sent shivers down the paymaster's spine.

"The next time it ever happens, I will kill you myself, whatever the consequences may be; and you can be sure that it's no idle threat."

Dawn would be breaking in about half an hour as Roy asked Elian to bring the charts as he doused the running lights before he swung the seventy-five-foot boat towards the coast and gunned the motor. The craft leapt forward as they headed towards the shore. Elian reappeared with the charts, and Roy told Connor to take the wheel. Roy and Elian scanned the map. The whole coastline for miles was sandy beach, and there was an estuary much further north, but if the patrol boat captain had any knowledge of the coast, and Roy had every belief that he was more than familiar with the local topography, he would have no difficulty in cutting them off. There would be nowhere for them to go. Roy had no idea how fast the patrol boat was, and if they did try to make a run for the estuary, they could be trapped whilst the patrol boat called for support.

It was still not daylight, and they either had to turn and fight, or make a run for it. Roy made his decision. They had already disposed of a body, he was carrying a boatload of drugs, and he had trained personnel and arms aboard his boat. He gave the order. Then, with Elian's assistance, he armed the torpedoes, and the trained recruits brought up the Sam7s and the rocket launchers. They armed each piece of equipment as Roy watched the patrol boat's movements as it made its way in their direction. The patrol boat had no way of knowing who he was or where they were headed. All they knew was that they had a large and fast boat running without lights or any identification. He instructed Elian to get one of the decals she had prepared, in preparation for changing the boat's identity, as he turned and headed back for the patrol boat, cutting the speed to less than half throttle.

The patrol boat headed towards them in gloom of the gathering dawn. The patrol boat radioed for them to stop and demanded that they identify themselves. Roy slowed to almost a crawl, and then, using an Aldis lamp, he sent a Morse code message saying that they were unable to use the radio as that and their transponder had been damaged by fire. They would stop and wait for the patrol to come alongside, and the unsuspecting patrol boat approached. Roy told the men to stay hidden. When the patrol boat was just under a mile away, Roy opened the throttles and the MTB leapt forward. At a distance of six hundred metres, he ordered both torpedoes away, and as they turned, he ordered the Sam7 missiles to be launched. The patrol boat never stood a chance; it was doubtful if they even got a chance to get an SOS away or report the attack. The patrol boat was struck by both torpedoes below the waterline, and both missiles hit the wheelhouse. The patrol boat exploded, sending lumps of metal and black smoke high into the air, mixed with the cries of men in the act of dying.

The ear-splitting noise was followed by an eerie silence as the twisted hull slipped below the waves. Roy headed away at almost forty knots, the debris from the stricken vessel dropped all around them, and several shards of metal hit the deck. Fiona gave a scream, partially from fright and partially from the guilt of it all. Elian put her arm around her and gave her a large brandy to calm her shattered nerves. As soon as they were out of sight of the sinking ship, with Roy at the wheel, they continued northwards, and after sometime, they slowed down and to avoid being at sea when the inevitable search for the sunken patrol began Roy headed for the estuary leading into Setúbal.

The entrance to Setúbal was a tidal estuary, and the tide was rising. Roy cautiously and slowly made his way up the estuary; he could see that there were a number of derelict wharves designed for large commercial barges around Santa Catarina showing on his new charts. It was Sunday, and Roy was hoping to make for one of them unchallenged. Heading along the edge of the shoreline, as Roy searched for the spot he had earmarked on the chart, the derelict buildings came into view. They were in luck, and unobserved, they slid into a deserted wharf; the rotting doors lay open, allowing them to enter slowly; once inside, they tied up against the wharf, hidden from all but the most rigorous of searches, from the estuary, and after they had dragged the camouflage netting over the boat, they were hidden from above. The chart showed that the wharf they were in was deep, and they were unlikely to be beached and left high and dry on the ebb tide.

Roy and the rest of the passengers and crew lay quiet for the whole day. Connor had put four trained men on watch, and the watch was changed every three hours. The men were armed with side arms and machine guns. Roy had walked into the stateroom where Elian still sat with her arms around Fiona. Roy went up to Elian and told her to leave Fiona with him. Roy sat beside her on the bed and shook her.

"Fiona," he said in a tone that snapped her out of the wretched and guilty mood she had sunk into. "Listen to me. You are aware who we all work for. Did you think we were on a buying mission or a joyride?"

Fiona looked at Roy, her face drawn and lined.

"All those people on that boat, we killed them. Oh God, how will I be able to go to confession with all that guilt?"

"Fiona, you must listen, and listen carefully." Roy said, his face drawn, and Fiona saw he was deadly serious. "You can never tell anyone what happened today, especially the priest. If you cannot promise me you can do that, you will never get back home. If our controllers ever found out that you had told anyone or betrayed the trust I am putting in you, they would kill you without a second thought. Fiona, look at me. Do you understand what I am saying to you?"

Fiona sat wide-eyed as the consequences of what she was hearing finally dawned on her.

"You mean…?" she whispered quietly.

"Exactly," said Roy, not waiting for the hapless woman to finish.

Fiona slumped forward against Roy's chest and began to sob. When the fear and guilt were finally expunged and, looking into Roy's eyes, her need to confess her guilt faded quickly, she forgave him for his rejection of her in favour of Elian and whispered,

"Oh God, I never knew. I'm becoming so unravelled I need someone to love and comfort me."

Roy stood and went to the door and turned the key. Fiona clung to Roy, her pent-up emotion at bursting point. She had to do something to wipe from her mind the sight of those blooded and broken bodies flying up into the air, and Roy's adrenaline was high from the excitement of the short burst of violent action. Both found the outlet for their frustrations as each began to feel their arousal soon, and there was a sudden rush to quench their individual needs. The two people fell on each other in sheer desperation. The resulting half hour was frenetic, Fiona let the horrors of what she had witnessed slowly fade from her mind, and sex was something she could relate to, as the tingle of excitement, still far off, slowly began to grow within her. Neither cared about the noise, both uninhibited by the fact that any of the passengers were well aware of what was going on behind the closed door. Finally, they found their release, and it was over; they lay beside each other, and the unleashing of their pent-up emotions had the effect of calming their adrenaline to a reasonable level; and the strain of the sexually inspired engagement told, for the two of them fell into a shallow but troubled sleep. Roy woke several hours later to the sound of knocking on the cabin door. Roy moved quickly and silently and, opening the door, saw it was Elian who had knocked to wake the sleeping pair. She enquired about Fiona and was pleased to see that she had recovered her composure when Roy pointed to the prone figure lying on the bed with a guilty look on her face and a smile on her lips. Elian left them; the moment had passed; they needed no more action as they showered separately before dressing, and Roy went back up on deck.

Everyone sat about tense and ready for any action. Roy whispered to Elian that now was the ideal time to use her prepared decals and change the name of the boat once again. The cruiser was to become a registered tourist passenger boat, 'The Rose of Tralee', complete with a crowd of tourists aboard. The order was given, and Elian, assisted by some of the trained mercenaries, peeled off the old decals, and in its place, the name 'The Rose of Tralee' and the registered number were stuck over the spot where the original name and registration number had been. Then, as the tide rose again, the camouflage netting was removed, and the cruiser with the mercenaries, dressed in their open shirts and shorts drinking beer and lolling on the deck, made its way down the estuary and up the coast. The news on the ship's radio was full of the missing patrol boat, which, according to the newscaster, was assumed to have hit a wartime mine and had sunk with all hands. The whole area was full of ships searching for survivors and looking for a full explanation of what had happened. The Rose of Tralee made her way up the coast of Portugal, and in the main estuary leading into Lisbon, they refuelled at the small fishing village of Casais. Roy asked what all the activity was about, and the harbour master said, hanging his head,

"Señor, it is one of our coastguard patrol boats. It has apparently sunk with the loss of all hands. Several pieces of wreckage have been found, and from all reports, it had been sunk by a massive explosion. The current explanation being given," he said reverently, his cap against his chest as a sign of respect for the departed, "was that it had stuck a wartime mine that had broken free and floated to the surface."

Connor paid for the fuel in euros and told the old man that he had to get this drunken crowd back to Ireland; he offered his sincere condolences to the families of the sunken mariners. Elian took the wheel and headed back out to sea. The crossing, for once, was calm, and they slipped by the huge freighters entering and leaving the entrance to the English Channel before heading back to the fishing village. They hove to, a couple of miles offshore, whilst the cruiser was once more restored to its original registration and name on the bows and the stern. They entered the harbour, disembarked the 'tourists' and topped off the fuel before heading around the coast to the drop-off point, where they aimed to be just after dark.

They dropped a deep-water anchor off the drop-off point to await the signal, and Roy sat Connor down in the lounge and finally was able to ask what on earth had made him load all those drugs on a run when he was carrying the trained mercenaries back to Ireland. Connor knew Roy's anger could flare again at any second, so he spoke quietly and quickly, saying, "If anyone knew what I am about to tell you, we would both be killed. You are fully aware that over the last few weeks we have changed from picking up arms and ammunitions to picking up drugs. Well, the supply from Europe is too small for our needs and very expensive."
Then, looking around as if he expected someone to be behind him, he nervously began to explain,
"With the settlement of Northern Ireland hostilities, this has meant that the inflow of funding for the IRA has diminished to a trickle, and funds are needed to keep the IRA together. It is inconceivable that they could or would just disband an organisation that is such a well-organised and tight knit. The decision has been taken, at the highest level, to continue to move against the British not with guns, as we have done in the past. This time, we shall be more subtle. We shall destroy England with drugs. The IRA has decided in its wisdom that if they cannot win the war with force, they will win it with drugs. It is their intention to undermine the youth by supplying huge quantities of dope in the drugs market at a cost lower than is currently available. It will not only achieve the destruction of the English society, something we have always wanted, but also the resulting money raised from the sale will keep the 'Organisation' together."

Connor went on to explain that he had been told not to tell this to Roy under any circumstances as he was an Englishman himself. Roy, who had sunk a naval patrol boat, disposed of a body, and run guns and drugs for the IRA, was not likely to be telling anyone what was happening, Connor reminded himself. Elian called down that she had seen the signal, and the two men climbed the steps into the wheelhouse and went alongside the jetty. The illicit cargo was offloaded on to the waiting pickup truck by ten men that appeared seemingly from nowhere. They had the consignment offloaded and secured in less than half an hour. Connor handed Roy the usual briefcase.

"Be careful with that," Connor said, pointing to the briefcase, "it's well worth stealing. Now get the hell out of here. I'm staying with this lot. It's my head if anything happens to it, and it's something I would not like to lose."

Roy and Fiona pulled the ropes aboard as the shore crew released them from their moorings, and Roy was relieved to be in one piece and finally heading back home. They had been away for well over a week, and he knew that Janet would be worried, especially if she had heard about the naval patrol boat. The trip up the coast was singularly uneventful, and it was with some satisfaction that they crept into the harbour under cover of darkness, and Elian jumped ashore and secured the shorelines fore and aft. She jumped back aboard, and Roy shut down the engines, and they decided to wait until dawn to check for damage to the superstructure from the shrapnel and debris from the unsuspecting naval vessel they had sunk so effectively. They had less than an hour to wait for daylight when they would have a better chance to get the boat up the slipway and into the boathouse. If Liam had been there, they may well have tried it in the dark, but without him, and as Fiona had never handled the retrieval operation of winching the boat up into the boathouse, they decided it would have to wait.

The three of them went up to the castle for coffee suitably laced with a good drop of Irish whisky. Being relieved at their safe return and the freedom with which the liquor flowed, the noise of their revelry woke Janet who came down to see what the noise was all about. As she opened the kitchen door, she put her finger up to her mouth and spoke as softly as she could,

"I know you are glad to be home, but keep the celebratory noise level down. You'll wake Sean and the rest of the staff."

"Sorry, love," said Roy. "We were just celebrating another successful trip."

"It looks and sounds as though you are overdoing it a bit. Why haven't you let these women go home?"

"We need to put the boat away and check her over, but we decided to wait until it was light, and we would have Bridget to help us."

"If you don't slow down with the liquor, you'll all be in no state to put anything away. Elian, you and Fiona can use one of the guest rooms upstairs, and Roy, you can join me in our room. Bridget will wake us at seven thirty, and she and the rest of you can get that boat of yours into the boathouse. Now, come on, all of you, before the whole household is awake."

They all downed the last dregs and went up to bed. Janet was about to speak to Roy when she came out of the bathroom, but he was in a deep sleep. What she had to tell him could wait until morning.

Chapter 8

The following morning after breakfast, Roy, Elian, Bridget, and Fiona, who seemed to have recovered from her guilt trip, winched the boat out of the water. Elian first began to go over the decking and superstructure and then below the waterline, looking for any damage from the explosion. She found several pieces of metal embedded in the deck and damage to the paintwork of the superstructure where shrapnel had rained down on to the boat as it sped away from the scene. She reported to Roy and told him that it would take her and Fiona two to three days to repair and touch up the slight damage. She looked below the waterline but all seemed well, and no damage to the hull was apparent. Roy walked back along the tunnel with Bridget, who came on to him at the foot of the steps leading up to the kitchen. She could be very persuasive, and despite Roy's initial resistance, as he could hear Morag and Janet talking, he could never resist the opportunity for long, and as Bridget was quite advanced with her pregnancy, he knew he could do no more damage. It was quick, and when it was over and he climbed the stone steps, he could hear Janet say,

"If Bridget's not back soon, lunch will be late. It's just too bad of Roy to keep her this long, especially in her condition."

Then she said to Roy, as he entered from the stairs,

"Where is Bridget? You know she has work to do. You should not keep her too long from her kitchen duties."

Bridget followed shortly afterwards, puffing and panting, her face red from the exertion she had expended in the rapid sex session with Roy.

"Sorry, Mum, I came as soon as I could."

Janet tutted noisily and beckoned Roy to follow her into the lounge.

"Don't tax her too much. I need her in the kitchen. I don't mind her just giving a hand now and then, but let her come back to the kitchen as soon as you've finished with her."

"I'll remember that in future. Now, is there anything else?"

"Yes! Whilst you were busy with the boat, I had a telephone call from the Delaney household. You know, from that woman you had to drive back on the night of the christening. Well, it's Mr Delaney. Some sort of big noise around the area, I believe. He wants to see you urgently. You are to ring him today without fail."

Roy's heart sank. Had he discovered his infidelity with his wife? He paled at the thought.

"Whatever's the matter, Roy? You have gone quite white. There's no trouble, I hope."

"No, it's just a bit unexpected. I'll go and ring him straight away."

When Roy returned, he looked more perplexed than ever and deep in thought.

"What's the matter, Roy?" Janet asked.

"I don't quite know what to make of it. I've been invited to some sort of meeting with the people that charter the boat. Normally, I just get a telephone message when they need me. This must be something new. The meeting is at 1 p.m. tomorrow, and I'm not to be late."

Try as she might, Janet could get no more out of him then or later when they were in bed. She knew it was important, and she hated to be left out of his affairs, but it seemed to be happening more and more with this charter business. She felt as though he only told her the bare essentials of what he was involved with.

The following day, Roy arrived at the huge gates and waited whilst the vehicle was identified. A voice from a small speaker asked him to identify himself, and when he said his name, the gates began to swing open. He drove up the wide entrance and was more impressed than he had been when he had driven Mrs Delaney home on the night of the christening. There were quite a number of cars parked around the huge circle, and he parked behind the last one. The house was large, and Roy guessed it had been built in Victorian times. It was very impressively built of red brick with several turrets and a portico entrance, obviously built for a gentleman of wealth. The grounds were immaculately maintained, and there was a helicopter parked on a pad to the left of the parked vehicles. It was obviously a gathering of people with money and, from the range of vehicles, a lot of money. The door opened, and Kate Delaney, who was accompanied by an older man with grey hair, came towards Roy's vehicle. As they approached, Roy took the opportunity to study the stranger. He was well dressed in what looked like an Armani suit. The man, who was a little taller than Kate, looked like a man who was used to being in command. He had an air of authority about him.

The man, Roy presumed, was Kate's husband; he smiled as Roy got out of his Range Rover and walked towards them; holding his hand out for Roy to shake it, he spoke in the voice Roy recognised as the voice of the man who had dictated where and when he was chartered.

"I'm Sam Delaney. I'm pleased to meet you at last, Lord Croft. I understand that you are already acquainted with my wife, Kate. Come inside and have a drink."

"Call me Roy, Mr Delaney."

"OK, Roy, but you will get used to us. We don't usually use names. We recognise each other without the need for labels."

Roy followed Mr and Mrs Delaney into a large reception room, and Kate asked him to sit down. Her husband walked to the drinks cabinet and spoke quietly,

"I understand you drink Irish whisky. Is that so?"

"Yes, I've been known to tackle the hard stuff from time to time," Roy replied with a smile.

Roy watched as Sam Delaney poured from a bottle that had 'twenty-five-year-old' on the label. He took the proffered glass and waited whilst his host poured himself a large French cognac and Kate a sherry.

"Lord Croft, Roy, if you prefer, you have done well in the time you have been with our organisation, and your dedication to your work has not gone unnoticed in our circle. It has been decided that we should approach you and offer you a greater participation in our organisation. I have asked you here to put that proposition to you. If you decline, we will continue as before. If you accept, you will be invited to our meeting after the vote."

Roy sat still, unable to believe his ears. He was an Englishman and a Lord of the realm at that, and here he was being offered the chance to become part of the inner circle of this section of the IRA. Just how senior the section was, he had no idea, but if he wanted more excitement in his life, it would appear now was his chance.

"I feel I have proven my dedication. I would be delighted to become more involved if that is the wish of the meeting," Roy said, realising that in agreeing to Sam Delaney's proposal, he was committing himself to a new level in his criminal activities.

"I'll inform the committee of your decision. If the vote is unanimous, you will be invited to join us in about an hour. Meanwhile, I'm sure, Kate, my wife, will entertain you until then. I see your glass is empty. Don't neglect him; just look after the man. Get the man another drink, Kate. He's dry."

Kate stood and poured Roy another drink, and when she had given it to him, she put her fingers up against her lips, indicating that he should not speak. She then beckoned him towards a door to the side of the room, and once the two of them were inside the small, badly lit space, more like a large cupboard than a room, she spoke softly,

"Every room and corridor in this house has a hidden camera and a listening device. This is the butler's pantry, and there are no cameras or microphones in here. Now, your Lordship, or shall I call you Roy? We have an hour, and I know exactly how I want to spend it after the way you impressed me the last time we met."

Roy groaned inwardly. This was far more risk than he wanted to take. He shook his head, but Kate had other ideas and was not going to take no for an answer. Her determination proved stronger than Roy's resistance, and it was half an hour later when they re-emerged. Kate's hair was unkempt and her skirt badly creased.

"Enjoy your drink, Roy, after that. I feel you have deserved it. There's more in the cabinet if you want it. We have to make sure you are relaxed. I've had strict instructions to ensure that you are happy whilst we wait, and I think I've done that. I'm just going up to the bathroom. There's one along the corridor if you need to use one whilst I'm away."

She smiled as she slipped out of the door, and Roy heard her running up the stairs. He was nervous. What if Mr Delaney found out? If that happened, heaven only knew what would result; the consequences did not bear thinking about. It could be the death of him. Christ, he was sure sex would be his downfall in the end. He wished he'd never seen Kate at his son's christening. How could he have been such a fool? He was caught like a fly in a web. All she had to do, if he refused to cooperate with her, was to claim that he had forced himself on her, and that would lead to his demise. She had told him as much when he tried to refuse her. She reappeared, looking totally innocent; her hair was back in place, and she was wearing a skirt very similar to the one that had been so badly creased when she had left the room.

"I see you have helped yourself to another drink, Roy. Now, excuse me. I must check on the snacks being prepared for the meeting. Good luck. I'm sure we'll be seeing far more of each other in the not-too-distant future."

The grin that crossed her face said it all. This was not a liaison he relished continuing, but he could not see any way out of it. She had not left the room many minutes when Mr Delaney reappeared.

"I have the pleasure of informing you that the ballot was unanimous, Roy. Now, come with me and meet the rest of the group."

The room Roy was shown into was like a boardroom of any large company. The table was long, and there were two vacant chairs: one at the head, which was obviously the chairman's, and the other on the left-hand side, about halfway down the table. All the men seated stood as they entered, and Roy was introduced. He stood as each member came up and shook his hand and commented on how they welcomed him into their midst, each one congratulating him on his escape from the Portuguese patrol; many of them commented on how he had kept his cool, in the aftermath of the explosion, ensuring the safe delivery of his passengers and his precious cargo. When all the handshakes had been exchanged, the chairman called the meeting to order.

"Gentlemen, we have to discuss the mole we seem to have in our midst. It's still not been finalised who our main suspect is and what we should do about it," Mr Delaney said.

"I think we all know who it is. Don't we, gentlemen? It's that bugger, Liam. I never thought it would be anyone so close," one of the men, whom Roy would get to know as Mr McGuiness, whispered grimly.

"I think we have to give him a chance to defend himself. We have always been fair in that way," the chairman said, "and as we speak, his suspected contact is being watched carefully. If he makes contact with the security forces, I don't think there will be much doubt about the man's guilt. You all know we lost the last consignment to England, and our man only just escaped capture. The loss of the drugs was bad enough. Thank God it was not a huge amount."

Roy blinked. *Liam, the man he had trusted so much. Could he really be the mole? If so, his own position and that of Janet and Sean could well be in danger of discovery. Was that why he had been brought into the fold?* The thought made him shudder.

The chairman gavelled, and the room fell silent.

"The matter will be kept on hold until the man returns from the training camp hospital. Then we can decide what must be done. Now, the next matter. I have managed to contact our American group to try and set up a delivery of drugs that will be easier and cheaper for us to operate. That's where you come in, Roy. You have to come up with a way to recover the drugs from the sea when they are thrown overboard. It will prevent us having to get them into a country and then get them out again, before you and your crew are able to deliver them back here. You and I will discuss the details after the meeting. Now gentlemen, is there any other business?"

"Yes," said a voice from one of the men opposite Roy. "I have my suspicions that the British Secret Service are becoming more active. I cannot prove it yet. It's just that I see the same face from time to time, a face I do not know, and it's happened several times."

"Now, Michael, don't get paranoiac on us. Let's just wait and see what happens when Liam gets back. Lord Croft will ensure that he talks to no one on his return journey, won't you, Roy?"

Roy saw that there was no alternative but to agree, and the meeting was closed. The entire group rose to go to the room off to the left, where snacks and drinks awaited them all. It was, Roy noted, just like any other board meeting he'd chaired himself in the past. He presumed the business side of the meeting and the finances had been discussed prior to his arrival. The conversation was casual, and each member reconfirmed how pleased they were to have him on board. Roy could only guess that it must have taken some persuasion for some of them to accept an Englishman into their midst, but it had happened and, for better or for worse, he was now inside the inner circle. He was concerned about Liam and that it would appear that the British Secret Service were becoming interested in their activities. What would have happened if they had taken Liam into custody? Under torture, Roy was positive that the British Secret Service were not averse to using such methods to make a man talk, despite their assurances to the contrary. Such tricks and the use of so-called truth drugs would or could be used to make anyone disclose his contacts, and Roy was one of them. Thank God, if it was Liam, who turned out to be the mole, he had not been captured by the British Secret Service.

Roy's thoughts fell behind him as the group began to break up and leave for their respective areas. Mr Delaney asked him to stay as he had things to discuss. For a moment, Roy wondered if it concerned Kate, but he need not have worried on that score. When everyone had left, and Mr Delaney and Roy were joined by Kate, his wife, in the reception room, it was the older man who spoke to Roy,

"I have studied your development, Lord Croft, or should I say Roy? From the cradle to the present day, there is little about you that I do not know—from your sex life, the strange mixture of your Accounting and Engineering career, your rise through the ranks, and the reason you chose the path you did. I can assure you that we will do our best to provide the excitement you crave in your life. But I'm sure you would know, from your own experience, that I would never have put you forward without such knowledge. Enough of that! I want you to go away and think of a method by which drugs can be thrown overboard by one vessel and recovered at sea by another. I want you to design the system and carry out the recovery. That's your challenge, and I have no doubt you will find a way to do it with little or no risk of losing the precious cargo."

Idea's flashed through Roy's brain, some hare-brained and others practical, and he was about to tell what he was thinking when Mr Delaney spoke again,

"I don't want you to bust a gut and solve it immediately. I want you to go home and present me with your final answer. It must work every time and be done in such a way that no one else could pick up our cargo or be able to identify where it is. Above all, the recovery must not be conspicuous or a long-drawn-out procedure that could draw the attention of passing vessels or watchful eyes. A tough one, but I'm sure it's possible. Now, let's go through to dinner. Kate assures me the chef has done something special. When we are alone like this, Roy, I want you to call me Sam, short for Samuel. I have a feeling, Roy, that our relationship will be beneficial for both of us, and long may it last."

The meal was all that Sam had promised, and Roy was only sorry that Janet could not have been there to enjoy it; by the time he left, he was quite tipsy from the effects of the wines and the whisky. He was glad he had, much to Sam's disgust, refused the large cognac before he left. The road home was along narrow tracks, in some places only wide enough for one vehicle, and once or twice, he could have sworn he caught a glimpse of headlights quite a way behind. He put his foot down, and all signs of the other vehicle disappeared. He was getting paranoid. Who the hell would try to follow him through this type of countryside? There was only one place he was going to, and that was home. The thought that someone would want to know who he was and where he lived, in the alcoholic fuzz he found himself in, never crossed his mind.

The following day, Bridget came to the breakfast table to inform Roy that there were two men at the back door wishing to speak to him. To

Roy's surprise, one of them was Connor, but the other was a total stranger. The three of them made their way down to the quay. The stranger was introduced as Padraig, whom Roy recognised as one of the young men who had held the rocket launcher at the sinking of the patrol boat.

"Padraig will be your new gardener and armourer until we find the outcome of the Liam story," Connor whispered. "Tomorrow, you will get an additional gardener who will help Liam's father, Quinn, until we decide if the old man is to stay. We cannot take any chances. If it turns out that Liam is the mole, the new arrangements are far too important to the organisation to put you or your family in jeopardy."

Roy showed Padraig where the armoury was situated, and he and Connor went into the workshop office where their conversation could not be overheard. When the door closed behind them, Roy whispered,

"It sounds as though you have made up your minds already and have found Liam guilty even before his trial," Roy said this in a voice full of concern for one of his, until proven otherwise, loyal workforce.

"That's not the case at all," Connor replied. "We know that the British have an agent in our midst, and we have set a number of traps, information that only he would know. If the British appear on the scene at any of the dummy arrangements after Liam's return, we will know it's him for sure. We still do not know how he communicates. We have had him watched for some time even before he got himself injured in Tangiers. The fact that not a single operation has been compromised since his absence is fairly convincing proof."

"Yes," Roy interjected, "but if the British were clever enough and knew you suspected or were getting near to one of their agents, they could well stop their operations, leaving you to put the blame on Liam."

"Your concern for your employee is commendable, but how would his contact know that Liam had been hurt or was recovering in North Africa. It does not make any sense," Connor said in reply.

Connor eventually left, and Roy sat down to fathom out the problem Sam had set him. The ideas floating around in his mind began to crystallise. It was essential that the packages be watertight, and the buoyancy had to be such that they would stay underwater at a predetermined depth and have a localised transponder with a range of no more than half a mile to a mile at very low frequency. That would be relatively easy. The location would be easy enough to solve; the person tossing the drugs overboard would need a hand-held GPS, and the latitude and longitude would need to be sent via a satellite uplink to a satellite phone on board the recovery vessel. The recovery vessel would need a rig designed to trawl the area and recover the cargo. It all sounded simple, but he needed to design the system and prove that it would work. He called Elian into the office, and they began to work on the system. Elian was as keen as could be. She pointed out that the time of the drop was absolutely critical as tides and currents could move the packages a long way in a short time, and with the transponder having such a short area of signal, they would need to calculate the approximate area for recovery, and time would be of the essence. A week later, they were ready to try the system out. Roy rang Sam, who was delighted with the news.

"What can I do to help with the test?" Sam asked.

"I want you to drop the dummy packages off the coast and use the satellite GPS coordinated phone to give me the location and time of the drop. Elian and I will then do our best to recover the goods using our recovery equipment. We may have to do it a few times over the next week or so to perfect the transponder signal and our pickup procedures."

Sam agreed, and it was arranged for the first trial to begin the following day. Roy arranged for Fiona to deliver the first of the dummy packages for the trial to the Delaney household. It took another two weeks to perfect the operation. With the transponder range being increased to a couple of miles and several changes of frequency, the sonar output had to be almost the same as the sounds of whales or dolphins but with a definitive sound that only Roy's equipment could recognise. Any submariner hearing the sound would be led to believe that he had found a subspecies of sea creature with an individual way of communicating. Sam then flew to his contacts in the Americas, where he made arrangements for a delivery to be scheduled for one month later. On his return, he phoned and asked Roy to meet him at the house.

"I delivered the empty containers and transponders. Hopefully, they will get to the point of origin of the suppliers, and they have arranged for the merchant seaman to have a GPS satellite phone for communicating the exact point of drop and the time. They will give us the approximate date of the ship being in the drop area. After that, it's up to you. I just hope it works. The sums of money involved are simply mind-blowing."

"We have to have an excuse to be seen in and around the area without drawing attention to ourselves. We could be hanging around for some time for the initial drops until a set routine has been evolved. NASA has satellite surveillance going on all the time, and it reports suspicious movements of vessels to various drug enforcement agencies, so we have to come up with an idea to cover that possibility. Perhaps a holiday charter in the Mediterranean area would be one of the ways, and if we were challenged, we would have an excuse to be where we were at the time."

"Leave that to me," replied Sam. "I'm sure Kate and I will come up with something."

Roy groaned inwardly. As much as the thought of spending days with Kate Delaney on board his boat was an exciting possibility, the danger of such a liaison might prove very dangerous if Sam were to find out.

"Come over on Sunday and bring the family, Roy," Kate said. "I'm sure Sam would love to show Sean his train room. It's his pride and joy, and I'm sure your wife would enjoy lunch."

Roy agreed, and as he drove home, he wondered why Kate, of all people, wanted him to bring his wife for lunch. He gave up. There was, he decided, no end to the cunning ways of women. He would just wait and see what happened.

The following day, Fiona was unwell. She seemed to have relapsed back into the post-traumatic stress state she had been in just after the sinking of the patrol boat. Nothing Roy could say seemed to make any difference; even the promise of sex did not do the trick this time. Janet suggested that Roy take her home; she told him that if she had not known where Fiona had been, she was sure that she was suffering from some kind of post-traumatic stress disorder. Janet believed that to be impossible. It must have been the thought of those poor souls aboard that Spanish patrol boat being blown up by a wartime mine that had made her the way she was. Janet firmly believed that as Roy and his crew were in the vicinity, Fiona must have been traumatised by the whole affair, believing that it could easily have been them that could have been blown up. Janet asked Roy to arrange for an appointment with a psychiatrist to see the young woman. Fiona was after all a member of his crew, and he was responsible for her welfare. It was obvious that Fiona had to be well enough to go with him on the boat, or he would have to find a replacement. Roy made enquiries and finally settled for a consultant at the Beaumont Neurosurgical Hospital in Dublin. The explanation Roy would give to the hospital would be that Fiona had seen a man blown apart at a local quarry, and she could not get over the sight of seeing a man destroyed in front of her. Roy took her home and was met by her married sister Cathleen at the door. Cathleen was beside herself with worry about her sister who had not been the same since she had been away on that trip on his boat.

"Oh, Lord Croft," she said, "I'm so grateful for your help. I'm hopeless with sickness. Poor Fiona wakes up at night, screaming. How long do you think it will be before we can take her to see the specialist?"
"Don't worry, Mrs Murphy. I'll collect her the day after tomorrow and fly her to Dublin."
"How am I going to cope with her? She looks so depressed and lethargic," Cathleen said, tears collecting in the corner of her eyes.
"The local doctor has prescribed some drugs to help. They will make her sleep. Just give her a dose. The doctor said that she will fall asleep and will not be any trouble."
Cathleen took Fiona to her bedroom and gave her the tablets from the doctor, and Fiona became drowsy and was asleep in less than fifteen minutes. She returned and was in a complete muddle. She could not seem to stop chattering. Having his Lordship in her home was something she had never expected to happen. He was so handsome, and she had heard stories about him, that would make any woman blush.
"Lord Croft, how can I thank you? Many bosses would just have sent her home. I'm so pleased you have arranged to take her to Dublin. Can I get you a drink? I've only tea or some of my grandma's potcheen. It's quite a strong alcoholic drink," she babbled on. "I have the secret recipe, but some of the ingredients are from long ago. They are available, but it involves herbs and roots. My mother gave me several bottles some time ago, just after I got married, and I've never opened it. She told me it had special properties. It's potent, she told me, so it's the only stuff I can offer you. My husband only drinks 'the Guinness', and that's only on a Saturday."

To calm her down, Roy agreed to have a drop of her Grandma's alcoholic mixture. Cathleen opened the bottle, and the cork came out with a loud 'pop'. The liquid was clear and had a colour not unlike whisky. She poured Roy a stiff measure and handed him the glass. The liquid had a soft aromatic aroma unlike anything he could remember ever smelling before, and, raising the glass to his mouth, he sipped the amber fluid. It was warm, and the heat filled his mouth and slid down his throat like a mature spirit. The taste was very pleasant, and the warmth spread down into his stomach. Roy drank more, and a feeling of elation spread through his system. Roy sat talking and sipping the liquid until his glass was dry, and he could not help noticing that he felt heady from the alcoholic content of the brew, but the other remarkable effect was as if he had taken Viagra. He was very sexually aroused, embarrassingly so. He could not get up for fear of Cathleen seeing what physical effect the drink had caused. Cathleen got up to make a pot of tea, and she looked down to see if the drink had had the effect her mother had told her about. She could see from the way his Lordship sat that her mother had been right. The bulge in Lord Croft's pants said it all. Why couldn't she get her husband to take the damn stuff? He was wary of potcheen, for he'd heard all about some of the effects that stuff could have on you. Cathleen was a simple woman who had no idea how she could get Lord Croft to make love to her. She had only ever had one man in her life, and to think of asking another man to have sex with her was out of the question. So she busied herself with her chores, and at the earliest opportunity, when she was out in the small kitchen, Roy made his escape. As he slammed the car door, Cathleen reappeared at the front door with the bottle,

"Take this with you, your Lordship. I've plenty more where that came from. It's the least I can do for you after you have offered to help with Fiona."

Roy took the proffered bottle and drove away. The ache in his groin was simply unbearable. He would have to gain some relief when he got back. He hoped Janet would be up to it. Janet was overwhelmed by his attentions and could not believe it when he took her to bed, and they made love until she could take no more.

"Whatever has come over you, Roy? I thought my second pregnancy would have put you off, but it's been some time since you were so passionate. I'm not complaining, just surprised, my darling. I'd begun to think the new women in your life were gaining the upper hand, but now I'm not so sure. Has Elian fallen from favour, or has she found another man?"

"Now, Janet, no jealousy. You've never been that way. You know it's you I love. With anyone else, it's just sex. No more, no less."

Roy put his arms around her and held her tight against him. She kissed him, knowing that what he said was true, but it did not stop her worrying that one day someone might come along and take him from her. She hoped it would never happen, but the worry never left her.

Roy took Fiona, accompanied by Cathleen, her sister, to see the specialist, a Professor McNulty. The professor was sympathetic and insisted that Fiona be admitted for observation and treatment. Roy opened a line of credit with his card to cover the expenses; he had known all along that it would not be cheap. By the time all the arrangements had been made, it was too late to get back, and Cathleen and he would have to stay the night. Roy booked two rooms in the 'Crowne Plaza', and after a satisfactory dinner, at which Cathleen seemed nervous and unsure of herself, they turned in. Roy's room was just down the corridor from Cathleen's, and as she thanked him for the meal, she stood outside her own door and watched Roy go into his room. Roy had no idea how long he had been asleep, or what had woken him up until he heard a soft tapping at the door. He got up, and slipping his robe about him, he opened the door to a pale-faced Cathleen.

"I'm sorry to bother you, your Lordship," she whispered, "but this is the first time I've been out of my village and I'm scared and lonely by myself. Can I come into your room? At least I feel I know you."
Roy was taken aback somewhat but stood aside and let her enter.
"You take the bed, and I'll take the chair," Roy said, getting the spare blanket from the wardrobe.
"I would not dream of it, milord. I'm a married woman. You will not shock me. You've nothing I've not seen before, and from what I hear from Fiona, you are not shy yourself. I'll take this half of the bed, and you can have the other."

When it happened Roy could not be sure, but during the night the two were in each other's arms, and the inevitable happened. Roy was more than shocked by the way Fiona's sister played the wanton woman. She gave Roy free reign, her mind and body totally relaxed at first and excitedly energetic during the tryst between them. The following morning, when Roy woke, she was gone, and neither of them mentioned the night's events at breakfast or on the way back home. Roy thought he could well have just imagined it, but it did give him food for thought.

Sunday morning arrived, and Roy once again made love to Janet. Now that he was aware of her worries, he was determined to make her feel loved and wanted. They left for the Delaney house just prior to lunch, and when they arrived, Janet stared at the house and its well laid-out gardens, and she whispered,

"You never told me they were that well off. This place must be worth a fortune. It's beautiful. The maintenance of the grounds alone must be expensive if our costs are anything to go on."

Before Roy could answer, the door opened, and Sam and Kate appeared. They welcomed Roy and his wife to their home. Sam was taken with young Sean and insisted that he carry the little one into the house. Sam seemed a different person around children; he was like a kindly uncle, over enthusiastic in his attempts to please the small boy. At lunch, it was Sam who insisted that he sit next to him, seeing that the youngster got two helpings of strawberries and ice cream. After lunch, Sam wanted to take him up to see the trains, and Janet went with him.

Kate sat down and began to tell Roy what she had arranged.

"Don't let on when Sam tells you about the trip. I don't want him to know that I have discussed the details with you. I have arranged with a few friends of mine to charter your boat for two weeks. We are going to go to the Mediterranean."

"How many of you will there be?" Roy asked. "Because you know we have restricted space on board, and outwardly, the boat looks like a princess cruiser but she is still quite basic."

"We shall not sleep on board, but we shall stay in a hotel at each port of call. Sam left it to me to choose the final passengers from my most trusted group of friends. Besides myself, I have chosen Lady Blanchester and her eighteen-year-old daughter, Karen, whom we shall drop off at Nice or Monte Carlo. It is intended that after being dropped off, the young woman would be going to finishing school in Switzerland. When I mentioned the cruise to Lady Blanchester, she specifically asked if they could go along. She felt it would broaden her daughter's knowledge. The poor girl had been a bit of a swot at school, and she has few friends."

"The two remaining passengers are close friends from America, both of whom will be staying with us at the time of the cruise. You'll love them. They are so much fun to be with. Tessa Buchannan is an oil baron's wife from Texas, and Millicent Casemann is the young wife of a fast-food chain millionaire, both of whom would not be averse to taking your attention away from me, given half the chance."

Kate was sure in her own mind that any idea of Roy having sex with Lady Blanchester, who was in her early forties, and her daughter Karen, who had just been let out of the convent, where she had spent all her school life studying, albeit to obtain six straight A level subjects, was totally out of the question. The young woman was going to finishing school for a year before she went to Oxford University to study languages. Her mother had asked if they might accompany Kate as a treat for her daughter, who had really done nothing in her life but study. Kate continued,

"Lady Blanchester has confided in me that the cruise will do her daughter a world of good as she needs to be brought out of her shell. I should have replies from the hotels tomorrow, and I presume that you and your crew will be staying aboard the boat. I will try to get a copy of the proposed itinerary before you leave. Now follow me," Kate whispered conspiratorially.

She waltzed across the room to the butler's pantry. No sooner had the door closed than she flung herself into Roy's arms.

"Jesus, Kate, not now, we'll get caught for sure."

"Oh, don't be so coy. Come here, you devil, I want a hug."

It was more than a hug Kate wanted, and when the frantic coupling was over, Roy could not wait to get back into the reception room, where the two of them sat having several drinks before Janet, Sam, and Sean appeared.

"What's wrong with you two sitting indoors?" Sam asked. "Look at the weather. Let's go out on to the patio. We can drink there. Sean will love it on the lawn," Sam said and added to Sean, "I can see us having to get you a bicycle for you to ride whenever you come to see your Auntie Kate and me."

The rest of the afternoon went well, and Kate surreptitiously handed Roy a sheet of paper with the itinerary for the trip as he and Janet were leaving. Roy took care not to comment or look her in the face. This liaison would be the death of him, he feared. He imagined that Sam was not a man to be tolerant, especially where his wife was concerned. The trouble was he could not see any way out of it until Kate got tired of him, although he had to admit that she was hot and he enjoyed being with her. Nevertheless, Roy hoped that it would end sometime soon.

Roy discussed the itinerary with Elian the following morning. The route was simple enough: Tralee to A Coruna, then to Gibraltar, Minorca, Nice, and, if possible, they would spend time in Monte Carlo. Elian checked each leg, and all were fairly easily achievable. There was no time to dwell on the matter. All too soon, the day rolled around for another trip to collect the trainees and take the next lot. They would need to be away early. The departure day, for some reason, had been brought forward, and they were to leave midweek. Roy had been informed that Liam had recovered and that nothing was to be said to him prior to getting back to their home port. Connor would take care of the rest. Roy was assured when the call confirmed the departure date that this time they would only be carrying passengers pending the new drugs delivery arrangements.

Chapter 9

Janet was sound asleep when Roy slipped from their marital bed; he slipped into Sean's room and kissed him on the forehead, but the youngster did not stir. Roy went downstairs, intending to have coffee, but to his surprise, there was a knock at the kitchen door. He went and opened it, and there stood Fiona's sister, Cathleen.

"Lord Croft, I came to offer my services for the voyage. With Fiona away, you will be a crew member short," Cathleen said.

Roy stood stock-still. Elian had already made arrangements for Kerry from the village to help in Fiona's place. The arrangements had only been confirmed late the previous night. Now Cathleen was at his kitchen door, and he already had a full crew. He did not want to disappoint her, but an extra crew member on this trip was not required.

"Come inside, Cathleen," Roy said, standing aside. "You look half frozen."

"Thank you, sir. It's a bit chilly, and I've walked over the headland," Cathleen said, looking at him and added, "I've brought you some more of that potcheen. You said it did wonders for you."

With that, she got a glass from the cupboard and poured Roy half a tumbler full. She handed it to him after taking a sip herself.

"Drink that, sir. It will warm you up in readiness for the trip ahead."

Roy was about to protest when she pushed up against him, putting the glass to his lips. She tilted it up, and to avoid spilling the liquid down his shirt, he took a deep draught. Like the previous time, he felt the liquid's warmth spread across his tongue down into his stomach and into his loins.

He turned to put on the kettle, but he could do nothing to stop the Viagral effect of the brew Cathleen had given him. He turned to find Cathleen drawing up her skirt and, seemingly unable to resist the temptation as his arousal soared, he lifted her up on to the kitchen table. In what seemed like seconds, Roy's trousers were around his ankles, and Cathleen's undergarments were somewhere close by, and the aroused pair were coupled in a frenetic spontaneous bout of wild, uncontrolled sex. The potcheen seemed to have the same effect on Cathleen's libido as she sought to seek her own satisfaction. Shortly after, Cathleen gave a cry as her body rose up to meet Roy as he gave a grunt of joyous fulfilment as he unhesitatingly released into the married woman's very core. When the urgent desire was finally spent, both of the participants were staggered by the suddenness and ferocity of their sex and the unpredictable speed with which the drink had worked on them. Roy was shaken as he quickly dressed and said,

"I'm sorry, Cathleen. I don't know what came over me. What's in that drink of yours? I cannot believe it worked so quickly or overcame my normal self-control."

"Nor can I, sir. My mother did give it to me soon after I was married, as I told you, and I've never known why. Now, I know the reason she had so many pregnancies, although only Fiona and I survived."

"I only hope I've not caused you to have the same fate, Cathleen. Your husband would be devastated."

"Only if he knew he was not the father, sir," Cathleen whispered, looking down as if embarrassed by the idea. "Now, do you want me to help on this trip or not?" she asked.

"I'm sorry to disappoint you, Cathleen, but Elian has arranged with Kerry to come on the trip, and she is on board, as we speak. I'm sorry, but I do not need an extra crew member this time. You could stay and help Janet in the house. With Bridget being well into her pregnancy; I'm sure she would welcome any help you could give, and I'm sure the extra money will help as well."

"Thank you, sir. I'll stay and help in the house. You're right. The extra money will help out at home."

Cathleen stood aside to let Roy out of the door, and she handed him the bottle and whispered,

"Take this with you, sir. You never know when it may come in useful."

Roy carried the bottle on board the cruiser and put in the top of his wardrobe in the stateroom and promptly forgot all about it. Elian and Kerry had stocked the necessaries, and he went up on to the bridge and signalled Kerry and Elian to cast off the lines. He felt full of well-being after his unexpected early morning bout of sex as he took the vessel out into the Atlantic swell. The smell of bacon soon assailed his sense of smell, and Kerry brought up two wedges of bread with a good helping of bacon in between and a mug of coffee laced with Irish whisky.

"I thought you might be hungry, sir. This will put you to rights on this chilly morning. Elian is below having breakfast, and she says she will be up as soon as she's finished."

Roy bit into the thick bread, and the tang of his favourite HP sauce fanned his tongue. *This is the life,* he thought to himself. *I feel like one of those buccaneers of long ago. Plenty of excitement, good food, and more sex than I care to think about. What more could a man want?* The journey to pick up Connor was soon over, and as Roy helped him aboard, Elian took the vessel out to sea and headed south to pick up the passengers.

Roy was surprised when only seven trainees joined the ship.

"Is that all there is?" he asked Connor.

"I'm afraid so," Connor replied. "It's more difficult to recruit since the settlement. It's a whole new board game now. The youngsters are more interested in IT than getting trained in the art of fighting. I suppose it's a sign of the times we live in."

Roy could only nod in agreement as they moved out to sea in the direction of the Bay of Biscay and the busy shipping lanes heading in and out of the English Channel, one of the busiest channels leading to London and the ports of Holland, Germany, and the Scandinavian countries.

They refuelled in A Coruna and headed south towards the Portuguese coast and North Africa. During the voyage, Elian and Roy did four hours at the wheel and four hours below. It was when Elian came up for the last changeover that she spoke to Roy about the way things seemed to be developing below.

"I am a bit concerned about Kerry, Roy. She is not like Fiona. She's a bit of a flirt, and the passengers are getting a bit out of hand. It's not these guys I'm worried about. It's the ones we're going to pick up. They will not have had the benefit of sexual relief for over six weeks. It's strictly forbidden for the trainees to have any kind of relationship other than as soldiers. If she carries on being a tease with them, the Lord only knows what might happen on the return journey."

"I'll go below and calm things down and try to give her some fatherly advice," Roy said.

"That's good, coming from you," Elian retorted. "You forget I'm wise to what you have been up to and with whom. But she needs to calm things down."

Roy went below and read the riot act to the raw recruits, which seemed to calm them down, but when he spoke to Kerry, she seemed to take heed to his warning, but she was still a bit flighty with the men as she served coffee.

Roy hoped his message had got through. He went to his stateroom to rest, and it was sometime later when Kerry came in and shook him awake.

"Elian says it's time to send the radio signal, sir."

Roy looked at her as he slid out of bed and walked into the small shower.

"Tell her I'll be up in a few minutes, Kerry. Just be careful and remember what I've told you about the men on the way back. I can't watch over you all the time."

Kerry just smiled as she walked out into the main cabin. Roy dressed and forgot about it as they made ready to meet up with the dhow as dawn was breaking. They radioed and got a burst of static and then a poor quality message that the dhow would be late. As far as they could make out, it was something about a serious illness in the camp. The passengers would not be back for twenty-four hours, and the rendezvous would be delayed until the following day. Roy cursed; he had thought things had been going well on this trip, so, taking the wheel, he headed back in the direction of Tangiers once again. This time, Roy was uneasy as they moved into the Puerto de Tangier, the inner marina; he seemed to think eyes were looking them over as an easy target; if they were, they were in for a big surprise.

Connor went through the usual ritual, and the slips of paper were placed in the passports, stamped in readiness for a quick exit. Roy called, and the "Movenpick Hotel" reception recognised his name from his previous stay, and confirmed that the presidential suite was available. Roy booked it and paid with his credit card. They all went to the bar for a drink, and Roy was careful to make sure that Kerry stayed with them at the table with Elian and himself. The trainees made use of the local girls, and Connor watched over them, ensuring that they did not get drunk. Roy and the two women took a cab up to the hotel and ate before retiring. Kerry, alone in the large king-size bed, lay awake, listening to Elian and Roy, and she felt unwanted and very frustrated.

They were up well before dawn, and as they slipped their moorings, Roy was ever mindful of the feeling of being watched; it never left him even when they were almost at the rendezvous point. The dhow answered the signal and eventually came alongside. Liam was the first to jump aboard. The six weeks had been kind to him; not only did he seem to be fully recovered from his wound, but he was tanned and looked much fitter than when Roy had last seen him. There were only eight men plus Gael, of the original twenty trainees, that boarded, and Connor was told that sickness had taken four of them and that the others were still in quarantine and would come back with the next group in six weeks' time. As the smaller group put their kit away, Roy did not like the mood of the men. They seemed a little too overconfident and full of their own importance. Roy's attention was particularly drawn to Kevan, the biggest of them all, who seemed too sure of himself by far. Roy listened to the chatter as Elian and Kerry showed them their quarters, and Connor paid the dhow captain, plus the bonus offered for the safe return of Liam. Roy took the wheel and headed north, back towards the Portuguese coast.

It was Elian who drew Roy's attention to the radar and the five boats, which seemed to be converging on their position. Roy watched as the boats closed in. He called Connor up on deck and said,

"I think we have a problem. I was sure we were under observation, and if you look at the radar, you'll see what I mean."

Connor glanced down and took one look at the radar and said quietly,

"You were right, Roy, when you said we were being watched. It looks like pirates. Will they never learn?"

"You must remember," said Roy, "we had not had the boat converted when we were attacked last time, and they must think we will be easy pickings. If they saw us with the dhow, they might think we have picked up a load of drugs. You had better break out the arms and hope these buggers have been trained well. We seem to have plenty of unwelcome company, and they are coming up fast."

"You're right, Roy. I'll get the weapons out and ready. They'll think World War III has broken out if they try anything with us, I can tell you that."

Connor had no sooner gone below than the approaching craft began to separate on the screen, the five boats fanning out, and Elian pointed out to Roy that they were not only very fast but looked as though they were trying to come at them from five different directions. Roy could see them now, through his binoculars. They were fast low boats used for ocean racing, known as cigarette boats. They were much faster than Roy's craft, being so much lighter, and he knew that he could not outrun them; it would have to be a fight. He thanked God that the men on board had at least been trained and appeared full of confidence and would be of some use to him in the forthcoming fight. If they had been raw trainees, he doubted if he would have been able to come out on top.

The arms were distributed amongst the trained terrorists; they consisted of Uzis, the Sam7 launcher, and the two rocket-propelled grenade launchers, each man under the control of Kevan kept out of sight, each one ready to open fire when called upon. Roy could now see the approaching craft, which were converging on his own boat. Their plan, it seemed, was to encircle him like a Red Indian raid of the Wild West, no doubt encouraged by the old films they had seen on the local television station. He could see that the men aboard were armed with guns, and all had bandoliers of bullets on their shoulders. Through his binoculars, he could see that they had quite an array of weaponry and looked a wild and undisciplined bunch. Roy called out to Connor,

"They are an armed and dangerous-looking lot. I suggest that we take advantage of surprise and attack first and ask questions later. Tell that bloody lot to take aim but wait for my signal."

That was when he saw Gael emerge from below with his new Sterling Assault Rifle. Roy had told Sam that he had been presented with one, and it had been one of the coveted prizes from his Bisley days of shooting. Sam had taken it upon himself to upgrade his rifle to the latest sniper's rifle, complete with its silencer and high-powered scope, the last time they had met. Roy felt a pang of jealousy watching her handle the weapon. Gael treated it as though it was something very precious; Roy had not even had the opportunity to shoot it himself, other than to line it up at targets and sight the weapon. Gael smiled at him as if she understood how he felt; her hands caressed the weapon in a sensual manner, and Roy felt he was witnessing something almost sexual as she took cover behind the bar counter, well hidden from the view of the approaching craft.

The sound of a loud hailer was the first challenge that came from the boats.

"Ahoy there! Rose of Tralee," the favourite nom de plume Roy used on the boat when on a trip such as this, "shut down your engines and prepare to be boarded. Do so now, or we shall fire"

One of the men standing beside the leader fired his automatic weapon into the sky to emphasise the warning.

"When you're ready, fire at will," whispered Roy.

There was a slight 'phutt', the sound of a silenced round being fired behind him, and the leader seemed to stumble backwards. A small red dot appeared in the centre of his forehead, and a spray of red mist seemed to explode from behind him, covering the men behind with a fine mist consisting of blood and brain tissue. He sank down and fell forward over the wheel. Gael had taken her shot. There was a whoosh, and the first Sam7 raced towards its target, the heat-seeking missile finding its predetermined target, and the boat to the right erupted as the smoke trail suddenly exploded, hitting the engine amidships. There was a cry of alarm from the boat nearest to the leader, and the high-speed boat abruptly changed direction. The rocket launchers went into action, and the first shot was a near miss, sending waves up into the air, almost swamping the boat it had been aimed at; the second landed on the deck of the boat on the left of the lead boat, exploding and sending men up into the open space above, their screams of surprise and pain breaking into the sounds of explosions.

Moans and screams of alarm of the injured filled the air, and before the startled pirates could recover from their shock, the second Sam7 hit the leader's boat, exploding in the engine bay. The boat, which had been stationary since Gael had shot the leader, seemed to bend in the centre. The engine erupted in a fountain of metal pieces and, aided by the fuel, sent flames and smoke in all directions. The hull sank almost immediately, taking what remained of its passengers into a watery grave. The carnage was shocking. There was wreckage spread far and wide, and men and the wreckage of their boat were raining down from where they had been cartwheeled up high into the air. The smell of cordite and burnt flesh lay heavy in the atmosphere, and the two remaining pirate vessels took off at a high rate of knots, leaving their comrades helpless amongst the flotsam and jetsam around them. Red seemed the predominant colour in the water as Roy pushed the throttles wide open, and the cruiser leapt forward, leaving wreckage and death in its wake. The smoke would attract the attention of any passing vessel, and Roy wanted to put as much distance as he could between him and the wreckage. He knew as well as Connor that the sharks would soon get the smell of blood, and he wanted to be away before the feeding frenzy began.

The original Lord Croft, who had shown such concern over the fact that he had blown up a patrol boat, was no longer there. That man had been replaced by the current version, and he was slowly becoming hardened to the sight of such destruction. Turning to Gael and Connor, he said huskily as the adrenaline surge ran through him,

"That will teach them not to assume that a cruiser will capitulate without a fight. Those bastards would have killed us without a second thought.

Elian, take the wheel, whilst I go and congratulate our battle-trained would-be terrorists."

Turning his head in the direction of the bar, he called out,

"Gael, that was damn fine shooting. I had no idea you could handle that weapon so expertly. I could not have done better myself."

Gael was pleased with the praise and went below to clean the weapon and return it to its case. Roy spoke to Connor, telling him to give the men a drink of whisky each as a reward but no more than that. The last thing he wanted aboard was a drunken euphoric bunch of lads not yet fully trained in the field. Then, going up top, he relieved Elian and instructed her to use the trained agents to get the weapons stowed away again. Connor, who had returned, moved closer,

"Roy, those explosions may well have been spotted by one of the satellites. I suggest that we make for the nearest port and get lost in the melee of boats in the marina before we head north for the Spanish coast."

Roy, whose head had cleared, and who was thinking logically, replied,

"OK, but that thick cloud cover may have saved us, but I will do as you say and head for Lisbon. We can hide in the traffic going through the narrows. We can refuel and get on our way. It will mean us being late into A Coruna, but what the hell. We can usually find a place to tie up. It's only overnight."

Roy had been right. It was quite late when they finally made their way into the port of A Coruna. They found a berth and tied up for the night. Connor insisted that he take the guys ashore for a few 'toots', as he called it. He persuaded Gael and Kerry to go, and Elian tagged on to make sure Kerry behaved herself. Roy stayed aboard; he wanted to keep a watchful eye on the cruiser.

It was almost dawn when Roy heard the sound of voices coming across the quay. To Roy's amazement, it was Elian, her voice raised in anger, calling Kerry a whore. Roy listened more closely and heard Elian's voice clearly.

"Do you have no shame, Kerry?" she called out, "letting those drunken brutes touch you like that? I could see a couple of them feeling you up in the bar, and you were standing there letting them. Roy Croft warned you of the consequences of flirting with those brutes, who have been without female company for some time. Not only have you ignored him, but you have let things go one stage further, you silly young fool."

"I like male attention," replied Kerry sulkily.

"If it's that kind of attention you want," Elian's raised voice questioned her subordinate, "you could earn money by selling your favours, and you could get all the attention you could ever want and make money at the same time. If you act the part of a whore, you might as well get paid for it."

The three women came aboard, and a tearful Kerry stomped off in a huff to her cabin. Elian and Gael, not seeing Roy anywhere around, went to the other crew cabin. They had decided that they would go to their cabin before the drunken louts came aboard; Elian was concerned that the drink had seemingly taken away their inhibitions and made them brave.

A short time later, Roy heard Connor and the rest of the group come aboard, and from the raucous sound of their voices, Roy could tell that Connor had been more than liberal in plying the group with the local beer. The returning recruits and Liam, Roy could understand, as they had been away from alcohol for weeks. There was no such excuse for Connor, who was so drunk that he was falling over as he made his way below where he fell on to one of the couches and was out of it. Roy heard one of the trained men, who sounded like the youngest, say to the others,

"That young one's game for anything, I tell you. Why don't you go in there and give her some of what she's been asking for? When you've finished, she can probably accommodate the rest of us as well."

Roy listened for any reaction and, hearing none, thought it was probably just the drink talking and that nothing more would come of it. Once everyone was aboard, Elian and Gael came up on deck to get some air; it was too stuffy below. Roy asked them to go down and cast off; whilst they were away, he could hear voices in heated debate. Only Gael returned to the upper deck as she needed to clear her head, and the breeze on her face was doing just that as Roy headed out in the first rays of the dawn sun. He had cleared the harbour and was heading out to sea when he heard one of the cabin doors open and Elian call out,

"Don't you come in here and try any of your tricks with me, my fine boyos? I'm armed, and don't you lot believe I won't hesitate to use it."

Roy looked at Gael, who shook her head sadly at the commotion.

"It's the drink," she said. "It's fatal, even trying to trust them. Give them a few bob and a few beers, and they become totally uncontrollable. That's why there was no drink allowed at the camp, and women were strictly off limits."

She stood beside Roy, watching the spray splash up over the foredeck as Roy headed out into the swell. Her arm was around his waist, and her head nestled into the crook of his neck. Beside this man, she somehow felt safe. She allotted him far more responsibility, for the way he had handled those damn pirates, than he deserved. In her own mind, Roy had handled the situation as though it were an everyday occurrence. Even though he had not himself fired a shot, it had in truth happened almost spontaneously. She wistfully remembered how she had let him take her on the way to the camp on the last voyage. He had been magnificent in bed, and the thought went through her mind that she might let him take her again should the opportunity arise, but with that crowd below, it was not likely to be happening any time soon.

It was about half an hour later when Elian raced up the companionway to find Gael leaning against Roy as he stood at the wheel. Hearing the clatter of her shoes on the companionway, Roy turned to see who it was and, seeing the look of alarm on Elian's face, asked her,

"How're things below, Elian?"

"I'd be a lot happier if you went down there and took control. They're up to something, and I don't quite know what."

"If we are going to have trouble with that lot below, better we are as far out at sea as possible," Roy said as he pushed the throttles wide open.

Elian nodded, and Roy could see her 9mm Beretta tucked into her belt as Elian took the wheel, saying,

"I agree, Roy. If we are going to have problems, we need to be as far away from the authorities as we can get. I think things could turn ugly down there. They're drunk, and Connor is out of it, so there's no control."

Roy stayed to ensure that they were well out at sea, and clear of the busiest part of the bay; he wanted to be way beyond the international water mark, before going back down to the cabin. Gael followed him cautiously. Roy could see Kerry's door open, and Kevan, the self-appointed leader of the group, was standing with his trousers round his ankles, and he was between Kerry's legs. His movements left little to the imagination. Kerry's cries were partially being suppressed by hands over her mouth whilst the other four held her arms and legs. Kerry was struggling, but Kevan and the others were too much for her to fight off. Roy went white with anger. He was incensed at this attack on one of his crew, and drunkenness was no excuse for rape. He grabbed his 9mm Beretta from behind his back and pulled back the slide to load a round in the chamber. He felt overwhelmed with rage and calmly walked up behind the big man and, without so much as a word, he put the gun to the back of Kevan's head and pulled the trigger.

The sound of the round going off in the confined space of the small cabin deafened Roy. Kevan went rigid for a split second, and the front of his head seemed to explode, sending blood and brains shooting out in every direction. Then, his body seemed to crumple as the nerves and sinews lost contact with its control centre, Kevan's fragmented and bloody brain. The others stopped dead in their tracks, frozen to the spot, as they saw what had happened to their former leader. Roy said firmly and quietly,

"I won't entertain drunkenness on board this boat, and rape is the worst crime in the world as far as I'm concerned. Now, either clear up this mess or make a fight of it. I don't much care which way it is going to be."

The four men sobered up immediately. Roy could hardly hear their response as the shot in the confined area of the cabin had affected his hearing. Gael, who was standing in the main cabin behind Roy, took over command, and in minutes, the whole group had Kevan's inert body wrapped in the bloodstained bedclothes after they had pulled him off a screaming and traumatised Kerry. Roy pulled her trembling and wailing into the stateroom, where he ripped off her bloodstained clothing before pushing her blood-spattered and naked form into the shower to wash away the gory mess that had formally been her attacker. Elian, who had had the boat running flat out and was about thirty miles offshore, throttled back, locked the steering, and set the engines to just maintain a forward motion. She came down the companionway to investigate the sound of the gunfire. She could hear Kerry whimpering and sobbing in the stateroom, and from the activity in Kerry's cabin and the mess, she could only surmise what had happened. She opened the stateroom door to see a white-faced Roy. Gone was the confidence he had displayed earlier, when they had defeated the pirates. Roy was trembling with fear or anger, Elian could not tell which. He had finally realised the enormity of his actions, and she could make out the naked form of a wet, trembling, frightened, and traumatised Kerry standing in the shower with rivulets of red blood and gore being washed from her body.

"Jesus Christ, Roy!" Elian exclaimed. "What the hell happened?"

Roy stood pointing to Kerry but, due to shock, he was unable to utter a word. Elian poured him a large Irish whisky and sat him on the bed whilst she pulled Kerry from the shower and rubbed her down with a dry towel.

Gael had organised the now sober group, who had taken part in the rape of Kerry, together with the others, who had roused themselves at the sound of the shot and the commotion that followed. They carried the inert body of Kevan up on to the deck, where she unceremoniously stripped the corpse. She then took two of the shocked and silent, but obedient, so-called trained terrorists to fetch two wartime ammunition boxes and ropes from the ammunition locker below. Gael knelt beside the corpse, busy with pliers, before they wrapped Kevan's body in a tarpaulin she had found inside the chain locker on deck; she then tied the body up with strong ropes before attaching the heavy wartime ammunition boxes to the dead man's feet. Then, with the assistance of the others, they slipped the grisly package overboard. The sound of the bulky package hitting the water was disproportionately quiet, bearing no true reflection of what it contained. It sank like a stone, leaving just a bloody mess on deck, the only trace of the untimely death of Kevan, the troop's one-time leader. She then detailed the four of them to clean the deck and the rest to clean the cabin, after drawing scrubbing brushes and cleaning chemicals from the cleaning store below decks and handing them to the still shaken men. Roy, who was still traumatised and shaken by the speed at which things had happened, went up to the bridge, and on the way up, he held on to the side rail and vomited up his last meal and the drinks he had consumed earlier. Roy needed to get some fresh air in his lungs to clear his head, so after making his way across the upper deck, he unlocked the steering. He opened the throttle wide and headed for Ireland at top speed. He felt he had to put as much distance between himself and the heinous crime he had committed as fast as he could.

Sometime later, Elian arrived with strong black coffee laced, just as he preferred it; he grimaced as the hot strong coffee and the smoky flavour of the whisky overcame his bile. Elian took over the wheel. She waited silently and patiently until Roy slowly recovered his confidence and began to tell her the whole story. She listened, incensed at what he told her. Sympathising with him, she responded,

"If I had seen a scene like that, I would, in all probability, have shot them all," Elian expressed indignantly.

"But you didn't. I did, and I will have to live with that action for the rest of my life. I was not part of a group action. I killed him with my own hands and under no one's orders other than my own anger," Roy replied, his head in his hands.

Elian suggested that he go down and comfort Kerry, who was still in a traumatised state in Roy's stateroom cabin. Roy stood up, nodding, and descended the stairs to the deck and the companionway to the lower cabin, glad he was going to do something to try and help. He felt incapable of taking control of the cruiser at that precise moment in time.

Gael had everything under control. She and the now subservient and silent men were cleaning up every sign of Roy's actions. The smell of fresh blood had already disappeared under the aroma of cleaning chemicals; clean linen for the bed was already drawn from the linen cupboard; and there were no signs of any of the bloodstained bedding. Roy walked silently into the stateroom. He sat on the bed where the naked but still trembling Kerry lay in a curled foetal position. He stood up and grabbed his terry towelling robe and wrapped it about her trembling shoulders. Then he put his arms around her, giving her comfort and support. The enormity of his crime slowly faded as a lethargic tiredness crept over him, and both fell into a shallow and disturbed sleep. The activity on-board finally ceased, and from the voices Elian could hear on deck, Gael had assumed full command of the still shocked and very subdued trained terrorists. She had them doing press-ups and exercises to get them battle-ready; the boat could still come under the inspection of naval patrols, and she did not want shocked troops unable to obey commands in case of trouble. Elian had to admire Gael's tenacity, strength, and training under such trying circumstances; she realised that Gael was also vying for Roy's attention. Elian reluctantly had to admit that the way Gael had reacted in the face of adversity proved that she was a worthy competitor and, in all probability, she would have to share Roy with yet another woman. Finally, the cruiser was quiet; the passengers lay asleep in the main cabin whilst Gael stood watch beside Elian on the bridge.

They were approaching the drop-off point where the trained recruits were due to disembark, and Gael whispered to Elian,

"If Connor will let me stay, I'm going to come back with you. I rather like the idea of being one of the crew on this boat. I'll get more excitement here than I will, being debriefed by some fat bugger who has never left the security of his own village, especially now that the agreement for peace has been signed. I'll have fuck all to do. What do you think, Elian?"

"I would love to have you with us, but it's up to Roy. He's the boss," Elian replied.

She had come to like the scrawny but strong and confident style of her probable rival.

"You had better see what Connor says and talk to Roy before we put everyone ashore."

Gael went below. She found Connor in conversation with Liam. Connor had now recovered from his sonorous bout of drink and drug-induced stupor. He had listened half comatose to what had gone on whilst he had been out of it. He realised that it had been his fault, and if he had not gotten so drunk in celebrating their victory over the pirates, he could, in all probability, have prevented what had happened. He looked like death warmed up and not very warm at that, and there was a deep sense of guilt reflected in his face. Gael knew that she could take full advantage of the situation; in his present state, Connor would not be in any fit state to argue against her request. She sat down in front of Connor, who was now well aware of her part in cleaning up his mess, and she explained in words of one syllable just what she wanted and he said,

"OK, Gael, I'll see what I can do. Whilst I phone HQ to see if it's OK, you had better put the proposal to his Lordship for, despite what anyone else agrees to, it would be up to him to make the final decision about his crew."

She found Roy in the galley with a cup of coffee in his hand.

"How's Kerry?" she asked.

"She seems much quieter now," Roy replied quietly. "I have given her a sedative from the medicine chest."

"There's something I want to ask you," Gael said.

"What is it? I have already thanked you for the way you handled the situation, after I shot that bugger Kevan?"

"No, that's not it. I want to stay and be part of your crew, if you will have me. I have my sea legs, and I can turn my hand to most things."

"What's Connor got to say about it?" Roy asked casually.

"He's checking with the boss when we land, but only if you are agreeable."

"If he says it's OK, then I'll give you a trial. I don't think Kerry is going to want to come with us for some time to come. If she ever wants to come again, so that leaves me with a crew vacancy. Can you cook?"

"I can learn quickly," Gael replied, a little too eagerly for Roy's liking. He'd already had enough trouble with women he'd had sex with without complicating his life further.

"Tell me, Gael, when I killed Kevan, it was my position as skipper, a person those men would respect because of my position in the pecking order. But you, a mere stripling of a woman, took command, and they obeyed you without question. How can you explain that? I'm intrigued."
Gael smiled. It was not often that she had the chance to tell her side of the story; she always seemed to be on the defensive with her peers. She began to tell him something of how she had proved herself amongst the tough guys.
"It began when we arrived at the island. After I'd had sex with you, I'd considered having sex with the guys, but the first time they had seen me in the shower, they had laughed at the size of my small breasts, saying, Eh, Kevan, having sex with young Gael here would be like having it off with a bloke, wouldn't it?" and hurtful comments like, "You were on the back row when they handed out the tits, love." She paused as though remembering her humiliation. Then, as if she drew strength from within herself, she continued, "I was determined then that I would prove that I could be just as good as they were. I would go on to show them that I could do over a hundred press-ups and run faster and further than any of them. I was informed by my instructor that my obstacle course work had been outstanding and my marksmanship exceptional. I was also told, to my indignation, that the reason I had not been given command was due to my small frame. It was felt that the men would just not be dictated to by a mere slip of a girl, although by the end of their training, they accepted me as one of the boys, so to speak."

Her cheeky grin made Roy smile, and she continued,
"I made friends, strictly of the no sex kind, with one of the Chinese instructors, who, for the whole time I was at the camp, had instructed me in kung fu, taekwondo, and kick-boxing. While the others had lain about resting, I was busy practising, pushing myself to the limit. It had been Kevan, the big man, who had taken command when we first arrived. He forced me to my knees and made me carry out a disgusting sex act in front of the others. I found the whole thing degrading and quite unforgivable. I bided my time, and before the tour finished, I challenged him to a free-for-all match. The terms were no holds barred and whoever either

knocked the other out or overpowered their opponent, so that they could not go on, would be declared the winner. If he won, I offered to repeat the act again as a penance. In the event that I won, he would have to carry out the disgusting action on one of his own men. He had thought himself invincible and readily accepted the challenge. After all, he was at least twice my weight. I could see from his face that the result in his mind was a foregone conclusion. The contest between us lasted thirty minutes, with the whole camp watching. Throughout the match, I avoided letting him hit me with the full force of his fists, although I took several glancing blows. Using the skills the Chinese instructor had taught me, I finally brought him to his knees, and the final kick had him face down in the sand unconscious. No one had dared laugh at me after that, and the men were careful not to cross swords with me over anything. In fact, they all treated me with the greatest respect."

Roy was impressed. She would prove to be a very useful member of his team, and he was pleased when Connor confirmed that, under the circumstances, Gael could join Roy's crew on a trial basis to make up his complement.

Roy walked up on deck and watched as Elian organised the refuelling, letting Connor pay as usual, and they headed for Connor's drop-off point. Connor pulled Roy to one side and said quietly,

"Liam is coming with me when I get off. As you are well aware, we have a few things to discuss," Connor said tongue-in-cheek.

Liam had no idea what was in store for him. He just got off the boat at the jetty and said to Roy,

"I'll see you when I can, sir," as he walked away with Connor. Looking back, he watched the cruiser move into deeper water.

Elian took the boat out and headed for the castle harbour, and when they had secured the boat to the quayside, Roy invited them both up to the castle for supper. Gael was struck by the size of the castle and the private harbour. At the first opportunity, she was whispering to Elian about the setup,

"I had no idea he was this rich. This place is massive."

Gael would have said more, but she got no further as Janet walked into the kitchen.

"Hello, Elian. Who have we got here then?"

Janet thought to herself, *This is not Roy's usual kind of woman*, as she took in the semi-cropped head, the scrawny but strongly muscled frame, the vest top, and the almost total lack of breasts. This woman did not need to wear a bra. She was more like a man than a woman.

"Oh, Lady Croft," replied Elian with a grin. "Let me introduce you to Gael. She will be replacing Kerry as one of the crew. I don't think Kerry is quite cut out for our type of charter work, are you Kerry?"

Kerry, who was still shocked and pale, shook her head. Janet's attention was drawn to the pale face. She stared at her hollow eyes with dark lines under each and, to the gaunt and frail-looking figure. "Kerry, are you all right?" she asked sympathetically,

Then to Elian, she said,

"Elian, Kerry looks sick. Whatever is wrong with the girl? She looks as though she would be better off in bed."

Then, turning to Kerry, she said in a soft motherly voice,

"Go upstairs and lie down, Kerry. You can use Bridget's room. She has gone home for a couple of days. She is getting very near, and she was exhausted yesterday. I'm sure she won't mind you using her room, under the circumstances. I'll come up and see how you are when I have spoken to Roy. Now, off you go. I'll bring you up some supper and a drink."

Kerry was feeling very low. She just nodded and walked, as if in a vacant daze, out of the room and up the backstairs to the staff bedroom.

"She looks terrible, Roy. What's wrong with her?"

"One of the men got out of hand after getting drunk and raped her. I think she'll be OK in a couple of days. The silly bugger brought it on herself flirting with the blokes who were quite drunk."

"Oh, Roy, that's a bit unfair. No one deserves that kind of behaviour, no matter what they do. These bloody men should understand that when a woman says 'NO', she means it. Have the police been informed?"

"I don't think that's really necessary," Roy replied.

"I do! Now, has she bathed or washed? It's important to retain a sample for the police."

"I've told you that it's not necessary. He's dead. He fell overboard, and in the swell, he sank before we could get to him. I don't think that in the state he was in he could swim anyway. Now let the matter drop. It's over and done with."

Janet gaped. Rape, drowning, what else had Roy been up to? She would have to have it out with him later. For the moment, the most important thing was that she had to go up and see Kerry before supper. Cathleen appeared dressed in her uniform.

"Good evening, your Lordship and you, Elian," she said. Then, seeing a strange face, "Who's this then?" Cathleen asked, her curiosity having got the best of her.

"Oh, hi, Cathleen," Elian replied. "This is Gael, our new crew member. What's for dinner? I'm starving after the journey we've had, I can tell you."

The chatter and banter continued, and life went on at the Croft household as usual as Morag came into the kitchen with Sean, who was delighted to see his daddy back home. Roy took him from her and left the women in the kitchen; he was happy to get himself a whisky and leave them to it. Sean hugged his daddy and watched as he downed an extra-large Irish whisky.

Chapter 10

The weekend passed without incident. Janet never did get to the bottom of what had gone on aboard the boat, and after several rebukes at her enquiries, she let the matter lie. She thought to herself, *Perhaps it's better that I don't know. I would only worry.* Janet resigned herself, and she had the pleasure of Roy's company the whole weekend. He had been so loving and attentive despite the fact that she was now showing her current state of pregnancy. She had felt that he really cared for her and young Sean. She had wondered if all these other women would have made him less loving towards her. She had been overly concerned after having seen him with Elian and Kerry, but from the attention she received over that weekend, she knew she could forgive him anything. On Monday morning, Janet heard the news that Bridget had given birth, a few weeks prematurely, to a little boy and that both Bridget and Billy, her husband, were very happy. Roy seemed to be overjoyed with the news, and Janet was certain that it was Roy's child. *Yet another*, she thought to herself, wondering just how many others he had really fathered.

On Monday, Elian sent Gael to fetch Roy down to the cruiser urgently. Roy hurried down to see what the problem was. Jumping aboard, Roy went down into the main lounge and saw that Elian had removed the bed in the cabin, where Kerry had been raped, from its anchorages on the floor and had triggered a hidden switch, whereby a part of the panelling behind the headboard had swung open. The space was packed with notes. Hitler's Deutschmarks, US Dollars, Old English white five-pound-notes, wartime French francs, and a whole host of other currencies. Elian had waited until Roy was aboard and, using her arm, she had manoeuvred the headboard away, and the whole panel swung away to give access to the currency.
Elian was obviously shocked with her discovery, and she looked at Roy and said,
"I don't understand why this did not come to light when Granville did the refit." She continued, "I was just making sure that there were no bloodstains left from Kevan, and I must have caught the switch by accident. It was very well hidden, and if I had not moved the bed, we may never have known it was there."

It hit Roy immediately that the reason no one at the MOD had checked on what was included in the sale of the castle, at the time he purchased it, was that it had in all probability been a double-agent operation, acting completely independent of the War Office for whatever clandestine operations were required. That was why it had operated in the country of Ireland, which had been friendly to Germany. The picture became clearer. That's why the records had shown that the MTB had been sunk with all hands, and no trace of the boat existed in any War Office records. It all became so much clearer, and he now fully understood why they had sold it as it was. The MOD could not have been seen to dismantle an undisclosed cache of arms and ammunitions in Southern Ireland so soon after the signing of the Good Friday agreement.

Roy looked at the bundles, and he instructed Elian to take the currency and destroy it. Most of it was probably counterfeit anyway, and he did not want to be caught with a boatload of counterfeit currency and the store of drugs if the castle was ever raided. He asked her to keep one note of each denomination for each currency as a keepsake and to burn the rest in the furnace in the workshop, adding that she should burn the old panelling as well, ensuring that the blast motor was running on the furnace, to make sure that no ash remained that could be identified. He went on to instruct her to replace the old panelling with a new one and to leave the opening mechanism so that they could use the void to hide anything they cared to smuggle in the future, adding that if he was to be the new paymaster, it would be an ideal place to hide the cash. Elian understood and proceeded to pack the notes in boxes for disposal. Roy walked back to the castle intrigued. No wonder Jeremy Strong, the War Department's expert, who had carried out the original re-commissioning of the MTB, had been so intrigued by the very existence of the place. There were no records in the War Department of the place ever existing, and they had sold it to avoid embarrassing the government. Roy had just been the right person to make an offer at the right time, and no one would ever suspect the existence of his cache of arms or his secret armoury.

Roy had received the call to attend the meeting of the new IRA central committee on Saturday morning. Apparently, Liam had confessed. When Roy arrived at the Delaney house for the meeting, he was full of trepidation. Had Liam given his details to his contact or had he not? Did MI5 know about him and his activities, and was his family under threat? Roy was met by Sam, who pulled him to one side and said to him in a whisper,

"Don't worry, Roy. The British know nothing of you. Even under strict persuasion, and believe me, it was very strict; Liam convinced us that he had never mentioned your name to any of his contacts. Even so, his chances of seeing the day out do not look good."

Roy felt sorry for Liam. He had been a good man, and his only real fault was that he had become greedy for money. A bit like Roy had been when he had taken on the IRA charters; and a shudder went down his spine, as he realised that one mistake could, and would, in all probability, mean he would have a similar end to his career. He would have to try and be more careful where his dangerous liaison with Sam's very attractive wife was concerned. They walked into the house, and Kate came up to him and greeted him. She said politely that she was pleased he had been able to come to the meeting at such short notice. When her husband turned to speak to one of the others, she whispered that he would hear all about the final arrangements for the charter in the committee meeting.

The hearing, about Liam, was almost a foregone conclusion from the start, with Liam himself agreeing that the only way he could be dealt with was his own termination, knowing in his own heart that he could never again be trusted. Finally, he was led away. He had known the consequences of his actions all along, and his only sign of remorse or contrition was that he had hung his head in shame. The meeting broke up into sub committees, and Sam pulled Roy to one side again, this time to confirm that the charter would go ahead the following Monday as arranged. The meeting was reconvened, and Sam stood to confirm to the committee that arrangements had been made for the new way of collecting the cargo from South America. He confirmed that Kate and four of her trusted friends would go on a holiday cruise, using the usual boat, ostensibly to the Mediterranean and the French port of Nice. Sam continued to tell the meeting that, during the cruise, he would be in the United States and would radio the approximate coordinates of the various pickups twenty-four hours before each drop would take place. The operative doing the drop would use a satellite phone to make a once-only call giving the actual GPS coordinates as the cargo went overboard, and the phone would go over the side never to be used or traced again. Roy would attempt the recovery of the packages during the night, and there would be either three or four pickups during the three-week-long cruise. No one on board but Roy and

Kate would know of the purpose for the trip. Elian ostensibly would just be told that Roy had certain packages to recover for 'the Organisation'. Roy knew full well, however, that she would know exactly what the parcels contained whether he told her or not.

Roy gave a full report of the incident with the pirates of the North African coast and how he had used the newly trained group to defeat the attack. Everyone present listened with open mouths as Roy described the attack and how it was defeated. Then he went on to report the death of Kevan and how he had summarily executed him for rape. He summarised by informing them that the personnel and the drugs had been safely delivered to the designated points on the coast. There was a hushed silence as the committee took in the report. The one man stood and offered Roy a vote of thanks for returning safely and said that the IRA was well rid of Kevan if that was what he was capable of when the worse for drink. The meeting stood and applauded Roy's actions and then sat down, and the whole committee again reiterated that they felt that Roy should now begin to play a greater role behind the scenes and avoid putting himself constantly at risk. He was becoming too valuable a member to be lost to renegades and pirates.

After the meeting, Sam looked at Roy hard as he added that he hoped he would be able to stay behind and join Kate and himself for dinner. Roy agreed, feeling he could not risk offending the boss by refusing to stay and have a meal with him. Sam went to say goodbye to the others, and Roy walked into the corridor just as Kate was opening the door of the lounge.
"I need to use the phone," he said. "I have to let Janet know I'm staying for dinner."
Kate beamed and led him inside and pointed to the telephone. Roy called home. Janet said she understood, but she begged him to be careful on the road,
"You know the risks of being there late at night. The country lanes are narrow. Be very careful of the more treacherous crossroads. Remember things that seem safe at the time can be very dangerous at night, so please be extra careful and don't let your concentration be diverted."
When she put down the phone, she hoped that he had understood the innuendo she had tried to inflect in her warning. She could not imagine life without him, despite all his shortcomings and his wayward sex life.

Kate grabbed his arm and walked through into the door leading to the butler's pantry. She was more than usually excited. She was bubbling with enthusiasm as she told him that she had spoken to Sam and told him she wanted a child. Roy looked at her with a deep sense of danger as he began to see where she was heading and he was horrified at the very thought. Kate continued to bubble over as she held on to him, and as she kissed his ear,

"Sam flatly refused to hear about my plan to have a child, at first," she whispered, "but after he had sat and given it more thought, he finally agreed. He told me he needed an heir to leave his estate to."

"Kate, what are you suggesting?" Roy asked incredulously, standing aghast at what he imagined she was going to tell him.

Kate smiled and said with a broad grin running across her face,

"Isn't it obvious? I want a child by you."

Roy's mouth dropped open.

"There's no way that could happen," he interjected. "Sam would surely kill us both."

Kate smiled with a cruel smile and said,

"He need never know. The cruise will be the ideal time. I told him I would stop my pill immediately. I shall not be ovulating until the second week of the cruise, so he can try as much as he likes this week, but there's no danger it will be his child."

Kate pulled Roy towards her. Roy tried to push her away; he was determined to stop this before it got out of hand. She pressed her compliant body against his, and he felt her breasts against his chest; her hand dropped, and as she began to caress him, his arousal soared; he knew he was lost. Kate knew she had won and, quickly freeing him from the confines of his clothing and pulling up her skirt, she whispered, the growing arousal making her speech sound husky with desire.

"It's going to have to be quick," she said "I don't know how long he will be saying goodbye to the others. Sam usually likes me to say goodbye to all the members, but he told me to keep you busy whilst they dispatched Liam. They know you were quite fond of him, and he did not want you to be there when it happened."

They were soon lost in the throes of their uncontrolled passion, unheeding anything else until, with a shudder running through Kate's arching body and a wild moan of triumph as Roy urged deeper, the moment was past. They knew they had not been long and both of them would have liked to continue, but it was too dangerous. They had to get into the lounge quickly.

Roy quickly tidied himself up, and Kate let her dress fall into place, and both of them walked into the large lounge. Only minutes later, they heard the sound of voices in the corridor, and both Kate and Roy, both slightly flushed from their recent sexual contact, walked out of the reception door in time to say goodbye to the last of the committee members.

Sam led Roy and Kate into the lounge, ringing for a domestic and asking him to pour drinks. Roy's whisky must have been half a glass, Kate's glass was a quarter full, and Sam drank a very large cognac. He pointed to Roy's glass of good Irish whisky and said,
"I'll have to convert you to brandy, Roy. That stuff will rot your liver."
Sam laughed at his own comment. The very idea that such a suggestion should be coming from a staunch Irishman seemed to appeal to his sense of humour. Dinner was an interesting affair with Sam asking Roy about his newly reconstructed cruiser, its speed, range, and passenger space.
"I have to tell you, Sam," Roy replied, "that originally the boat was very basic. It was built to be a hit-and-run boat for men and officers. I have had her converted, and outwardly, she looks like a luxury cruiser, but it does not change the fact that it had formerly been a wartime MTB. Even now, the comfort, although considerably better than it was, is not really what you would expect from a modern luxury cruiser built for comfort and not for speed. The cabin space is still small by comparison, and the lack of crew's quarters below restricts the number of passengers and their comfort. The original design had deck guns that, together with the Vickers machine guns, provided some sort of defence, but the torpedoes had always been the main attack weapons. Since the new conversion, the main armaments on board now are still the two torpedo tubes, which are always loaded, only ready to be fired once the actual fish are armed. The Sam7s could be used as attack or defence, and the rocket grenade launchers and the Uzis are there to be used as backup. It's hardly what you would expect wealthy ladies to put up with for a two-week cruise."

Roy paused to see what Kate's reaction would be and how Sam would react to his wife having to rough it on a basic cruiser with few luxuries; in addition, he was keen to pass on Elian's idea that they should fit new turbo boosters to the engines.
"Elian has proposed that we fit new turbo boosters," he commented, "and then, given that she would be running light, the boat should be able to achieve between fifty-five and sixty knots. I believe, however, if she was

pushed much above that, she could become somewhat unstable in the water as it's much faster than the hull was designed for. As for passenger capacity, she was originally designed to have a complement of thirteen, but the cabin facilities were very basic. Even now, the term stateroom is a bit of an overstatement. The other cabins have been refitted but are not much more than extended bunk rooms with a bed and a tiny toilet facility. The main cabin was originally the captain's room, and the other cabins are very small. Originally, they were meant for the officers to bed down, if necessary. The boat was originally designed for use overnight and return the following day. The main lounge, now a day lounge, was where the crew spent their time when there was no action. The galley was never intended to be a place where gourmet meals were prepared. There is no way my boat, although converted for peacetime use, could even now be called luxurious when compared with modern fibreglass boats." Roy paused to see what reaction her was getting, then he added,

"These modern boats have much more room below decks and even have staff quarters away from the passenger's accommodation. I do not feel my cruiser could be used for overnight sleeping accommodation of several women passengers, especially your wife who is used to the comforts she has here. Running during the day as a base travelling from port to port for the passengers to go ashore to sleep ashore would be the only option I believe under the circumstances."

Sam nodded as if in deep thought. Roy went on to say,

"The boat is capable of high speed, but the comfort at high speed can only be rated as extremely poor. To pick up the underwater packages at high speed with the special grappling gear is an easy matter. The total range, but only at considerably lower speeds, is now up to three thousand miles, but even then, that distance could only be achieved by carrying deck fuel tanks or towable floats that are designed to be jettisoned when empty." He summed up by saying,

"If this trip is to go ahead and, as you suggest, we carry female passengers for a leisure cruise, the maximum should be three or four, plus I, Elian, and one other would be needed to see to the passengers' comfort during the trip."

"Could you run from here to Nice or Monte Carlo in a single day?" Sam asked, pondering over the problem.

"No," said Roy emphatically, "not with ladies aboard. To make it comfortable for them, I would suggest that at least two nights stopping in pre-designated ports would be the ideal. Running with myself and a crew, who are used to roughing it, we could do it non-stop."

Sam suggested making it seem more like a leisure cruise.

"We should make it a four-day trip, with three nights at ports to be decided by you and Kate. If there is any doubt with the crossing at the Bay of Biscay, an extra day should be allowed for the personal comfort of the ladies in, say, one of the ports on the Spanish Coast, or Porto on the Portuguese coast."

Roy nodded, then, looking in the direction of Kate, he secretly winked to let her know that he was playing her game and not letting Sam know that he knew all along what had already been decided. Then he continued speaking to Sam,

"I am in complete agreement with your suggestion." Roy then added, "A Coruna would come to mind as an ideal first stop. I would suggest Gibraltar for the second night and Minorca for the third night, finally reaching Nice the following day."

It was finally agreed, and Sam said,

"I will leave Kate to do the hotel bookings. After all, she has to make sure her friends are comfortable and well cared for."

The departure date was set for the following Sunday morning—to leave early in the morning, subject to the tide, from the small harbour of Tralee, weather permitting. Roy shook hands on the price, and they sat for another hour, talking about nothing in particular. The two men parted after making final arrangements for the recovery of the valuable cargo. Roy was informed that Sam could only give the approximate time of the drops of the cargo twenty-four to forty-eight hours before he had to make the pickup.

"Could you run from Nice to pickup points off the North African coast and be back in that time?" Sam asked.

"It would be possible but not with the guests aboard. It would mean a fast trip both ways," was Roy's only comment.

Kate took the opportunity and rejoined the two men in conversation. When the opportunity arose, she asked Roy,

"Roy, would it be possible for us to take five passengers, including me, on the outward journey and return with four? One of the group," she explained, "would be going on to stay in Switzerland."

Roy readily agreed that they could handle that, providing the guests slept ashore. The two men were fast becoming good friends and, after a couple more drinks, Roy suggested that the next be the last. The 'one for the road', as Sam called it, was a very good cognac with Sam, and when he saw how much Roy appreciated his favourite tipple, he said, seemingly in a happy and buoyant mood, that the arrangements had gone well.

"I'll have a case delivered to the castle as soon as I can. It's nice to see that you can appreciate the good things in life, my Lord."

Roy drove back to the castle deep in thought. He would have to provision the boat to cater for light snack lunches for his passengers, as well as food for himself and his crew for breakfast and dinner. The bar would need to be completely resupplied. He could not imagine his female guests drinking red wine, beer, and whisky. He would speak to Kate and then order whatever she suggested. He swung into the garage and walked slowly up the stone steps through the kitchen and into bed; he knew that he had drunk too much and was soon in a deep sleep.

It was Fiona that brought in their morning tea, and Janet thanked her, saying,

"Thank you, Fiona. I shall be down shortly. I have to go for a check-up with the doctor this morning, and Lord Croft was in late last night and is still asleep."

Janet, knowing that he had not got in until late; decided that she would let him sleep for a while. After she had showered and had breakfast, she let the gardener drive her to the doctor's, and as soon as Fiona saw her leave, she walked upstairs to take Lord Croft some fresh tea. He was still asleep when she entered the room, and knowing that no one was likely to disturb her, she quickly undressed and slid naked into bed. Roy woke with a start.

"Where's Mrs Croft?" he asked.

"She's gone to the doctor's, sir," was the breathy reply. "The gardener has taken her in the Land Cruiser. It's the day for her check-up with the new baby, sir."

It was some considerable time later, when Lord Croft gave a deep sigh of satisfaction. Fiona lay back, her body satiated, and her breathing slowly returning to normal.

"Fiona, that's what I call early morning tea. Whenever Mrs Croft is out, that's how you must bring me tea in the morning."

He walked through to the shower, and when he reappeared with his towel wrapped around him, Fiona had left to get on with her daily chores.

Roy had decided that Gael would not be needed on this trip, and he gave her the chance to take a holiday after she had checked that there was nothing Janet wanted her to do around the house. Gael asked Roy if he would mind if she went on a course to try and get her mate's ticket so that she could be of more use on the charters. Roy agreed and offered to pay the course fees. Roy and Elian were busy during the next few days loading the provisions and preparing for Sunday morning. They managed to snatch some time alone together, both realising that, with the passengers aboard, there would be little opportunity during the voyage. His relationship with his skipper was safe and secure, one fully approved of by his wife, who was getting closer to the time she was due to give birth to his second child. She had broken the news to him that the doctor had informed her that it was going to be a girl.

Saturday night was a tearful event for Janet, who really did not want Roy to be away for the next two to three weeks. They both knew that she could go into labour any time, but she understood that he had to go out on a charter once he had accepted it. They made love carefully, for the last time prior to his departure; she knew he would have every opportunity for sexual satisfaction with five ladies as passengers and his crew of two. She sighed and knew that it was of her own making. She had made him what he was, and she had no one to blame but herself. She slowly sank into a deep sleep, only disturbed by the thought of the possibility of him being caught 'in flagrante' by Sam, Kate's husband. *What would be the outcome of that?* she shuddered to think.

The cruiser pulled into the quayside at Tralee at 8 a.m., and the five ladies came aboard. The luggage they had brought with them seemed to Roy as though they were moving house. Elian stored it in the hold, hoping that none of them would need anything during the initial four-day part of the cruise; in addition to the hold luggage, each one had hand luggage to defy the very meaning of the description. Once the passengers and their luggage were safely loaded aboard, under Elian's skilled hand, they finally pulled out of the small harbour and headed towards the south. As the cruiser cleared the south-west corner of Ireland, the Bay of Biscay was calmer than either Roy or Elian had ever known. It was like a protected lake, as calm as could be. Unfortunately, Karen, Lady Blanchester's daughter, was still seasick, despite Fiona giving the poor young woman "quells" to suppress the sickness. Roy had allowed her to rest in the stateroom during the voyage. Late that afternoon, they pulled into A Coruna, and all the ladies were eager to go shopping. Karen, who looked very pale, said weakly that she was too sick to go, and Roy offered to stay behind to allow Lady Blanchester to go with the others. Roy told Elian and Fiona that they could also go with the passengers, for shopping and eating in the Spanish port did not interest him in the slightest. He was still remorseful of the fact that he had killed Kevan after a visit to this very port. He offered to stay behind and keep the boat secure, and he sat alone in the main lounge of the cruiser after the women left in the small tender.

It was not long after they had gone when a bleary-eyed eighteen-year-old walked in and asked,

"What's that you're drinking, Lord Croft?"

"Oh, hello, Karen. Call me Roy, for heaven's sake," Roy responded cheerfully, "I really have no time for all that formality between any of Kate's friends or members of their family. I'm sorry, but I thought you were asleep. This fine spirit," he said, pointing to his half-filled glass, "is a fifteen-year-old Irish whisky."

"Could I try some of that?" Karen asked innocently. "Having been in a convent for most of my time at school, I've never had the opportunity to try alcohol in my life,"

Roy instantly poured the young woman a hefty tot; she picked up the glass and took most of it in one swig. The fiery liquid burned her throat and she coughed.

"Oh my God, that's so strong." She coughed at the unexpected strength of the spirit. "I never expected the tangy strong flavour. I can feel it burning. It was down into my stomach, but it's not unpleasant once you get used to it. Could I possibly have some more?"

Roy refilled her glass and sat back to see how things developed. He had not expected his first conquest of the trip to be the young innocent daughter of Lady Blanchester, *but if that's how it was meant to be, so be it,* he thought to himself. From what Kate had told him in confidence, it seemed that the young woman had spent her whole life in a convent. Now that she had drunk a fair amount of the amber nectar, the young woman seemed keen to tell Roy her life history. She began by telling him about her time in the convent and then, suddenly, she changed the direction her conversation was heading. It came unexpectedly, with the emphasis on her being an innocent. She looked him straight in the eyes and explained to Roy that she did not want to arrive at finishing school a simple schoolgirl up from the country. Roy had been surprised at the brazenness of her approach. He was aware that the alcohol had much to do with the ease and confidence she showed in her eagerness to get the situation she found herself in off her conscience. Her inexperience, however, could not be disguised; even so, it was an opportunity he had no intention of turning down. Her seduction was easy. She let him do as he wished, the drink giving her courage far beyond her experience. The moment of entry had been painful, but she had been determined to go all the way. She cried out as her innocence was lost forever, but minutes later, after recovering from the initial shock, her instincts took over. She became a lover of note, her body rising and falling, matching Roy's energy; her excitement seemed never ending as she headed towards her ultimate climax.

The experience was dramatic for both of them, and finally, the deed was done; they lay in each other's arms. She had been somewhat inhibited at first but had soon let Roy take full control. Now that it was over, she looked a mess, the front of her skirt up around her waist, her hair tousled, her top up around her neck, and her bra, still fastened, was bunched up together with her top, but she was at last a woman.

"Oh, I never thought it would be like that, Lord Croft; sorry, Roy. I am finally a woman, and no one will laugh at me for being an innocent country girl. I've heard so many stories about how they laugh at young women who have no experience in those schools. They will never be able to do that now, will they?"

They dressed, and Roy was surprised that she showed no remorse over what she had done. As she sat on his lap with her arm around his neck, she whispered to him softly that she was so happy. She had been dreading losing her virginity and was pleased it had been done by someone like Roy and not at the hands of a rapist, or the fumblings of a young, inexperienced schoolboy, or, worse still, at the hands of one of her school friends' or even one of her own brothers. She said she felt glad that she was now a woman, not a schoolgirl. She had gone into one of the other cabins, and Roy had retired to the stateroom intending to sleep.

It was about half an hour later when he heard the tender bump against the side of the cruiser. Elian and Fiona had returned. Roy slipped on his robe and went to see them aboard. Karen's mother was with them. She looked enquiringly at Roy standing in his robe, noting the slight flush in his face.

Although she suspected something may have gone on between him and Karen, she decided to keep quiet for the time being.

"I came to take Karen to the hotel, if she's well enough," Lady Blanchester said.

The confident new Karen, still recovering from her conversion from a girl into a woman, appeared and said to her mother,

"Oh, don't fuss so, I'm fine now. I feel ready for anything."

Lady Blanchester looked at Roy more closely, but neither he nor Karen gave anything away. Karen followed her mother as she walked across the deck towards the skiff and, in the voice of an innocent, said,

"Thank you for the trip, Lord Croft. I'm sorry I was so seasick, but I'm happy to say I'm so much better now and would like to thank you for *everything.*"

Roy thought it was fortunate that her mother failed to notice the emphasis on the word everything. However, Lady Blanchester had noticed it, and an idea began to form in her mind. They climbed aboard the small boat, and Elian started the motor and eased the skiff away towards the shore. When they arrived at the quayside, the two women climbed ashore, and they waved to Elian as she returned to the cruiser. Later, when the three of them were enjoying a nightcap, Roy asked Elian and Fiona if they had enjoyed the evening. Both of them said they had, and Roy left them to make a late night milk drink and went off to bed.

Roy woke to the sound of the small tender leaving to pick up the passengers. They had a very early start; Fiona was making breakfast for everyone in the galley. Roy, as usual, had woken sexually aroused; he put on his robe and walked into the galley. Fiona was alone preparing breakfast as the ladies would be leaving the hotel long before the kitchens opened. Roy walked up behind Fiona as she bent forward over the counter top, pushing himself up against her. She turned, startled for a moment,

"Oh God, it's only you, Lord Croft," she said.

Taking that as acceptance of his evil intentions, Roy began his move. He needed relief, and here was the only opportunity he was likely to get that morning.

"Oh, your Lordship, they will be here shortly. I don't think we have time," Fiona babbled, her body rapidly reacting to Roy's attentions.

She cried out, but the sound was lost in the confines of the small galley. Both were soon lost in the euphoria of the moment until they both became aware of voices as they were carried across the water, and Roy could hear the sound of female voices as the party began climbing down into the tender.

"Oh God, they'll be here in a minute," Fiona muttered, conscious that they may be caught."

Roy redoubled his efforts, and Fiona bit down on to the towel as her body began to shake as she rose to meet their joint culmination, the critical climax of their joint effort. The sound of the tender against the side of the boat came all too soon, and with a grunt and a sigh of satisfaction, they broke off their sexual embrace and moved apart. Roy pulled his robe about him and let Fiona's skirt fall back as he walked towards the main lounge to greet his passengers.

As they came through the main cabin door, Roy realised that he had nothing on under his robe; he hurriedly opened the stateroom door.

"Good morning, Roy," Kate said as he was shutting the door.

"Good mooring, all," Roy responded. "I'll be with you shortly. Please take a seat. Fiona will bring breakfast as soon as she has it ready."

He shut the door and slipped into the tiny shower and washed before dressing and going out to talk to the passengers. Fiona looked hot and bothered as she put the plates before the passengers and Elian. Roy winked at her perspiring face as he walked past her to the galley, where the smell of cooking mingled with the strong smell of Fiona's arousal and the heavy scent of recent sex. Fiona came back and squeezed into the galley as Roy picked up a plate.

"Oh, Lord Croft," she whispered conspiratorially, "You'll be the death of me. We almost got caught."

"Fiona, it's all part of the thrill," Roy replied with a smile. "Don't you get a buzz from the chance of being caught? I know I do."

Roy helped himself to breakfast. The fan had taken away most of the remaining aroma of their hurried sexual escapade as Elian, having finished her meal, came up behind Roy and rubbed herself against his back like a cat.

"I'll see you up on the flying deck later," she whispered.

With that, Elian went out of the cabin and up the steps to prepare the vessel for departure. Roy explained to the still-yawning passengers that this part of the trip could still be choppy and suggested that they remain inside the main lounge cabin until they had seen how the weather was going to behave. The forecast had predicted light to medium onshore winds. There were some moans from the ladies as they wanted to get on to the deck to bathe in the sun, but they agreed to wait a while, for it would not be pleasant in a rolling sea. Roy could see that the voyage was going to be a real challenge, if he was not going to get caught at some stage. This, however, was what he enjoyed, and to hell with the rest of the world. Sex, crime, drugs, and the risk of being caught were the adrenaline he had sought when he had given up his mundane way of life. Safe though it may have been, it did not have the challenges he had now. He smiled as he went up on to the flying deck, the wind and spray blowing his hair back, and the open sea stretched out in front of him like a painted canvas.

The waves were being blown towards the shore, and the vessel was rolling as it gathered speed. Roy felt Elian turn out into the waves, and the rolling motion eased. There was a small cheer from within the lounge, and Roy climbed up to the flying open deck to plot the day's course with Elian. The tanks were still two-thirds full, and they chose a wide course that would take them well out to sea before turning back towards the entrance to the Mediterranean and Gibraltar, the harbour chosen for the night's stopover. The sun was shining, and Roy stepped up behind Elian as she steered the vessel at a fairly easy cruising speed.

"It will take us around ten or eleven hours to get to Gibraltar unless I push her a little,"

Elian said.

"As you wish, Captain," Roy replied, and he moved his hand around her waist.

"What about the passengers?" she asked, moving away from him.

"I asked them to stay in the cabin for a while until we saw what the weather was going to do. After all, we do not want an audience watching what we are doing, do we?"

"I'm sorry, Roy, but there's no way I'm going to expose us to the chance of being caught with all those passengers on board. Let's get this straight from the beginning. The answer is no. Get down and sort out your passengers. It's going to be a long day, and I'll want you to relieve me at the wheel in three hours."

Roy grinned wickedly,

"No, not that way. You know what I mean. Behave yourself. We have business to get on with."

Leaving her, he went below to see that the passengers were comfortable. After all, this was supposed to be a luxury cruise. That was the cover for the operation. Roy walked into the main cabin; he gave a smile as he saw the tiny brief bikinis on Kate's friends, and addressing them, he said throatily,

"If you ladies want to sunbathe, you can, but at this speed, you will get wind burn quite badly. Today will be quite a long trip, but we shall have you all in Gibraltar tonight."

Kate smiled to herself thinking that could be taken either way. *I don't know about anyone else, but if I have my way, Roy will certainly have me tonight, Gibraltar or not.* Roy went below to check the engines. The noise in the engine room was quite loud; the three supercharged diesels had no soundproofing inside the enclosed area; the walls and deck above had all the soundproofing needed to give the passengers and crew comparative quietness. Roy checked the gauges, and all was well; they would refuel in the harbour tonight and take on more fresh water.

Roy spent most of his time up on the bridge with Elian, and the trip went without further incident; the sun was low on the horizon as they entered Gibraltar harbour, where they were directed to an empty spot well out in the harbour. The ladies grabbed their overnight bags and climbed aboard the tender, and as it was Roy's turn to go ashore; he started the motor and sailed towards the customs and excise wharf. The only problem was the two Americans. He should have known that all was well, for they would have had to have European entry visas to get into Ireland, so they had the necessary visas for Europe, and the formalities were soon over. Once ashore, they took a taxi to the hotel. Kate had her own room, the two American ladies shared a room, and Karen shared a room with her mother, Lady Blanchester. Kate spoke out saying,

"Oh, Roy, we are in such close proximity on the boat. If you want a shower before we have dinner, you had better use the one in my room."

Kate had been going to say you can share mine, but it may have shocked Lady Blanchester, and she had thought better of it. Roy replied to her offer that he would be up shortly; he needed a quick drink from the bar before he showered. Roy deliberately took his time, and when he went upstairs, he tapped on the door, and Kate let him in.

"Oh God, I'm so wired up I could scream. I was hoping you would be quick, but now there's no time. I will finish getting ready quickly, or the others may become suspicious. The last thing I want is for Lady

Blanchester to mention to Sam that I had spent a long time in my room with you. The fat would really be in the fire."

Roy let Kate go down to join the others in the dining room, saying that he would join them in a few minutes. That way, Lady Blanchester would think he had gone into Kate's room after she had left. The meal was wonderful, and everyone remarked on how the sea voyage had put colour into everyone's cheeks. Even Karen had lost most of her pallor. Lady Blanchester commented that Kate seemed as happy as she had seen her for a long time, for she was fairly bubbling with energy. Kate whispered to her that she had been speaking to Sam, and he had made her feel so wonderful. Lady Blanchester and her daughter went up to bed after coffee. Roy sat with the other three until the Americans finally retired and then he slipped into Kate's room. It was not until the early hours of the morning that he finally escaped from Kate's clutches, and he excused himself, saying that he needed to get back on to the boat. He caught a taxi, and once on the quayside, he climbed aboard and drove the tender back to the cruiser. Then he tied up and climbed aboard. Elian and Fiona were sound asleep in their own cabins, and in a short time after Roy had entered the stateroom, he had fallen into a deep sleep, despite the exciting and arousing thought of having sex with Kate for once, without the fear of being caught by her husband.

The following morning was almost a repeat of the previous one. Elian got up early and took the tender. Roy had once again taken advantage of Fiona in the galley. The passengers were much later than the previous morning, and Roy was still in the shower when he heard the tender bump against the side; he dressed and walked out to meet the passengers, noting the sparkle still in Kate's eyes. Whilst the passengers enjoyed breakfast served by a florid-faced Fiona, Elian, with Roy beside her, cleared the harbour and headed out into the Mediterranean. The waters were much calmer and the journey much shorter; it was late in the afternoon when they anchored off the island of Minorca. The ladies, all except Lady Blanchester, wanted to go on to the beach. Roy took everyone ashore, leaving only Elian and Fiona aboard. They took a taxi to the hotel, where they checked into their rooms, and the bikini-clad ladies went on to the beach leaving Lady Blanchester alone in her room. Roy, as usual, went down to the lower-level bar for a drink; the bar was situated below the ground floor and was beside a delightful pool. Roy was on his second whisky gazing at the bevy of beautiful women all around him; he was genuinely surprised when he was joined by Lady Blanchester; that afternoon's experience was one he had never considered would ever happen. Lady Blanchester had shown that she had a considerable capacity for alcohol by drinking a number of large martinis, the speciality of the house. She had impressed him with her capacity for drink, and after consuming several potent martini cocktails, she had appeared somewhat the worse for wear. She had asked him to help her to her room. Roy had been too polite to refuse.

When he was alone with her in the lift, her ladyship had been all over him in the guise that she was under the influence of alcohol; however, once in her room, all pretence fell away. Her passion had known no end; she had been the aggressor in their sexual tryst; the eagerness of their sex and the passion she showed as they achieved sexual satisfaction. She lay back and whispered, the excitement still evident in her voice,

"I knew you were a very sensual man the first time I laid eyes on you, Lord Croft. I have always enjoyed sex, and my passion, once raised, knows no bounds. I assume from the change in my daughter that you took her virginity that first evening on the boat. I recognised the flush in your cheeks and that sparkle in Karen's eyes. I assume you took her without any precautions, you wicked man. I thank God she was not ovulating. She was innocent of what the consequences of your actions might have been. I do not have that worry, so come on. I need you to take me again."

Roy had enjoyed the older woman, surprised at her casual approach to sex. She showed that she was no novice at the game and was eager to show him her unrivalled ability to please a man. They began again. Lady Blanchester was surprisingly agile, and she gave a wild cry as she achieved yet another pinnacle of excitement. They continued to move together until Roy gave a contented grunt as he achieved yet another joint satisfying orgasm deep within the matriarch beneath him. Roy had been glad to escape from her room and was back in the bar before the others returned from the beach. He had refused to consider the invitation that he had spent the night in Lady Blanchester's room. Karen would have been shocked, and what might have ended up being a ménage à trois was avoided. Unknown to the rest of the party, after dinner Roy had spent the night in Kate's room. He was glad that he had his hip flask full of Cathleen's potcheen with him at the time.

The following morning, Roy rose early and waited patiently in the reception area. Lady Blanchester had a glint in her eye as she and her daughter joined Roy in the hotel reception. Shortly afterwards, he was joined by the others. Kate settled the bill, and they all took a minibus taxi back to the dock. Thankfully, the tender was where he had left it, and they rode out to a worried Fiona and Elian. Both showed their concern but suppressed their eagerness to question his absence, even though they were curious to know what had happened to him. When the passengers had gone to their rooms, the two women told him that they had gone into the stateroom and had seen that he was not back. They had been worried about his safety, but in view of their not having a second tender, they had waited anxiously for his return. Roy informed them that it had got too late. He had had too many drinks into the bargain, and he had just taken a room for the night. Elian and Fiona looked at the passengers and wondered which one Roy had slept with. They could not even guess it had been Kate, but they had no idea that it might well have been with Lady Blanchester or her eighteen-year-old daughter; both of those aristocratic women looked as though butter would not melt in their mouths, and Lady Blanchester seemed more aloof than ever this morning.

They set off for the last leg of the journey to Nice. Roy knew that the harbour would be full of cruisers just as big, if not bigger than his, but much more expensive, and as a result even with his title, the anchorage they would be given would not be one of the better ones. It was very hot when they anchored, and it was decided that, instead of Fiona preparing the usual snacks, they would send for food from one of the better restaurants, a routine that many of the visiting boats and the restaurants favoured. It was not cheap, but the better restaurants sent a waiter with the food; the motor boat delivered both the waiter and the food, and the vessel waited whilst the meal was served. The seafood and iced champagne was exquisite as they sat on the deck beneath the stars. No one seemed in a hurry, and it was quite late when the party decided they were going to the hotel. Only the two American women said that it would be a sin and they would hate to sleep inside on a night like this. They asked Roy if he could provide them with a couple of lilos to enable them to sleep on the deck. Elian and Fiona went below and returned with two mattresses off the bunks. Elian loaded the rest of the party aboard the tender, and they headed for the hotel at the other end of the bay. Fiona, who had worked hard all day, seeing to the

"It's about 150 miles to the Straits of Gibraltar and then fifty miles to Cadiz. I suggest we aim to anchor there overnight and move out in the morning. What do you say?"

"That sounds good to me. We can anchor in the outer harbour overnight and move out early in the morning. We are due to rendezvous at the drop point in the evening, and the rough coordinates are about 250 miles from Cadiz. It will give us a leisurely morning after our race today."

"I'll call you as we approach Cadiz. Now get below before you fall asleep on your feet."

Roy went below. Before he turned in, he decided to go below and check up on Fiona. He had not seen her or heard of her for hours. Going below and through into the lower hull of the Cruiser, he caught sight of her. She was concentrating on wrapping the weapons in oily clothes before replacing them carefully in their proper places. Fiona looked up and grunted,

"Christ, is it that time already? I have been so busy I lost track of time. There's no supper ready or anything. I'll get right on to it now."

She stood up, her hands covered in gun oil and her face smeared where she had rubbed her eyes with her oily hands. Roy still thought she looked remarkably attractive, but he was just too tired to make any move on her.

"Don't worry about it. I'll eat later," Roy said. "I'm just too tired to wait. Talk to Elian, and call me when she's off Cadiz. We're going to hold over there until morning."

Fiona apologised again and began packing the weapons back into the store before going up to clean up and begin to prepare the meal. As she stood up, she realised that she was bloody starving. *I'll prepare something that will keep and I can take up to Elian to eat whilst she's at the wheel*, she thought to herself as she made her way up towards the galley and the heads. Roy had, in the meantime, gone into the stateroom and stripped off before falling naked on to the bed; he was asleep in seconds. The next thing he knew was Fiona shaking him.

"Roy," she whispered, "It's time to get up."

She stared at his nakedness, seeing his muscle-bound chest and realising just how good-looking he was. Her eyes were drawn lower, realising that he was somewhat aroused as he woke from a deep sleep. Fiona, far from being embarrassed, was already pulling her top over her head and, minutes later, had joined him on the bed. It only took a few seconds before Roy was fully awake, refreshed and ready to join in the fun, and when the fervent sexual furore was over and he lay back beside her, he said throatily,

"Fiona, if that's the 'entrée', I'm looking forward to the main course."
"It was not only for you, Roy," Fiona replied. "A girl has her own needs as well, you know. Unfortunately, that's all there's time for. Your meal is in the galley. Now, let me get dressed. Elian will wonder where I am."

Roy got off the bed and dressed, and as he closed the door behind him, "I'll leave you to use the heads and get dressed," he said quietly. "I'm so hungry I could eat a horse."
He went up to the galley and the smell of the food drew him to the hot meal. By the time he reached the galley, his stomach was rumbling with hunger. He ate his fill and went up on deck as Elian was rounding the San Sebastian headland. They headed for the outer harbour with the lights of Cadiz on their right until the marina was in view. They anchored in the outer section and settled down for the night. Later that morning, after a hearty breakfast, they moved out and headed for the rendezvous area. They were thankful they had made the effort to be early. At lunchtime, Roy received the call showing the coordinates.
35° 53′53, 40 N
9° 22′41, 47 W
Roy checked their position and found that they were about half an hour away. He gave the information to Elian and went down to assist Fiona to rig the recovery equipment. He went back up top and switched on the receiver, waiting for the transmitter on the submerged cargo to sound. The half hour was up, and they were at the exact point the cargo had been jettisoned, and the receiver was still silent.

Elian looked at Roy quizzically, a deep frown across her brow, and she said quickly,
"Turn the volume up to full, and I'll begin to circle until we get a signal," Elian said.
"Wait," said Roy. "I'll check the tide and current details for the area."
When he had checked, he pointed to the screen,
"It appears there's a current running south. That's where we need to head. The speed and strength of it varies according to the time of year, but it would appear to be fairly strong at the moment."
Elian headed south, and ten minutes later, the receiver gave a faint signal. They began to sweep the area, and the signal grew in intensity.
"Elian, try to keep the signal as strong as you can. I'll pay out the line attached to the recovery hooks and then, using the fish finder, you can

begin to trawl back and forth until we engage the cargo. Don't go too fast. We don't want to rip the cargo open, as this is the first time, and we don't know how well they've followed our instructions."

Elian nodded and put her thumb up to indicate that she understood. Roy was glad she had been on fishing boats as she seemed to understand exactly what to do. Within a few minutes, they had snagged and recovered the first of the parcels. Repeating the manoeuvre, they recovered the second, but it took half an hour to recover the third as it had been some distance from the others.

Roy sent the signal as arranged *mission completed* before returning to base. Elian turned in a wide circle as Roy and Fiona dismantled and stowed the recovery arm and gear. Then they hid the cargo in the specially constructed hold, ensuring it was hidden from view to the most thorough search. Roy was under the firm belief that the hull would need to be stripped before its presence would be spotted. They headed back towards the Straits of Gibraltar. With the first part of their mission behind them, they would aim to stay in Gibraltar harbour for the night and have a drink to celebrate their success. Anchoring offshore, Roy opened the bar, and the three of them settled down for a long session. Fiona was the first to succumb to the alcoholic excess, and Roy and Elian carried her below and tossed her casually on to her bunk.

"Do you want another drink, Roy," Elian whispered, "or shall we go straight to bed?"

Roy, who had already consumed more than he should, nodded, and the two of them entered the stateroom as naturally as if they had been a couple. The following morning, after another burst of sexual energy that drained them both, they showered and dressed only to find that Fiona was still out of it and no preparations for breakfast were anywhere to be seen. Roy went up on to the bridge and tidied up the bar area whilst Elian went to wake the bleary-eyed Fiona. A few minutes later, Elian followed Roy up on to the bridge and asked,

"What do you want for breakfast? It looks as though I'm on breakfast duty; Fiona's out of it. When she wakes up, she will have a hangover of note."

Roy rolled his eyes and grinned sheepishly.

"You have had all you can from that department," Elian said, "Roy. Be serious. Will a bacon and egg sandwich be OK?"

"If that's all that's on offer, I'll have to make do with that." he replied, the broad grin still running from ear to ear.

"You get breakfast, and I'll get underway. Is Fiona getting up?"

"Yes, but I don't hold out many hopes. She still looks the worse for drink. How much did she drink last night, for heaven's sake?"

"Best part of a bottle of vodka, from what I could see," Roy replied.

"I don't think she'll be up to much; best you leave her in bed. If she gets up, she will only be like a bear with a sore head," Elian pointed out.

"I think you'd better have a quiet word with her Elian. You should warn her that she should observe moderation at all times."

"Oh, yes! That's good coming from you. You should think of that, Lord Croft."

Roy looked guilty. During the voyage so far, he'd managed to have sex with his crew and his passengers. Moderation, as far as sex was concerned, was not Roy Croft's style. If it were that obvious, he would have to be more careful in future. The last thing he wanted Sam to know was that he was sleeping with Kate, and his stomach turned over at the latest proposition that she was trying to make Roy the father of her child. She would be the death of them both, taking such risks. He put the thought at the back of his mind as the wind blew his hair back as he headed out to sea. He wanted to be back in Nice by nightfall. Then who knew what pleasures awaited him with five women to choose from? The other two would be on the way to Switzerland.

Chapter 11

Roy anchored in the outer marina at Nice and secured the boat. Then, leaving Elian and Fiona to get the boat shipshape for the passengers, he left to tell Kate that he was back. The three women were nowhere to be found, and Roy asked at the desk, only to be told to try the beach. He walked through the foyer and the open bar leading to the pool down the steps and on to the beach. If they had not called out, he would probably have walked right past them for, in the French tradition, they were all topless, and their skins had turned a delightful golden brown. The crowd of admirers turned and looked in Roy's direction; it appeared that Kate and her American friends had not been alone whilst he had been away. The three of them waved their admirers away and clustered around him. It was Kate who spoke first.

"Oh, Roy, it's good to see you again. Everything went well, I hope."

Roy nodded, not wanting to go into too much detail.

"When are you going away again?" Kate asked as she pulled his shirt up over his head and began to massage and rub his shoulders with sunscreen whilst pressing her breasts against his back.

"Sam tells me it will be about a week before the next cargo is due," came the reply.

"With Lady Blanchester away, we wondered if you would take the three of us down to Monte Carlo. We could book in at a hotel. I've asked. This place has a sister hotel there, and they are quite agreeable to us transferring for a few days. Millie and Tess would love to go there. Will you take us?"

Roy felt he had no option, and agreed. It would give Elian and Fiona a break. If they anchored near the hotel, the two crew members would be able to sunbathe as well. Roy felt it would allow them all to relax whilst being able to keep a watchful eye on the cruiser. The resort was only a few miles up the coast, and Roy saw no harm in granting them what they wanted.

The hotel was some way out of Monte Carlo itself and had its own private cove. Its beach was secluded, and Roy was surprised to find out that the speciality of the hotel was that its beach catered for nudity. Roy was pleased that he had been pre-warned and, as a result, was not surprised when he dropped anchor off the beach and realised that everyone was nude. With Lady Blanchester away, all three women unhesitatingly sunbathed naked, letting their bodies soak up the rays of the sun. Elian disapproved at first, but seeing how relaxed they were with their nudity, it was not long before she and Fiona joined them. Roy was in his element, with five women on board, all naked from morning until night. He joined them, and for him the week passed all too quickly, giving him the opportunity to enjoy the favours of all five women at different times. Basking in the feeling of total sexual freedom as he unreservedly had wild and unashamed sex with each one of them with no prudish reservations. Roy was somewhat relived in that, even with the five women on board, the opportunity to have questionable benefit of two of them at the same time never presented itself; but that did not prevent them all having a good time when each had the chance to be below decks with his Lordship. Unknown to Roy, the only one safe from the possibility of pregnancy was Elian, who had been given a contraceptive injection that lasted three months. The others relied on the pill. None of them had taken into consideration that each at some time had been seasick and broken the cycle of their contraceptive protection. At the end of the week, Roy anchored off Nice, again allowing the three ladies to go ashore to their hotel, where they were joined by Lady Blanchester, and the four of them settled down whilst Roy, accompanied by his crew of two, headed back to the Atlantic for the second pickup.

After the usual race through the Mediterranean to get to the rendezvous on time, they arrived at the set coordinates and switched on the radio receiver to pick up the transponder. The result was once again silence. No signal was either being sent or received, and Roy became concerned as they slowly widened the search and as the result was still silence. When they had covered an area of approximately seven square miles and still had not picked up any signal, Roy, using the emergency satellite telephone, rang the emergency number. The voice that answered asked what the emergency was and Roy asked if the pickup coordinates had been changed. The voice said that they would call back when more information was available, and they should remain where they were until further instructions were received. If no instructions were received in twelve hours, Roy was to cancel the pickup and return to collect his passengers. Elian and Roy sensed that there was a problem and rigged a sea anchor before going below. Roy was worried about remaining at the point of pickup, concerned that they could be picked up by one of the drug agencies, worried that this was not going as planned.

They were lying in open waters and possibly under the observation of any satellite, and he was just about to tell Elian to head back when the satellite phone rang.

The voice of Sam informed him that the coordinates had been changed without authority. Seemingly, the crew member responsible had almost been caught, and he had to wait for the next opportunity, and the parcels could be found at the new map references. Elian checked, and the new coordinates were some sixty miles south of their current position. They pulled in the sea anchors and set the course to recover the packets from the new site. They approached the area cautiously, the radar searching for any sign of a patrol boat. Thankfully, the area was deserted, but taking every precaution, they decided that they would wait until darkness fell before attempting any recovery. Elian stayed aloft to keep within reach of the pickup site using the sounds from the transponder fitted to the drug packages to track the drift whilst Roy went below. Fiona was in the galley preparing supper. It would be getting dark in an hour, and Roy liked to eat early. He walked into the tiny galley and, walking up behind the unsuspecting cook, he caught her around the waist and spun her around in his arms. He kissed her on the lips and felt her instantly relax in his arms.

"Oh, Lord Croft," she mocked. "I was beginning to think you had deserted me and preferred the company of the more wealthy passengers. I thought you did not want me, a poor girl from the village, any more." Her face was a picture of sarcasm and mock censure.

"I think it's time we dropped the Lord Croft. It's Roy," he said.

The change in his voice gave a clue to the sudden rise in his arousal as he reached behind her and turned off the heat on the gimbal stove and swept Fiona, unresisting, up in his arms and walked into the stateroom. Roy's concern about the change of the pickup point had raised his adrenaline, and suddenly this charge of energy was directed towards his sex drive. In minutes, the two of them were in the throes of lustful sex. Elian was on the bridge, totally unaware of what was taking place below. When Roy reappeared, she guessed what he had been up to.

Elian could recognise the symptoms as well as Janet; she could see that his face was flushed, and he had showered, always a sure sign.

"I can guess what you've been up to, Roy. Your face gives you away every time."

"I know that's what Janet tells me as well," Roy replied with a broad grin.

"I just hope it's not taken the edge off your concentration. It's getting dark, and we need to make our move to recover the goods. I've turned off our radio transponder, and I've deliberately not put on the running lights. Where's Fiona? Is she ready to give a hand getting the stuff on board?"

Fiona put her head up through the companionway and smiled. No, it was almost a grin of self-satisfaction.

"I'm ready for anything now, Elian. Don't concern yourself. I'll give Roy a hand. Just shout when you begin the run."

Roy went down to join her. It was easier to rig the recovery gear this time, and Roy gave the signal that the gear was in place. In less than thirty minutes, they had recovered the packets and stowed them safely below. Roy ensured that they moved from the spot, and an hour later, they were well out of the area of recovery and were in the shipping lanes heading for the mouth of the Mediterranean. They cleared the narrows and, once inside, they headed for Minorca. At the high speed they were travelling, they arrived late in the afternoon, and Roy decided that they would stop overnight as all of them were tired and had only had snacks for a couple of days. They showered, changed, and secured the cruiser from the possibility of an intruder getting aboard, and then the three went ashore for a meal.

The hotel had provided them with an excellent supper, and the wine had flowed steadily when they headed back to the berth. Roy had no idea what went on with his crew, or what was said, as he climbed into bed. Whatever the arrangements were, it was Fiona who stood watch and Elian who joined him in the cabin. The night was long, and by the time he fell asleep, the food, the wine, and the sex had had its effect.

The cruiser anchored off Nice early the following evening, and after securing the vessel, they went ashore in the tender. None of them were in the mood for a crowd, and so they slipped quietly into a street café and had a quiet meal together with a bottle of local wine. They sat and ate a splendid seafood meal and were on their second bottle of wine when a voice called to them from the street. It was Kate. She had been shopping on her own and had decided to get a drink. She came across to the table and asked if she could join them. After several brandies, the conversation began to get a little loose, and finally, Kate said that she was going to ring the others and tell them that she would not be back as she was going to spend the evening with friends. The four of them went back to the boat and, to the surprise of both Elian and Fiona, Kate announced that she was going to sleep with Roy in the stateroom. Elian and Fiona stared at her in amazement. Both knew that, in all probability, Roy had had sex with her at some time, when everyone sunbathed naked, but no one really could be sure.

"But you are married to Mr Delaney," Fiona said in all innocence. "What would he say if he knew?" she asked.

Everyone in the county knew what kind of man he was, and both Elian and Fiona knew very well what the consequences would be for both Roy and Kate if he ever found out. Kate was adamant and also very merry as she said,

"You two have had this man all to yourselves for the last few days. I would like him for tonight. If either of you breathe a word to the others or anyone else, I shall personally have to arrange for your demise," she slurred.

Both women knew that she had drunk far too much, but they also knew that, drunk or sober, she had meant every word of what she threatened to do, and they had no doubt that she also had the means to carry out the threat.

Kate strolled into the stateroom and stripped off her clothes, which she cast on to the floor. As Roy came through the door, she ran to him, almost tearing off his clothes.

"Oh God, Roy, I have missed you. I spoke to Sam, and he told me there was a problem with the drop off coordinates. I was so worried whilst you were away. I need you. I'm ovulating. I only hope we have not missed the time."

Roy had been worried enough that she had broken the news to his crew that she intended to sleep with him. The more people who knew of his relationship with her made it a possibility of Sam getting to know of her infidelity and his own involvement. Now this, and his heart sank; she was obviously determined to go through with this madness. Janet had warned him not to get involved; he knew now that she had been right. If it was to be, then so be it; he would enjoy the moment even if it killed him; he climbed into bed beside her and drew her into his arms.

Whether it was the time of the month or for some other reason, Kate was more aggressive and responsive than he had ever known her to be; she made no attempt to keep the obvious sounds of her enjoyment at what they were doing. After it was over, Roy lay beside Kate. His heart pounded, and he was sure that if the intensity of her sex drive had anything to do with her ovulating, she would surely be impregnated. Kate, on the other hand, lay quietly as her body regained a sense of normality; she felt as though her whole world had changed; she had experienced something wonderful; she only hoped that she was pregnant; she had stopped taking all her pills, but wow, she thought to herself, what an incredible orgasm. Roy always seemed able to make her feel wonderful, and she knew that sex was never like that with her husband Sam. Perhaps, regrettably, it was that she had lost something over the years with Sam, and sex with Roy was comparatively new. Thoughts of the pleasure she had experienced were still racing through her mind as she made her way to the tiny heads to wash away the perspiration and the evidence of her sinful escapade with the latest man in her life. She stood beneath the shower, feeling the water cleanse and cool the heat she had experienced. Hearing Roy waiting outside the small cubicle, she stepped out and allowed him inside. Then, as she dried herself with the large bath towel, she watched him shower. She stood totally naked as he rubbed himself dry before they both returned to the bed they had shared so recently. They lay together with their arms around each other for some time before finally falling into a deep sleep. Kate woke before it was light. Her body craved more of Roy, and she was determined that he would be the father of her first child. She began to caress him, and Roy woke, and with a sigh, he complied with her obvious need; he had given up worrying about the consequences of their actions. Unbeknown to either of them, the inevitable had occurred. Kate illogically somehow felt she was impregnated and would be carrying Roy's child for the next forty weeks.

Elian and Fiona had heard the all too obvious sounds of Roy and Kate having sex; both of them looked at each other and agreed between themselves that they would be sworn to secrecy and would never tell anyone what they had heard. Otherwise, Roy and Kate would surely die at the hands of Kate's husband, Sam Delaney. Fiona prepared a light breakfast in the tiny galley whilst Elian checked the oil levels and turbo boosters in the engine room, ensuring that the vessel was ready for sea at a moment's notice. When Roy emerged from the stateroom, breakfast was ready, and Elian reported that everything was running perfectly; the vessel was ready for the next part of the voyage. To ensure that Lady Blanchester did not get wind of the fact that Kate had spent the night in Roy's bed, it was arranged that she would go ashore and check out with the others. It was Elian, accompanied by Kate, who took the tender ashore after breakfast to pick up Tess, Millie, and Lady Blanchester, after first checking all of them out of the hotel and, together, with their travelling cases, they boarded the tender. After everything was loaded aboard the cruiser, they set out to return to Minorca before moving on to a short stay at Cadiz.

Roy intended to leave the ladies in Cadiz whilst they collected the last cache of drugs, then return and collect them and head up the Portuguese coast on their way home. That was the plan, but even the best laid plans sometimes go wrong. The ladies were finally set up in the San Miguel Hotel, a mixture of old and new decor, and Kate ensured that each room overlooked the pool. The message came in, confirming the coordinates, and Roy, with Elian at the wheel and assisted by Fiona, cast off; Roy had a funny feeling about this last pickup. It was some distance from the last two, and although it could have been explained by the commercial vessel taking a slightly different route or heading for a different destination, Roy was not happy. The weather began to deteriorate, and the sky began to cloud over. Elian said to him as he stood beside her on the bridge,

"I hope the clouds stay in place. It will protect us from any satellite surveillance."

"So you feel the same as me about this last pickup after the delay with the last on? We were out there exposed for far too long," Roy confided.

"The weather is the only thing I am happy with this time out. I have a bad feeling that something is going to go wrong."

"I do too," replied Roy. "I can't put my finger on it, but I agree with you. I'm not often wrong, and neither are you. Let's get out there quickly and get this thing over with."

Elian nodded, and as soon as they had cleared the headland, they moved swiftly out to sea. They had roughly fifty miles to go before they could expect to pick up the signal.

"It's too damn close to the mainland for my liking, Elian," Roy said, as they neared their target. "Why they chose a spot that is close to the coast I'll never know? We could be spotted so easily that we have to make the pickup quickly. No hanging about. We have to get it right first time, or the cargo will have drifted out into the main shipping lane or if the tide is strong, it could end up on the beach."

"Would we have to abandon it if it did?" Elian asked, thinking of the money involved.

"It would be far too risky to try and recover it. We would be spotted by either the North African Patrol or, worse still, the Spanish. We are too far south for the Portuguese. Yes! I'm afraid we would have to abandon it," Roy affirmed.

"I can't see the boss being too pleased about that," Elian said.

To herself she thought, *or the fact that you have slept with his wife, you randy old bugger you'll get us all killed with your constant need for sexual satisfaction. Have you no shame? You would sleep with the devil's wife if you had half a chance, if you haven't done so already.*

It was fortunate that they located the signal on the first pass by the coordinates and recovered the packages with only two runs. The cargo had been stowed and the recovery gear packed away, and the decks had been hosed down only seconds before Elian called down to Roy,

"There's a vessel that looks like a patrol boat approaching us fast. Is everything stowed?"

Roy ran up the companionway to the flying bridge and looked at the radar screen. It did look like a patrol boat, and it was coming in their direction fast. Roy took the wheel, and they headed for Cadiz fast, but not too fast as to cause the approaching vessel to be suspicious of their movements. They were about half an hour out from the port when the approaching vessel increased its speed and came closer.

"Shall I get the weapons ready?" Fiona asked.

"I don't think so, Fiona. We have done nothing wrong and the cargo is stowed in the secret lockers and we have hosed the decks clear of any traces of the cargo itself. As far as I know they have not put sniffer dogs on patrol boats yet, and besides, I don't think we could hold them off with just the three of us, do you?"

Fiona shook her head in agreement; then she went below to make coffee to give her something to do to calm her nerves. She hated officials of any kind and, with the cargo they had aboard, no matter how well hidden it was, there was always a risk that it would be discovered. She knew that Roy had a pistol up top in the strong box under the bar, but she had nothing. Contrary to her instructions, she went below and helped herself to a Beretta pistol and hid it in the galley.

When the vessel came closer; as suspected, it was identified as a Spanish Customs and Excise Patrol boat, and it called on them to 'heave to'. The patrol boat closed in on them, and as they slowed down, the official patrol came alongside. The officer approached the side of the boat as Roy went down to greet him.

"Is there anything wrong?" asked Roy.

"May I come aboard?" the officer asked politely.

Roy knew that to refuse would cause them to be suspicious, and so he nodded, and the officer jumped aboard, followed by a second figure. The second officer stared at Roy and said,

"Hello, Lord Croft, do you remember me? We met aboard your MTB sometime ago."

"Officer Catalina Cordoba, if I'm not mistaken," Roy said, smiling into the face of the pretty officer.

"Officer Cordoba, do you know this man?" the first officer asked.

"We have met before," she replied, "when we checked his other boat, an old wartime MTB. It was an unforgettable experience being aboard one of those old boats. It was almost nostalgic," she added with a smile.

To herself, Catalina thought, *Lord Croft is such a handsome man. I could hardly forget the combination of the two.* With the knowledge that the master of the vessel was an English Lord and Officer Cordoba had met him before, the approach of the first officer changed slightly as he asked,

"How many of you are there on board, Lord Croft?"

"There are three of us at present. I am the owner. My skipper is Elian, and my general crew is Fiona. I have a female crew to deal with my all-female charter party who are at present in the San Miguel Hotel in Cadiz."

"Where are you bound for, and where have you been?" the first officer enquired.

"We are out to test our engines. We had a spot of trouble yesterday while coming from Gibraltar, and we did some minor repairs and were trying them out. We are on charter to some very aristocratic ladies, and the thought of breaking down with them on board would be a disaster and would do my charter business no good at all. We shall then head up the coast, stay overnight, and then head back to Tralee."

"I would like to see your log, and Officer Cordoba would like to take a look below, if you don't mind."

"Elian, show the officer the log, will you? I will show the other officer below."

"Lord Croft, now that I am below decks, I see you have modified your old MTB into this cruiser. Is that for your charter business? She is now much more attractive to look at but not so nostalgic," Officer Cordoba said.

Fiona, hearing the sound of voices, popped her head out of the galley door and asked,

"Coffee anyone?"

"No, thank you. Perhaps next time. I am just looking over the boat."

Roy pushed open the stateroom door, and Catalina Cordoba stepped inside.

"You have made some wonderfully comfortable changes, Lord Croft, or is it Roy? I seem to remember that was your first name."

The door swung behind them, and as Catalina turned to look to see if her memory had been correct, Roy bumped into her. He put his arm out to steady her from falling, and she fell into his arms. Their faces were so close it seemed perfectly natural, and their lips touched just for a moment. They moved apart, and Catalina said, in a voice that had lost some of its officialdom and was a little breathy,

"Why, Lord Croft, Roy, are you trying to seduce me?" Catalina asked wryly.

"No! That was not my intention, but you must admit you are a very attractive woman, Catalina. Given half a chance, I could be tempted, I must admit," Roy responded.

"Another time, another place, and I might just be tempted myself," Catalina replied. "Perhaps another sample may help make up my mind," she added with a grin.

Catalina's arms went up around Roy's neck, and she kissed him on the lips. Her lips were soft, and to Roy's surprise, the full lips parted, inviting his tongue to enter. The kiss was passionate, and Roy could feel himself respond. They broke apart, and Catalina straightened her uniform and whispered,

"I knew I was right. I can usually judge a man. You are a man of considerable passion. I have no time to go any further, but there may come a day in the not-too-distant future when we shall meet again. Until then, show me the rest of this boat."

The search was once again cursory, to say the least, and when the two of them reappeared on deck, the first officer looked enquiringly. Catalina smiled and confirmed that Lord Croft's boat had a clean bill of health and that there was nothing suspicious below decks. She thought to herself *he might well have something interesting down there,* as she glanced down towards his groin, *but there was nothing illegal about that.*

"We shall wish you good day then, Lord Croft. We may need to check you again sometime. Have a safe voyage."

The first officer made his way to the rail, closely followed by Catalina, who smiled at Roy as she boarded the patrol boat. The boats parted, and it was with a sigh of relief that Elian waved as they moved away. Elian looked at Roy and she enquired,

"What happened below? I hope you were not foolish enough to make a pass at our pretty customs officer, Lord Croft? I don't think even you would get away with that."

"Au contraire," Roy said in a mocking French accent. "On the contrary, Elian, I think she was the one who made the pass. Rest assured that, although tempted, I resisted, but I'm not sure we've seen the last of Officer Cordoba."

They headed back to Cadiz in a lighter mood than when they had left that morning.

They went ashore to join up with the ladies at the hotel, and they were all in the bar when, to everyone's surprise, they were unexpectedly joined by a striking Spanish lady. Elian hardly recognised the woman. She had long, shiny black hair that glistened with health, and she wore a dress that had been designed to show off her female attributes, the off the shoulder top, and the split skirt, all carefully chosen to be the centre of attraction. Roy recognised her immediately; it was Catalina Cordoba, the Spanish customs and excise officer from the patrol boat.

"Hello Señor, sorry, Lord Croft. What an unexpected pleasure. I had arranged to meet a fellow officer here for dinner, but he seems to have made alternative arrangements; but I am disturbing you with your guests I'm sorry for the interruption."

"Please, Catalina, join us, and I'll introduce you," Roy said politely.

Catalina took the seat proffered by Roy as he stood to get the attention of a waiter. When the extra chair had been brought to the table, Roy asked her what she was drinking. Catalina looked at the table where several jugs of Sangria stood half empty.

"Sangria will be fine for me. Just ask him to bring another glass, and I'll join the rest of the ladies."

As Roy introduced Catalina to the rest of the guests, for some unknown reason, he had decided not to divulge Kate's surname.

"Fiona and Elian, you have already met on board the cruiser, and this is Lady Blanchester. This is Kate, a friend of her ladyship, and her friends from the United States, Tess and Millie. Everyone, this is Catalina Cordoba, an officer in the Spanish Customs and Excise Navy Patrol. As your escort for the evening seems to have let you down, I hope you will join us for dinner, Catalina."

Catalina, who was somewhat disappointed not to have Roy to herself, gave a nod in agreement and immediately fell into conversation with Kate and the others. During the time they were in the bar, however, she took every opportunity to touch Roy's arm and spoke to him with soft tones of endearment at every occasion as it presented itself. She placed herself next to Roy at the table and continually pressed her thigh against his, and Kate sighed. She knew that a last night of sex with Roy was going to be out of the question. She, of all people, knew that if Roy snubbed the precocious Catalina Cordoba, she could well ensure that whenever Roy or his boat were in the area, it would be stopped and searched. She knew that eventually some more determined officer could well find its illicit cargo of drugs or weapons. She would retire gracefully and leave Catalina to reap the rewards of her efforts.

Roy left the table and spoke to Elian, suggesting that it might be better if they went aboard without him and she should book him a room in the hotel as he did not want to offend the pretty raven-haired Catalina just in case she decided to stay over. Elian made the booking and slipped Roy the key. His perception of the situation had been correct, and as the others left to go up to their rooms, Miss Cordoba remained at the table with Roy.

"Are you staying at the hotel, Roy?" she asked with a sensual look and a glint in her eye.

"I am, indeed," Roy said, pulling the key to his room from his pocket. "Would you care to join me for a night cap?" he asked.

The flash of her eyelids and the broad smile on her face said it all, and they left the table and walked slowly to the lift. The room Elian had booked in Roy's name was one of the luxury suites overlooking the water and the bridge. Catalina sat on the edge of the bed as Roy broke the seal on the mini bar and asked her what she would like to drink.

"I think it's time for a brandy, your Lordship, don't you? Or alternatively, you can open the bottle of champagne provided by the hotel in the ice bucket. I seem to remember that they serve a fairly respectable bottle to its guests in their luxury rooms. Pricey, but who's counting the cost of tonight?"

Roy popped the cork and poured two glasses, and as he turned, Catalina's dress fell to the floor, leaving her standing in a fragile set of underwear, designed more for what it revealed than for what it hid. Taking the glass, she touched glasses with Roy and drained the contents. She then began to undo the buttons on Roy's shirt. In minutes, they were on the bed naked, and Roy discovered that she was no novice in the sex stakes. She was a veritable wild cat, and for the next two hours she not only enjoyed the pleasures he could offer but taught him some new ones as well.

Eventually, even with the boost of Cathleen's potcheen, they were finally unable to continue. Roy's groin ached, and he knew when he had had sufficient for one night. They lay beside one another, drained of energy, trying to get their bodies to regain some semblance of normality.

"I knew I was right the first time I laid eyes on you, Lord Croft. I just knew you were that kind of sexual animal; it is the aura you generate. You certainly did not disappoint me, and I hope the same applies from your point of view."

"Catalina, you have surpassed my wildest imagination. How will I be able to look you in the eye in that uniform and not remember this moment? You were a revelation."

Roy knew she was excellent in bed but he was aware that Janet could outperform her on a good day, but, being a gallant gentleman, he avoided putting his thoughts into words, and the last thing he wanted was to upset the pretty naval officer. He knew well, that even after the time they had spent together, she was an ambitious woman, one who would not hesitate to turn him in, if he upset her by telling he had had better elsewhere. In no time, they had both fallen into a deep sleep. When she woke the following morning, Roy had showered and was dressed.

"Going so soon, your Lordship? I was hoping we could have spent the morning in bed. It's my day off."

"Nothing would give me greater pleasure, Catalina," Roy said. "Unfortunately, I'm on charter, and we have to get going. I'm due in port in Northern Spain and then home tomorrow, so I'm sorry to disappoint you. Perhaps you would join us all for breakfast, but I'm afraid it would only cause speculation in my charter party. Perhaps breakfast in the room would be a better option for you."

"I think that would be the better option. It's a pity you cannot join me, but I understand. Perhaps we shall meet again in the not-too-distant future. Come and give me a goodbye kiss, and I'll let you go with some reluctance, I must add," she whispered softly.

Roy crossed the room and took her in his arms and kissed her. Then, not falling into the honeyed trap, he walked towards the door and said in his throaty tone showing his desire,

"Goodbye for now. I hope that meeting will not be too far away."

Roy closed the door behind him and went down to the reception area to join the others. He used his credit card to pay for the room, instructing the staff to send breakfast up to his guest and to charge whatever she wanted to his account, certain that he would be able to use the liaison with Catalina to his best advantage at some time in the future.

Roy rejoined the others, and Elian arrived to transport them all back to the cruiser. Once aboard, Roy had put paid to everyone's questions about his previous night. They had been disappointed when he told them a gentleman never kissed and told. They would have to speculate as he would not divulge anything to besmirch a lady's honour. The conversation moved on, and Elian headed north to A Coruna, where they would spend the last night before heading back to Ireland. Roy saw to the clearances, and Elian organised the refuelling. Fiona took the ladies ashore to the hotel after Roy apologised and said he would be staying aboard to ensure that all was ready for the crossing to Ireland the next morning as the forecast did not look good. He had retired to bed, and Elian and Fiona had taken the opportunity to get an early night in preparation for the crossing the next day, which, by all accounts, was going to be a rough one. Suddenly, Roy woke up. A boat had bumped against the side of the cruiser, and he could hear the sound of voices. Someone was trying to climb on-board. He reached into the drawer at the side of the bed and pulled out his Beretta. Quickly, he pressed the release on the base of the handle and checked whether he had a full load. Then, sliding the barrel, he pushed a round up into the firing chamber. Should he wake the others, he wondered? He decided against it and slipped up to the deck. He could hear movements but could not see anyone. He could hear the sound of the boat moving away when the door opened, and there stood Kate. She looked at Roy and began to laugh quietly.

"What's so funny, Kate? I could easily have killed you," Roy said sharply.

"You only have to look in the mirror," she said. "There you are standing naked with a pistol in your hand, and you ask me what's funny. Put it away, and let's go to bed. I asked the water taxi to collect me in an hour, so let's not waste any time."

Watching her go after their torrid mating, Roy shook his head; Janet had
been so right. Kate Delaney could well be the death of him if Sam ever
discovered his intimate affair with Kate, his beloved wife. What fascination
Roy held for her, he did not understand; but he could never pass up the
opportunity regardless of the risk. He turned to find Elian shaking her
head, but with a cup of hot coffee.

"I hope you know what you're doing Roy. You are on dangerous ground
with that one. Now, drink this, and let us all go back to sleep. I've put a
good measure of whisky in it, and that, combined with the energy you
expended on our visitor will, I'm sure, knock you out for a couple of
hours. We are going to need the rest. I can feel the storm beginning to
strengthen even in the shelter of the harbour."

They went back to their separate beds, and by dawn the storm was at its
height.

"There's no way I'm going out in this with those women aboard, Elian"
Roy said, looking at the dark storm clouds overhead. "I think we should
see how the morning goes. The storm may blow itself out by midday. Let's
wait and see."

"I'd better go ashore and tell them to be ready by lunchtime when we can
review the situation," Elian said with a resigned sigh.

Elian took Fiona with her and went ashore to break the news to the group.
Roy was surprised to see them all come back in the tender. It was Kate who
spoke first when questioned by Roy.

"We felt that if the storm blew over, we should be aboard, so that you
could leave at the earliest opportunity. So here we are. We put ourselves
entirely in your hands, so to speak, and we will go as soon as you feel it's
safe to do so."

The others nodded in agreement, and Elian and Fiona stowed the luggage
safely, and by midday, the storm had begun to ease, and they moved out
into the rough sea. Even though the gale dropped from force six to force
four, the swell was quite bad, and Fiona was kept busy below whilst Roy
and Elian were at the wheel. It was very late that night when they made
their way slowly up the estuary, on a full tide, into Tralee. All the passengers
had been seasick at some time on the journey, and Roy still wondered why
they had been so insistent on returning that day and not waiting until the
storm had passed.

Roy eased the cruiser up against the quay in Tralee as a minibus drove up
to collect his passengers. Two men got out and helped Elian and Fiona to

load the luggage into the back of the bus. Roy's phone rang, It was Sam Delaney.

"Glad you made it back safely, Roy. We have a meeting tomorrow. Be there at 12 noon. I have something to discuss with you. It's urgent. Don't be late."

"I'll be there. What do I do with . . . ?"

"Not on the phone. I'll discuss it with you tomorrow."

After the luggage was loaded, the passengers got into the bus after saying their goodbyes to Roy and his crew. With Elian at the wheel, Roy and Fiona cast off, and she turned the boat around and headed down the estuary on a rapidly falling tide. They made it and headed back to the castle with its deep water harbour where, after a couple of attempts in the rising swells, they tied up and Elian said,

"Roy, I want to get her into the boathouse. I just have a feeling that something is very wrong."

Roy agreed, and between them, they winched the boat up into the boathouse. When they had chocked the boat into position, Elian began going over the boat with a fine-tooth comb. Roy stood and watched in amazement as Elian gave a gasp and yelled,

"Yes, I found the little bugger. Come here, Roy. Look at this, will you?"

"What have you found, Elian?" Roy asked, his interest raised instantly.

"It's a transponder! A bug! A tracking device, I recognise it from the similarity to the ones we use on the packages. It's not one of ours. Look for yourself," Elian whispered as if the transponder could hear.

"Is it live?" Roy asked.

"I don't think so. It has a sort of timing device attached to it, and the LED is not showing any form of life," She whispered.

"Can we remove it?" Roy wanted to know. "Here, let me have a look."

Roy inspected the device, and as if making up his mind, he went into the workshop to return with a variety of tools, just as Janet arrived to find out what the delay was. She had seen them arrive, but when they had not appeared after putting the cruiser in the boathouse, she had become concerned.

"Roy, for heaven's sake, can't you leave your damn boat for two minutes to say hello to your family after being away for more than two weeks? Whatever is wrong, can't it wait until morning?" Janet asked crossly.

"Hello, darling, I'm sorry, but I will come as soon as I have managed to find out who the hell is trying to track my movements. I love you and

Sean, but this has to take pride of place. It's important to all of us. I'll be with you both as soon as I can," Roy responded, although he was sympathetic, he needed to get to the bottom of the problem Elian had discovered.

"It comes to something when your boat is more important than we are," Janet shouted venomously; with that she whirled on her heels and slammed the door behind her.

Elian and Fiona stood and stared as Roy shrugged his shoulders and began to remove the device from where it had been strategically placed.

It took about half an hour to remove the object without breaking or damaging the transponder. Then he turned to Elian and asked,

"What aroused your suspicions, Elian?"

"I saw a strange car on the quay. It's not tourist time, and besides, it had only men inside. Whilst we were busy with the luggage, they disappeared, and when I was retrieving the cases, I noticed a couple of lines of bubbles surfacing between the end of the quay and our boat. I looked at the car, and it was empty. When we had loaded the bus and we came back on board, the bubbles were alongside. I started the motors, and the bubbles moved in the direction of the quay. By the time we had said our farewells and turned the boat around, the men were back in the car."

"Well spotted, Elian. I have to admit I saw nothing out of the ordinary. Now, we have to decide what to do about it. Let me go and make some sort of peace with Janet. You and Fiona, go and get some food in the kitchen, and I'll inspect it more closely."

Roy and his crew made their way along the subterranean passage and up into the kitchen. Cathleen was there preparing supper.

"I hope you've made enough for all of us," Roy said. "Look after these two whilst I go and see Janet and Sean."

Roy let the door shut behind him as he raced up the stairs to find his wife.

Chapter 12

Janet was annoyed with Roy, but she had never been able to be upset with him for long. She loved him too much for that. Roy explained that he had found some sort of bug or tracking device aboard his boat and had been worried who had placed it there.

"It could be another charter company or, more likely, someone trying to track my movements for the IRA contract. I'm sorry, darling, but I'm going to have to sort it out. It's not active at the moment, but it could become active at any time, and I don't want this location to show up on the equipment of whoever has us under surveillance. I don't ever want you or the children to be under any sort of threat."

"It's a bit late for that, Roy. You always wanted more excitement in your life, and this is the result. You are under investigation by someone. You better find out who it is, and do something about it. I don't want Sean or our unborn child threatened in any way."

Roy kissed her and went down to the kitchen where the two women were eating.

"When you two have finished, you'd better come through to the workshop. I need to find more out about that bloody device."

Both the women nodded in agreement, their mouths too full of food to answer. Roy turning to Cathleen, instructed her,

"Cathleen, you had better come and tell me when the evening meal is ready. I don't want to upset Mrs Croft any more than she is upset already."

He rushed headlong down the stone steps and hurried along the passage to the workshop. He looked at the device and unscrewed the antenna carefully to avoid the unit sending or receiving any outside contact. Then he had a closer inspection. As an engineer himself, he could see that this was no cheap piece of equipment. It was state of the art, if anything military quality. It had to be some government department. He made up his mind and ran back to the kitchen.

"Elian, see if Gael is back. If she is, I want you both to come with me and bring the wet suits from the stores, will you? I have a feeling we shall need them in the not-too-distant future."

Without question, Elian pushed aside her plate, leaving Fiona open-mouthed as she ran up the back stairs calling for Gael.

When Elian returned with Gael, they could tell from Roy's expression that he had made up his mind to do something, and he obviously wanted to do it in a hurry. They ran down to the stores and grabbed the wet suits, the air bottles, and the handgrip of underwater tools. They met Roy at the car after he had been up to tell Janet his plans. He drove fast towards Tralee and pulled up on the outskirts of the village. It was already dark, and after checking that there was no sign of the mysterious car and its two male occupants, Roy drove on to the unlit car park and, changing into the wet gear, they made their way towards the harbour. Anyone seeing them could have easily mistaken them for a bunch of divers from the nearby diving school. Roy paused and scoured the harbour. There was the local hire cruiser, 'The Rose of Tralee', and a French registered boat, the 'Esprit de la Danse', not too dissimilar in design to his own and that of the local boat.

"We'll use the French boat," Roy said quietly.
The two women knew just what he planned to do; they all put on their wet suits, tanked up, and slipped quietly into the water. It was cold, even with the wet suit, and both women knew that without them they would have been shivering in the cold in minutes. Moving with grace and skill, they swam underwater. It was pitch dark and very murky with the tide at its highest point, and Roy was glad they had thought to bring the underwater torches. They swam slowly, going deep so as not to arouse anyone's suspicions, with the glow of the torch light. They had marked the distance of the French registered cruiser from the shore, and the hull came into view. Roy and the two women worked as quickly as the freezing coldness would allow. They first had to drill two securing holes in the bottom of the hull, where the fibreglass was thickest. The last thing they wanted to do was to make a hole in the boat and let water in. Roy worked the small hand drill, avoiding the vibrations from a motorised one. The work was slow, and the two women held the torches illuminating the work area. Roy stopped several times to listen with his ear against the hull, ensuring that no one aboard had raised any alarm about any noise he was making. Finally, Roy was satisfied and, using a screwdriver, they finally secured the device to the hull. When they had done so, Roy carefully checked that it was secure and replaced the antenna, switching the device to the on position. The tiny red glow from

the LCD glowed for a moment before once more extinguishing all signs of activity; from what Roy had discovered when he had inspected it, it showed that it was on but that it was still awaiting the signal to make it live and send the location signal to wherever the receiver was situated. Roy was certain that it would be aboard a naval vessel offshore. Satisfied that they had completed the job they had come to do, they made their way from under the boat's hull.

The crew of the French cruiser had either been away or occupied with something more important than to listen for anyone placing a device on the underside of their boat. The three clandestine divers swam back to the harbour wall, and surfacing, they listened carefully before Gael removed her flippers and climbed the metal ladder attached to the harbour wall. She looked around, and all was silent. She signalled the all-clear, and Elian and Roy climbed the ladder and stood beside her. Then ensuring that they were unobserved, they made their way cautiously back to the Land Cruiser and, stowing the gear in the back of the vehicle, rubbed themselves dry. They dressed and sat for a moment reflecting on the consequences of their actions.

"That will give whoever planted that on our boat a surprise when they move in to intercept that French boat when it eventually returns to France," Elian said grinning at the thought.

"Not as much as the innocent French couple. I only hope they are not trying to smuggle anything out of Ireland or into France. They could be in for a nasty surprise, and the look on whoever tries to make the arrest will be priceless. Now let's get back. I'm late for supper, and I do not want to antagonise what is a delicate situation with Janet any more than I have to."

They drove back quickly, but not in any way dangerously, and Roy was aware enough to keep a close eye on the rear-view mirror to ensure that he was not being followed. He knew that if anyone was on to him, he would need to be wary and not take anything at face value. Roy parked the Land Cruiser and walked to the front door. Elian and Fiona were left to return the diving equipment to the store before they retired for the night. Janet was waiting to have dinner, and as soon as she heard Roy at the door, she asked Cathleen to serve the meal. It appeared that Roy was back in Janet's good books, for an expensive bottle of red wine was open and breathing as he entered. The meal was excellent, and Janet seemed to have recovered completely from her mood and was eager to hear what he had found out about the listening and tracking device.

"Now, Roy, tell me what did you find out about that little tracking device? You dashed out of here like a bat out of hell. What's it all about?" Janet enquired.

"Well, to be perfectly honest, I'm puzzled. The device was not your usual run-of-the-mill device. It was very sophisticated, too sophisticated to be anything but government. If it's anyone checking on our connection with the IRA, they seem to be going to an awful lot of trouble, tracking what is now considered a defunct organisation. They will be even more puzzled when they follow the French boat lying in Tralee and follow it all the way to the French coast. The owners of the boat will have red faces if they are trying to smuggle anything into France," Roy replied with a grin running from ear to ear.

"Won't whoever is trying to track you be mad and come back spoiling for your blood?" Janet asked; the concern could be heard in her voice.

"No, I don't think so. They'll probably think their agents just got it wrong. Ha! Ha! Bloody funny though, don't you think?" Roy said guffawing at his own prank. Moving to the drinks cabinet, he turned to Janet and said casually, "Enough shop. Let's have a drink. The usual for you, darling. I'm having a large Irish to celebrate."

Janet refused the alcoholic drink and settled for more coffee. They sat and talked about nothing and everything for the next few hours before finally retiring to bed. Janet was surprised, but happy, that even in her pregnant state, Roy still wanted to make love to her. When it was over, she lay with her arms around him, his head resting in the crook of her neck.

"I did not think you fancied me anymore. I'm ugly and fat," Janet said softly.

"I love you anyway. Now go to sleep before I start all over again," Roy replied.

As he said, it she noticed the cheeky smile as it crossed his face, and she gave him a nudge in the ribs. As soon as Janet had fallen into a happy, deep sleep, Roy slipped out of bed; he was just not satisfied; he needed more, or he would be tossing and turning all night.

Roy padded softly down the stairs, and he crept down the stone steps and along to where the cruiser was at the head of the slipway, well and truly chocked in place. Roy hoped either Elian or Gale would be sleeping aboard the vessel. Roy walked up the ramp and on to the deck, then down into the main cabin, and he stood still, listening for any sound of movement. There was nothing, not even a squeak. He ignored the stateroom, which he usually occupied, and opened the door of the cabin next to it; he was in luck. Elian lay on the bed. Even in the gloom, he could see that she was awake, and a broad smile indicated that she had recognised the intruder.

"Hello, Roy. I thought I heard someone come aboard. I hoped it would be you, but I thought you would have been with Janet tonight."

"It's the baby. I think she's tired and not really up for a wild night. How about you?"

In answer to Roy's question, she simply threw back the bedclothes and beckoned him towards her. Roy needed no second bidding and, pulling the cord securing his robe, he let the garment slide off his shoulders and fall to the floor, revealing his already very aroused state.

"I see you are already in the mood," she said laughing.

It was almost light when Roy made his way along the subterranean tunnel back to the kitchen where voices alerted him. Morag and Cathleen were already at work. Morag was preparing Sean's breakfast; the young lad had never got out of the habit of waking as soon as it was light, and Cathleen was busy getting things ready for breakfast.

"I was about to bring up your tea, Lord Croft. Would you prefer it down here or in your bedroom?" Cathleen asked.

"Upstairs. I had something I needed to attend to, in the workshop, and it could not wait," Roy said to the two women, but fooling neither, as he slipped past them and went up to the bedroom where Janet lay fast asleep. He walked into the bathroom and into the shower. He did not want Janet to smell Elian's perfume on him when she woke up. He was somewhat shaken when the shower door opened and Janet walked in to join him.

"Do you feel better now? I'm sorry I was not up to your expectations last night, but this baby is not like the first one. I feel so tired all the time. It must be a girl."

Then, getting no reply from Roy, she said,

"I asked you if you felt better now. I'm sure Elian or, maybe, Fiona or Gael would have satisfied your carnal desires."

Roy shrugged and stepped out, brushing past Janet's swollen form.

"I know you don't really mind who it was, and does it really matter, anyway, to you? In reply to your question, yes, I do feel better, thank you. Now, let me get something on. Cathleen will be up with the tea any moment."

"I'm sure she won't mind seeing you like that. It would not be the first time, would it, you wicked oversexed animal?"

Roy pulled a shirt over his head and his underwear and trousers on and was sitting on the bed wearing his socks when there was a knock at the bedroom door.

"Come in, Cathleen."

When Cathleen came into the bedroom carrying the tray.

"I've changed my mind, Cathleen," Roy said. "Leave the tray, but I'll have my tea downstairs. I'll be down in a moment."

Cathleen glanced at the bathroom door as Janet appeared with a towel wrapped around her, and, seeing the look on her face, Cathleen nodded a greeting and walked smartly from the room.

"I can see you are in the mood for an argument, Janet, so if you don't mind too much, I'll leave you to get dressed, and I'll go down and have my breakfast early."

Roy had just started to drink his morning brew when the telephone rang shrilly, the metallic sound disturbing and adding to the growing headache he usually got when he had words with Janet. *Oh God, what now?* he thought as he walked over to pick up the telephone. It was Sam.

"We have a problem," Sam said quietly. "I want you to come over when you can. I've called a full meeting, but I want to speak to you first," Sam said quietly.

"I'll be there as soon as I can," Roy replied, recognising Sam's ultra-serious voice.

"We may be here for some time. You'd better bring Janet with you. I'm sure Kate would love to see her, and I would like to show Sean the trains again," adding, "if we have the time."

Roy finished his tea, and there was still no sign of Janet. He made his way upstairs and into the bedroom. He opened the door fractionally.

"I have to go out," he said through the half-open door. "It's business, Sam and Kate asked you to come if you wish. If not, I don't know when I'll be back. It could be a long day."

Janet snapped out of her pout and said,

"I'd love to come, but you will have to give me some time to get ready. Tell Morag to get Sean ready for me, will you? I'm sure she will welcome the break and have some time to herself without him."

Roy shut the door and hurried down the stairs. He was worried. What could possibly have gone wrong now? He popped his head around the kitchen door, called Morag before giving her Janet's instructions, and then went into the lounge to wait. It seemed to be taking Janet forever, and he began to wish he had not invited her. At last, she was ready, and Sean was delighted to be going out with his daddy. Unusually, Roy seemed unresponsive to the young lad's eagerness, and Janet realised that something was worrying him. Knowing that she had already added to his worries earlier, she decided not to press the matter, and she amused Sean herself. Roy was getting more and more concerned as to why Sam had called a meeting, and why he wanted him there early. Had he discovered his wife's infidelity? If so, there would be no need to call a meeting; Roy would just be disposed of, so that was not the reason. He was no wiser when he swung the Range Rover into the parking place outside the front door. Sam opened the door. He looked grey with worry as he welcomed Roy and Janet and gave young Sean a pat on the head.

"Janet, Kate is in the study waiting for you. We shall see you after the meeting."

Then, turning to Roy, he said quietly,

"You had better come into the study."

Roy followed him apprehensively, waiting patiently for the bad news. Sam sat at his desk and pointed to the chair in front.

"It's Connor. He's been arrested by the British, and the fool had Padraig with him."

Roy's mouth opened in disbelief as he asked Sam,

"When did it happen? The bloody fool knows better than to have Padraig with him, backup yes, but not together. Did they lose the whole shipment?"

"It happened a few days ago, and no, thank God, they did not lose it all," Sam said, some faint signs of relief showing in his face. "They were delivering the last batch to one of the distributors. It was bad enough. The street value of that package was 1.5 million euros. The other problem is that they were still driving the van with Irish registration plates, which will have alerted the port authorities to the fact that drugs are coming across from Ireland. We may well have to make use of you for deliveries in the very near future in addition to collections. I know it increases the risk, but you will be well paid for your trouble."

Roy sat and thought before he spoke quietly, saying,

"I think I would rather be paid offshore in the Cayman Islands or Mauritius," he added calmly. "The payments in cash are becoming a problem. I have so much cash at home that it would be very difficult to explain if the house were ever to be raided."

Sam understood the problem and immediately agreed to do the next payment using the American banks. They sat and had a couple of drinks, commiserating over the loss of the two men.

"What do you think they'll get?" Roy asked.

Sam's response shook Roy to the core,

"It looks like about fifteen to twenty years, but the lawyers are doing their best to get them the lower rather than the higher sentence. They should be out in seven to ten with good behaviour."

Roy could not imagine being away from his family for that length of time, or in fact being away from women in general for even a week, let alone ten years. From that moment on, Roy's whole position began to change. He decided that, come what may, he would somehow be planning his retirement from this sullied business and was determined to open a charter business in the West Indies far away from the IRA. He sat stone-faced, not wishing to alert Sam to his decision. He had no idea at that moment how he was going to achieve the break from the committee, but the decision had been made. He would manage to do it somehow. He was determined. If he were to do the deliveries as well, his exposure would be twice as great.

Roy's thoughts were interrupted as Sam coughed and said,

"Snap out of it, Roy. That's why I've had to call the meeting. You will have to be the paymaster on the next trip, and I'll have to first break the news to the others and get the agreement to the idea of using you and your crew to do the deliveries."

"Is there likely to be a problem with that?" asked Roy.

Sam watched as Roy cocked his head to one side in an attitude of inquisitiveness, his eyes darkened, giving the impression of being somewhat dazed, or was it shock as his mind reeled at the prospect of an increase in his personal involvement.

"No, but I feel I should at least let the rest of the group know what we are doing. You know they have been worried in case you were caught doing the collections. I don't know how they'll react to you doing the deliveries as well," Sam replied.

They sat drinking coffee, laced heavily with liquor, and after some thirty minutes, the others began to arrive. Sam and Roy rose to meet them and take them into the meeting room, where drinks were waiting. The general hubbub continued until the last member arrived; the group was called to order and everyone was invited to take their seats. They sat looking apprehensive, and Roy saw the look of dismay on their faces as each one took in the news of the arrest of Connor and Padraig.

"Has Connor's wife been taken care of? Does she have everything she needs?" asked Billy O'Shea, a member sitting at the end of the table.

"She has; as usual, she was the first to know, and everything is in place to ensure she has everything she needs," replied Sam.

"What happened? Was it a tip-off? For Christ's sake, what's happening? We thought we had got rid of all this when we made Liam pay for his treachery," said another.

"We are looking into that. I have my sources trying to find out where the tip-off came from. I have no doubt we shall get to the bottom of it eventually, and God help the man or woman involved."

There was a general murmur of consent, which ran around the members, at the last remark.

"Is there any chance either of them will talk?" Tom O'Shaunesy asked.

"Both have been with us for a long time, well enough to know what happens to informers" was the reply from Michael McGuiness.

"Even so," asked another, "have we made provision to silence them, if it became obvious that either one of them would turn Queen's evidence?"

"It has indeed been arranged just in case," replied Sam gravely. "But I don't, for a moment, believe either would be so foolish. It would not only affect them but their families as well."

Roy gulped; his breakaway would seem to be more and more difficult as he listened to the feelings of the meeting. It would appear to be an almost impossible task. The IRA had connections everywhere; it seemed that nowhere was one safe, not even in jail, at home, or abroad. The general babble continued until Sam called the meeting to order and began to explain that if they were to continue with the deals in place, it would be necessary to get Roy more involved. There was a sudden lull as everyone listened very carefully to what was being proposed. They had been worried about Lord Croft's safety before, but what was Sam going to propose now? In the silence, Sam continued,

"I feel we shall have to involve Roy in the deliveries, and, following the arrest of Connor, I am of the opinion that we have to stop using the ferries and road for the time being at least. The logical answer is that, for the next couple of months, any new deliveries will need to be done by sea until things quieten down."

There was a pregnant pause. Then it seemed as though everyone began speaking at once. Several suggestions were put forward that Roy himself should take a back seat and involve his crew members more. Roy was much too important to risk; he was the man bringing in the supplies; the hubbub continued as the cacophony of angry voices rose until Sam banged the table, bringing instant order to the disarray. Michael McGuiness, a longstanding and revered member of the group, raised his hand:

"This committee has already made it quite clear that Lord Croft is far too important a member to lose on a drugs delivery."

It was O'Gilliagan that came up with the suggestion that Roy had a fully trained crew and that he could arrange everything but not be involved in the actual deliveries. If Roy felt Elian, Gael, and Fiona were not up to it alone, then help could be arranged from one of the other groups. The proposal was put to the vote, and all agreed. Roy would have to be involved, but not directly. The committee felt that, with Connor gone, they had to conserve the important links and the lesser people should now take more of the risks. It was even mooted that, if necessary, the committee would be prepared to assist with half the cost of a second cruiser. Roy sat dumbfounded that they could account for up to two million pounds, no mean amount of money for the group to fund. The matter of a second boat was put to the vote and passed unanimously. Roy stood up and thanked the committee and informed them that he would begin to look for a boat, but it would not happen immediately because he would be looking for a boat that would need considerable changes, including the engines to give him speed and manoeuvrability. The committee agreed to let Roy take his time and find the right craft suitable for his purposes but informed him that the money would be set aside and be available when he needed it.

Later, when the others had left, Roy sat with Sam, having a quiet drink, and he spoke quietly but with a new determination.

"Sam," he said, "I did not go into this business with the desire to sit back and let others take all the risks. Elian and Fiona are good, very good, but I never intended that they would take all the risk. I don't know if they would be prepared to do that."

"Roy," Sam replied, "You forget I supplied them to you. I know what they are capable of, so don't concern yourself."

"I am not prepared to sit back at a desk for the rest of my life. I could have done that before I left England. No, whatever you or the committee say, I will not take a back seat on these jobs. Especially now that we have deliveries to contend with."

Sam sat back, his hands crossed in his lap, as he looked at Roy, knowing just how he felt. He had felt the same way during the struggle when he had been pulled out of the front line and raised up through the ranks.

"I understand, Roy, and no, I'm not asking you to take a back seat completely, but with the extra responsibilities you are now taking on, it becomes imperative that you do more of the planning than actually take part in something as simple as delivering to the British mainland. By all means, go with the crew until you are satisfied they are fully competent. Then take a back seat for a while. You have a new baby to look forward to, and after today, you will have to source a new boat and get it converted. You will be too busy to go on every delivery, believe me."

Roy understood and could see the reasoning behind Sam's argument, but his resolve to find a way out had not diminished in anyway.

The two men walked back into the lounge where their respective wives sat talking. Sam picked up Sean and said to him with a broad grin on his face, which was equalled by the look of expectancy on the young boy's face.

"Would you like to see the trains again with Uncle Sam?"

Sean nodded eagerly but looked at Janet enquiringly.

"OK, your mom can come too, if she wants," Sam said,

Sam walked towards the door with Sean in his arms. Janet rose and followed him, looking back and shrugging her shoulders. Kate waited until the footsteps could no longer be heard before she drew Roy into her arms.

"I did not know if we would have the chance to be alone together today."

She pulled him towards the door leading to the butler's pantry and, once inside, she gave herself to him unreservedly. Roy, in turn, took her with a vengeance. It was only when they calmed down and she lay back, her hands clasped behind her head as she lay replete, That she smiled and whispered,

"I don't know if Sam has broken the news yet, but I can tell you as I've told Janet. It's confirmed that I'm pregnant."

Roy looked somewhat aghast at the news.

"Oh, Roy, come on. Don't act so innocent. You must have suspected that it was always a possibility. It happened when we were on the boat. I told you I was ovulating at the time."

"Are you sure it's mine?" asked Roy incredulously.

"Yes, it's yours. I'm sure of it. I worked out the dates to perfection."

"Oh God, does Sam know?"

"He knows I'm pregnant, but not that it's yours. He's delighted with the news. If it's a boy, he will have someone else to play trains with, and if it's a girl, I'm sure she'll have to like trains as well as dolls."

Then, as if she suddenly realised how long they had been, she sat up and said,

"Oh God, help us. We've been here too long. Hurry. They will be down shortly."

They dressed quickly, and they had only been sitting in the reception room for a few minutes, drinking from a hastily refilled glass, when the door opened and Sean ran in, throwing his arms around Roy's neck, and cried out,

"Daddy, Uncle Sam let me drive the trains."

Janet followed at a more sedate pace with Sam close behind her.

"Oh, Kate," she said. "Sam took the opportunity to show me around. You have such a lovely home. If it were mine, I don't think I would spend so much time in America."

Janet spoke with sincerity, trying hard to give the impression that she was completely innocent of what Roy had been doing with Kate, whilst Sam had been showing her around the house. Kate smiled, saying,

"You should see the house in America. It's on the beach, fully air conditioned, with a swimming pool and all the extra trimmings. You really must come and see it in the near future and bring his Lordship," pointing to Roy, "with you."

Sam, who was standing beside his wife, agreed.

"That's a wonderful idea, Kate. I could introduce Roy to the American connection. We will make a plan in the very near future. They will be delighted to meet our English connection and a Lord into the bargain."

Roy felt the world was getting smaller. Once he was known to the Americans, he would be roped into their group, and he knew from reports that the American patrol boats took no chances. They fired first and worried later.

On the way home, Janet asked Roy if Kate had told him her news. Seeing the reaction and guilt written on Roy's face, she had her suspicions that Roy could well be the father. When Janet did the calculations in her head, she realised that the date could well coincide with the trip on the cruiser to the Mediterranean with Kate and her friends. She put it to the back of her mind. Even Roy could not be that stupid, she thought. She was sure Sam would kill them both if he ever found out. Then she said,
    "I'm sure that's not what's worrying you. What is it? Although I could not fail to notice, you were both quite flushed when we got back from the tour of the house. Tell me it's not so."
    "It must have been the Scotch. I have had rather a lot, and so had Kate. It must have had the same effect on her. The reason I looked so concerned," he told her "was that one of my connections, you know Connor, the guy that usually goes on the long trips with me, has been arrested in England. It looks as though he will be in prison for quite a long time."
    "But the conflict with the IRA and England is over," Janet said, a genuine look of puzzlement crossing her face.
Roy, with not much else to say for fear of letting her know the real reason, replied,
    "The English have long memories and are somewhat unforgiving."
Fear replaced the puzzled look.
    "It's not going to happen to you, is it? I don't think I could stand you being locked up."
Roy looked at her unflinchingly and whispered,
    "Nothing is going to happen to me. The English do not even know I have any connection with the IRA, as far as that is concerned. I don't believe they know I even exist."
But the fear of being caught was strong at the back of his mind; he would have to be doubly careful in future.

They arrived back at the castle, and Roy had a message. It was from Lady Blanchester. She wanted to charter the boat over the weekend up the coast of Ireland and back, and the message implied that there would be two passengers, herself and one other. Roy hoped, but realised, that it was a vain hope that her young daughter Karen would be the second passenger.

This was one charter he would enjoy. There would be no risk this time. It would be a straightforward charter for the day with no fear of being chased by patrol boats. Roy was glad of the chance to have a regular charter. It would give him the chance to get things into perspective. He needed time to think things over and plan for his future. One thing he did know was that if he accepted the offer to go halves on a new boat;, that would tie him into the group even more. Then, he believed that he would never be able to break free.

Chapter 13

The following day, Roy confirmed the charter arrangement, and Elian stocked the boat for the trip. Fiona was coming along as the cook, waitress, and general handywoman. It was early on Saturday morning when the cruiser pulled into the harbour at Tralee. Roy had to look twice at the other passenger. It was a woman. From what Roy could see of her, she could easily have been mistaken for Karen but looked slightly older. Roy put her in her mid-twenties. Lady Blanchester fairly bounced aboard and, after embracing Roy like an old lover, she introduced the other passenger as she came aboard.

"Lord Croft, let me introduce you to my other daughter, Erica, otherwise known as Lady Donegal."

Roy acknowledged the greeting and asked to be excused for a moment as he helped Fiona cast off. Once that had been done, Elian headed out into the Atlantic before turning north towards Galway Bay. Lady Blanchester sat in the main cabin and began her tale. She told Roy that her daughter was married to the young Lord Donegal, like Roy himself her daughter's husband was a peer of the realm. Apparently they lived in a castle at Ballyshannon. Lady Blanchester continued,

"Don't be overwhelmed by his title. He is not at all like you. He is a weak-looking specimen of a man. I never understood what Erica could see in him, apart from his title and the family fortune. He had been in London at her coming out and had apparently been besotted with young Erica. He had taken her everywhere and proposed even before the end of the season. Erica had been captivated by the young man's attention. He had seemed to know everyone. They had dined with royalty, and the engagement ring had been the size of an egg."

Roy sat bemused at the tale, never guessing for a moment what was coming next, as Lady Blanchester, dropping her voice just above a whisper, said,

"Poor Erika's sex life, however, is a different story. What she had considered to be gentlemanly behaviour during their whirlwind romance turned out to be his lack of desire. He made love to her once a week in order to get an heir, but she had confided to me that she had never had an orgasm with her husband, and he had been the only man she had ever let into her panties."

Lady Blanchester continued to inform Roy that the idea of the trip had arisen during one of Erica's many tearful sessions when she had sobbed, telling her mother that she felt as though she would never have the child she desired more than anything in the world. Lady Blanchester paused for the story to sink in, and then she confessed that she had told Erica about Roy, Lord Croft, and how he had behaved on the trip to the Mediterranean.

"She had stared at me in amazement when I told her that you were the kind of man I and any mother would have wanted for her daughter and that you had even got into the panties of Karen, otherwise known as Miss Iceberg by her brothers."

Roy deduced from her attitude that Lady Blanchester had not confided in Erica that she had also been a part of the voyage when Roy had slept with every woman on board, including the haughty and somewhat superior Lady Blanchester.

The conversation ended as Erica came into the cabin from the deck where she had been standing, watching the coast from the flying bridge where she had been beside Elian at the wheel. She had come down as the wind had changed direction, and there was a decided chill in the air. Fiona brought out breakfast, and when the two ladies had finished and had taken coffee in the lounge, Erica asked,

"Oh, Roy, I may call you that?" she asked. "Do you think I could lie down for a while?"

Roy showed her into the stateroom and returned to speak to Lady Blanchester. She looked up and said in an exasperated voice,

"What are you doing here? I thought I had made it quite plain. My daughter wants a child, and her husband is incapable of giving her one. She needs a man to help her, and I have recommended that that man be you. Now, unless I'm very much mistaken, you find Erica almost as arousing as you did Karen, so don't stand there with your mouth open. Get back in that cabin and strut your stuff. I know only too well that you are very capable."

Roy understood perfectly what Lady Blanchester had planned despite the fact that he felt like a stallion put out to stud; he walked back into the stateroom and asked if the young woman lying on the bed needed anything else. The young married Erica said shyly,

"I have been told by my mother that you were the man who deflowered my younger sister."

Roy nodded his head, trying to look shameful and failing miserably. "Well," Erica said, "I don't quite know how to phrase this. I'm not like my mother, but I'm led to believe you are more than capable of what I have in mind. I am advised by my own mother that you are skilled in the art of sexual pleasure, and if I am correct in my assumptions, you would not be averse to letting me see you aroused."

Roy was glad that Lady Blanchester had briefed him. Otherwise, he would not have known how to react to such a request, especially from a peer of the realm's young wife. Roy's response was still cheeky as he said with a broad grin on his face,

"I'll show you mine if you show me yours."

Erica was at a loss for words, but determination had been bred into her, and she nodded. She started to undo the buttons of her dress as Roy unzipped his trousers. Roy pulled them off his feet, removing his shoes and socks as he did so. Erica's dress pooled around her ankles, and she stooped to pick it up carefully, folding it and putting it over the back of the chair. Roy pulled his T-shirt up over his head and stood with just his boxer shorts covering the slowly growing bulge between his thighs. Erica looked so much like Karen that Roy remembered clearly the moment he had taken her chastity, and he felt the bulge grow larger as the memory of that moment's pleasure was clearly pictured in his mind. Erica stood beside the bed, dressed in a tiny pair of panties and a bra that barely covered her nipples. As if by order, the cold breeze caused the hidden nipples to harden, and they pushed against the flimsy material.

Surprisingly, Erica took the lead and, in minutes, the two of them were embracing. As Roy's lips touched hers, he felt them part, and the passion of the kiss deepened. It was as though they had been lovers all their lives, and there was no hesitation on either side as they fell on to the bed and began to make love. Roy imagined he was with Karen again, and he held nothing back. Erica gave her all and was overwhelmed by Roy's skill as a lover as he brought her to climax after climax. Finally, they lay beside one another, both replete for the moment, and Erica struggled to get her breath back.

"Oh my God, Roy, that was way beyond my expectations. I hope we shall have the pleasure again before I leave after this weekend."

Erica was carried away in a blissful mood as Roy, always keen to please, rose and got the potcheen from the cupboard and poured himself a shot in a whisky glass, and nature did the rest. Roy felt so good, but the feeling was inevitable that, with each new conquest, he could never get over the fact that very few times in his life had he ever had to make the first move; women just seemed to come to him; he was pleased to think it had more to do with the way Janet had taught him than his own features, his pheromones, or his physique.

This time, Erica was elated; she had responded to Roy's skill with a need and a desire she had never experienced before.

"That was a truly wonderful experience," she whispered breathlessly. "I really feel like a woman at last. I just wish you were my husband. But then, I would have had to share you with my sister Karen, wouldn't I?"

Roy put his mouth close to her ear, and with a sense of wickedness.

"You would have had to share me with your mother too," he whispered.

Erica could not believe what she was hearing.

"You have had intercourse with my mother as well? I can't believe she would do that." "Well, you will have to ask her if you don't believe me" was Roy's response.

It was quite some time before Roy reappeared and sat by Lady Blanchard, who was delighted that her plan had gone so smoothly. She knew what had happened. She had listened at the door almost the whole of the time Roy had been in the stateroom. She hoped her plans to hire the boat exactly on the day her daughter would be at her most susceptible time for fertilisation would pay off. Roy walked up to her and whispered in a stage whisper,

"You are as cunning as they come, aren't you?"

Lady Blanchester just smiled.

"I hope you've saved something for me on the return journey," she said in a whisper that left no doubt what she had in mind.

Roy ignored her plea and looked at his watch; they would be approaching Galway Bay in about thirty minutes. Lunch had been booked at a small hotel by her ladyship, and oysters were on the menu to fortify Roy on the return trip. The five of them, Roy and the crew, together with Lady Blanchester and her daughter Erica, ate their fill and drank a couple of bottles of champagne before returning to the boat for the return trip.

The return journey went as planned, and Roy finally went up on deck. He could feel the cruiser running well, but the swell seemed to be increasing as he arrived on deck and could see the storm clouds gathering from the west.

"How long has that been coming," Roy asked Elian, who had donned her waterproofs.

"It's been coming up over the last thirty minutes," she said. "It looks like it could be a bad one."

Roy, concerned for his passengers' welfare, said,

"I'll speak to Lady Blanchester to see if she wants to risk returning to Tralee, which will be a nightmare to get into if it blows up to gale force three or more. We could take shelter in the Shannon, or we could make a run for home. What's the latest radio forecast say?"

Elian, quite used to sailing in almost any storm, replied quite unconcernedly,

"The forecast indicates that it could get up to gale force four, but the storm has increased much faster than they predicted."

Roy ran down the companionway and broke the news to the two passengers, neither of whom were particularly good sailors. It was agreed that they would put into Shannon for the night and complete the journey to Tralee the following morning. Roy called Janet and told her the story; she said that, under the circumstances, she had to agree that she would be much happier if he stayed in Shannon. She had been worried ever since the TV had broken the story of the storm, which seemed to come from nowhere. Roy gave Lady Blanchester his phone for her to call home and say that she would only be back the following day. Roy went into the lower wheelhouse and called up on the intercom for Elian to shut down the flying bridge and come down to the lower controls. Roy handled the craft until a windswept Elian arrived to take over.

The storm built quickly, and the decision to go into the River Shannon had proved to be the right one. The seventy-five-foot craft was being tossed about like a cork, and Elian had to use all her skill, obtained on the fishing fleet, to keep the boat heading in the right direction. The sea broke over the small craft, washing the decks and spilling down the slipways. Roy went below to ensure that the bilge pumps were coping and that the lower areas were not flooding; the excellent design of the wartime MTB hull proved its worth as they raced through the storm into the Shannon estuary. They made their way upriver and eventually passing 'Glin', securing a berth at 'Foynes' for the night. They secured the lines rigged for stormy weather and walked through the wind and rain to the Harbour Inn. Supper was plain but good, and the hotel had rooms for them. Elian and Fiona declined the offer to stay at the Inn, insisting that they would stay on the boat. Roy told Lady Blanchester that he would also sleep on the boat, but he would stay a while and have a well-earned nightcap with his passengers. Lady Blanchester retired just after nine, leaving Roy and Erica together in the bar. The storm by now had reached gale force four and showed no signs of abating.

"You had better stay. You are not going to walk back in this. You can stay in my room," Erica said.

They walked up the narrow stairs to Erica's room, which was plain but clean with a double bed. The widow frame howled as the wind whistled around the old window frame and the pair of them stripped off and climbed between the sheets. The bed was cold, and they clutched at each other for warmth. The heat began to build between the sheets, and Erica slowly became aware of not only her own arousal but also Roy's. They made love with an unrestricted passion, never worrying or even considering the inevitable outcome of their wild tryst. Eventually, all good things had to come to a close, and with Erica's head in the crook of his arm, they slowly drifted off into a deep sleep.

Roy woke early. The wind had subsided, and the storm had blown itself out almost as quickly as it had arisen; he quickly dressed and slipped out of the front door of the Inn; he made his way across the harbour to the cruiser. It was still pitch dark and not yet five o'clock; using his key, he unlocked the door to the companionway; he made his way silently down into the lounge and into the stateroom where a semi-clad Fiona lay sprawled across the bed. She looked so inviting, but Roy was learning that he had limitations. His groin ached. He knew better than to push his luck. Perhaps the opportunity would arise later in the afternoon when he had recovered somewhat. He quickly changed and went up to the bridge and folded the cover away to begin preparing the cruiser for the short trip home. Hearing noises from the bridge, Elian woke up and raced upstairs, wearing just a thick sweater that finished just below her waist, unheeding that as she was dressed, she was showing her panties to all and sundry as she hurried up the stairs.

"God, Roy," she said, "you gave me a fright. I thought someone was trying to break in."

Roy looked at Elian, her brief panties clearly on view.

"If I were you, I would put something more than that on. If I had been a thief, you would not have stood a chance. You would have easily been meat and would have had little chance of escaping being raped in that outfit. I must add, it's rather fetching," he said with a broad grin.

Elian looked at him without any animosity in her voice for, like his wife, she knew that no one woman would ever be able to control Roy's wild lust and love for women; he liked nothing more than new conquests to add to his list.

"I would have thought you would have had your fill after yesterday. You should be ashamed of yourself. I did not think you were into older women. You really are completely incorrigible. I hope that Lady Donegal is feeling alright this morning or was Lady Blanchester the one who offered you comfort in the height of the storm last night? I have no doubt you were too occupied to give scant thought to us aboard this boat in the harbour."

With that, she turned and went below to dress in a more practical manner.

The two passengers had to be chased up by Fiona; she had to go to the Inn to hurry them along. They climbed aboard, and Elian took the cruiser out into the still fairly high swell of the Atlantic and, once clear of the river mouth, she opened the throttle and felt the raw power of the turbocharged diesels below. A couple of hours later, they pulled into Tralee, dropped off their passengers and, with a wave, they were on their way to the castle. They tied up, and Elian suggested that they put the boat into the boathouse so that she could give the boat a check-up after the storm and before they went on the long voyage to North Africa. Roy agreed, and he rang the house telling Janet that he was back and asking if she could spare Bridget for about an hour. He explained that he needed Bridget, who had returned to work after the birth of her child, to help get the boat up the slipway. Janet was pleased to know that he was safe. She sent Bridget down the steps to operate the winch. Once the operation had been completed, Roy walked up the stone steps from the subterranean tunnel, having chocked the boat and leaving Elian and Fiona to check over the hull.

On the way back to the kitchen, Bridget had told him she thought there was a possibility that she had another child on the way and Billy, her husband, was delighted with the news. Roy had by now lost count of the number of children he had fathered; he just enjoyed good, unprotected sex wherever he could get it. Janet ran forward, throwing her arms around his neck, and kissed him with fervour. Roy sent food down to the boathouse for the crew and sat down to have a late lunch. Bridget had prepared one of his favourites, a ploughman's lunch. Janet sat at the table and felt the kick of the developing child within her,

"I wish you did not have to go on this week's charter," she said. "I am getting very near my time, and I would love to have you with me when I give birth. It's so comforting when a woman's husband is present at the birth of her child. It confirms that he cares."

"I understand, Janet, but you know how it is. I get the occasional charter outside, but the majority of my work comes from Sam, and until things change, he calls the tune. I don't feel that Elian is ready to do the North Africa run with only Gael and Fiona as support."

He was about to elaborate, but the phone interrupted him. He picked up the phone and listened. His face had a hard look about it as he nodded his head, as if the speaker at the other end of the line could see him. He said grimly,

"OK. If you think it's really necessary, I will, but what's all the rush? Can't it wait until I get back?"

Switching off the phone and replacing it on the holder, he said,

"That was Sam, and I'm going to have to go to England. I have to go and see him tomorrow at lunchtime. You are invited if you are up to it."

"I'll see how I feel in the morning," she replied.

Janet sat back, unable to hide the disappointment in her face. He had been away over the weekend, and now it looked as though he was going to be away this week before he left for North Africa. Kate had told her that the 'charter group' had offered to pay half towards a second boat. She had been against it at first, but that way, he would have to train a second crew, and at least he would spend more time at home. She would discuss it with him after the baby was born.

Chapter 14

Lunch at Delaney's' was usually a leisurely affair, but this time, when Roy arrived, Kate welcomed him and told him to go straight into the study where Sam was waiting for him, whilst she entertained Janet and young Sean. When Roy opened the door and walked in, Sam was at the desk, his face dark, and worry lines were more pronounced than Roy had seen on his face in a long time.

"Grab a seat, Roy. Help yourself to a sandwich. We could be here for some time."

Roy walked to the side table and pulled back the white cloth covering a couple of plates of assorted sandwiches. He took some and put them on his plate and, turning to Sam, asked,

"Do you want any?"

Sam shook his head.

"Perhaps later. Pour me a brandy, and help yourself to whatever you want."

Roy poured the drinks and carried them back to the desk and retrieved his own sandwiches.

"What's this about, Sam? You look terrible. Have you been up all night?"

Sam nodded his head and beckoned Roy closer.

"I've been worried about the new arrangements. It appears that our contacts in England were the ones who got careless. The police were following them when they met with Connor. The police had never suspected an Irish connection, and they are treating it as an isolated event. They have not tied the trafficking of drugs back to us. Even though it means a longer sentence, Connor and Padraig have refused to cooperate with the drugs squad in England. As a result, their families will be taken care of during their incarceration."

"That's good news, isn't it, Sam? That's what we wanted them to do," Roy answered.

"Yes, but with the connection in England now under surveillance and probably penetrated by drug squad operatives, we have to set up new connections, and the risks involved in that are difficult, to say the least. You know I can't go to England. There is still a warrant out for my arrest from the bad old days. I would be arrested the second I set foot on British soil."

"How does that affect me?" asked Roy, still not clear where this was leading.

"You are going to have to go and set things up in England. You are the one person in the organisation the drugs squad would never suspect."

Roy sat back, the half-eaten sandwich still clutched in his hand.

"You want me to negotiate with those gangs. I don't know if that's really my style."

Sam raised his eyebrows and smiled.

"Roy, from what I learnt about you, before you joined us, you never held back at any board meeting. You could negotiate with the best. Your negotiations with Charlie to get the castle fit for habitation were not strictly legal now, were they?" Sam asked.

"How the hell did you find out about that?" Roy queried, wondering what else from his past Sam was privy to.

"Oh you would be surprised; I know that and much more. Now what's not your style?"

"Negotiating with drug lords or their gang members; Company boards are one thing, but negotiating with criminals is another. Company directors do not kill you if things go wrong," Roy replied, emphasising his concern.

Sam threw back his head and laughed. Tears began to run down his face. Roy looked at him askance and, with some indignity, he demanded,

"What's so bloody funny, Sam?"

"You! You still look on yourself as a normal citizen. Oh, I'm sorry, your grace. You still think of yourself as a Lord of the realm. You sanctimonious bastard, you've committed murder, sunk a naval patrol boat, run drugs, weapons, and sunk several pirate vessels, and yet you don't consider yourself as a criminal. You are no better than them. Don't you realise that?"

The realisation of what Sam had said struck Roy like a hammer blow as he sat open-mouthed. Sam was right of course. He had never considered that fact. Yes, he was no better than the very same drug lords Sam was asking him to negotiate with.

"Christ, Sam! You're right. I never considered that. It's a sobering thought, but OK, I'll go. How do I contact them or is that your job?"

The mirth went out of Sam's voice, and he became serious again.

"Yes, that's my job. I'll set up the meeting," Sam said, watching Roy's reaction.

"I want to be as prepared as I can be, when I start negotiating with them just as I was when around a board table. I want a full dossier on each group, especially on the group leader. I don't want to go in there with only a wing and a prayer. I want to know exactly what I'm up against. I don't want to die for something I had not been warned about," Roy emphasised, his face reflecting the seriousness of what he had said.

"Already taken care of. Don't you worry about that. I'll give you as much support as I can, but I think on more than one occasion you will be on your own," Sam replied.

"I want to set the meeting place, or it's a no-go. I don't want to end up dead in some bloody dark warehouse or an unlighted parking garage. It will be out in the open where I can see if the bastard I'm talking to has any undisclosed supporters I should know about. Oh, and I want to take Elian and Gael with me as my backup, notwithstanding any others you provide. Is that fully understood?"

Sam sat and looked at Roy in a new light. Roy may only have just realised how the outside world would see him, but he had embraced the situation, and his mind was already getting to grips with the new position he found himself in. That was why Sam had selected him for the inner committee, despite the fact that he was English. His analytical mind was just what the committee needed. It was time someone else took responsibility and eased some of it off Sam's shoulders.

"I'll make that a condition of any meet. After all, you will be meeting them in their territory, and you will be the one at risk. Now, enough shop for the moment other than the fact that I'll contact you when the meetings are set up, one in London and the other in Manchester. Let me get you a refill. I can see your glass is empty."

They rejoined Kate and Janet, but Sean was nowhere to be seen.

"Where's Sean?" Roy asked, looking around.

"You might know he's found a new friend in the kitchen, the cook. She promised him some chocolate, and we haven't seen him since. I'd better go and see where he is," Janet said.

"I'll join you if I may," Sam replied. "I'm sure, if he is not too full of chocolate, he will either want to see the trains or ride that bicycle I got for him."

They left Kate and Roy alone. She put her finger to her lips to keep Roy from speaking and grabbed his arm and pulled him into the butler's pantry.

"I may be pregnant, Roy, but I still have needs," Kate whispered, her desire expressed in the tone of her voice and the urgency she dragged Roy through the door.

Roy sighed and resigned himself to the inevitable, but he whispered,

"We will have to be quick. They won't be long, and we don't want to get caught, do we?"

They had just closed the door behind them and taken their seats in the reception lounge when Janet returned; she spotted the flush in Roy's and Kate's cheeks and knew that the previous twenty minutes had not been wasted. Roy had satisfied Kate's growing hunger. *Jesus,* she thought to herself, *did she want them to get caught? Heaven knows what Sam would do if he found out about their affair. This was no casual sex like the others. This was getting serious.* Janet hoped that Roy would come to his senses, but she knew how determined Kate was to have him at every opportunity.

"I think we should see about going back, darling. Sean is getting tired, and I'm just about all in myself. This baby takes far more out of me than Sean ever did."

Roy stood, and as Sam entered with Sean on his shoulders, Roy and Janet made their excuses and left. As soon as they were in the car, Janet looked at her husband and said quietly, so as not to upset the young man behind them.

"Jesus, Roy, You will get caught for sure. What were you thinking of? We were only away for less than half an hour. I'm sure you can't be that desperate, or is Kate taking over from me in your affections?"

"Don't be so silly, Janet, you know she is the driving force in that relationship. I'm afraid if I say no, she will tell Sam that I came on to her, and then the fat would be in the fire. I'm trapped. I really should have refused at the beginning. You know how I am. I find it difficult to say no to any woman."

Janet sat back, wondering if she should believe him. She knew that Kate was pregnant and she hoped against hope that the child was Sam's and not Roy's. This trip to England worried her. She was concerned that Sam had not mentioned it when they had stood and watched Sean ride his new bicycle. She had tried to draw the information from him, but he had just said it was business. She worried about Roy. He seemed so preoccupied with the committee and the charter work that he never seemed willing to discuss anything about either these days. She sat quietly until they pulled into the garage to park the Land Cruiser. Then she turned and kissed him fiercely and whispered,

"God knows I love you, Roy Croft, for all your faults. Just be careful; you seem to be getting far too involved. I don't want anything to happen to you."

Roy was surprised. It was out of character for Janet. He wondered if she guessed the danger he would be putting himself in, in England, or whether she was referring to his liaison with Kate. He had still not worked out the answer when they retired to bed later that night. He resolved that he would try to find out later. He had a fairly restless night as he ran Sam's proposal and Janet's behaviour though his mind.

The following morning, Sam rang. Roy picked up the phone and listened,

"The first meeting is on Wednesday in London with Ivan Romanoff and the next on Friday in Manchester with Baba Abasha, and I feel we must meet today to discuss our strategy."

"I agree," Roy replied. "Come over to us, and after the meeting, we can have a bite of lunch. I'm sure Janet would welcome the chance to entertain you for a change."

"We'll be there about eleven," Sam said.

The reply had come a little too quickly for Roy's liking, and he wondered what Sam knew that he didn't; he hoped there wouldn't be any more complications. Roy broke the news to Janet that the Delaney's would be over there later, for lunch. Far from being happy, she scolded him for not giving her more notice.

"Oh, Roy, how could you? Kate always gives us such lovely meals, and now I have to serve lunch back with no notice. Oh God, I don't even know what I've got to give them. I only hope Cathleen or Bridget can come up with some ideas."

Janet, still muttering under her breath, hurried through to the storeroom off the kitchen, and that was the last Roy saw of her for some time. He walked through to the workshop where Elian and Gael were working on the boat. He called them into the office and broke the news about the meeting with the drug barons in London and Manchester. The two women were concerned for Roy's safety and expressed their feelings forcibly. Roy put their minds at rest by telling them that he would be choosing the actual meeting place and only giving the location at the last minute to prevent them setting up a reception committee. Then, continuing, he informed them,

"These meetings are only preliminary meets, where we shall be discussing the principles of mutual cooperation and our supply. No money or drugs will change hands other than perhaps a small sample to let them gauge the quality of what we have to offer," Roy said.

"I don't like getting involved with people like that. I can only presume it's going to be the Russians and the Nigerians," Gael said grimly.

"Gael, you amaze me. I had no idea you were so well informed about drug barons in England."

"I may be female and live in Ireland, but don't think just because I chose to be trained as a terrorist that I am unintelligent, because, if so, I could feel insulted." Then, looking at him through half-open eyes, she continued, "You would not like to see me mad now, would you?"

"Not unless I had a cocked gun in my hand. I saw how you handled those others on the boat after I shot Kevan. Those guys showed you a lot of respect and obeyed you without question. That sort of respect has to be earned," Roy said with a grin.

"I'll tell you about it some time. Believe me, it was tough going for a time," she quipped back.

Roy broke the news to them that they would be driving to the United Kingdom as it would be easier to conceal weapons in the Range Rover or the Land Cruiser than it would be to fly. He informed them that they would need to start out on Tuesday and get back on Saturday and be ready to leave for North Africa before dawn on Sunday.

"Fiona will have to see to the food stores being loaded, and Gael and I will see to the weapons and ammunition today," Elian said.

"Sam Delaney is coming over to go over the fine-tuning, and I'll tell you the rest as soon as I know myself," Roy said as he stood.

The two women left the office, and Roy could hear their voices as they discussed the pros and cons of the forthcoming meetings. Roy pulled open the bottom drawer to his desk and pulled out his 9mm Beretta and began to clean and oil it. He heard Janet's voice calling as he reassembled and reloaded the pistol. Then, slipping it back into its hiding place, he made his way back to the house. As he approached it, he could hear Kate's voice coming from the kitchen. He ran up the steps two at a time; on hearing him approach, she turned and, putting her arms on his shoulders, she politely kissed him on the cheek. Janet looked on and smiled, knowing full well that if she had not been there, Roy would have been getting more than a polite greeting.

"We wondered where you had got off too. I have poured Sam a brandy, and he is in the lounge waiting for you." Janet said.

Roy hurried through to the lounge where Sam sat waiting. He rose as Roy entered, and they shook hands.

"I took the liberty of pouring myself a second and a drink for you. I poured Irish. Is that OK?" Sam said taking a sip and appreciating the quality of the brandy

"That's great," Roy said. "Now, let's get down to business. Are we sure that talking to these guys is a good idea? I have a feeling they will agree to take our drugs at the cheap rate but will not pass the benefit on to the users. You know our plan was to flood the market with cheap drugs and destroy the young society of England. That's not going to work if these Russians and Nigerians take our drugs and make a bigger profit. We'll just look like idiots for selling the stuff too cheaply."

Sam pondered for a while as though turning the matter over in his mind and considering what Roy had said.

"What are you suggesting we do?" Sam asked. "We have plenty of stock with our distributors at present, so the matter is not urgent. It would have been a lot better if that stupid bugger Connor had not got overconfident and had taken precautions to see that the other party was not under surveillance."

"That a bit harsh, Sam. It was surely up to the McGuire's to see that they weren't being followed. You can hardly blame Connor for that. But that aside, what do you think?"

"You're right, Roy. I was not thinking correctly. I was thinking they would receive our drugs and pass them on to our distributors acting as middlemen, but I can see that that will not work. They will keep the drugs and sell them at a huge profit, and we should be the losers, big time. What are you suggesting we do instead?"

Roy had been running the alternatives through his head all night and he said, not very convincingly at first but sounding more and more sure of his facts, as he proceeded to lay out his plans.

"I feel we are opening ourselves up to these Russian and Nigerian bastards. We know nothing about them other than that they are supplying drugs to the same people as we are. The difference is they are charging far more than us, and we are gaining ground on the market share. I am sure that it's their intention to take us out and try to disrupt our organisation. They have no idea just how big we are, or how far down the chain our fingers reach. Far from dealing with them, we should disrupt their organisations by meeting with them, letting them believe we are foolish enough to fall for their proposals and then take them down at the first exchange."

Sam sat back, his face a picture of surprise and his eyes wide with excitement as he thought of the possibility of the committee being powerful enough to take down the largest drug barons and take on their market.

"Jesus, Roy that's a great plan, but don't you think they would crucify us?" asked Sam.

"We have sleepers all over Britain, people who have the Irish cause close to their heart, people who have been trained in clandestine operations. If they were willing to help us plant bombs, I don't think they would be averse to helping us with our newest plans to destroy the youth of Britain by whatever means, do you?"

"It's a point I had not considered," Sam said, deep in thought. "How do you propose we would get the larger quantity of drugs to England?"

"My plan would be to get everyone who has both a connection with the cause and any reason to go to England would act as a carrier. We would send them over in small parcels carried on ferries, which could be posted or handed over to the sleepers all over the country. None of the parcels would be big enough, on their own, to attract any attention, but cumulatively they would be big enough to swamp the market," Roy replied with equal enthusiasm.

"I think you should propose it at the next committee meeting. What do you want to do about the meetings in the meantime?" Sam said excitedly.

Sam was so enthusiastic at the thought of reactivating all the sleepers in England, that his mind was already calculating the logistics of Roy's proposal and how the idea of taking down the two biggest drug lords would cause confusion in the market.

Roy looked Sam in the face and asked,

"Do they know it's the IRA who are making the approach?"

Sam thought for a moment, then replied,

"No. The arrangements have been set up by a third party, who was instructed not to disclose the source, only that we could be relied on to meet the demand for top-quality merchandise."

"You realise that we shall have to get rid of the third party when this is all over. We want no way that any dealings with either party can be tracked back to the committee. The meetings can go ahead as planned, and I can set up the time and place for the planned exchange. If we plan correctly, we can take both gangs down at the same time."

The two men agreed that that was the best way to go forward. Sam was interested to know why Roy was so keen to carry out their plans. Sam could understand where the new IRA was coming from, but Roy Croft, no, Lord Croft, a peer of the realm, was being prepared to bring down the very country that had nurtured him. Roy's answer shook Sam to the core.

"I joined you to bring excitement into my humdrum life. You told me what I had become yesterday and, realising there was no way back and how I am now fully committed to my new life, I am fully aware of what England would do to me if I was caught and put on trial. I am, therefore, as committed to your cause as any Irish national. You gave me what I wanted, and I will give you my fullest cooperation in exchange. Now, let's put that behind us and move ahead, shall we?"

The two men shook hands and embraced, sealing all agreements between them. They returned to join the ladies. Both men had a satisfied gleam in their eyes. Both knew the commitments they had agreed to, and both were more than ready to move ahead.

Tuesday arrived, and Janet waved Roy off. He was accompanied by Gael and Elian. She had asked why he needed them both, but Roy's answer had been vague, and she had not pressed the matter. She had seen that Roy, like Sam, had not wanted to discuss the trip at all. She was curious but worried about his safety. Elian and Gael would not let any harm come to Roy if they could help it. She did not know how well trained Gael was in the art of defence and her ability to kill without scruple; if she had, she might have been even more worried. Roy normally told her something of what business he was going to be doing, but this time he had been so secretive. Today she knew he was putting himself, together with Elian and Gael, into danger, and she could not fathom out why. He had money, respect, a title, a loving wife and son, and a new baby on the way. She would never understand this desperate need to put himself at risk. It was one quirk in his character she would never understand. As the vehicle disappeared down the long drive, she turned away sadly and, clutching Sean's hand, she went back inside.

Sam had rang the third party and requested the meeting to be arranged according to Roy's wishes. He waited for the confirmation that the gang leaders had finally agreed that the precise location be given only one hour before the meeting.

Roy drove to Dublin and intended to take the ferry to Holyhead, the shortest ferry trip taking just over one and a half hours. Holyhead presented no concerns; the customs were slack, and they would not make any fuss about his title. The three of them could slip into the Welsh port and drive down to London, stay overnight, have their meeting with the Russians on Wednesday before returning to Manchester. Roy drove the Range Rover hard to the ferry and then kept strictly to the speed limit as he drove down towards London. He was tired by the time he arrived and booked a suite in one of the larger hotels. Once he had checked in, he rang a hotel in Reading and booked two adjoining rooms for the following day in the name of Fergus McNally. When they asked for his credit card, Roy used the one supplied by Sam, which would be cancelled after this trip, to reduce any trace-back pointing to Roy. He rang Sam and told him to communicate with the third party, informing them to set up the meetings at the Post House Hotel and give the time for each meeting, emphasising that the information should not be given until one hour prior to the actual meeting. Gael and Elian were somewhat disappointed when, after supper, Roy retired to bed alone, telling them that they had to be awake early to get to Reading by nine o'clock the following morning.

Traffic was heavy, and Roy, Gael, and Elian arrived at the Post House Hotel at 09.15 a.m. He parked the Range Rover some distance away from the hotel car park, and they walked to the hotel. Roy did not want his vehicle on the hotel surveillance cameras, in case of trouble, and he avoided going to the desk, sending Elian to pick up the keys, before they went up to the rooms. Roy had decided to play the part of a lecherous Irishman not really clued up about the meeting. He explained to the two women what he wanted, and they stripped and got on to the bed. Roy changed into a hotel robe and waited for the reception to inform him that he had visitors. When the phone rang, he asked for the visitor to be sent up.

"Oh, Mr McNally, there are four of them. Do you want me to send all of them up?"

Roy had expected as much, and he asked the receptionist to send them up in five minutes. Roy told Elian and Gael to get into bed and rumple the sheets as though there had been an orgy, instructing them to be on their guard, weapons cocked in case of trouble. They knew exactly what Roy wanted, and they lounged back with a sheet barely covering their nudity, their hair tousled and untidy. Both were armed with a pistol, and under the pillows were concealed a silenced automatic Uzi. They were ready for anything.

Roy left the adjoining door, where the girls lay, ajar and waited for the knock. He went forward pistol in hand.

"Who is there?" Roy asked in a broad Irish brogue.

A voice thick with Russian overtones replied,

"Who are you expecting? Open the door slowly and, if you are armed, show your weapon."

Knowing that the two women would have him covered, Roy complied. The door was thrown open, and the four men pushed Roy aside. One of the men grabbed Roy's gun.

"Are you alone?" the man Roy took to be the leader asked.

"I have female company next door. I was tired of waiting around."

One of the Russians moved to the door and opened it. His gaze settled on the two naked figures lying on the bed.

"You should see this, Ivan. There are two of them. It seems our friend likes more than one at a time."

"Are they any threat, Gregoff?" the leader demanded.

"Only as a distraction. I'm getting hard just looking at them," Gregoff replied with a lecherous grin.

"Leave them. We're not here to have fun. Let's get this over with." Then, to Roy, he said, "I understand you have a sample for me."

Roy nodded and opened his case; one of the others drew a weapon and pointed it at Roy.

Roy pretended to be concerned and took out a small packet and threw it to Ivan.

"Look, you. Whoever you are, I'm merely the messenger. I was told to bring that sample. I was to give it to you and emphasise that if you were satisfied with the quality, we could meet any quantity demand you need. I understand that the price has already been agreed."

"If the quality is as good as you say, why so cheap?" asked Ivan.

"I don't know. I'm just the messenger. I'm being well paid, and I don't get too involved. Over the years, I've learnt it doesn't pay," Roy replied, glancing from one to the other as though nervous.

Ivan tore the end of the packet and poured some of the white powder on to his finger. Then he rubbed the whitened finger over his gums. His face broke into a smile.

"It seems good to me. How do I know you can commit to a large order of, say, 40 kilos of the stuff?"

"I was told you can have as much as you want, but the arrangements must be made with whoever set this up. I'm not involved with that side of the business. I only make deliveries and collect the money."

"Leave him. Let's get out of here. He's not much help. I'm sure he has other things on his mind. Let him get back to what he was doing before we arrived. Throw his gun on the bed," Ivan said gruffly as the four of them backed out of the room.

Roy waited a few minutes to make sure they had gone. Then he whispered,

"Doss badanya suckers" and walked into the other room where Elian and Gael had left the confines of the bed and were standing relaxed.

Gael was sporting the Uzi, and Elian had a Beretta clutched in her hand. Both were naked, and Roy's smile broadened into a grin.

"Jesus, you two look like a kinky pair ready to audition for *Annie Get Your Gun*. Put your weapons down, and let's make use of the room. After all, Sam's paid for it."

They stopped for a late snack on the motorway on the way to Manchester. Then they repeated the performance of the previous day, checking into one hotel for the night and then the Post House Hotel for use on the following day. Roy, as usual, parked the Range Rover far enough away in a side street. The set-up went much the same until the phone rang to inform Roy that he had visitors.

"Do you want me to send them up to your room?" the receptionist asked.

The tone in her voice clearly showed that she was concerned about that group of black men, who looked suspicious, in so much as they wore business suits but avoided letting her see their faces. She was concerned about letting them all go up to one of the guests rooms; as she watched the group carefully when they went to sit down as directed, until Mr McNally was ready for them to go up to his room. She added,

"If there's any trouble, Mr McNally, call me. I'll send up security. I don't really like the look of them. Are you sure it's all right?"

Roy was grateful for her concern but was apprehensive that she had noticed them and made a mental note to use a different hotel next time.

"I'm sure, miss, don't worry, I've dealt with them before. They look worse than they are."

The knock came as expected, and once again, Roy asked hesitantly, his voice sounding unsure and nervous,

"Who's there?"

"Who the fuck are you expecting, the queen?" came sharp answer. "Open the fucking door, and don't be stupid."

Roy opened the door and stood back, his hand resting on his weapon. They came into the room, swaggering with the arrogance of men who were not afraid of anything. Pointing to the half-open door,

"Who is in there?" Baba asked, unsure he had not walked into a trap.

Before Roy could answer, the powerful, well-built black man said,

"Obed, check that room."

Obed complied, and the other two drew their weapons as if expecting trouble. Obed's eyes opened wide as he saw Elian and Gael, obviously naked, on the bed.

"Der's two naked white chicks on dah bed. Dis honkey has been entertaining his-self and I'll bet he's been up to no good while he's bin waitin for us."

"Keep an eye on them, Obed. We got business to discuss wid this man, an' I don't wan no interruptions." Then, to Roy he said, "You got da stuff, white man?"

Roy pointed to his briefcase,

"In there," he said.

Baba waved his gun in the direction of the case and said,

"Check it out, Juba," and to Roy he said, "No tricks, mind. I can be very nasty when I want to be."

Juba opened the briefcase and took out the small packet, handing it to Baba.

"You wan' check it out, Baba?" he asked.

Baba tore off the corner and ran a line along the side of his hand and then sniffed the powder into his large nostrils. A smile crossed his face as the effects hit his system.

"Oh yea! That's good stuff, man . . ."

Before he could say any more, there was a commotion from the other room, and Obed came back with blood running down his bare chest. His trousers were open at the front, and he called out,

"Hey, Baba, that white bitch cut me."

"I didn't tell you to try anything on wid the white trash. Get dressed. I don't want to upset this man. He deals in good stuff. I'll be in touch with the man and order what I want. Now let's go, Obed, before your dick gets us into any more trouble. Sorry, man! No harm done."

Roy went to the door where the two women sat smiling.

"The bloody arrogance of that prick. He thought we were his for the asking, cheeky bugger. He got more than he bargained for. He should think himself lucky it was his chest I cut," Gael said, wiping the blade on a tissue and putting it back under the pillow.

"Did he see the guns?" asked Roy. He was pleased when Elian shook her head. "Let's get out of here whilst we can. That silly clown might decide to come back for a second try, just for fun."

Both women laughed at the thought of Gael cutting off Obed's genitals, and they shook their heads as they began to dress. A few hours later, they were on the late ferry back to Dublin. On such a short crossing, there was no time for any hanky-panky, and they settled for a couple of drinks in the bar. Roy rang up Sam and told him that the mission was accomplished without any problem.

"Phase one," he whispered, "completed satisfactorily."

Chapter 15

Sunday morning arrived all too quickly for Janet. She and Sean had barely had time to realise Roy was back before he was on the move again. It was with sadness she watched the boat move out of the harbour with a crew of three women and her husband, making a total of four. This time, there were no trainees to take out, only the last batch to return. On this trip, Roy was not only the skipper but the paymaster as well. Sam's chauffeur had delivered the briefcase containing the required funds the night before. When Roy opened the briefcase, he was somewhat perplexed to find a note telling him that the pickup was delayed for twenty-four hours and that he was to collect a drugs drop off the coast of North Africa on Tuesday morning. The exact coordinates for the drop would be sent as soon as the drop was made. Roy knew better than to phone Sam even on the safe phone, so he broke the news to the three women.

With no Connor aboard this time, Roy was able to enjoy the favours of each of his crew members without fear of discovery. It was a much better arrangement all round. Roy refuelled at A Coruna, as usual, and was heading down the coast in the direction of Cadiz, where he had decided to call in readiness for the drugs collection. As they approached the southern coast of Spain, the radio broke the silence. Roy answered with his call sign and was pleasantly surprised to hear the voice of Officer Catalina Cordoba,
"Is that Lord Croft?" she asked. "I thought I recognised the boat."
Roy gave a start. Could it be a coincidence, or was she lying in wait to catch him in the act of recovering drugs? He hid his fear well as he replied,
"Officer Cordoba, what a pleasant surprise! What can I do for you?"
"It's Captain Cordoba now, your grace. I was wondering where you were heading this fine day."
"I'm calling in at Cadiz," Roy informed the enquiring captain.
"What a surprise! So am I. If it is of any interest to you, I'm off tomorrow. I have to have the patrol boat serviced. Perhaps we can meet for supper if that's OK with you."
Roy had an idea that he could keep Cordoba busy in the morning and the three women could go out and recover the drugs; they had all had

enough experience, and at least he would know where the patrol boat and its customs officer was whilst they were out there.

"I would very much appreciate that, Captain. Shall we say the San Miguel Hotel in Cadiz at 7.30pm. We shall dine at eight o'clock, and I and my crew will look forward to entertaining you once again."

"I'll see you there, my Lord," Captain Cordoba said with mock subservience in her voice.

"Despedirse, Capitanía Cordoba."

"Gracias Señor, Lord Croft," she said, adding, "I had no idea you could speak my language."

"Until tonight, Desde el lunes el viernes mi Capitanía."

Elian looked at Roy in surprise as he replaced the microphone.

"I had no idea you could speak Spanish, Roy."

"I thought we might meet up with our Catalina Cordoba again, and I learnt a few phrases just in case. You never know, do you?"

"I know enough to warn you to keep that in your pants. It could compromise you," Elian said.

"Now, now, Elian, live and let live." Roy said with a grin. "I can keep her occupied tomorrow whilst you take the boat out with Fiona and Gael to recover the goods. Our erstwhile captain will be too pre-occupied to notice you are missing, and if she does, I'll say that you have gone in search of our late arriving passengers. Something good can come out of most things."

Elian shrugged her shoulders.

"You would get away with murder, my Lord."

"I already have, as well you know," replied Roy, grinning.

As he pulled Elian close to him and kissed her on the lips, his hands were roaming over her tight buttocks and groping between her thighs. She playfully struggled, as if to free herself, replying,

"You are just too much, your grace, save yourself for the Spanish Captain."

But she returned the kiss with fervour. Despite the risk of other boats in the area being able to see what was going on, Elian leant forward, pressing herself against Roy in an open invitation to take her on the bridge. Roy never had any intention of going that far, but he could never resist temptation when it was offered and, minutes later, they were in the throes of wild sex.

Later, as they entered the harbour of Cadiz, Roy was allocated a berth near the N443 highway. He went ashore to clear customs, and Elian arranged for the refuelling. They all caught a cab and were driven up to the San Miguel. Roy booked rooms and arranged to meet his crew at the poolside bar in thirty minutes. Roy was on his second whisky when they arrived clad in scanty bikinis, which drew the attention of most males in the area. Roy ordered snacks, and they relaxed in and beside the pool until it was time to change for dinner. They sat overlooking the pool in the bar, and the public address system requested Lord Croft to take a telephone call. All eyes in the bar followed Roy as he left the crew to take a call on the house telephone. Roy hated it when his title was used in such places. Everyone looked at him. It drew far too much attention. Roy picked up the phone, and reception informed him that a Miss Cordoba was at the reception waiting for him. Roy smiled to himself. So Catalina wanted people to see her with an English Lord. He wondered who she was trying to impress. He had no intention of disappointing her. She might well prove to be useful in the future.

Walking into the reception, he saw her standing at the desk, dressed in an off-the-shoulder evening gown designed to show off her assets. It did just that. The support under her breasts lifted them high, displaying her cleavage to the full, and the skirt was slender with a hint of a split up the side. Roy approached her, and she turned and kissed him on the cheek. Roy took her arm and, linking it with his own, escorted the lady back into the bar where all eyes followed the couple. They joined the others, and Roy could hear comments from other men about what a title could do to attract women, and how lucky Lord Croft was to have such a following. Roy revelled in the company of beautiful women, and the drinks flowed.

Over dinner, the conversation was all about boats, and anyone around would have been disappointed if they had expected sex to be on the list of things discussed in the conversation. Roy, however, noticed that Catalina was letting her hair down, and the drink was clouding her judgement as she edged closer to Roy at the table until her thigh was touching his. She became more and more touchy, and she took his hand and laid it on her thigh exposed by the slit up the skirt of her long dress. Roy had not realised how high the slit went until then as she drew his hand higher under cover of the table cloth. Roy turned and looked at her. She smiled openly as she drew his hand higher; she leant forward and whispered something in his ear that the others could not hear. Roy's eyes opened wider as his hand confirmed what she had whispered. She was sans panties, and the invitation for fun later was confirmed. Catalina drank more champagne, and the group finally retired for the night. Roy's crew wished him goodnight as they went to their own rooms in the knowledge that Roy would engage Captain Cordoba well into the night and, if he ran true to form, most of the following day as well. That would be one less patrol that could possibly spot them recovering the drugs from the ocean. Roy had given Elian the satellite phone, and she had to board the boat before dawn with the others and await the coordinates. The three of them would have an early start. None of the three bore Roy any ill feelings, even if all of them felt envy for Captain Catalina Cordoba as she held the place of honour for the night.

Lord Croft opened the door to his room, and Catalina, a little the worse for drink, pushed passed Roy into the room. She stood and faced him and, putting her hands behind her, she caught the zip of her dress and drew it downwards. Roy heard the sound and watched as the dress slid down the young woman's body and fell around her feet. The dress had a built-in support for her breasts, and Roy stood staring at her nakedness. The dark hair emphasised her face and was reflected by the dark wisps of hair under her arms and the untrimmed bush of hair covering her mons pubis. Her breasts were full and firm, her waist slender widening out to her hips and her legs tapering down to well-shaped calves. She half turned, displaying the tight, firm cheeks of her bottom, and she turned back, looking at Roy, completely at ease with her nudity.
"You like what you see, my Lord? Don't stare like that. After all, you have seen it all before," Catalina said, her voice thick with desire and under the effects of the alcohol.
"I know, but not quite so starkly. You are beautiful, to say the least. I did not appreciate your beauty when you were in bed the last time, as I recall it," Roy replied, taking a drink from his hip flask and taking off his own clothes, unable to disguise his arousal and feeling himself respond to the vision before him.
In minutes, he had pushed the dark-haired Spanish beauty back on to the bed, and they were kissing and petting, both becoming more aroused by the minute. Roy moved over her, and she sighed deeply as he entered her, and they began to rut like a pair of animals in heat. Roy felt her orgasm several times before he released into her. They lay together, recovering their breath, and Catalina spoke first,

"Señor, Lord Croft, you get better each time we meet. I know I am high on alcohol, and that has made me more relaxed, but I enjoyed that. It was much better than last time. Perhaps I am not so overwhelmed by being bedded by a Lord."

Roy rolled to one side and lay on his back, his hands behind his head, totally uninhibited by the fact that he was lying naked beside one of the strikingly most beautiful women he had seen in a long time.

"Tell me, Catalina, why you came on to me so hard tonight? You could not keep your hands off me. I'm not that good-looking, and there are plenty more men around that would give anything to be where I am at this moment. Is it my title, my money, or the fact that I'm married and present no threat to you?"

"You are far too clever for me, my Lord, but none of those apply tonight. I am to be married to a captain in the Spanish army in just over a week. He announced two days ago that he was going away with some fellow officers for a few days. How do you say in your country a bachelors' retreat? I have heard about these things. They have wild bouts of drinking and girls of the night to pleasure them. I just wanted fun myself before I got married. I just felt I wanted more than a gigolo. I wanted a man. I don't know anyone who fits the bill more than you. Now, let's not waste time. I need more."

Roy was shaken by her frankness but thanks to the potcheen, he took advantage of her offer, and it was long after they had talked when they finally fell into an exhausted sleep. Dawn was just breaking when Roy heard a soft tap on the door. He left Catalina in a deep sleep as he went to answer the soft tap, tap, tap. It was Elian; she showed no surprise at Roy's nakedness as he opened the door.

"I'm sorry to disturb you, Roy, but I had to let you know we are off. I had the signal that the vessel was in the area, and I want to be at sea before the actual coordinates are sent. I see Catalina proved worthy. I hope you have saved some of that for the rest of us, you rogue."

She pushed the door open a little more and kissed Roy on the mouth.

"Get off with you. I will try to keep the captain busy until you get back," Roy whispered.

"I'm sure you will feel it is your bounden duty to protect your crew," Elian replied as she turned away from the door and hurried towards the lift.

Roy went back to bed, and when he woke up later, he was surprised that Catalina was keener than ever to continue where they had left off the

previous night. It was mid-morning when they had breakfast served in
the room, and they showered and went down to the pool. The pool deck
was crowded, and at Catalina's suggestion, they returned to the room and,
thanks to some of what remained in his hipflask of potcheen, he was able
to comply with her demands and resort to another wild bout of sex. This
time, Roy lay back after they finally completed their goal, and he knew he
had done enough. His groin ached, and he had to admit that Catalina had
drained him for the time being. They showered again and dressed before
going down for a late lunch.

"Where's your crew today, Señor, Lord Croft, or shall I call you Roy?"
Catalina asked "I feel we know each other intimately now. Do you
mind?"

"Call me Roy by all means, Catalina. I think the crew are either checking
the cruiser or have gone in search of our charter group. They seem to be
arriving late for some reason. Have you heard from your army captain, or
are you not expecting him back just yet?"

"I have not heard from him. I don't expect to hear from him for a couple
of days. When are you due to leave? I hope not too soon, I feel we have
unfinished business to complete. I don't know if we will get another
chance."

Roy groaned softly to himself. He knew where this was heading, and he
knew he would have to comply reluctantly. He would need the rest of the
potent potcheen in his hipflask, tucked in the pocket of his overnight bag;
he smiled at the thought; after all, he had to protect his crew from the
clutches of Captain Cordoba and her crew.

Roy felt completely drained, physically and mentally, when he and
Catalina were joined by his crew in the bar just before dinner. Elian fairly
beamed at him and whispered in his ear,

"I see you have done your duty. I have done mine. The goods are safely
aboard, and we can pick up the group at dawn at the usual coordinates. It
means we will have to check out after dinner."

To her surprise, Roy seemed pleased that they would not be spending
another night at the hotel. He turned to Catalina and said,

"I'm sorry, Catalina, but we will have to leave tonight. I have just heard
that we have to pick up our group at dawn further along the coast. Please
excuse me, but it's a well-paid contract, one that I would hate to lose."

"I'm sorry too and disappointed that we must part so soon, but I
understand business is business. Catalina said, her face registering her

disappointment that she would not have another night with his Lordship. "We shall meet again, soon I hope. But let's enjoy dinner before we part, even though we will all have to restrict our wine intake. You because you're sailing tonight, and I because I have an early start tomorrow. I had better go up and get my things together."

Roy looked at her with suspicion. It was the way she said that she had an early start. Something about the inflection in her voice did not sound quite as it should. He would need to look out for Catalina. She was not quite what she appeared to be.

After dinner, Catalina and Roy went up to his room. Roy grabbed his overnight bag and apologised once again for having to leave. As soon as his Lordship left, Catalina rang reception and enquired if anything had been delivered for her. She asked for the parcel to be brought up to Lord Croft's room. The overnight case contained her uniform, and as soon as she had showered, she dressed, putting the evening dress in the overnight bag, which she left at reception to be collected. She rang her second-in-command and asked,

"Lord Croft's boat. Has it left yet?"

"It's pulling out of the marina now, Capitan. What do you want us to do?"

"Get ready to follow them. I will be with you as soon as I can. Don't alert our HQ. If we are going to catch him with what I suspect he is going to collect, I want it to be our catch, not anyone else's. I want a full report on what the boat did yesterday when I arrive."

She had been suspicious of Lord Croft for some time, but the first time she had been distracted, and the second time she had been more suspicious. Her desire to bed him had clouded her judgement but now she had got that out of her system, she could concentrate on getting her man. The arrest of a British Lord with a haul of drugs on board would go well on her record. She wanted to show her husband-to-be that she was every bit as good at her job as he was at his. This was her big chance.

Aboard the cruiser, Roy called the crew up top.

"I want everyone on their toes. Catalina Cordoba's well-contrived meeting, her arrival at dinner, and the subsequent sexual aftermath, I believe, were a ploy. She suspects us and, if I'm correct, she will not be far away. When we dock with the dhow, she will believe we are picking up a drug delivery and will want to board us."

The crew looked shocked at the news.

"Are you sure. Roy?" "If so, she put on a very good act."

"Were you followed yesterday when you recovered the drugs?" Roy asked.

"No, I don't think so. Nothing came anywhere near us, although on several occasions there was a boat on the periphery of the radar scope." Elian admitted.

"Why didn't you tell me? It's small things like that that could get us caught." Roy emphasised.

The whole crew piped up, each trying to make a point.

"We all knew there was a boat out there, but it never came anywhere near." Gail retorted.

"It was too far away for us to identify it." Fiona commented.

"They could not have seen what we were doing. There was too much cloud for satellite surveillance, and we would have heard a plane." Elian pointed out.

Roy held up his hand to stop the cacophony of voices.

"Enough. I understand, but you should have mentioned it to me. It's enough for them to know you were hanging around in an apparently deserted part of the ocean. We have to come up with a reason."

Gael spoke first.

"We are meeting the dhow today, and if you're right, Captain Catalina and her crew will not be far away. How do we explain that?"

Roy thought for a moment and said,

"That's it. We'll brief the passengers that they have been away for a stag weekend . . ."

"There are two women in the group. Explain that," was Elian's comment.

"With AIDS high on the agenda, they took their own strippers," was Roy's quick response.

The crew broke out into laughter,

"Trust you, Roy, to come up with that," was the comment from one of them.

Roy could not ascertain which one, but he continued,

"Our cover will be that you went to meet them at the given point and there was a no-show. You were contacted last night and given new coordinates. Elian, enter it in the log. It's a perfect cover. Get some beers out, not too many. We don't want those bastards drunk, just relaxed. I want them dressed casually and the two women dressed provocatively to make the point."

"Do you think we will get away with it, Roy?" asked Elian.

"I don't see any reason not to, do you? If it is Captain Cordoba, she will have every reason to believe our story; her fiancé has gone away for a similar weekend, something I don't think she was too happy about. Now, get below and make sure everything is put away so that even a detailed search will not reveal any of the secret compartments. This will be our first real test. Something must have aroused her suspicions on a previous occasion."

Roy took the wheel whilst the crew dispersed below to check and recheck that no trace of the weapons or the drugs would be seen on even a detailed examination of the boat.

Catalina Cordoba and her crew followed at a discreet distance, just maintaining radar contact with Lord Croft's cruiser. She was convinced she was right and would wait for the right moment to pounce. She had been suspicious of the amount of instruments and radar equipment aboard the last time she had searched the vessel. She had no proof, and it could have just been that Lord Croft was wealthy and had a thing about gadgets and safety equipment aboard his toy. She was only too well aware that he enjoyed the services of his female crew and she knew how satisfying he could be in bed, but if she could catch him with a consignment of drugs aboard, it would make her career.

Roy arrived at the designated coordinates, and they waited patiently. The dhow was late as usual. Elian spotted the sail as the dhow approached from the shore. The rendezvous went well, and the group boarded. Gael took them all below, and whilst Roy paid the dhow master, she explained the plan. When Roy came below, he was amazed to see that they all wore slacks and loose shirts and the two women were nowhere to be seen. Roy asked,

"Where are the two girls? I can't see them. Gael, it's imperative that they play their part."

"Don't worry, Roy. If you look in the main cabin, you will see what I mean."

Roy pushed open the door, and the two girls were down to a pair of tiny panties and a couple of scarves and a broad grin. From the looks on their faces, they were going to enjoy convincing the Spanish captain that they were a couple of strippers that could whore with the best. Roy smiled and pulled the door to. A few years earlier, he had no doubt that he would have slipped inside the cabin and had unrestricted sex with both young women, but at the moment he had other concerns. Captain Cordoba was one of them. He wondered if he could have given anything away in his sleep. He doubted it. No one had ever complained that he talked in his sleep before. What could have alerted her? He had to get to the bottom of it, but how? Had he have realised that last night would have been the ideal opportunity, but that was behind him, and from the looks of things, he would not have that pleasure again. Going back up on deck, Roy saw that Elian had headed back in the direction they had come from and her heading would take them back in the direction of Cadiz.

Catalina was delighted. She had observed the two vessels converge and had seen movements between the two boats, albeit too far away to be sure of what was being transferred. She could only surmise it was drugs. She had no idea it was trained terrorists playing the part of men on a bachelor party. It was a dangerous game she was playing. If she was right, she would be acclaimed a star in the service. If she was wrong, and Lord Croft complained of harassment, she could well be in trouble. She put the thought out of her mind; Lord Croft struck her as a modern-day buccaneer, an adventurer, womaniser, and a man who was not afraid to take chances. She likened him to characters played by one of her favourite actors, Errol Flynn, of the black and white screen. She had watched the old movies in her village as a child. Modern films could not be shown on their tiny cinema, and they could not afford the cost of new equipment. She could almost imagine herself as the captain of a ship of the line boarding the pirate ship and capturing the swashbuckling pirate captain herself. She was dragged out of her reverie by her first officer.

"Capitan, they are heading back. The dhow is moving away, and Lord Croft's vessel is heading towards us. Do you want to report to HQ and obtain permission to stop and board the vessel?"

"This is our arrest. I do not want to alert anyone else." Captain Cordoba advised her second in command.

"But you know that where the aristocracy is concerned, we ought to report in. Don't you remember Captain Gomez? He got into so much trouble when he arrested Prince Rainier's boat and the Prince was not even aboard." The first officer queried.

"Captain Gomez did not know whose vessel that was. We know exactly who owns this boat and that Lord Croft is aboard," Catalina snapped back, taking her second-in-command by surprise. "They will say nothing when we return with them in tow and the drugs aboard our own boat." The first officer shrugged his shoulders. He had done his best and raised the question. If Captain Cordoba wanted glory, she had to take the risk; it might backfire, and he did not want to go down with her. He would not, however, go as far as reporting the matter to HQ or make any comment in the ship's log. Captain Cordoba gave the order to head south. She did not want it to be obvious; they had lain in wait for Lord Croft; she wanted to approach from the direction they would normally have been patrolling in.

Lord Croft's cruiser was turning to go up the Spanish coast towards Portugal when Catalina made her move. They approached fast from the south after announcing their arrival by radio and requesting *The Sea Nymph* to heave to and wait to be boarded. Under normal circumstances, realising that it was Captain Cordoba, Roy would not have given it a second thought. He gave the signal, and the festivities began below. The high speed patrol soon came alongside, and Captain Cordoba, in her most official voice, requested that they be allowed to board as it was suspected they were carrying illicit cargo. Roy threw the crew of the patrol a line and welcomed them to come aboard. The music from below could plainly be heard as Roy's entertainment equipment pumped out music.

"Good morning, Captain Cordoba. What a pleasant surprise? We seem to bump into one another with alarming regularity. Is this an official visit? You sounded so formal on the radio. Now what is this about illicit cargo? The only cargo we have aboard are revellers. We picked up our bachelor and his friends, and they even brought their own entertainment with them. I hope you won't be too shocked by what you find? I always believe in live and let live so long as no damage is done to my boat."

"Lord Croft, I am in no mood for jokes. This is serious business, and I demand that you allow us to search this vessel. Refusal will mean that I will escort you to the nearest port under arms and carry out the search there."

"So formal, Captain, be my guest, search as you will. I will have one of my crew accompany you rather than myself. I would not like to distract you or your officers from carrying out your duties. I must add, though, that I find your attitude disturbing and intend to formally lodge a complaint that we seem to be subject to a continual harassment by your patrol whenever we are in Spanish waters. As you have no proof that I have done anything wrong and no real authority as we are still outside Spanish waters, I take the matter very seriously. Please continue and note that I have not resisted your illegal boarding or your unsolicited demand to search this vessel."

The search crew from the Spanish patrol moved along the deck and opened the door leading down to the main cabin. Captain Cordoba stopped and stared. There was a woman clad in nothing but a thin silk scarf gyrating in front of a group of men, with cans of beer in their hands, lewdly commenting on the attributes of the stripper. The presence of uniforms drew the attention of the leader, who rose and turned off the music. He beckoned the stripper, who went over and, without a word being spoken, she sat on his lap, her scarf falling to one side, and her nudity was complete. Captain Cordoba opened her mouth to speak when the master cabin door opened and a second girl, wearing only a G-string and a scarf around her top, put her head out and asked,

"What's wrong? The music stopped before Beryl's dance finished?"

Her eyes followed the direction the others were staring, and her mouth hung open in mock surprise.

"Oh, I'm sorry. Are you another strip group? We were not told about that," she said.

Captain Cordoba glared at the girl in the doorway, her face clouding with anger that anyone would confuse her with a common stripper.

"Get dressed, both of you. I'm here to conduct an official search of this vessel, and that means all of its passengers."

Connie, the girl in the doorway, laughed, and she was joined by Beryl. Both stood and walked towards the glowering captain, and Connie said,

"I don't know much about searches, duck, but I don't know where I'm going to hide much contraband in this outfit, do you?" Adding, "If it will turn you on, Lady Captain, you can body search me here and now I'm sure the boys would love that. They would think it was all part of the entertainment. Pity you did not arrive later. You could have joined us in our act."

Captain Cordoba brushed past and went down to the lower levels to begin the search with her second officer. The first thing that struck Catalina was the extra fuel tanks. She knew what the hull should look like from plans she had studied. Nothing had prepared her for what she could see. There were extra tanks everywhere with crossover fuel pumps to balance the boat as fuel levels dropped. She could see that some tanks could be flooded in a rough sea to retain stability. It was obvious to her that this conversion was no ordinary one, and the range of the cruiser was considerable, possibly even enough to cross the Atlantic. She wished she had the opportunity to strip the hull down, but without evidence, it would mean her job was on the line, if it was not there already. More hands would have helped, but the first officer had remained on deck to ensure that no one left the cruiser. The search took two hours, and a very disgruntled Captain Cordoba reappeared; her annoyance at finding nothing was embarrassing her in front of her crew. She knew Roy Croft was carrying drugs, and apart from pulling the cruiser to pieces, they had made as thorough a search as possible and had come up with nothing.

Roy smiled as she came up on to the bridge and, in a somewhat contrite mood, she began, "Lord Croft, I can only offer my sincerest apologies to you, your crew, and your passengers. I only hope my brusque and rude behaviour has not affected their enjoyment. It is obvious that the tip-off we had was incorrect, even though it was from a reliable source. I beg your forgiveness and wish you well and a safe passage back to Ireland. We will meet again in more congenial circumstances in the not-too-distant future, I hope."
"I accept your apology, Captain. If it were not for the vigilance of teams like yours, I'm sure more smugglers would get away with their crimes. Now, I am going to be late back with my group, so excuse me. I must be on my way. Good day, Captain."

Captain Cordoba and her officers re-boarded the patrol boat. The lines were cast free, and Roy gave Elian the nod, and they headed north on their way back to Ireland. Captain Cordoba stood and watched as the cruiser and its passengers moved away, the gap between the boats widening with each second. She was certain in her own mind that there had been drugs aboard, and her senses told her so. She could almost smell them. Why couldn't they have sniffer dogs aboard patrol boats? She was sure they would have been able to spot the haul. She knew she had blown the only chance she would get. She would never dare to challenge Lord Croft again without good reason and, unless a miracle happened, it was unlikely that that would be the case. She gave the order to recommence the patrol. Remembering how good the bastard was in bed, whatever the outcome, she had got something out of her meeting with the elusive Lord Croft.

The music had started almost as soon as the two boats separated, and Roy had gone below to re-establish some decorum. He made it clear that he was not in the habit of running a floating brothel, and now that the danger of discovery was over, the two women should get dressed and the men should settle down. There was no more beer. One was sufficient to paint the scene. They were welcome on deck, but his crew were strictly off limits to all passengers. He went back on deck grinning. Elian looked at him. She was sure that if he had been given the chance, he would have loved to take Beryl and Connie into the cabin and pleasure them both. Both were attractive women and not averse to a little fun and deception on the side. Gael appeared from below, and once she had joined Elian and himself back on deck, Roy took the opportunity to ask Gael how the search had gone.

"It was a very thorough search, Roy. They crawled into every crawl space we had. They tapped and prodded, but thanks to the skill of the armourers and the Williams's boatyard crew, they found absolutely nothing. I think that little minx was out to get you. What did you do to her last night? It's not like you, but for some reason, she must have been disappointed."

"If she was, it was with the search, not the sex. I can assure you on that point," Roy said, grinning like the proverbial Cheshire Cat.

Gael and Elian smiled. Both of them knew that, in all probability, Roy was right. He did not have many sexual encounters where his partner was disappointed. In fact, it was something they had never considered.

The rest of the journey went without incident, and Roy offloaded the trainees in the village where they were met by IRA representatives. The group climbed on the bus provided, and Roy and his crew moved out into the Atlantic. They had been tried and tested once again and proven to be almost invincible once again. It was late when they got back to the small harbour at the castle, and the crew decided they would sleep aboard and put the boat with its illicit cargo in the boathouse the following morning. Roy felt drained. Captain Cordoba had put a lot of worry on his shoulders, and he just needed bed. He had had enough excitement for one day to last him for some time.

Chapter 16

Janet had been sound asleep when Roy fell into bed beside her, and when Cathleen brought in the morning tea, Janet had been relieved to see him asleep beside her. Shaking him awake, she gave him a kiss on the cheek and asked him,

"Why didn't you wake me when you came in?"

"You were sound asleep, and with the baby so close, the last thing I wanted was to startle you. Thanks for waking me. I have to get the boat in the boathouse. She needs a check on the hull. We scraped the bottom on a rock, going too near the shore. No real damage, but we just need to check."

Roy knew that it was a lie, but it would explain getting the boat out of the water and allow him to transfer the drugs haul to the airtight safe in the armoury two floors below. He showered and dressed before going down to breakfast where his crew was already awake waiting for him.

"I have not mentioned our little incident with the Spanish captain. I told Janet I had scraped the bottom getting too near the shore, so if she asks, you know what to say."

They nodded their agreement, well aware that Roy had never told her what he did on charter work. She would have worried too much if she had known. They finished breakfast and went through the passage to the workshop. They missed Bridget. It was her day off, and Elian took over the winch. Roy was glad they were not handling the corroded shells as the recovery was nowhere near as smooth as when Bridget worked the recovery winch. Finally, they had the boat chocked and secure and began to unload the soft watertight packs of white powder and transfer it to the safe below.

Once that task had been completed, Elian suggested that as they had a few days free from charter, could she service the motors and make enquiries about new turbochargers to give considerably more power to the engines? She had heard about a new product that increased the output of the engine by as much as twenty per cent over that generated by standard turbochargers.

"They would give us a faster pull-off as well as a better top speed. They may reduce the range, but not significantly, only if we used them to the full all the time, and we know that's not what we need. The power would be there when we need it."

"That sounds an excellent idea. Elian, go ahead and just check the cost with me if you want to go ahead with the conversion and let me know if you have strange engineers in the workshop. We would not want them to see anything out of the ordinary now, would we?"

Once Roy had the office to himself, he rang Sam on the private secure cell and broke the news about the boarding and then confirmed that the collection of both people and goods had been completed satisfactorily. Sam was concerned that the cruiser had been the subject of such a thorough search but was happy everything had turned out for the best.

"Why don't you come over and tell us all about it, Roy?"

"I would rather leave it. Janet is pretty close, and I don't want to risk her going into labour whilst I'm away. She has managed to last this long. She was worried she would start whilst I was on the last charter."

Roy was still talking when the door burst open, and it was Cathleen,

"You best come now, sir. It's the missus. I think she started."

"Got to go, Sam. It looks like my hunch was right. Speak to you later."

Roy ran along the passage and upstairs. Janet was coming down the wide staircase with her bag in her hand.

"Sorry, Roy, but I think you had better take me in. I know I'm close. I made a bit of a mess upstairs. Tell Cathleen to help Morag clean up, will you?"

Roy took the bag off her and swung her up into his arms.

"You are two stone lighter already. Now, let's get you in the Land Cruiser and down to the hospital. I'll come back for your bag in a minute."

The journey to the hospital was uneventful, but Janet's pains were established on a regular basis by the time they arrived. She was admitted into a private ward, and Roy was allowed to sit with her. Two hours later, she gave birth to a little girl. He had stayed with her throughout the birth, and now she lay back, clutching the small bundle against her breast. He stayed, giving Janet encouragement and telling her how pretty the new born child looked. Then he was asked to let his wife get some rest and told that he could see her the next day. Roy drove home. New born children to him were all the same, pink, their features as yet unformed, their tiny faces wrinkled, and he hoped that the child would look better in the morning when they had managed to clean her and her wrinkled face had become more normal.

Roy called in at the Delaney household, although it was late. Kate and Sam were pleased to see him. They congratulated him on his new daughter and asked what he was going to call her. Roy had no idea. He had not had any chance to discuss it with Janet before the birth. He had been too busy. Sam opened a bottle of vintage champagne to wet the baby's head, and they sat drinking for a couple of hours. "I have to get back home. I have to break the news to the staff." Roy said.

"Roy, you can't drive in your state. I'll ring and tell the staff." Kate said seemingly concerned for Roy's safety. "You can go up to the guest room. You can shower and go from here in the morning. If you want, I'll send the driver, and he can fetch you some clean clothes and bring back Sean for you to take and see his new sister."

Sam seemed worse than Roy, and the two of them went upstairs, leaving Kate to telephone and make arrangements with the chauffeur for morning. Roy had just climbed into the clean sheets when the door opened. It was Kate in her robe. She crossed the room and came to the side of the bed. She pulled the tie, and the robe slid down her body and pooled on to the floor.

Roy was sober in a second,

"Jesus, Kate. What are you doing? Sam is only next door. We can't do anything now."

Kate, far from halting what she was doing, pulled back the covers and was pleased to see that Roy was completely naked in bed. She climbed in beside him and whispered,

"I slipped something into Sam's last brandy. He will be out of it for a few hours. Now, I know Janet will be no help tonight. Let's see what I can do. You don't object to having sex with me in this state, do you? After all, you got me this way."

When the housekeeper brought in the tea the following morning, Kate was nowhere to be seen, and as Roy stepped out of the shower, he could hear Sean's voice calling him. Wrapping himself in a bath towel, he opened the door and called out,

"I'm here, Sean."

Sean bounded along the corridor and leapt into his father's arms, his face beaming with a broad grin.

"I have a new sister," he boasted proudly. "Did you know, Daddy?"

Roy smiled, nodding his head, as he hugged the young lad who had asked the question in all innocence.

"Hurry up, Daddy. I want you to take me to see her. Come on, you old slowcoach, get dressed. Breakfast is ready and I'm starving. Uncle Sam and Auntie Kate are waiting for you at the table."

Roy set the lad down and picked up the bag left at the door.

"I'll be with you as soon as I'm dressed. Now, go down and tell Auntie Kate I'm coming as fast as I can."

Roy followed his son, and they all ate a hearty breakfast. Kate, for some reason, seemed to be the hungriest of all. Her appetite seemed endless. Sam put it down to the fact that she was eating for two.

Roy took Sean to see the new baby, and they were both pleased that the new child was pretty as a picture. Her round face looked up from her mother's breast, and she gave a windy smile and turned back to continue where she had left off seconds before. Sean was in raptures. He seemed enchanted with the latest addition to the family and ran along the hospital corridor, announcing that he had a new baby sister.

"What are we going to call her?" Roy asked his wife.

"Well, to keep it Irish like Sean, I wondered how you would feel about Sheenagh?" Janet whispered softly.

"That sounds good to me. Sheenagh it is then. How long are they keeping you in here? You know I'm fairly hopeless organising domestics. I stayed at Sam's last night after having a few drinks to celebrate Sheenagh's birth."

"I hope that's all you had. Was Sam home?"

"Yes, he was, and I slept in the guest room next door, so don't worry your head about that."

Janet studied his face. She could not make up her mind if he was being truthful or not. Not to worry. He was here, and that was what mattered. She told him to let Cathleen or Bridget organise the food.

"I've told them what to do whilst I'm in here. Now, I'm not sending you away, but I don't think the hospital staff are enjoying our son racing about. I will see you this evening. Now, get off home, the two of you."

Roy returned home, and Bridget had lunch waiting. When he had finished, Morag took Sean off for his lessons, and Bridget cleared the table and served the coffee.

"Anything else I can get you, sir?" she asked.

Making it perfectly clear what she was offering, she seemed quite disappointed when Roy refused her offer and walked along to the workshop. His mind wandered to Elian's idea of improved turbochargers on the boat and was keen to discover what she had done about it. Elian was poring over papers and making calculations on a sheet beside her. Hearing him come in, she looked up and smiled.

"I've spoken to the manufacturers, and when I mentioned that it was for Lord Croft, they were prepared to send down a couple of technicians to confirm the suitability of their product and to ascertain if they would do what we wanted."

"That's fine, Elian, but I need to know the cost and how quickly they can be fitted."

Elian told him the cost and said that if he was agreeable, they would be able to send two technicians to do the survey, and if they were satisfied, they would fit the new turbochargers at the same time. Roy enquired how soon, and Elian's smile broke into a broad grin.

"Tomorrow. I told them to go ahead."

Roy looked at her with mock severity and moved towards her. She rose and put her arms around his neck and whispered,

"I understand that congratulations are in order. Janet is not going to be much help at the moment, is she? Why don't we go aboard? I can think of a wonderful way to celebrate the new baby and the new power we shall have on the boat. Although from what I can feel, turbochargers are not going to be necessary for what I have in mind."

When Roy got back to the kitchen, Sean was eating his supper and would soon be ready for bed. Roy ate quickly and, after reading his son a short story, left to visit Janet at the hospital. He would be glad when all this was over and he could settle down to a routine and get back to sea. That, however, was not going to be the case in a hurry. Sam rang and told him that there would be a committee meeting to discuss his proposals with regard to the joining or taking over of the two drug barons' areas. Roy arrived to be met by Kate, as usual, and she kissed him on the cheek. They are in there waiting for you, so go give them your best. Roy opened the door and walked into the board room. The chairs around the table were filled with faces he recognised and respected. The vacant chair was next to Sam, always a good sign. They had been briefed, and now Roy had to convince them why he felt they should not share but take over.

Roy spoke at length, explaining each and every point, emphasising the importance of keeping the flow of drugs going and the price cheap. He told them that it was his belief that if they joined, then the other parties would accept the drugs the committee had on offer and sell them at their own inflated prices, pushing the price out of reach of the very targets they were aiming at, the young men of England. His speech had them enthralled. He spoke like a true Irish patriot, pointing out how men had died trying to push the British from Irish soil and how many of their Irish compatriots had died during the potato famine and been forced to leave the country during that time. He had pointed out how men had died for the cause during the struggle, and now that the new strategy was beginning to take effect, the committee wanted to water down the force by joining gangs with no stronger objective than pure greed. By the time Roy had finished, Sam believed the whole committee would have risen as a man and followed him into battle and to certain death. They gave him a standing ovation, something Sam had never ever witnessed them doing before. It was agreed that they would transfer the drugs using sleepers and not join the gangs but take over their territory, whatever the cost. When everyone had gone, Sam sat with Roy and, taking him into his embrace, whispered,

"That speech you made today was truly inspiring. I believe you are becoming more Irish by the day, a true believer in the cause."

"I learnt well after you brought me to my senses as to what I have really become. Gone are the old days and the old ways. I treat each challenge as I did in the boardroom, and I give it my all. It has to work in life whatever you do. If it's something you believe in, then you give it everything you've got."

Sam smiled and, going to the cabinet, he reached down for some Napoleon brandy.

"I'm told this is from the very boat destined for Elbe, but not all of its cargo arrived. We Irish diverted some of it for better days, and I happen to have a couple of bottles. I think today's business deserves a drink for both of us."

The next few days saw Janet back home with Sheenagh. New turbochargers were fitted to the cruiser, and Roy started making preparations for another visit to England. He had to first go over his plans and proposals with Sam. The meeting was set up, and Roy drove over to the Delaney household with Sean, leaving Janet at home with Sheenagh. Sean could hardly wait to arrive. He wanted to ride the bicycle Uncle Sam and Auntie Kate had brought him. The grounds at the house were so much flatter than the gardens at home, and when Daddy had finished the meeting, he was hoping Uncle Sam would play trains with him; he loved trains. The constant chatter from the young man kept Roy's mind from dwelling on the meeting and the inherent dangers of his trip to England, for no matter how well he planned the takeover of the drug barons' domain; they could always be one step ahead. He could be the one compromised; he knew he was not infallible. Good planning in these matters was absolutely essential. Finally, they pulled up in front of the huge gates protecting the entrance to the Delaney estate. The vehicle number plate recognition system identified the Range Rover, and the camera scanned the driver and any other occupants and, finally, the body heat scanner checked for hidden bodies that might be concealed from view. The computer voice welcomed him,

"Good afternoon, Lord Croft. I'm sorry for the delay. Please park at the front of the building."

Roy was impressed. Sam had upgraded his security over the last few days, and he would speak to him about it at the meeting. The huge steel gates swung open to admit him, and he drove to the front of the building where Kate stood at the open front door. As soon as the door locks were released on the vehicle, Sean was out of the car and running towards Kate. She bent down and swept him up into her arms and gave him a hug. Roy stepped out of the vehicle and called out,

"Be careful, Sean. Auntie Kate should not be lifting you in her state of health." Kate grinned back.

"Don't be such an old woman, Roy. I'm fine. I'm having a baby. I'm not ill. Go on through to the study. I'll take Sean. I'm sure he can't wait to get on that bike."

Roy kissed her on the cheek and patted her swollen belly.

"How's this one going?"

"Fine, thank you, sir. Not long to go, I hope. I seem to have been pregnant forever." Kate replied

Roy rubbed Sean's head and left them to go through the house whilst he turned and walked along the hall to the study where Sam sat waiting for him.

Sam stood and walked towards Roy, his hand extended to shake Roy's hand. They shook hands and embraced as family, and Sam said,

"Good to see you, Roy. I'll get you a drink. The usual?"

Roy nodded, and when he had sat down, he commented,

"Beefed up the security. I see it must have cost you a packet."

"I felt I could not be too careful with the baby on the way. The last thing I want is bloody intruders on the property. You should think about it yourself. You know you can't be too careful these days, especially in the business we are in," Sam responded.

"I've always worked on the assumption that the more security you have on show, the more people think you have to protect, but I'll bear it in mind. Now, let's get down to business."

Roy outlined his plans for both London and Manchester and told Sam what he wanted in the way of backup.

Sam sat and listened, nodding his approval as the details were laid out.

"Are you sure four men are enough besides the camera crew?" he asked.

"Any more would draw attention, and I have Gael and Elian as well. I believe it's more than enough. I'll detail the arms they are to carry as soon as they contact me," Roy replied.

"It's a good plan. Just be careful. I don't want you too exposed on this one. I've made arrangements for our agents in the area to move up a notch and let it be known that they have adequate supplies of drugs available, and that message will go out the instant your plan has been put into practice and the opposition has been eliminated, not a second before. Then, if, for any reason our plans fail, we can still transact with the London mob as we originally planned until we get another chance. The drugs will have to be the real thing at the time of exchange. Let's hope no authority wants to check them. Ha! Ha!"

"I hope to God we don't have to do that. I could be dead if that happened," Roy said, a deep frown crossing his forehead.

The two men went over the plans several times, adjusting and simplifying every detail, trying to ensure that nothing would be left to chance. Finally, they were satisfied, and Sam agreed to set up each meeting. By the time the meeting was over, it was getting quite late, and Roy declined the offer to stay for dinner.

"I'll get back with Sean. He has to have his bath, and you know Morag. She will be getting impatient that her charge is not home."

The following morning, Roy went over his plans with Elian and Gael. Both were impressed with the fine detail and could not wait to get going. Elian slipped away to get the boat ready and ensure that the new identity and the nationality flag was aboard. The boat was to be out of Falmouth, and a boat called *Wave Dancer* had been identified and its name port of registration and ID number had to be in place before they set sail. The weapons were identified and checked over, silencers and ammunition on board, and the other equipment were stowed in the hold as soon as it arrived. The weekend arrived, and they were ready to go. The others would join them in London. Sam had assured Roy that they were trained men who knew how to handle themselves, from the old days, and were not afraid to kill when required to do so. They would be more than adequately rewarded for their efforts.

Janet watched them go still concerned as to why Roy had to resort to the cloak-and-dagger methods of changing the name of the cruiser. It all seemed so dramatic to her, but she shrugged her shoulders. After all, if Roy wanted to play games, why should she object? It was what he wanted, and if changing the cruiser's name added spice and excitement to his life, so be it. She wondered if it was legal or what the outcome would be. She only hoped he would be safe. What with his involvement with the new IRA and his secret meeting, who knew where it would all end? The boat headed out into the North Atlantic and was gone. She went back into the house to wait; she knew he would not contact her again until whatever he was doing was all over. It was something she had got used to over time.

Elian headed south. They would go up the English Channel and into the Thames. A berth had been booked, and the others would meet them on Monday morning. Confirmation had been received that the required vehicles had been stolen and cloned with other similar vehicles so as to not draw attention. Permits had been applied for and granted, thanks to Sam's connections. They were ready to put the plan into action. They moved up the Channel under the watchful eyes of the coastal radar, a situation that Roy hated but realised was a necessity; the Channel was not very wide, and a lot of shipping used the strip of water, a gateway to the northern European ports as well as London and the container ports on the British East Coast. Without the system, similar to air traffic control, it would be bedlam. Finally, they entered the Thames and began to move upriver. They had a berth booked for two days under the guise of making a film. All the permits had been granted, and the meeting was set up for the following day. The special berth booked on their behalf was near the Embankment Gardens, in the very heart of London. The Marriott Hotel overlooked the area perfectly, and a suite had been booked on the top floor, perfect for an assassination shot. They tied up at the berth and displayed the special permit in case of inquisitive eyes or the arm of authority. They checked into the suite in the name of Mr and Mrs McMillan and Miss D. Ottery. The hotel had been warned that, for filming, the suite had to be available for the full three days, although it might not be occupied for that length of time. The suite was not to be serviced during the period of occupation. Gael set up Roy's sniper rifle in readiness for the following day and, during the night, she fired two shots into a small target near where the meeting was to take place.

Sam set up the exchange explaining that, for the first one, they wanted security in one of the most public places so that no funny business could occur. This would be the arrangement until full trust had been established between both parties. Sam had explained to Ivan that he felt his men would be safer if the exchange took place in broad daylight and in as public a place as possible. Ivan had reluctantly agreed, telling Sam that was not the way they usually did business. Their way was always at night and at the back of a busy club or in a quiet car park. Sam had emphasised that it had to be this way or not at all. The Russian's greed had clinched the deal. If these amateurs wanted it that way, so be it. The drugs were of excellent quality, and if the fools wanted to sell them at that price, who was he to argue? The deal was too good to miss. The exchange was set for 3 p.m. exactly. The main pathway would be where Roy would stand; he would be wearing a grey coat and a trilby hat and carrying a red bag containing the drugs. Ivan would approach and hand Roy a briefcase. He could have someone with him to check the bag and, once the exchange had been made, Roy would walk away, and Ivan and his man could take the red bag containing the drugs. Ivan was even more convinced that he was dealing with stupid amateurs, and he smiled as he agreed. He would have four of his men in situ earlier to ensure that everything was OK, before he got anywhere near the exchange point, just as a precaution.

Three o'clock arrived, and Roy stood nervously in the spot, checking that the others were in place. There was Elian on a bench nearby, a man with the sweeper's cart across the oval, a tramp on another bench, and a policeman walking up and down. The vehicle was parked on the road, in readiness, and the van was parked behind it. The tape and notices were hidden but ready. Roy saw Ivan walk towards him with Gregoff, his number two. They were obviously nervous as Gregoff kept looking around, but he relaxed as he saw the London bobby saunter away from their man. No one was going to try anything in full view of the police. Even so, four of Ivan's men were sitting on benches close by. Ivan spoke softly as he approached Roy,

"This is all very melodramatic, my friend, and so unnecessary. We will not be doing this your way again. Next time, it's my way, get it?"

Roy nodded his agreement as Gregoff bent down and unzipped the bag. He used a small knife to slit one of the plastic bags and slipped his finger inside and licked the end. It's OK, Ivan. It's the real thing. The next second, a van with a camera crew drove into the park, and Ivan looked round.

"What is thi . . . ?"

That was as far as he got. A small red hole appeared in the centre of his forehead, and a spray emanated from the back of his skull. Gregoff pulled out his gun, but even as he drew it, the front of his head exploded in a red spray of blood. The supporting four ran towards Ivan as he fell forward: one was taken out by the policeman, one by the tramp, and the other two by the man with the sweeper's cart using a silenced Uzi. The crowd stopped dead in its tracks and a woman screamed, but almost as the first shot was heard, the vehicle with the cameras on the back appeared and everyone believed that it was all make-believe. The van arrived, and the bodies were loaded into the van with the camera apparently filming it all. Roy and Elian walked away slowly, carrying the bag and the briefcase. The camera crew threw buckets of water on to the spot where the blood had run and then drove away to the applause of the crowd. No one was any the wiser. The tapes announcing the movie shoot were left in place, and the van and the vehicle with the cameras on the back edged back out of the park. The Russians had not got off a single shot. Roy walked into the Marriott, and as soon as he was in the suite, he sent a message to Sam using the cell phone. The signal was sent and the announcement was made; there were new drug boys on the block. Sam confirmed with his men that the bodies in the van should be disposed of and that evening a raft for an office block would be cast, but under the hard-core base would be six bodies belonging to the Russian gang. There were many Irish crews building in London. Any of one them could have been contacted by the old IRA. using the network set up for just such a job. The first part of the takeover had gone smoothly. Everything was packed aboard the cruiser, and within half an hour, they were on their way downriver heading for the sea. No alarm had been raised, and the six o'clock news would report that an apparent shootout in a London park was a false alarm. It was only the scene of a film set, for which full permits had been granted by the authorities. Roy was only happy when they had reached the mouth of the Thames and were once again in the traffic going through the English Channel towards Falmouth and Land's End in Cornwall.

The next day saw Roy heading up through the Irish Sea and the coast of Wales towards Anglesey. The original name was now on the bow and the stern. Once Roy had cleared the Isle of Anglesey, he turned, and from there they made it to Granville Williams's boatyard. Roy knew that the cruiser would be safe in Granville's yard, come what may. Roy and his team had decided to park the cruiser there and hire a Range Rover to get into Manchester. The ship *Canal* was fine, but it was long, and they could be stopped almost anywhere along the waterway if anything went wrong. The vehicle had been hired in Birmingham and driven by one of Sam's men to the boatyard. Roy accepted Granville's offer to take him, Elian, and Gael out to supper, but he spent a long time on the phone with Sam discussing the next operation. Both decided that the last method, although extremely effective, would not work with Baba. He was too wary. Finally, after Sam had conferred with his contacts in Manchester, they came up with a plan. Roy rang off and waited for Sam to contact Baba Abasha, He would come back to him as soon as the arrangements were made. The meet was to be in a public car park near Manchester Airport where the controversial runway extension was being made, if Baba would agree.

Roy was eating when his cell phone rang. Sam simply said,
"Tomorrow night, 10 p.m. Place as arranged. Good luck."
Roy nodded to the two women, and shortly afterwards, Roy apologised for their early departure but promised Granville and Kirsty that they would make it up next time. Roy packed an overnight bag and joined Elian and Gael. The weapons and bags were carefully placed in the Range Rover, and they set off for Manchester.

They checked in at the airport Holiday Inn and drove to the site through New Mills. Then, following the signs for the new car park, they took a left into Small Lane; they followed it round until they reached Hobcroft Lane and on to the newly laid road leading to the runway extension site and the recently laid car park. The lengthening of the runway had been necessitated by the introduction of the new Airbus 380 and the new car park to cater for the increased number of passengers the larger aircraft would carry. The gate to the site was unlocked as arranged and Roy dropped off Gael with the sniper rifle. They climbed on to the roof of the temporary buildings housing the site office, and there was the hide, ready as arranged. Gael checked and found it easy to slide into, and her view over the newly developed car park was excellent. She slid the weapon into the hide and resealed the entrance. They stood back; even with the glare of the sodium lights from the site, unless you knew where to look, the hide was virtually invisible. Roy had insisted that the hide should not be able to be seen from the ground, the air, or the roof itself, and whoever Sam had got to do the work had done an excellent job. They left the site and drove back to the hotel to grab a few hours' sleep. The site would not be so quiet during the week, so they wanted to get there early in the morning to set up the reception for Baba and his Nigerian gang of drug dealers.

The next day was busy. Once Gael was ensconced in her hide, Roy and Elian made sure that the backup team knew what to do and where to stand. The Nigerians would have no hesitation in shooting first and asking questions later, if they bothered with questions at all. They would simply pick up the drugs and drive away. Once Roy was satisfied, he checked with Mr O'Flynn, the night superintendent, and the necessary arrangements were made. He had he promised that the backup truck would be nearby, but out of sight. All was set. Roy and Elian drove to New Mills and had a meal before driving back to the rendezvous. As Roy had expected, Baba and his men had arrived early and sussed out the site. Roy drove on to the car park and parked in the spot he had arranged with Mr O'Flynn. Roy flashed the headlights as prearranged, and two men alighted from the first car. Neither of them was Baba. They moved back to the car, parked to the left and slightly behind, and opened the rear door. The two men drew weapons, and Baba got out. The driver and the passenger alighted and stood behind Baba; they also drew weapons. Roy got out and pulled the bag of drugs from the rear door and set it down on the ground. Obed got out of the rear of the first car, and Baba said,

"Mr McNally, bring da bag to da middle. I want Obed to check da stuff."

Assured of his backup and with the added security of his protective vest, Roy walked to a point midway between the Range Rover and the spot where Baba stood flanked by his bodyguards.

"Is all this drama necessary?" Roy asked, pointing to the guns.

"Dat's for me to decide. Check da stuff, Obed, and God help you, Mr Fucking McNally, if this is some kind of trick."

Roy stood to one side whilst Obed bent down, unzipped the large holdall, and rummaged around, going deep into the bags packed inside. He drew out a packet and jabbed it with his knife. The powder spilt on to the back of his hand, and he drew his tongue along the white dust. He replaced the bag, then took out a second, and after slitting it, he poured a line along his forefinger. The white powder was stark against the blackness of his finger. He bent his head down and sniffed the line up into his wide nostrils. He smiled. The whiteness of his teeth seemed almost to glint as he said,

"It's da same as before. Good stuff. It's OK, Baba. It's on da level."

Baba reached into the car and withdrew the briefcase. He said,

"You may want to check the money before we exchange, Mr McNally. Obed, come get the case. We have work to do."

"Send one of the others. Obed can stay with the goods." Roy shouted, "I want no one saying we switched the stuff whilst you were not watching."

"Enjiro, do as the man says."

The driver's door of Baba's car opened, and a tall man stepped out. As he stood, he dwarfed the others, and he took the proffered briefcase and slowly but deliberately walked with confidence towards Roy. As he approached, he undid the locks and opened the lid. Roy could see the money stacked in bundles, and just as he stretched forth his hand, there was a soft thud. A startled cry came from the roof of the temporary building, and a black figure holding a rifle toppled off the roof. Gael had spotted him take a line of sight on Roy, and she was taking no chances. She shot him with her silenced 9mm Beretta, hitting him in the chest. She took aim. The big black man standing in front of Roy was partially blocking the shot on Baba. She took aim and squeezed the trigger. Enjiro gave a gasp as his face crumpled and he fell backwards. The briefcase fell, and wads of notes lay scattered on the tarmac. Baba dived for cover inside the car The sodium floodlights behind Roy came to life, effectively blinding Baba's guards. Roy threw himself to the floor, drawing his own gun out at the same time.

Bedlam broke out with bullets flying in all directions. Gael could see the car with Baba inside but could not see well enough to get a kill shot. One of the guards jumped into the driver's seat and started the engine. Gael lined up the shot. A hole appeared in the centre of the windscreen, and Baba was covered with what remained of the guard's head. The guards fired in all directions, but they were blinded by the lights. The rest of Roy's team appeared from nowhere, and the sound of silenced Uzis and the clunk of bullets hitting metal was all that could be heard. Baba tried to make a run for it, but he could not escape the brilliance of the sodium glare. Gael finally had him in her sights, and he gave a lurch to the left as the sniper's bullet found its mark in his right temple. Then the guns fell silent, and the only sound was the revving engine of Baba's car. Roy walked towards it and reached in through the shattered window and turned off the key. Silence fell on the scene of total devastation; the bodies of Baba's guards lay still, their weapons lying beside them. Roy checked around and found that there were no casualties on his side; the floodlights had done the trick, and the guards had been firing blindly, unable to locate any of Roy's band of men and women.

The silence was broken as the site came to life. The bodies were carried out on to the prepared runway and placed deep down into the recessed trench. A huge cement mixer arrived, and several tons of concrete were poured into the deep recess, bringing the level up to that of the rest of the area. A large flatbed truck appeared and, using its grab, it lifted Baba's car and dropped in on to the flat area. Then the grab lifted the guard's car, partially crushing the roof, and placed it partially on top of the first. It pushed down, and a chain was thrown over the load, securing it in place. Then the lorry drove away. Next, a water cart appeared, and water was splashed on to the surface. Then a road sweeper drove over the wet area and washed the surface of the car park free of the blood stains, brushing up the scattered bullet casings at the same time. Roy had, in the meantime, packed away the holdall and picked up the bundles of money. Mr O'Flynn stepped forward, holding out his hand. Roy counted out the amount, agreed by Sam, from the briefcase. Mr O'Flynn smiled and said,

"Give my regards to Sam, the old devil. Tell him anytime he needs us, we are there for him. The contractors will be here at dawn, and several layers of tarmac will cover up any signs of our friends lying under that concrete. The painters will be setting out the parking spaces, and the car park will be open to the public at the end of the week. There'll be no trace of anything that's gone on here. Long live the Republic. Now, be off with you. I'll make sure there's nothing left for anyone to find."

Gael had joined Elian, who had been in the Range Rover in case anything had gone wrong and she had to get Roy away quickly. Roy climbed into the passenger's seat, and Elian drove away from the second phase of the operation. Sam was overjoyed when he heard the news from Roy, and he alerted the men poised ready to take over Baba's contacts. The small packet trade across the Irish Sea was well underway. None of the sleepers travelling would carry any significant amount of drugs, but the tide of traffic was swelling by the day and stocks were building fast. Enough drugs would soon be in place to provide sufficient supply for the newest areas of acquisition.

Roy drove back to the Holiday Inn, and the three of them slept soundly, too stressed out for any sexual interplay that would come later, when they were back on the boat. The following morning, they drove back to Granville's yard. Roy stopped off to buy papers, but there was no news of anything from the London papers or the Manchester papers to indicate that any of the IRA's activities over the previous few days had been discovered. Granville complained bitterly when Roy told him that he was leaving straightaway.

"Oh, Roy, you can't go yet. Kirsty will be so disappointed. Do you have to go?"

"I'm afraid I do. Janet is at home with the new baby, and I've hardly had time to see the little girl. I know she won't know that, but Janet will, and I'm in her bad books already. I'll see you again soon. Give Kirsty my love, and tell her I'm sorry to have missed her."

Granville stood and watched as Elian took the cruiser out of the yard and headed out towards the sea. Once they had cleared the Isle of Anglesey, they headed west. The weather in the Irish Sea was bad, but surprisingly, the Atlantic was calmer. The wind was blowing up from the south and not the west for once. The three of them gathered around the wheel on the upper deck, and Roy asked Gael the question burning in his mind.

"Gael, what happened? I did not give the signal to shoot."

Gael, who had been expecting the question, had prepared her answer in advance.

"Well, Roy, I was lying in that hide. I'd been there all day and was feeling decidedly stiff. I was about to break cover when I heard a noise behind me. I lay there wondering if it was one of your men coming up to check on me, and fortunately, I waited. Then I heard the sound of a weapon being assembled, and I just knew that treachery was afoot. I watched as he lay down beside me totally oblivious of my presence. He lay there for hours, and when it began to get dark, he sighted the weapon. I watched in horror as you moved away from the Range Rover and he followed you in his sights. When you reached forward to touch the money, he tucked the weapon against his shoulder, and I saw his finger begin to curl on the trigger. I could not wait for your signal. Your life was being threatened, and there was no way to let you know. I had the Beretta on the floor by my side in readiness to defend myself, so I reached down and picked it up and half turned to aim it. I must have made a noise as he half turned towards me just as I fired. He saw it coming, but he had no time. He screamed a split second before the bullet struck home and toppled forward, dropping his rifle and falling off the roof. I had no choice. I had to kill Baba, but that big guy was partially blocking my view. I shot him to get a clear sight of my prime target, but as he fell backwards, Baba was diving into the back of the car. I saw the other guard climb into the driver's seat and start the car, and knowing that we could not let him drive Baba away, I fired a shot through the screen, killing him instantly. The result was that the windscreen was damaged, and I could not see Baba at all. He might have been alive today if he had not tried to make a break for it. I saw him leave the car, and I had a clear shot. I took it and killed the bugger instantly. Did I do right?"

Roy smiled and put his arm around her waist.

"You did just what I expected of you. I'm sure you saved my life."

"I can't take credit for that. Mr O'Flynn has to take the credit for that when he switched on those bloody lights. Christ, it was like daylight. The poor bastards didn't stand a chance, Sam's guy's cut them down like straw in a wind. The bloody cars must have weighed twice what they were designed to weigh. There was so much lead embedded in the metal of the body."

"Perhaps you're right, but the speed and efficiency of the clean-up was remarkable. In less than half an hour, there was no trace of what had happened. I'm just glad he was on our side. Aren't you?"

Elian, who had been silent up until now, spoke up,

"Jesus, Roy, I hope things like this are not going to happen every day. I don't think my nerves would stand it. How I didn't start that car and drive between you and those black guards I don't know. I was so worried for your safety. Do you think we can stop over before we get back. I just need to hold you close to me?"

Roy agreed and then, in Donegal Bay in the fishing harbour of Killybegs, away from the cluster of busy fishing boats, the three of them lay in the main cabin, simply enjoying the feeling of being alive. Sometime during the night, Roy enjoyed both of his companions' sexual delights. The following morning, after breakfast, they headed south, and once they had passed Tralee, it was only a short time before they entered the small harbour belonging to the castle. The money was stowed in the safe, and the drugs in the special store in the underground ammunition store below the workshop.

Roy hurried along the corridor and up the stone steps to the kitchen. Cathleen and Bridget gave a little curtsy, and both said in unison,
"Morning, your Lordship."
Bridget piped up,
"Madam is in the lounge. I don't think she expected you home yet, sir."
Roy pushed open the lounge door and found Janet feeding Sheenagh at her breast.
"Oh, Roy, why didn't you let me know you were coming back today. Look at me. I'm not dressed, and I'm feeding Sheenagh. What will you think of me? I can't look very exciting."
"Janet, you look the picture of domestic bliss. Just what I need at the moment. I've had enough excitement over the last few days to last me a month, so don't give it a second thought."
He walked over and gave her a kiss and one on Sheenagh's head. Janet looked at him, wondering what on earth he was referring to. Janet had no idea what excitement Roy was talking about. She wondered if he had enjoyed Elian over the last few days, and that was what he was talking about. Roy, however, did not give her any further information, so she just smiled, hoping that, in a couple of weeks, she would be back to normal and would have her looks back. Then she'd show Elian a thing or two. It was enough for now that he was back safe and sound.

Chapter 17

Roy gave a full report to Sam the following day as he sat in Sam's study. Janet had brought the new baby, and she and Kate were busy talking on the terrace. Morag was kept busy watching Sean on his bicycle. Sam was in one of the best moods Roy had ever seen. Sam explained that the takeover in the two areas Manchester and London had gone smoothly and, from the reports he was receiving, sales had jumped tremendously.

"It went far better than we could have imagined. The pushers and sellers just allowed our guys to continue the supplies once they became aware that Ivan and Baba's gangs were no more. I don't think they care who supplies them so long as they have a safe and ready stream of reasonable quality drugs. The idea that passengers on the ferries carry small packets has gone well, and stocks on the mainland are ahead of demand. You are going to be kept busy picking up drug drops from cargo ships for quite some time. It will be safer for all of us than trying to deliver them the old way."

Roy sat back. He felt that running drugs on a regular basis would become as boring as being chairman of his old board, but he said nothing, preferring to bide his time until he felt the time was right. He knew that, with his last escapade, he would have proven his loyalty beyond any shadow of doubt. The right time would come, and when it did, he would recognise it. He was sure.

Sam studied Roy's face. There was a far-off look in Roy's eyes as though he were some place far away.

"What's wrong, Roy? You seem unusually quiet, and you have hardly touched your drink. That's not like you. Come on, tip it up. I'm ready for another. It's celebration time. We've made it to the big time," Sam said, unable to contain his enthusiasm.

"That's what's worrying me. I'm sure now we shall be attracting more attention from the powers that be." Roy replied

"The way we are doing things now, no big deliveries, no big payments, it's amazing." Sam argued, "There's nothing to attract the attention of bankers. Small transactions are going into different accounts offshore, where the payment to the suppliers in Colombia are carried out carefully, so as not to attract too much attention. Those banks handle millions every day. Ours is just one of thousands of such transactions with no way of tracing any of them back to us," Sam said, still bubbling with the success of their achievements.

"Just be careful, Sam. Overconfidence is the way to get us caught. I think we should lay low for a time. Just carry out the bare minimum of pickups. Perhaps larger quantities would help," Roy suggested.

"I think you're worrying unnecessarily, Roy, but I'll give it some thought. The difficulty with larger quantities is control of the men aboard ship. They tend to be basic crew and not of a very high intelligence. If they jettison a cargo or don't send the right coordinate or send them too late, we would never recover the goods. The bigger the drop, the bigger the risk, and this stuff costs an absolute fortune in its uncut state," Sam said, some of his excitement evaporating under Roy's apparent gloom.

"OK, Sam, but don't say I haven't warned you. Now, where's that bloody bottle? I need a large one this time." Roy said his hand reaching for the glass.

Sam brightened. This was the old Lord Croft, the one he recognised.

"That's better, Roy. I thought you were going soft on me."

The two men sat and talked, with Sam absorbing every detail of the operation as Roy related it once again. It was two hours later when they rejoined the ladies. Kate looked up and said,

"It looks as though coffee is called for, and you had better stay for supper. Morag can bathe the children and put them down whilst we eat. You have the carry cot, so Sheenagh won't be disturbed when you go, and I'm sure Sean will sleep on the back seat with Morag. So let's have no refusals. It's all agreed."

Roy looked at Janet, who simply shrugged and smiled. It was no good arguing with Kate when she had an idea in her head. The evening went well, and when they left, Janet could not help noticing how Kate's kiss seemed to linger for a moment too long. She looked at Sam, but he seemed too busy with getting Sean into the back of the Range Rover to notice. They waved good night, and Roy drove slowly back. He knew he had drunk far too much and was aware he had his family in the car. The roads were as usual deserted, and they arrived back safe and sound.

The next few weeks went without any trouble. Roy made several trips to areas off the coast of North Africa. The shipping routes heading for the

English Channel were always a bit more risky, but no one challenged them, and the northern shipping routes gave no problems, with Roy picking up a couple of drops off the Hebrides. At the same time, he began to beef up the security around the house. He put burglar alarms on doors and windows around the castle and beefed up the ones on the boathouse and workshop. He became even more determined to get away for a time, but it would not be easy. There were lots of things he had to put in place before he could begin to put a plan in order. He would need to have building work done, and Gordon would need to make a visit once again. The thought of seeing Megan again stimulated him, and he smiled. He rang Gordon's number, and his receptionist apologised and said that Mr Gordon O'Leary would contact Lord Croft when he returned to the office. He was away on business with another large client. Would an associate be able to help? Roy declined the offer of one of Gordon's associates and asked her to get Mr O'Leary to give him a ring when he returned.

Half an hour later. the phone rang. It was Gordon O'Leary.

"Hi, Roy. I gather you wanted me? I'm out of the office for a week or so. It's a government contract, but I am interested in hearing what you have to ask me. Give me an idea of what you need."

"I did not want, or expect you to come back so urgently, Gordon. I just need to sit and discuss a few things with you, security for one. I have considered the possibility of having a long break in the West Indies and need a few changes to be made to leave things secure from prying eyes," Roy said, not really sure of what he wanted.

"What's going to happen to the place whilst you are away? Have you considered leasing the place for a short term?" Gordon asked.

"I had not given it much thought, but that sounds a good idea. Ring me when you get back and come over for a weekend. Janet's had the baby, and it's a little girl. We've called her Sheenagh."

"Megan would love to come. She's always happy to come to see you and Janet at the castle. You know she lost the last baby. She had a miscarriage, and she's been low for ages about it. The prospect of a visit will cheer her up, I'm sure. She always seems brighter after a visit with the two of you. I'll ring you and make the arrangements when I'm finished here."

The line went dead, and Roy could feel the response in his loins. Megan always excited him. Even after the children, there was something that attracted them to each other. They just seemed to meld. It was something to do with their genes or pheromones or just plain lust, he could never fathom out which.

Putting the lecherous thought of Gordon's red-haired wife out of his mind, Roy walked back into the lounge where Janet sat reading. He sat down and she looked up.

"What's wrong, Roy? You seem preoccupied over something. Tell me what you're worried about? It's not like you to mope about."

"Oh, I don't know. I feel we need a break. A long holiday in the West Indies or somewhere similar. I've mentioned it before."

"Yes, Roy I know, but Sheenagh's too young. She's still a baby, and Sean would not be safe on the boat. He's not old enough."

"Oh, I don't mean straightaway. I have a lot to do before we could go. I have to set up another boat for Sam and make changes to this place to make it safe whilst we are away. What would you think about leasing it out on a short-term basis whilst we spend time abroad?"

"I hadn't given it any thought, Roy, but I suppose we could if we could find the right tenant."

"I've been talking to Gordon O'Leary, and it appears there are agencies to find the right sort of people. Large country houses are leased all the time these days. We vet the tenants before any contract would be signed. We have the final choice and say in how the agreement is worded. I would need to get the workshop altered to prevent anyone touching my spares and my underground storage space. I mentioned it to Gordon, and he's agreed to come up for a weekend."

"Oh, Roy, what will he think of us? We only ask him to come when there's work you want him to do. He must bring his wife, you know that woman with the striking red hair, Megan. She has two children, now I believe. She sent me a card when the second was born, and I sent her flowers and a gift."

"Yes! She was at Sean's christening, if you remember? That was the last time we saw them. She gave Sean that silver christening mug. You must remember that."

"Oh yes, I remember. I had an idea she was pregnant again. That husband of hers is worse than you. Can't he keep his pecker in his pocket? It seems every time Megan comes to see us, she's pregnant again."

"Gordon told me she had lost the last one, a miscarriage, and she has been depressed about it for ages."

"Oh, the poor girl. I'm sure I'd be depressed if it happened to me. When are they coming?"

"Gordon's going to ring me when he finishes his current work. A couple of weeks, I think."

"Give me as much notice as you can. I want to make it a special weekend for her; I'm sure you'll do whatever you can to help."

Roy felt himself become a little aroused just at the thought of making it a very special weekend for the fiery red-haired Megan.

Roy arrived early at the Delaney's'. Kate was nowhere to be seen, and one of the domestics, recognising him, showed him into the study. Sam looked up with a start.

"The meeting's not until after lunch, Roy. Is something bothering you?"

"Yes, Sam. I have been wondering if there could be any possibility of me taking a holiday?"

"Why, of course, you can, Roy. Why do you ask?" Sam enquired.

"A long holiday, perhaps as long as a year. I feel I need a change. I need to get away from this business for a while. After that business in England, I keep having the feeling I'm being watched. I know it's only my imagination, but nevertheless, it's very real to me," said Roy.

Sam sat and pondered. Roy was now an important part of the group and to be without him for a year could prove difficult.

"What about the collections? How are we going to manage those?" Sam asked.

"The committee offered me funding towards another boat. If we got one, we could train a crew and operate it out of one of the fishing villages up the coast, or even Cork, relieving me to go on holiday," Roy replied, already thinking on the spur of the moment.

"A new crew? Why not the crew you already have?" asked Sam.

"I would need them to be with me. The crossing is dangerous, and I could easily train a new crew to pick up the cargo. The recovery method is easy to handle now that we have perfected the technique," Roy said, getting more and more sure of his ground.

"Mm, let me think about it. Don't bring it up at this meeting. Let me do my sums. I'll discuss it more with you, and we can put it on the agenda for the next meeting. Now. I have a few things to complete. Kate is around. Find her, and get yourself another drink. I hate to see a man dry."

As Roy walked out of the office, Sam sat back and asked himself, *What the hell was that all about? I understand his Lordship may be getting cold feet and wants a rest. If I let him go, I need to be sure he's coming back. I'll have to make sure he has plenty to do whilst he's away besides sitting on a beach. I'll need to speak to a few friends before he goes.*

Roy walked through the large house and finally found Kate reading on the patio. She looked up and saw Roy with his glass almost empty.

"Hello, Roy, where's Sam?" she asked.

"He's going over his agenda for today's meeting. There was something I had to discuss before the meeting. But there's no rush. We can bring it up at the next one. It's not important."

She checked that no one was about before she kissed him on the mouth, her swollen belly getting in the way as she tried in vain to put her arms around him and pull him closer.

"I'm not much good to you at the moment. I've only about a week to go. It won't be long now. What do you want to drink?"

"Sam has been pouring drinks like there was no tomorrow. I'd better have a coffee, or most of the meeting will go over my head."

Kate gave a grin and said,

"He's so pleased that the last project you did went so well. I'm sure he has a surprise lined up for you, so act as thought I have not warned you."

She poured black coffee. Roy sipped the dark-coloured bitter liquid, and he could feel it dampen the effects of the alcohol almost immediately. His head began to clear as he finished his second cup.

"I know you, Roy. What have you been up to? Sam would not normally send you out here unless he wanted to think about what you had told him. Now, come on. What is it? Tell me," she demanded.

Kate listened intently whilst Roy explained what he had told Sam. She began fidgeting as she realised he was proposing to go away.

"You won't be going for good, will you? Oh God, Roy, I'll miss you."

"No. I won't be going away for good. Sam asked me the same thing."

"I bet he did. You know almost as much about the IRA's business as Sam does. He could not let you be out there as a loose cannon."

Roy paled. Kate had put into words the very thing he was worried about. Would they ever let him go? He doubted it. He knew too much. Faithful servants, no matter how good, often told tales when they left their master's service. Roy knew that Sam could not afford that to happen. He had to come up with a plan that would placate Sam and enable him to get away, albeit for a year at least.

"I will have to get another craft. I had thought about a fishing boat, but that would attract attention in this day and age where boats are being made idle by the new fishing rules and regulations. A fishing boat that constantly went out and never landed a catch would soon be noticed by the authorities. No, it has to be another cruiser. The cover of going out on charters seems to have worked well in my case. It should work whoever does the trips."

Roy's gaze wandered again, and Kate left him to his own thoughts as the baby kicked and moved around. Her lump was becoming very uncomfortable, and she was grateful that Sam had decided she should have the baby in Ireland. Miami would have been far too hot. She stood up and moved around. It seemed to offer some relief. She was glad when the butler put his head out of the patio doors and stood until Kate beckoned him towards her.

"Yes, Browning, what is it?" Kate asked him.

"I beg your pardon for the interruption, Madam. It's just that Mr Delaney has requested Lord Croft to go through to the meeting."

Roy followed Browning into the house, leaving Kate to try and get comfortable again.

The meeting commenced with every member congratulating Roy on the success of his mission; everyone wanted to shake his hand. Roy was overwhelmed by their conduct, and he waited until Sam had called the meeting to order when he stood and thanked everyone for their congratulations but pointed out that the projects had only been successful thanks to the whole team that had taken part.

"Each and everyone did their part well and helped to bring the operation to a satisfactory conclusion," Roy said as the committee began to clap. "I could not have done it without them."

Sam called the meeting to order again, and the business of the day was discussed and either passed or approved. Then under the heading of any other business, Sam stood and said,

"Some time ago, we had suggested that Roy buy a second boat and we would fund half of it. I suggest that we renew that offer, but this time we offer the full cost and help train the crew from our own resources. Roy has shown that he is a capable member of this committee and one we would not like to lose under any circumstances. He has become a real asset to us, and at some time we should be able to offer him a break."

The room fell deadly quiet, wondering where this was going.

"Roy has a family, and we have taken up a great deal of his time and put his life on the line many times. Roy has asked me today if, at some future time, he could take an extended holiday. I have thought it over carefully and, if he can buy his second boat and train a crew to successfully carry out the front line collections and occasional deliveries, I feel we should grant his wish."

There were murmurs of discontent amongst the committee members, but Sam raised his hand.

"I understand your concerns, and we must be certain that the new crew are fully capable. I suggest that we give Roy up to six months to show us that his second crew are fully capable of carrying out our operational requirements. We've been saying that Roy must not expose himself in the day-to-day running, and this would be the golden opportunity to achieve that aim. Do I have your full agreement to go ahead with this and report back before we consider Roy's application for extended leave?"

The committee began to talk amongst themselves, and slowly, one by one, they raised their hands in agreement until every hand in the room was raised. Sam looked around the room and said,

"Thank you for your vote of confidence in me for putting such a controversial proposal forward and for having the confidence that Roy can deliver the solution still under his command. Now, if there is nothing else, I propose we break for drinks, and I'm sure Roy will be only too pleased to answer any of your questions, even though he had no idea I was going to put this matter on the agenda today."

The meeting broke up, and Roy was bombarded with questions by each and every one who thought the backup crew and cruiser was a brilliant idea, which would allow Roy to be more involved with planning new ways to achieve their goal and less time being exposed to arrest and capture on day-to-day activities. Roy was glad when he sat down with Sam in his study after the rest had left.

"That was a bit of a surprise, Sam. I thought you wanted to leave it until the next meeting."

"The mood of the whole group was just right. I wanted to get the feeling of how they would view you being away for some time. It's never been done before, and I needed to put feelers out. Usually, they would have said no, but after your last performance in London and Manchester, I thought it was just the right time. Even stalwarts like McGuiness and O'Malley had to agree that there was no risk that any group would be able to turn you. I listened to the undertones before the vote. You have certainly earned the complete trust of them all, not to mention my own. Roy, you have truly become one of us."

Roy was glad to get away. For once, he felt uncomfortable with all the accolades Sam and the committee had showered upon him. It did not, however, change his mind, and he now had the way out delivered to him on a plate.

At the earliest moment, Roy phoned Granville and told him that he was looking for a second cruiser; he explained that he wanted a sound boat that would be suitable to be upgraded for speed and similar storage places and long range fuel tanks as his own. He also informed him that he would want him to do the conversion and that he would need a price for the boat and the engine upgrade and the below decks changes as soon as possible. Granville was delighted and promised to ring Roy back in a few days. Roy called Elian into his office and broke the news.

"Elian," Roy said, when she sat in his office, "I would like to get your views on my latest project."

He went on to explain that he wanted to get away for a year or so, and the opportunity was there for her to go with him as crew or to skipper her own cruiser whilst he was away. He pointed out that if he obtained a second boat whilst he was away, that crew would do what charters he did for the IRA at present. She would be fully responsible to him for all operations. Elian raised her hand to stop his diatribe.

"Roy, we've been together almost from the start. I hope you are not trying to get rid of me and the others. Thank you for the offer, but I know I speak for Gael and Fiona, and we all want to stay with you. We will help train the new crew, but we all want to go with you wherever you head for."

She stood up and walked towards him in a provocative sort of way and whispered suggestively,

"We have not had much time to be together and, seeing as we are alone, I want to take advantage of the moment. It's time you had a bed placed in this office, although, come to think of it, I don't think it would go down well with Janet."

Roy rose to embrace her, knowing where it would lead, happy that his crew preferred to be going with him. He would contact Sam and ask him to send a couple of prospective skippers, from the men at his disposal, to be interviewed by Elian and himself. With the fishing boats not being able to renew their licences and the tighter fishing restrictions being imposed by Europe, there would be plenty who would give their right arm for just such an opportunity.

The next two months were busy for Roy, leaving Granville to find a cruiser that had fire damage, preferably in the engine room and cabins, but leaving the hull in sound shape and suitable for a full refit. Roy, on the other hand, had been kept on his toes to find a new crew, people who could be trusted and have the necessary skills, and this took up most of his time. Elian, Gael, and Fiona did several trips to recover drugs successfully, convincing Roy that with the right crew he could safely leave for his proposed extended holiday in the Caribbean. During that crucial time, Sam had sent several men for Roy to interview, but each one had some kind of hang-up. They were clearly fishermen who were not ready to do as Roy wanted, and none of them really showed that they wanted to change their way of life. Roy, together with Elian, had interviewed each one and rejected them all. Granville had had the boat delivered to the yard. He had asked Roy to come and see it, and as Roy and his crew were going by boat, it would be an ideal opportunity for Roy to visit his mother; he felt that he had been neglecting his duty of late. They docked in the yard and looked at the cruiser Granville had found. It looked to be in a sorry state, but Granville had been so enthusiastic about the possibilities that none of them had the heart to be despondent about its prospects. They went out to supper, and when they returned, Fiona and Gael went into their cabin, and Elian joined Roy in the stateroom. After they had enjoyed sex, they lay talking about the prospect of the holiday in the West Indies, and Elian said,

"Will Janet be coming with us? The children could be a nightmare on such a long trip. We would be forever watching if they were safe."

"No. Janet will fly out to the Caribbean and wait for us. She will only be with us on short island hops. How many of the crew do you think we will need to take with us?" Roy asked Elian to see how keen she really was about the whole trip.

"We'll need Fiona to cook, and we really ought to take Gael, but she will want to share you with Fiona and myself. I'll have to see about some sort of rota. I know it seems clinical, but it will save any ill feeling between the three of us, don't you agree?"

Roy had not given that side of the trip much thought. Pushing that aside, he asked her to check the long-range forecast to see which route they should take.

"When would we be going?" Elian asked;

"Hopefully, sometime within the next two to three months. It all depends on us finding the right crew to leave behind and us being successful in training them," Roy replied.

They discussed their plans for the trip, and when they were too tied to continue, they fell asleep.

Roy went to visit his mother, leaving his crew to go over the plans for the rebuild with Granville. Roy's mother was pleased to see him but scolded him for not coming to see her more often. She asked him when he was going to get her new granddaughter christened as she had not seen her yet and it would give her the opportunity to visit. Roy had hardly given the christening of Sheenagh a thought, but the chance to get his mistresses in one place again seemed to stimulate the idea. He rang Janet and discussed the prospect with her, pointing out that with the prospect of them going away, it should be sooner than later and left the final arrangements to her. That evening, Roy took his mother and her companion Shilpa out for a meal. Shilpa had not lost the implications of the glances that Lord Croft had been giving her throughout the meal and could not wait to get back and see that Roy's mother was safely tucked up in bed. Roy sat by his mother's bedside, and they talked about old times and how Janet was and how the grandchildren were faring. The conversation dragged on for what seemed hours before she finally said she was tired and would see him in the morning. Roy closed the door and went downstairs. Shilpa sat in the lounge dressed in her robe with a whisky poured in readiness for when he came down; as Roy opened the door, she rose and moved towards him, embracing him and kissing him with the fervour of a lover who had been separated from her desires for some considerable time.

The whisky lay forgotten as they renewed their lust for each other. Roy delighted in her erotic movements during their most intimate moments. The movements of her muscles, which had so excited Roy, had been the side product of the muscle control she had learned during her time spent in mastering the art of Indian dancing. Once their initial need had been assuaged, Roy carried her upstairs and into his room where they continued well into the night. When Roy woke, he was alone, and his mother stood at the open door with a tray of tea and a slice of toast.

Roy sat up and said with surprise showing in his voice,
"Mother, why didn't you ask Shilpa to bring that up? You are supposed to be recovering, not waiting on me."
His mother replied with a broad grin,
"I have always brought you breakfast, and I'm quite capable of continuing. I had no thoughts of sending that young woman up here with you in your usual state of undress. I remember catching you in bed with her sister a long time ago, and I'm not encouraging you in the ways of wickedness. Now, drink your tea and get some clothes on. Your breakfast is being prepared by Shilpa, so don't take all day."
Roy spent the next couple of days with his mother, to her delight, although his mother was innocent of the fact that he spent the nights with Shilpa in his bed, enjoying all she had to give. Both women were sorry when he announced that he had to go. Roy drove back to the boatyard and was astounded with the changes to the cruiser; what had been a sorry-looking wreck was beginning to look more like the boat he had expected to see when they arrived. Elian insisted that she stay and supervise the reconstruction, and Granville agreed; they had booked her in a small guest house nearby for the duration of her stay. So it was Roy who took the cruiser out with Gael and Fiona as crew and, on the way home, Roy took the opportunity to stop over in a fishing village on the Irish coast and enjoy the sexual favours of both members of his crew, one in the evening and the other the following morning. He arrived back at the castle in an excellent state of mind. Janet was delighted to see him and began to discuss the arrangements she had made for Sheenagh's christening.

Later that day, Sam rang up to say that he had another skipper for Roy to interview.
"I think you will like this guy, Roy. He's an Irish American who has been sailing in and around America for quite some time. He's an older man with many years under his seafaring belt. I'll send him round this evening."
Roy waited for Fergus O'Malley to arrive and liked him from the first moment he set eyes on him. Fergus was in his late fifties, early sixties, with a round, weather-beaten face, a cheery smile, and a character to match. Roy asked him to sit and, without asking, poured him a large Irish whisky. The

older man took the glass in his strong hand and smelled the ambrosia of the mature spirit; his eyes sparkled as the amber fluid touched his lips.

"Thank you, your grace. That's a nice drop of the hard stuff, some of the nicest I've tasted in a long time."

Janet sat and watched the interplay between the two men; it was obvious to her that Roy had found his skipper. She sat and listened to the banter between them and what Fergus had been doing all the years he had been at sea. She was as fascinated with him as Roy was, and it was in the early hours of the morning when she left them to it. When she woke up, Roy had been to bed and had got up early, showered, and when she went down to the kitchen, he was talking to Fergus who had obviously stayed the night in one of the guest rooms. She watched them as they walked out of the kitchen and along the quayside towards the cruiser.

Roy introduced him to Gael and Fiona and then asked Fergus to take the cruiser out to sea to demonstrate his skills. Fergus was delighted to get his hands on such a delightful boat and was even more delighted when he realised just how powerful she was.

"Oh be Jesus, your grace, she handles like a dream. The instrumentation is just what I would be needing to take a strange boat out of an unknown harbour and into an area of sea I've never been in before. If the boat you want me to skipper is anything like this one, I'll be as happy as a man with two heads."

Roy instructed Fergus to take the cruiser into Tralee and then return to the castle. When they had tied up in the harbour, Roy walked back to the castle with Fergus for a bite of lunch. Roy waited until they were alone and asked the question that had been on his mind since they had met.

"Has Mr Delaney given you any idea of the kind of work you will be doing for us?"

"Don't you worry your head about that, Lord Croft? I was involved with Mr Delaney and his associates in America. Lord bless you, your honour. I've carried all sorts of stuff in my time and done things I hope the good Lord has forgotten by the time he comes to take me."

Roy smiled at the older man's candour and enjoyed the way he put things in that easy and relaxed way. Both men knew exactly what sort of things he had done, without the necessity of having to spell it out in too much detail.

"The cruiser is being refitted. as we speak. Now what about a crew for you? Have you any ideas? I feel if you are going to have to rely on men, you should be the man to select them, don't you? I'm not going to impose people on you that you may or may not get on with. I have seen a few that may be suitable, and I'll give you their names, but you are under no obligation to take any of them. You will have the final say."

"Thank you, your Lordship. I have a few ideas but leave that with me, and I'll get back to you in a couple of days. I understand you have a few trips you want me to go along with. Let me know when I'm to come over."

Roy watched him go and sat back relieved that he had found the right man for the job. He had come highly recommended by Sam himself and was used to doing work outside the law. Roy's extended holiday seemed to be getting to be more than a distant pipe dream; it was slowly becoming a reality.

Roy asked Fergus to go with them on the next collection of drugs. This time the drop-off had been executed off the coast of England, near the mouth of the Bristol Channel. The drop had been made on the rip tide, so they had to track the parcels over quite some distance. The whole thing went off without a hitch. Fergus was amazed at the ease with which the parcels, although they had drifted far apart, were located and recovered. The second collection was off the coast of North Africa and again went very smoothly The third delivery, however, which took place, of all places, just off the coast of the Isle of Wight, did not go so well. Whoever the idiot was who had jettisoned the cargo in such a ridiculous place was a mystery to Roy. Roy had a bad feeling from the time they set out; everything felt wrong. The outward journey went well but the cargo was difficult to locate, and with the constant change in tides in the busy channel, the recovery took longer than usual. Roy had a distinct feeling that they were being observed throughout the entire operation. He was glad when the last parcel was aboard, and they headed for home. The feeling of being watched persisted until they rounded the southern Irish coast.

They arrived home just after dark and, for some unexplained reason, Roy requested that they pull the boat up the slipway. The four of them finally got the boat into the boathouse, and Fergus and Gael chocked the hull in place. Gael was the first to spot the problem. She called out to Roy, and they went to see what she had found. There it was! Another tiny sending unit attached to the hull, like a smaller version of the one they had discovered last time. This time, the small item had been attached to the rudder magnetically like a limpet mine. Roy detached it, and he ran up to the castle and told Janet that he had to go out for a while urgently and would be back in a couple of hours. Janet stood back amazed. *What the heck was wrong now?* she wondered. He had only just got back from one of his shorter trips, and now he was away again without so much as a kiss or a hug. Roy and Gael and Fergus jumped in the Land Cruiser and drove south towards Cork. Roy had no time for another trick like last time. He wanted to get rid of the bloody thing as quickly as possible. He drove down to the old port of Cobh, which had a harbour that served Cork. It was an old town, and he knew that container ships often called in to collect and drop off cargo. He was in luck there. Out in the harbour was a container ship with the last few containers ready for loading. Roy let Gael chat up one of the dock officials whilst he, with Fergus keeping watch, sidled up to the container and stuck the small unit on its side. He caught Gael's eye and gave her the thumbs-up sign that they had carried out the task successfully. Much to the official's dismay, he had believed he was on to a good thing when he got off duty. Gael broke off her chat-up line, disappearing around the buildings, where she rejoined Roy and Fergus in the car park.

She climbed into the vehicle, and smiled.
"That boat is on its way to South America," Gael said, "so they will have a fair old trip to get it back, and we did not have to get wet this time. Who do you think planted the damn thing, Roy?"
Roy pondered for a while before answering,
"I don't know, but that's the second time it's happened, and I really don't like it. It makes me believe we have one of the security branches on our backs, and the sooner we can get underway for our holiday, the better I'll like it."
Gael had been eager to sit in the middle, and now she leaned across and put her head on Roy's shoulder and rubbed up against him like a large cat. Fergus just looked at the scene and said nothing. He knew the score. Roy smiled. He knew one or two places on the way back where they could both get rid of their frustrations. He would drop Fergus off near Tralee, and he knew he was going to be later back at the castle than he had thought. He hoped Janet would understand. She usually did.

Chapter 18

Roy was determined to go away as soon as he could manage it. Elian called to say that the boat was ready for delivery, and Roy arranged for Fergus and Gael to fly to collect the craft. It had been registered in the name of a new company as 'Pride of Waterford' in Cork. Roy, for the first time, showed little interest in the new addition. He would never sail the boat, and the least he had to do with it, the happier he would be. He had asked for the boat to be stored in Cobh, near Cork, well away from the castle, and Fergus had taken a small cottage on the outskirts of the area. He asked Elian and Gael to go out with the new crew and report back when they had done a couple of collections and a delivery to the pickup point they used to use when Connor had been with them. The trips went without a hitch, and Roy was satisfied that Fergus could manage. Sam had appointed another paymaster to pay for the fuel and other expenses in place of Connor, who was still languishing in an English jail. Roy was a much happier man when Elian and Gael finally returned to get the cruiser ready for the longest trip it had ever made.

The day of the christening drew nearer; Janet visited the gynaecologist and was given the all-clear. Roy took the opportunity to make passionate love to his wife each and every evening when they retired. Although Roy was a philanderer, he loved his wife dearly. Their passion transcended the wild sexual cavorting he enjoyed from his range of mistresses. Unbeknown to Roy, Janet had invited the same people for this christening as the previous one, and he was quite surprised when Shilpa and his mother arrived, closely followed by Megan and her architect husband Gordon together with their growing young brood. Kate had sent her apologies as she and Sam were in the United States following the birth of her son. Janet had invited the guests, other than those from the village, to come on the Friday and stay for a few days.

Roy took the opportunity to pull Gordon to one side and asked him if he had come up with plans that would ensure that, if they let the castle whilst he was away for a year or so, he could isolate the underground store and armoury so that no one would know it was there. Gordon's mind had been working on the problem almost from the time Roy had phoned him, but there were details he had to check. He told Roy that he wanted to look at the workshop and the second-level underground stores to make a few notes. To Roy's joy, Megan asked if she could leave the two children with Morag whilst she joined Roy and Gordon. She grabbed a note book, and the three of them walked down the stone steps along the underground corridor towards the workshop. Gordon explained to Roy that the corridor would be easy to hide; he would simply brick up the passage, leaving a small room at the foot of the steps, and rack it out as a wine cellar. The boat house would remain with the large workshop behind; they would brick up the entrance to the tunnel from that side and put a workbench in front of the new brickwork. The lift and hoist areas from the storage areas below would be bricked up and rendered with a coating of cement to give the appearance that it was a concrete wall against the hillside, and the steps leading down to the equipment store and the lower level would have a new concrete raft cast over the entrance. Roy showed Gordon around, and Megan wrote down as Gordon dictated. Gordon went down the stone steps, checking supports and power supplies; he needed to isolate the power supply to give a control box for the above ground areas, so that no indication of the heavy cabling below would be obvious even to a more detailed search of the premises. He disappeared from view, saying that he would be some time as he had to trace the wiring back to the main box.

Taking the opportunity, Roy caught Megan's arm and steered her into his office. He pulled her to him and kissed her on the mouth. His growing arousal surged through him. As his hands roamed and explored her body, he realised that she had thickened in several places but her eagerness to please him had not diminished in any way. Whatever it was that attracted them to each other, was as strong as ever. Then, as if realising where they were and with Gordon only down the steps from where they stood, she whispered urgently in Roy's ear,

"Oh dear God, Roy, we can't do this. Gordon will be back any minute. Please, not now. We shouldn't."

Ignoring Megan's pleas for him to stop, Roy's hand moved down until he could feel the hem of Megan's skirt. and he moved under the material. Megan groaned softly, knowing she was putty in this man's hands. She knew it had been a mistake to come with Gordon. This was what she had known would happen all along. She felt his mouth on her breast and, in a last attempt to put a stop to what had gone too far already, she whispered,

"Oh God, Roy! We can still stop now! Roy, please don't! Gordon could walk in on us anytime," she moaned.

She knew it was useless to try to object. Again, she surrendered to the inevitable.

"Oh God," she said. "Please stop."

But there was no intensity in her plea. She lay back, her body responding to Roy's skill. She was intoxicated by Roy's very presence. She always had been since the day she first met him. She felt herself rise against her lover, knowing he was not protected. Her body shuddered as she felt her climax peek. The joy of the moment was followed almost immediately by her cry,

"Oh God. No! Stop, pull out, don't, not again. Oh God forgive me!"

Roy was relentless, totally oblivious to her warning, and when they lay still, she pushed him away, a strong feeling of guilt reflected in her face. It was too late for remorse. The damage was done. She had let herself be taken by Lord Croft again. She had been determined this time that she would not let it happen. So much for her resolve! They straightened their clothing and walked out of the office just as Gordon emerged from the stairwell covered in dust.

"Oh, Gordon," Megan said, her voice sounding full of remorse, either for her latest sexual escapade with Roy or her exasperation with her husband's constant habit of ruining his good clothes. "Just look at the state of your suit. I will have to sponge it when I get back to the room."

The three of them walked slowly back to the kitchen stairs whilst Gordon continued scribbling on his notepad. They climbed the steps, and Janet met them at the top. She stared at Gordon's suit covered in a layer of cobwebs and concrete dust. Then, turning to Roy, she cursed him, saying sharply,

"Oh, Roy, you are so terrible. I did not ask Gordon and Megan to come for the weekend for you to drag them off into the depths of your inner sanctum. It's always the same whenever you get Gordon down here. If Gordon wants to do business with you, I suggest they stay on after the christening for a few days, and you can get him to design any changes you wish, but no more shop talk today. That's final."

With that, she grabbed both of them and whisked them off into the lounge, turning her head at the last minute to inform him,

"Oh, and by the way, Shilpa and your mother arrived a few minutes ago. Please go and give them a welcome. They are in the reception lounge. Morag and Bridget are getting their cases from the taxi."

Roy went through to see them, and his mother asked,

"Roy, you're neglecting your mother. Why weren't you at the airport to collect me? It's a good job your father was not there. He would have had something to say."

Janet had arranged for a car, but Mother felt he was neglecting his duties. Roy tried to explain that he had been busy with seeing to other guests. His eyes wandered to his mother's companion. Shilpa, wearing a Western-style suit, looked so inviting, a pleasure Roy hoped he would have later that evening. Shilpa walked forward and kissed Roy politely on the cheek and whispered,

"Don't be hard on her, Roy. She sometimes is difficult like this. It's her age."

They hugged, and Roy whispered that he would see her in the main lounge to discuss it further after everyone had retired to bed. The gathering in the dining room was a busy affair, and Roy was lavish with the drinks, plying everyone with an adequate supply to ensure that everyone would be ready for an early night. Eventually, after long a long session of talking about everything and everyone, the party finally broke up, and everyone retired. Roy went up to bed and waited until Janet had fallen into a deep sleep before he got out of bed and, putting on a robe, he walked down into the kitchen and, expecting that he would need it, he helped himself to a slug of Cathleen's potcheen from the cupboard. It was going to be a long night after a very tiring day. Then he made his way to the lounge where Shilpa was waiting as arranged.

The following morning, everyone went aboard the cruiser for a short boat trip round to Tralee, and Roy brought everyone lunch at the inn on the harbour. Everyone seemed full of food; on the way back, Roy, seeing almost everyone asleep either in the cabins or in the lounge, went up top to see Elian. Roy asked what she had found out about the long-range prospects for the weather forecast for the following month.

"The second and third months seem to give promise for the best weather. It's the lull between the seasons," Elian said.

Roy had a lot to do. If he was to be ready in time, he had to get the builders in and make sure all the work was complete before he left. He had to put the castle up for rent or, alternatively, appoint a caretaker to manage the place. Elian was disappointed as she watched him go back down the stairs without him even giving her a hug. Roy got his cell phone and called Charlie. He apologised for calling him on Saturday, but he urgently needed some more work to be done on the castle and asked him how soon he could get his team across to Ireland. Charlie replied,

"It'll take me a couple of days, Roy, but they could be with you by Wednesday or Thursday. How long do you reckon you'll need them?"

"Oh, about a couple of weeks," Roy said, guessing the time needed. "I would think. I'll have the materials and the equipment delivered by the middle of next week."

Charlie told Roy he would phone and confirm the day of his team's arrival so that Roy could arrange transport from the airport in Cork. Roy discussed the terms, and a price was agreed for the team for a two-week period.

Roy's mind seemed so much easier now that the decision had been made. Elian, skilfully and from having plenty of practice, slid the vessel alongside the quay, and Fiona and Gael tied the securing lines. Everyone went back up to the castle to change and dress for a light supper before retiring. Roy went down to the lounge after Janet had fallen asleep, but Shilpa was nowhere to be seen. Roy was restless, and he walked down to the quayside where Elian was sitting wide awake studying charts in the lower wheelhouse. She was surprised at Roy's entrance and showed him the two alternate routes depending on the weather at the time of departure. Roy leaned over the charts to see what Elian had planned. Elian turned her face and kissed Roy softly on the cheek.

"We could discuss this in bed," she whispered fluttering her eyes in a mock display of provocativeness.

Roy never could refuse such an offer. When he left her, it was the wee hours of the morning, and it was the day of the christening; the household would be up early with food and drinks to get in place before they left for church. Roy slept late, and when he got downstairs, the house was a hive of activity. The day went without a hitch, and for once, Roy spent time with Janet and Sean until the children were finally put to bed. The adults were having a quiet drink in the evening when Gordon called Roy to one side and asked a few questions about sealing the lower levels.

"Roy," Gordon said quietly, "I've ascertained from the plans that there is an escape route in case of fire. It's well hidden and would give you emergency access if required. It has a thick steel door that could be locked to prevent any unlawful person entering the subterranean passage."

"You mean, even after you have sealed the lower levels I could still gain admission to the stores without anyone staying at the castle, being aware I was even close by?" Roy said, pleased with the news.

Gordon nodded. Roy was intrigued at the possibility, and he agreed, cautioning Gordon,

"That sounds a good idea, Gordon. I agree but only if you can make it secure, it could remain," Roy said, his mind always on the caution side where safety and survival were concerned.

"That door is so thick it could take a direct hit from an RPG and still not open," Gordon assured him before asking, "When are the builders going to arrive?"

When Roy informed him that they would be arriving the following Wednesday or Thursday, Gordon replied,

"I'll need to go back to the office on Monday and get the Quantity Surveyor to detail the requirements before returning. I'll fax the detailed schedule of quantities through for your approval, and I could get the materials delivered from your local suppliers, as you requested." Adding, "As I am only going to be away for a couple of days, I wondered if Janet would mind if Megan and the children could stay at the castle whilst I'm away."

Roy told him that it would be no trouble at all. He was sure Janet would love to have her company for a few more days. The thought of having Megan and Shilpa at his disposal, for more time, made Roy smile. The prospects for sexual dalliance were definitely looking up. He would have ample opportunity with Janet busy planning her trip; she would be flying out and staying in a hotel on Barbados with Sean and Sheenagh, accompanied by her trusted nanny, Morag, to take any of the drudgery out of her holiday. She was really looking forward to the rest, the holiday promised. The agents had rung to say that they had received some enquiries for the castle and would vet each one before submitting them to him for consideration.

The next meeting of the committee went as planned with Roy informing the members that he was at last satisfied that Fergus and his crew were more than capable of recovering the drugs and could, when required, deliver to places off the UK coast in an emergency. Roy broke the news that he had found a second tracking device on his own cruiser and warned that it would appear that one of the security agencies, he had been unable in the short time to discover which one, was stepping up their surveillance. He was obviously being targeted, and that was why he had decided if the committee was in full agreement to grant him leave for his extended holiday sooner rather than later. The committee asked him to leave whilst they discussed the matter in detail as they did not want him embarrassed by anything that might crop up during the discussion. Roy left somewhat shaken by their request. He wandered through to the reception where Kate sat reading.

"What's wrong?" she asked.

Roy explained and she smiled,

"Sam told me that might happen. It's just that one or two of the older members are still a bit sceptical about your proposed long absence. It's nothing to worry about. I'm sure they will all agree in the end. Now, follow me. I have a plan in mind."

Roy groaned inwardly as she opened the door to the butler's pantry. He had hoped that now that she had had her son, things might not need to continue. Kate had other ideas. She had even had the room redecorated and, in place of the old massage table, was a padded couch, and the facilities had been upgraded. There was now a shower, a toilet, and a hand basin.

"What's this?" asked Roy, pointing to the new equipment and facilities. "Won't Sam be suspicious?"

"Of course not, silly. It's now designated a visitor's cloakroom. Sam thought it was such a good idea. The couch was my own addition, just in case anyone felt faint. I have a funny feeling that I am going to have to take advantage of that particular facility, sooner rather than later, don't you?"

They had just closed the door behind them and were walking back to the settee in the lounge when one of the domestics arrived to say,

"Would Lord Croft please go back into the meeting. They are ready for him once again."

Roy smiled and followed the man back to the committee room where he was greeted with smiles all round. He was informed that the meeting had granted his application, and he would be pleased to know that it was the committee's opinion and strong recommendation that, during his time there, if he could be of any assistance to their contacts in the area, his services were to be offered. On that condition, they were more than happy for him to be away for the full twelve months or longer, but he had to keep in contact with Sam on a regular basis in case the committee needed him back in a hurry. Roy smiled, seemingly pleased with the outcome of the committee's closed session. He looked slyly at Sam, knowing in his heart that the suggestion that he become available for the Americans or whoever was Sam's idea.

He was not too pleased at the prospect, but he would have to see how things panned out. At least, he had the go-ahead. It would really test the boat and his crew; he was only glad he was not doing the trip in a yacht. The winds as well as the waves were so unpredictable in Roy's eyes. Engines were much more reliable if you had the fuel to drive them. That was still a problem he had to solve. He would have to speak to Elian to see if there were any places to refuel on the three-thousand-mile journey from Cadiz to the nearest town in Brazil, and he realised that he would have to do a lot more work on the project. He could not leave it all to Elian. He had to get to grips with the problem himself.

The meeting finally closed, and after they had spent some time chatting over the snacks provided, Roy was left as usual with Sam. He sat down in the study with a large Irish whisky in his hand, and he quizzed Sam on the question of the American contacts.

"Well, Sam, you got your way. It would seem I have no choice in the matter. I will still have to work during my holiday. So much for a rest! Tell me who and what are these guys like? Are they reliable? I don't want to jump from one problem into another."

"We have a number of associates in America, ranging from the Mafia to the Irish American IRA, who are involved, as we are, in many sides of business. That's all I can tell you. The rest you will get to know on a need-to-know basis. You would not have it any other way if the arrangement were reversed now, would you? You would not like any organisation to come over here and know just what you did without your knowledge of what was being said about you now, would you? Be honest."

Roy had to agree reluctantly, and after he had had supper served with Kate and Sam, he drove home happy that his trip was approved but somewhat dismayed that the Americans could contact him and he would, to some extent, be in the dark unless they chose to enlighten him.

Roy spent the next few days poring over charts, calculating fuel usage, and each time he came up with the same answer. The margins were too close. He discussed the matter with Elian, and she promised to recheck his calculations. His concentration, however, was interrupted when the letting agents rang to say that they had two possibilities of tenants for Janet and him to interview. Roy went to speak to Janet again. He was not too sure whether he really wanted tenants in the castle or not. He could well afford to leave it empty. Money was not any problem. He was not relying on the rental income to pay for the outgoing on the property. He spoke to Janet,

"Janet, I'm not so sure we should lease the castle. What about any damage to our own furniture and belongings? I know we could easily replace them, but that's not the point. Some things are of sentimental value to either or both of us."

Janet looked at him. He was always the same in business. He made up his mind and carried out the plan without a second thought, but where she was concerned, he always seemed to want her approval. No, that was not what she really meant. It was not approval he sought but her input. It was as though he wanted the final decision to be hers.

"Roy we have discussed this over and over, but if you are still uncertain, let's do the interviews and make up our minds. If you don't like either of them, we will just put in a caretaker. I know you will agree to that at least. We can make the final decision only when we have seen what's on offer. Now, let's leave it there, and come and give me a kiss. I'm going to miss you whilst I'm in the West Indies."

Roy hugged his wife and whispered to her,

"Just behave yourself whilst you're there, my girl. I don't want bad reports about you when I arrive."

Janet pushed him away with a look of incredulity on her face.

"You have the cheek to say that to me. I have never once complained about your behaviour. Who would want me, an old married lady with two children hanging around her apron strings? I should be so lucky it's you that wants to behave, not me. You will have three beautiful younger women on board with you and no one to supervise your behaviour, so let's not hear any more about me, or else I might be tempted to go looking. I hear there is plenty of talent in Barbados."

Roy gave up trying to persuade Janet either way and decided to deal with the matter her way; he rang the agents, setting up meetings with the prospective tenants. The appointments were arranged for the following week, one on Monday and the second on Tuesday, and both parties wished to see over the property.

The first couple arrived, and Roy showed Henry and Stella Francis around the property. Both were suitably impressed with the accommodation, and Stella wanted to see the harbour. She sailed a thirty-five-foot sailing boat and wanted to inspect the harbour facilities. Leaving Henry with Janet, Roy walked Stella down to the harbour and aboard the cruiser. She met Elian and wanted to know details about the depth of the harbour. The two of them made several depth soundings before Elian took her up on to the flying bridge where she used the depth finder to ascertain the approaches and the harbour itself. Elian excused herself and went up to the boathouse to talk to Gael; Roy asked Stella if she would like a drink. She readily accepted his offer, and he asked,

"Stella, do you like Irish whisky?"

"Is there any other?" Stella replied, a glint appearing in her eyes.

Roy poured her a generous tumbler, and she looked at him, saying,

"Are you trying to get me tipsy, Lord Croft, because if you are, you're certainly going about it the right way?"

After several glasses, she visibly began to relax. Her rather forced accent slipped, and the broader Irish brogue that was more in keeping with her natural upbringing came to the surface.

"Dat's fuckin' lovely stuff, my boyo," she exaggerated the Irish drawl. Then, returning to her natural speech, she continued, "I like a drop of the hard stuff occasionally, but my husband does not approve. That's why I sail. He can't see what I'm up to when I'm out at sea."

She lay back completely relaxed and at ease in Lord Croft's company. She felt he was more like herself than any Lord she had ever known and, what's more, she lay back in what could only be described as a provocative posture. Her skirt had ridden up, displaying her well-developed thighs and occasionally giving Roy a glimpse of her delicate French knickers. Roy would normally have taken advantage of the situation, but some self-preserving instinct held him back. This was a little too easy. Stella had not had enough to drink to make her act this way, and the effects of what she had drunk could hardly have affected her so quickly. An eighteen-year-old innocent was one thing, but a self-confessed drinker was quite a different story, and he wondered what game was afoot.

Stella, on the other hand, wondered what was holding this man back. From the reports she had read, he was the sort of man who would take advantage of a woman somewhat intoxicated. She thought to herself that something she had done must have spooked him, but she could well understand women falling for him. He was a Lord, rich, very handsome in a rugged celebrity film star, actor sort of way, and he had that allure, which she could not quite pin down; he seemed to ooze sexual attraction, and he was so confident around women. She lay back, watching his eyes roam up her legs, and she eased them apart to give him just a glimpse of her underwear, not too much to be obvious, but just enough to entice.

Roy decided to just see how far she was prepared to go, and he moved closer and, taking the lead, he bent to give her a kiss. As he kissed her, Stella's mouth opened wide, letting Roy's tongue slide over hers. Roy felt her pull him down as she lay back, totally complacent. Roy pulled back, the warning bells ringing in his head; this was just too easy, and he stood up, moving away before his arousal got too far.

"What's wrong?" she asked, a look of disappointment crossing her face.

"Nothing. It's just going a bit too fast for me," he replied. "I know nothing about you. Your husband is in the house with my wife, and here you are offering yourself to me as if we had known each other all our lives. Something is not right here. What's your game, Mrs Francis?"

Stella protested her innocence.

"I don't know what you mean, your Lordship. We are both consenting adults, and if I find you attractive enough, and if you are willing, why should I not entice you into a closer relationship?"

"I hear you, but something is not quite right here. You mean you would give yourself to me on the chance that I might be tempted to let you lease my home to you at an advantageous rent? That's little short of prostitution, Stella, and you don't seem the type to me. There's more to it than that. I can feel it in my bones. Get up. Let's get back to the house."

Stella struggled to her feet. She had to continue to appear a little more inebriated than she had to carry on the façade. It would be more than her job with the agency was worth to let him guess the truth. She pretended to be angry that he should think she would go to those lengths just to get a reduction in the rent.

"I'm sure I don't know what you mean, but I certainly had you wrong. I was sure you were the kind of man who would not spurn the charms of a woman in need. I have an open marriage, and both my husband and I have other partners. I just misjudged the situation. That's all I'm guilty of, Lord Croft. Let's get back to the house. I am sorry if I have blown any chance of getting the lease. I just love the castle, and the harbour is the perfect anchorage for my yacht. I shall be sorry if I've upset you in any way. Please forgive my indiscretion."

She straightened her clothes and blatantly took his arm and walked back along the quayside towards the kitchen door. Gael and Elian saw them and looked at each other. They had overheard the sound of raised voices and had wondered what had gone on between the pair. There had not been enough time for any sexual contact, and she was an extremely attractive woman. Arriving back in the lounge, Stella ran towards her husband and said excitedly,

"Oh, darling, it's just wonderful. The harbour is just what I had in mind for the boat. It's sheltered, and there's plenty of depth for the yacht. I do hope we can get it."

Roy looked on, mystified at her ability to chop and change her character. There was more to Stella Francis than met the eye. He would have to find out more.

Janet had tea served, and Henry and Stella asked the usual questions like when they could have the site on lease. It was just as though the interplay between Stella and Lord Croft had never taken place. Roy was still not convinced. Something deeper was afoot.

They finally left, and Janet turned to Roy and said,

"They seemed a nice enough couple, just the sort I had in mind. He was very quiet. She seemed the one who ran that marriage. She was so bubbly. How did you get on with her down at the harbour?"

"She came on a bit strong. It just didn't seem right somehow," Roy said, his mind going over the incident but not really coming up with any answers.

"Oh, come on, Roy. That's not like you. What was wrong with the woman? She certainly was very attractive. I would have thought you would have jumped at the chance of adding another conquest to your collection."

"Am I that obvious? It just did not seem right. I can't explain it. Some inner warning told me to be careful. I never go against my instincts. They have never proved me wrong. This close to us getting away for a long break, I just felt she was a bit over the top, too much too soon, that's all. Now I need a drink, your usual?"

Even before Janet had answered, he had poured her a drink and one for himself, and as he sat down, Janet could see he was far away, deep in thought.

"What's wrong, Roy? You seem so preoccupied. Did she have that much effect on you?"

"No, it's not that. I just had a bad feeling about her. That's all. I may be mistaken. Let's forget about it, shall we? I'm just glad she did not want to see the boathouse before the builders had it completely finished."

Janet knew better than to bring the matter up, and she left him to his own thoughts whilst she went off to find Morag and the children. Perhaps Sean could snap his father out of his depressive mood. *That woman certainly got to him*, she thought to herself. *I wonder why?*

Henry and Stella Francis drove away from the castle, and Henry asked, "How did things go, Marion? Were you were too quick off the mark or did you rush things? Why didn't he take the bait?"

"I don't know what it was, but I thought he was going to go for it, and suddenly, he went cold. He seemed spooked. I don't know if it was something I said or if, as you say, I went a bit too far and a little too fast. We can look at the tape when we get back to HQ. I'm sure they will want to analyse it as much as I do."

"That's not like you, Marion. Seduction is your speciality. You must be losing your touch. The chief won't like that. We were supposed to get this tied up and in the bag. The chance to have a whole year to search that place would be too much of a lost opportunity. We know he has connections with the IRA, but they are a defeated group, and we don't know what they are up to. It will be bad for our record to have failed in our mission. The chief will have to think of something else," Agent Cosby, alias Henry, stated, more than a little concerned that they had failed in their mission.

Agent Marion Stewart (Stella) sat in the passenger seat as they travelled quickly through the narrow lanes, her mind trying to analyse just where she had gone wrong. The divisional head of the Irish division of the British Secret Service had planned the operation down to a tee. He had explained to Marion that the man was a philanderer and had been as he had risen through each promotion in industry. It had almost been his downfall for, when he had been put forward first for a knighthood and later as a member of the House of Lords, the London agency had been worried about his womanising ways. It could, however, never be proved that he had ever forced a woman to have sex with him. He had never been known to rape anyone, nor could it be proven that he had never, when asked to stop, pushed the other party to go further. It had always been the case that he simply switched off and waited until the next opportunity had arisen. The man, it seemed, had never had to wait long. Women simply fell for him. Marion had to admit she had felt that her attraction had been more than a job for the agency; she had really wanted him to make love to her and that, in her case, was a first.

They drove back in silence, both deep in thought, towards their HQ in Dublin. What the chief would say, or how he would report their failure through to his chief, they could only guess. They could not, in their wildest dreams, have known that the London head of section had prepared for just such an outcome and had a contingency plan in place. He had not intended to fail after the amount of work they had done investigating Lord Croft, and all to no avail. The womanising man seemed to have done nothing wrong during his ascension to the very top of his career. The section head had been envious of the man's success with women, and it had seemed to him that no one got to the top just by hard work and tenacity; it was just not possible. Especially when he considered his own rise to be the head of the section, he had taken many dubious steps, not always legal or even by the rules. He was determined to get to the bottom of the reason for Lord Croft's change in life. He had given up what any man in business would do anything to achieve; he had bought a castle on the west coast of Ireland and was seemingly involved somehow with the now supposedly defunct IRA. He just had to get to the bottom of things by means fair or foul. It had become almost a personal vendetta between himself and the too-good-to-be-true Lord 'bloody' Croft.

The following morning, the next couple arrived with their new baby, which was about two months old. Morag took over charge of looking after the young child whilst its parents looked over the property. Carl and Camilla were Americans. Carl was on a sabbatical, to study the flora and fauna of south-west Ireland, from the University of Illinois. Camilla was very pretty; her figure had obviously recovered quickly from the recent birth. She wore a yellow sundress, a bit cool for the time of year, but she probably had not expected the weather to be this cold so early. Janet offered to show Carl around the garden as his main interest was the local vegetation. Once they had seen around the house, Roy asked Camilla if there was anything she wished to see again.

"I would like to see that wonderful big bedroom upstairs," she said, "and the nursery. It is just so cute."

Roy climbed the stairs behind Camilla. He tried to avoid looking eyes but the woman had such good legs, something that had always been one of his failings. Unable to resist another look, his eyes gravitated upwards. She wore no stockings, and he could see up the wide-flared skirt. Her thighs were just as good in shape as her calves were; his attention was drawn to a glint of red, and that intrigued his sense of propriety. *Why would anyone wear red panties with a yellow sun dress?* he thought to himself, his mind not really concentrating on where he was going. Then, as Camilla came to a halt at the top of the stairs, she half turned to ask him to point out which doorway was the bedroom in question. The corridor was long, with lots of doors, and she had not really noticed which of them had been the master bedroom when they were shown around earlier; Roy had not sensed her sudden halt, and he bumped into her from behind.

"I'm sorry," he said, a little embarrassed. "I did not see you stop. My mind was far away."

"No, Lord Croft, it was my fault entirely. I just stopped without thinking. I just wanted you to tell me which was the main bedroom."

Lord Croft's close proximity made her feel a little uncomfortable. He had put his hand out to steady her and save her from falling, and she had grabbed out at him. They were standing on the edge of the stairs in each other's arms. Up close and personal, she looked at him in a different light. She felt that he certainly had something going for him; he was good-looking, in that rugged sort of way; she could imagine him as the hero of many a film. He was also, from what she had seen, very wealthy, and his wife and children seemed really happy. The main thing that made her move away was that they were both married and not to each other. She came from a God-fearing family that looked down on infidelity. She had been born in the Midwest and had met her husband at Oklahoma University. He had been a professor in her botany classes, and after she had qualified, she stayed on to do research. Carl had been a perfect gentleman. He had never seemed to be interested in her whilst she had been an undergraduate, but when she had taken up her research post to do her postgraduate course, he had courted her. Camilla's father had been put off Carl, for the simple reason that he was a Brit who had no real church or religious upbringing. She had, she had had to admit to herself, fallen head over heels in love with him and, despite her father's concerns, they had been married. Her father had finally given up trying to persuade her otherwise, and eventually, the ceremony had been carried out by her own father, who was a pastor. Camilla had desperately wanted a child and, after only a year of marriage, Carl had agreed, but from the moment she had broken the wonderful news, that she was pregnant, he had never touched her sexually even once. He seemed to be completely put off by the fact that she had another life growing within her and, despite her pleadings, he had left her completely alone, even down to the fact that he had stopped sharing her bed.

Then, to her complete amazement, out of the blue only a couple of weeks ago, he had suddenly announced that he was going on a sabbatical to Ireland, for a year. She had thought it would be a wonderful chance for them to be away from her dogmatic family, always on the lookout for a reason to find fault with the man she loved. Now that her daughter had been born, she had hoped that Carl would begin to take up their life as it had been before she had become pregnant. They had been a wonderfully happy married couple that had been so deeply in love. She pulled herself away and stepped back, allowing Lord Croft to gain a safe footing. Roy apologised for his clumsiness once again and showed the young woman the large master bedroom used by him and Janet. He stood and watched as she looked once again into the large shower and took in the dressing room with its twin double wardrobes.

"My, your Lordship, that shower is large enough to hold a shower party in, and the space you have here is wonderful. I've been used to roughing it with Carl. He goes on these field trips all the time, and sometimes, the accommodation leaves a lot to be desired. This is just wonderful. Let me see that nursery again." Then, as if she found the arrangement strange, she asked, "Oh, are you sure it's all right leaving Cheryl with Morag, your children's nanny, all this time? She seems such a blessing. She must be a godsend to your wife."

Roy smiled to acknowledge Camilla's comment; it showed to the young American a pretty picture of what most Americans would perceive to be the perfect way of life as he showed her into the nursery. Roy was trying not to show how bored he was getting and how anxious he was becoming to get back downstairs. He had realised too late that he really should not have involved himself with the actual showing of the house, but Janet had been so insistent that they show an interest, for it would also give them an insight into how the prospective tenants felt about the property. Most people could not hide their feelings when they saw something for the first time, she had insisted.

Camilla spent time looking around and seeing where Morag slept and where the baby slept nearby. She thought, *how strange it was to let another person take full charge of your child, especially at night. The child would get confused as to who its real mother was, and it was not for her.* She was satisfied, and as she walked out of the nursery door, she asked,

"Lord Croft, would you excuse me. I need to use the bathroom."

"I'll wait downstairs, Mrs . . ."

"It's Camilla, your Lordship," she interrupted.

"All right, Camilla. I'll wait for you downstairs," Roy replied.

Roy was glad to be away from domesticity. He had never really involved himself in that side of life and preferred to leave that to Janet. *Where was she?* he wondered. She surely couldn't still be showing Carl around the garden all this time. Roy walked downstairs and gently pushed open the door to walk into the lounge, He stopped dead in his tracks at the sight before his unbelieving eyes. Janet was lying back on the settee. From what Roy could make out, her skirt was up around her waist, and Carl lay between her open thighs, on top of her, his trousers around his ankles. It was only too obvious what was going on and, to Roy's utter astonishment, far from struggling to get free, Janet was giving as good as she was getting. He watched as Carl ripped open the front of her dress and began kissing Janet's breasts. Roy stood stock-still. He was the philanderer, not Janet. As far as he knew, she had remained faithful to him from the day they had got married. He had never had reason to think otherwise. He backed from the doorway, hiding the hideous and painful view from his unbelieving eyes; for once in his life, he seemed at a loss for words. *God,* he thought to himself, *what the hell has gotten into her?* She has never shown any interest in anyone before, and now, here she is having wild and fully compliant sex with a complete stranger. He heard a sound from behind his back. It was Camilla coming down the stairs.

The sounds coming from the room could hardly be interpreted as anything other than two people having sex. The slap of flesh meeting flesh and the soft grunt and moan of pure pleasure stopped Camilla dead in her tracks. She looked enquiringly at Lord Croft as Janet's voice could be heard as she said,

"Oh, Carl, I never thought I would ever see you again after you left University to go to America. We had such great times then, and after that, all I can say is you are as good as ever."

It was Carl's voice that affected Camilla; she had hardly dared to move after hearing Janet's voice address her husband. He was obviously trying to get his breath under control as his deep sighs interspersed his words,

"Janet, I had no idea you lived in Ireland. No one told me you were married to a Lord, for goodness sake. The last I heard was you had married some old geezer, who was some kind of accountant. None of us could believe it."

Then, a few minutes later, Camilla heard her husband say,

"God, Janet, It's been a while since I had any sex, but I don't know what's come over me. I can't believe it. I'm so excited I'm ready again."

Before Roy could stop her, Camilla had pushed the door wide open, and she stood and gasped, seeing her husband having sex with Lady Croft. She could not believe her eyes, and she cried out, the sound coming from deep within her,

"Oh my God, Carl, how could you? I love you with all my heart, and now you have taken everything away. I can never forgive you, you bastard! My father was right. I should have listened to him. Oh my God, Cheryl, what will she think when she's old enough to know what you have done?"

With a cry of anguish that seemed to come up from her very soul, she burst into tears, unable to believe her own eyes. Carl, who had turned his head and seen Camilla standing there, gave a strangled cry of horror, and his face went white. He attempted to stand, making matters far worse, and cried out,

"Oh my God, Camilla, it's not what you think."

Camilla brought her hands up to her face to shut out the scene before her eyes and she ran from the room; the sound of her crying sent shudders through Carl's heart.

Carl was horror-struck; his mind went back to the time when he had been recruited at the university by British intelligence. He had just been glad of the money to help pay his way through varsity. There had been several weeks of training and all that cloak-and-dagger stuff. It had all been one big laugh to himself and several of his friends who had been similarly recruited. To the group as a whole, the entire escapade had seemed totally unreal at the time and quite an adventure. Carl and his friends had been warned then that they would be sleepers and might never be called to active service. Together with the others, Carl had signed the Official Secrets Act, and when he had finished university, he had gone on to get his doctorate and settled in America. He had never heard anything from his contacts until a few weeks ago. Then he had been called and reminded of his official status and the fact that he had been in receipt of a retainer each year. He was now required to put into practice what he had been trained to do.

The agency had offered him the opportunity to do a year's research on the west coast of Ireland to study the effects of climate change on the flora and fauna, an opportunity he had accepted eagerly. The drawback was that he had to take a tenancy of a castle in the area so that the intelligence services could go over the premises with a view to discover what its present occupant was up to. They had told him that the current owner and occupant was an English Lord and he was somehow involved with the IRA, which was supposedly defunct, but the agency had informed him that the group Lord Croft was involved with seemed very active and they needed to find out the whys' and wherefores' of the whole set-up. It had seemed so simple, at the time, but when he had seen Lady Croft, he had recognised her. Whilst they had been in the garden talking, Carl, who had always had a beard at university and was now clean-shaven, had made himself known. Lady Croft had stood stock-still; she had thought something about Carl had seemed familiar; now everything had become clear. She had thrown her arms around him and kissed him. Carl had been one of Janet's many lovers, and when they had got back into the confines of the lounge, nothing seemed more natural than to renew her embrace, and she kissed him again. This time, the kiss had been more passionate, and their arousal had progressed rapidly. Carl, who had not made love to his wife through the whole of her pregnancy, found that Janet's presence was affecting his libido, and his craving had been inflamed. His desire had grown like a brush fire in California. Janet's reasoning seemed to melt under Carl's seduction. She had been transported back to the days at university, and as Carl aroused her, she had offered no resistance. *Now*, he thought, *just look at the mess I have got myself into. To hell with the agency.* He was still in love with his wife.

Carl stood. He realised at once that he looked ridiculous. He made a grab for his trousers and, pulling them up, he rushed past Lord Croft, who still seemed spellbound at what he had witnessed. Otherwise, he would in all probability have killed Carl, 'the bastard'. Janet pulled her top together and fastened the buttons. She stood and let her skirt fall back down her legs, and then she sat down. Her hair was awry, and she looked sheepishly at Roy who, by this time, had sat down on another armchair, looking so crestfallen. Janet recovered her decorum and said simply,

"Don't you dare ask me to justify what you have just witnessed. I do not really have to give you any explanation. I have allowed you total sexual freedom since I first met you. I have a perfectly good explanation, but I will not have you looking at me in that disapproving manner. What is good for the gander, in this case, Roy Croft, is also good for the goose."

"Janet, it is not for me to judge you. As you say, you have given me every freedom a man could want. If you feel I have treated you shabbily, you should have told me. You have never condemned my activities, as far as I know, but you did tell me you would never want me to be monogamous. I have no intention of judging you in any way. I was just surprised, that's all. You have never shown any interest in another man, and now suddenly this."

Janet took pity on the man she loved. She did, after all, she acknowledged to herself, owe him some kind of explanation. She began telling him that in the garden Carl had told her who he was.

"At university, he always had a beard," Janet said as though that explained everything.

"I suddenly recognised him. Carl was an old friend from my university days."

Janet's face seemed to hang in one pose as she remembered something from time gone by.

"It was when we were in the garden that we realised we knew each other. I just kissed him as though it was an everyday occurrence. Time seemed to have stood still, and we lost track of the time reminiscing about old times and old friends. We came back into the lounge and, when we embraced and he kissed me, it was just like we were back at varsity. When he made his move on me, I simply, out of old habits, let him make love to me. It was as though we had never stopped being lovers. I gave him free reign just as I had done all those years ago at university. I knew I was safe, and he had confessed that he had not made love to that young wife of his since she got pregnant, so he had an awful lot of time to make up for. He always was a skilful lover. I must admit it gave me back a feeling of youthfulness. I felt young again, and I have to confess that I really enjoyed the experience."

Roy nodded sadly. Although he could not object to his wife's infidelity, he felt something had gone out of their marriage for ever, but before Roy could respond, Camilla and Carl came into the room. Camilla was still weeping bitterly. Carl attempted to offer some kind of apology, but Janet rose and took him aside and spoke quietly. He pulled away from her as though being by her would make matters worse. Then he picked up his briefcase from the coffee table, and Janet escorted him out of the room. Camilla was beside herself, and Roy stood, putting his arm around her, to comfort her. She turned on him and said vehemently,

"I don't want any comfort from you, Lord Croft. I think your wife has done enough damage already. I don't want to give my husband any opportunity to say I was compliant with what he did, so please leave me alone. Despite appearances, I could never have let my desires get the better of me. I still love my husband, and we have fences to repair. I believe your intentions are good, but I want nothing more from you. Now, if you don't mind, I would like to collect my daughter and leave. I have had enough of Ireland to last me a lifetime. It's a den of iniquity. I'll be glad to get back to the bosom of my family. I'm sorry to sound so unsympathetic. You must be as distressed as I am, but I must go. Goodbye, your Lordship."

Roy felt suitably rebuffed as he watched Morag hand the baby girl to her mother. She looked at the tears running down the young woman's face and stared at Lord Croft as though it was his fault. She was not used to seeing women so upset in the Croft household. They normally looked happy and contented. This was something new, and she did not understand any of it.

Janet came back into the room. Roy had disappeared. He had walked out of the kitchen door and was cooling off on the quayside. He had to adjust to things and vindicate the new Janet. He knew it was irrational to feel the way he did, but he could not help it. He tried to get his mind around things; Janet had seen him with Elian on the boat; she had told him so, and he knew that she had seen him with Kerry and others. He could not come to terms with how she had put up with him over the years; he could only put it down to the fact that Janet had been the woman who had instructed him in the art of pleasing a woman before they were married. She had, at that time, had no intention of leaving her husband, and she had told him she never expected him to be faithful to her. But that, he tried to reason, was before they had got married. Perhaps she had felt that once she had given him permission to be promiscuous, she could not go back on her word. *Oh God*, he thought to himself, *I will never understand how the mind of a woman really works. All I know is that I was horrified when I opened that door.* He would have carried on, but he heard Janet call from the kitchen that the meal was ready. He went back inside in a very subdued frame of mind. Janet, on the other hand, seemed to have put the whole incident behind her, and the meal was conducted in a mood of indifference, with no arguments Sean was sitting with them. When the meal was over, Morag came in. It was time for the young man's bath.

When Roy and Janet were alone, Roy said,
"Janet, we have to make a decision about the lease, and I'm sure as hell not going to let lover boy Carl have it after tonight's performance. Although I must admit his wife looked very attractive, perhaps we should reconsider. I'm sure she may want to get back to her husband. It would appear that they do not, as we do, have an open marriage."
"Roy, you are incorrigible. I'm sure Camilla would think you are too old to have a fling with, even to get back at Carl. I would think from what she said tonight that her religion would simply not allow it."
Roy looked at Janet with a glint in his eyes,
"That comment would not seem to apply to local girls. They seem to have no hang-ups with their religion, even though they may be damned for what they do. I've heard one or two of them say it's a mortal sin. If so, who cares? The other couple, Stella and Henry, what do you think about them?"
"It would appear you turned the woman down. You may never have a second chance. Sleep on it for a couple of days and make up your mind then. I've got to finalise my own travel arrangements well before you finalise any lease arrangements. I think we should put the whole incident behind us and get on with our lives," Janet said, looking at Roy, almost daring him to comment.
Roy was not in any hurry to have an argument about either his or Janet's infidelity; it was a dangerous ground, and he knew it, so he let the matter lie. He thought to himself that if the price of his sexual freedom was Janet's occasional fall from domestic bliss, he would just have to put up with it. He smiled and put the sordid matter behind him.

Chapter 19

The next few days were a hive of activity. Gordon arrived alone for once, and the workmen from Charlie were on site, as were all the materials. Roy called Gordon to one side and told him that he wanted whoever leased the place not to be able to discern that new work had been carried out. Gordon understood and said,

"I've had quite a bit of experience with that type of work. Quite a lot of my contracts since the practice has grown to its new level have been to do with restoration work on listed buildings, and if we had not been able to disguise the new cement, it would have stood out like a sore thumb. Leave it to me. I'll have a word with the foreman."

Gordon disappeared, and Roy carried on working in the office. He was trying to decide how to carry the extra fuel he would need to get them across the Atlantic by whichever route they took. He was trying to decide if it should be a disposable deck tank or a towable tank between two rubber inflatable floats. Gordon stuck his head around the door and smiled.

"I've spoken to the foreman and explained what I wanted, and he understood immediately. Charlie's got a good man there. Now, I need to know if you want to seal the staircase down to the old ammunition store. I understand you will want it reopened at some time in the future, so I have made provision to seal and separate each level using a concrete raft that will merge in with the old concrete floors."

Roy could not avoid being impressed as he saw the men slowly transform each level completely, isolating one from the other. Roy wondered how they would cope with the lift. Well, ammunition hoist would have been a better term. Under Gordon's supervision, the team dismantled the lift itself. The winding gear, supports, and slides were dismantled and stored in the lower level. Then the rafts were cast, isolating the floors, until there was no sign that the lift had ever existed, and the only way into the lower level was through the escape tunnel that Gordon had described when he had studied the original proposal. The back wall of the workshop was bricked up and rendered so that no trace of any of the secret areas was visible to the naked eye, and even if someone broke through to the rear workshop, no trace of the stairs or lift shaft would be discovered. It looked perfect.

Gordon proudly showed Roy when the job was finished and took him through the grounds to the rear entrance. Using the secure key, he opened the door and switched on the lights. The tunnel opened up before them, and Roy followed the wartime shaft through until he arrived at the lower level. He could still get to the arms and ammunition, but there was no way he could load torpedoes, and he was glad that Elian had remembered to load and check the two tubes on the boat before work had commenced. There was no way into the spares store from this level now, that could only be accessed from above via the new entrance created by Gordon in case they should need spares for the boat when they returned. Roy could not see anything past the newly built wall at the rear of the boathouse. The underground tunnel leading from the kitchen had been bricked up at both ends, and the kitchen end had been racked out as a wine cellar. The brickwork had been treated with some equipment that Gordon had brought with him, and the wine cellar looked as though it had been there since the original castle was built, cobwebs and all. The outside of the boathouse looked untouched and Charlie's men had been scrupulously clean so that no trace of their work was visible at all. All the work and cement mixing had been carried out at the lower levels. It looked perfect from every angle, and Roy was convinced that no one would find their way beyond the back wall.

Elian had checked and rechecked the boat, ensuring that everything was as near perfection as she could make it. She had gone over the stores with Gael and Fiona, making sure every contingency was covered. The boat was ready. Gael had checked the weapons and the ammunition and ensured that everything was in its place in the hidden compartments below decks. Elian had done both options: the northern route via Greenland and the southern route down to North Africa and across to Brazil. They would choose which one according to the weather forecast when Roy decided the final date. Janet had finalised her travel arrangements, and she had booked a suite at the Sand Piper Hotel in Bridgetown, Barbados. She had been told by Kate that one of her friends had highly recommended the hotel as being ideal for a family. It had a private beach, and some of the family suites were right on the sand with its own area of the hotel's private beach. To Janet, it had sounded like a dream come true. She was all prepared to leave within the next few days.

The phone call came out of the blue. Janet answered the call and, to her utter surprise, it was Carl.

"Hello, Janet. I'm sorry we rushed away, but Camilla was inconsolable. I had to get her out of the house. She has calmed down now, and we are going to stay on to do my research. We found a small house up along the coast north of Tralee. She seems to have accepted our little dalliance better than I ever expected. She is still wary and does not like me to leave her alone. It will get better, but I won't be able to see you again before you leave for Barbados."

Janet sat up, stunned. She had not mentioned to him that she had any intention of going to Barbados. She had only finalised it a few days before. How on earth could he have known where she was going?

"I'm sorry to hear that, Carl," Janet said, her mind still registering the fact that he knew where she was headed.

"I had to tell you that another of our mutual friends from university is nearby where you are going. It's Dr Michael Crosby. I was talking to him yesterday and mentioned that you would be arriving soon and that you would be staying at on the island. I expect he will call you to have a drink with you. Oh, I must go. I hear Camilla calling me. She must have seen I was not in the kitchen. Bye. I'll see you again soon, I hope."

The line went dead as he replaced the receiver. Janet's heart was pounding. She had heard from no one from university for years, and now, out of the blue, she had met one lover and would soon be hearing from another. Michael, of all people! God, her heart was pounding. He had always been one of her favourites. He was so good in bed. She had lost contact with him when he went off to the West Indies to do research into Marine Biology of sea life. She had never heard from him since he left. The trip to the West Indies was beginning to look more and more interesting. She put the matter of Michael to the back of her mind for later. What was predominating in her thoughts was how Carl had known where she was heading. She would have to mention it to Roy, but then he would have to know that Carl had called her. Was it worth the upset? She would have to wait and see.

Lord Croft was alone in his study. It was a corner of the boathouse now that the workshop had been all but isolated, and there was no longer any means to get into a large part of that area. He had had the telephone moved from his old office to the new study, and he was at his desk calculating the fuel he would need, including a reserve, to do the crossing. The sharp ring of the telephone shook him from the deep dark thoughts, where his mind was imagining the worst that could happen during his proposed crossing. Roy's concentration was broken as he picked up the receiver.

"Lord Croft here. Can I help you?"

The voice that answered was broad Midwestern American; the only person he knew with that accent was Camilla. She sounded hesitant at first.

"Lord Croft, I really want to apologise for my rude behaviour the other day. I really should not have snubbed your offer of condolence as I did. What happened was really not any fault of yours. I'm sure you are no more responsible for the actions of your wife any more than I am for those of my husband."

"Camilla, I understand things were not normal. I fully understand how you felt at the time. I have to admit I was a little taken aback myself," Roy replied.

With his mind racing over the possibility of seducing the young woman as retribution for Carl's actions, he was, however, still curious as to why she had rung him. He did not believe it was just to apologise.

"Lord Croft, I don't know where to begin, and if I ring off, it's because Carl has walked into the room. I hope you can make more sense of this than I did. He told me some story about being recruited by some Secret Service agency when he was at university."

At the words Secret Service agency, Roy's ears pricked up. She had his full attention, and he listened intently as she went on to explain how he had told her about his training, how he had remained as a sleeper, and finally how he had been restored to active duty in order that the agency could lease his castle with a view to searching the premises. The agency had told Carl that there was little or no chance that they would ever obtain a search warrant with the flimsy information they had. They were aware that he was involved with the IRA, but not why or for what reason. If they had a year to search the castle, they hoped to find evidence to clarify the situation. Camilla stopped speaking as though she was listening and then continued,

"Lord Croft, I hope that helps you in some way. Carl told me that he expected them to be annoyed with him when he recognised your wife, and they, well you know, when they had sex. They seemed happy to overlook his indiscretion and told him he had done an excellent job. I don't understand any of it but . . . Oh, I hear him coming, I have to go."

The phone went dead, leaving Roy agog at what she had told him. It explained the bugs he had found on the boat, the feeling of being watched.

They had nothing on him at all, only an unfounded suspicion. He had to make doubly sure there was nothing to see. He pulled out the plans he had received from the MOD when he had purchased the property. No doubt the agency, whoever they were, would have got hold of a copy themselves. The drawings showed the castle and the boathouse but not the underground passage or the workshop and the armoury two levels below, which had obviously been carried out by the clandestine branch of whichever agency had used the castle during the Second World War. The changes had never been updated on any MOD plans. Roy released a sigh of relief. *Thank God for small mercies*, he thought to himself. At least, if they gained entry, they would not know where to look. He rang Sam and relayed what Camilla had told him but omitted to tell him what had caused her to tell him. He told Sam that she was shocked to learn that her husband was some kind of spy and was just against what her husband did in secret behind everyone's back, including her own. Sam was shaken to the core by the news and asked Roy to go over to the house when he had done some checks with his contacts.

The result of what he had learned from Camilla, added to what he knew before, was that it made Roy even more determined to get away as quickly as he could. He did not mention it to Janet in case she worried unduly. If he was caught, so be it; but there was no use in Janet worrying her head about him until something happened. He would just make provision. He knew there were thousands of euros in the safe hidden two storeys below. He would just tell her where it was. He walked into the lounge where she sat reading. The children were in the nursery with Morag.

"Janet, I want to discuss something with you," he said.

"What's the matter, Roy? You look worried," Janet enquired, looking at him closely.

"It's not that I'm worried about anything in particular," he lied convincingly, "but if you ever needed money in a hurry or if you had to come back before me or at any time and I was away on one of my trips," Roy began, not quite knowing how to put the matter so that she would not worry even more.

"There's always money in the bank, Roy. Why should I ever be without? I'm not a spendthrift."

"Listen to me, Janet. I go away on these trips, and you know the sea as well as I do. I could get injured or, even worse, so listen to me, will you? I'm trying to explain."

Janet looked at him hard.

"I don't want to think about that, Roy. Why are you telling me this now? Do you think something is going to happen to you?" she asked, her heart fluttering in her chest and her stomach churning at the thought of being without him.

"No. Just listen to me, will you? I will show you a secret entrance that no one but you and I and Gordon are aware of. It leads to an underground store, and in that store, there is a safe. The combination to open it is your name, using the position of the letters in Janet, and you turn the dial to zero, and from that point, you turn the dial right and left alternately. So right ten, left one, right fourteen, left five, right twenty. It's not complicated, but never write it down."

"All right, but you worry me telling me this now of all times. Why tell me now when I have just shown you that I cannot be trusted. I had sex with Carl, and I know it upset you."

"Let's not get into that again. You know I would give you all I had, and start again. I can accept what you did. It just came as a shock, that's all. You and the children are everything to me. With everyone else, sex is just that; sex plain and simple. There's no love attached to it, whatever you may think. I trust it's the same with you."

"Yes, Roy. It just made me feel young and alive. I was elated to think I was still attractive to other men despite having had two children. It was just good for my ego. I will do my best, but I cannot promise it will never happen again. It made me feel that I was twenty again, and I have to admit I liked the feeling," Janet said, a little too eagerly for Roy's liking.

Roy sighed. It was something he would never get used to but, as she had pointed out, what had been good for him over the years had to be good for her. There was no denying that. He decided to change the subject.

"Janet, let's talk about something else. What are we going to do about the castle? I don't think we can let it to Carl and Camilla after what happened. I'm sorry, but that has to be that. On the other hand, there is always Henry and Stella. They are the only ones who made any sort of offer. It's either them, or I have to employ a caretaker."

"There's always Fergus," she said. "He could operate the charters from here just as you do."

"I had thought about that, but I don't want him doing IRA work from here whilst we are away. You know it's not quite legal, and the last thing

I want is for our property to be seized through no fault of ours. So, no, I don't think that is an alternative."

"But I thought you said you did not think she seemed quite right as she came on to you too fast. I would have thought that would have been right up your street. I'm still surprised you did not take her up on her offer."

"It just didn't feel right. We have had no other offers, so unless I start looking for a caretaker, I think we have to accept their offer, don't you?"

"I leave it up to you, Roy. You make the decision. If you feel it's all right, you've taken enough precautions, so test them and let her have the place for a year. It will certainly prove one way or another if you are right."

"That's decided. Then I'll ring the agent and set things up. When are you due to leave?"

Janet explained that she just had to confirm the date to the travel agent, and she could go as early as the following week. Roy had been delighted, and it was left to Janet to finalise the date of departure. Roy took her out behind the castle and showed her the hidden door and showed her where the key was kept hidden in the wall. There is another aboard the cruiser just in case this one gets lost, and Gordon has a spare locked away in his office. Janet understood but was still worried why now of all times he had told her where his cash was kept, but once again, she did not push him for an explanation.

After they had returned to the castle, Roy had to go and see Sam before he left, and hopefully, he would be leaving to go on his long cruise at around the same time as Janet was flying or shortly after. He could not wait to get away from the thought of being under surveillance by whichever British Secret Service agency. Perhaps in a year's time, they would finally give up and leave him alone. Sam, for all his contacts, had been unable to locate which Secret Service agency had Roy under surveillance. If anyone knew, no one was talking. It seemed a mystery. Roy arrived at the house and was shown into the study. Sam rose and greeted him with a warm handshake and a hug.

"Good to see you, Roy. Sit down. Now, I'm sorry to have to tell you I have been unable to find out which brach of the Secret Service is keeping an eye on you. My contacts either don't know or, for some reason, they are not telling me. Both reasons give me a bad feeling, and I'm glad you are going to get away for a while. I'll see what I can find out whilst you are away."

He handed Roy a stiff measure of Irish whisky. Roy took a more than ample drink and relished the warmth as the smoky flavour fanned the inside of his mouth, and the warmth of the rich spirit flowed down into his stomach. It made him feel a little better but did not lift the sense of foreboding.

"That's a drop of the best, Sam. You're spoiling me," Roy said, smiling, to hide his concern.

"I can't do too much for a good friend, Roy. I'm going to miss you whilst you're away, and I know Kate will miss you. She thinks the world of you," adding, as if to cover what he had just admitted, "as well as Janet, and the children. When are you off?"

"Janet leaves next week, and I shall go as soon as I've tied up the lease on the castle. I've asked one of the couples to come and see me again. That's Stella, the one with the yacht and her husband Henry. A singularly mismatched couple, if ever I saw one. I don't know how they could live together for more than a couple of months, let alone years. They just do not gel as a couple. Oh, by the way, keep an eye on the place whilst we're away, will you?"

"I'll make sure the gardeners tell me everything that goes on. I'm sure Bridget, Cathleen, and Kerry will be in touch if anything goes awry inside. Don't you worry about a thing. You forget they are all handpicked."

Roy looked quizzically.

"Kerry and Cathleen?" Roy asked, shaken by the depths of the intertwined tendrils and connections of the people he employed Sam was so readily admitting to him.

"Both!" Sam said. "You forget I have quite a bit of control over what goes on around here, even down to the priest and the curate."

Roy smiled, remembering how Janet and he had worried that they would not be able to get Sean christened, and how surprised they had been when he had so readily agreed, even down to asking about their health.

"OK, Sam, I understand. I shall not give the place a second thought. I'll leave everything in your capable hands."

Roy drove back feeling a lot more reassured that things would be looked after during his absence. He rang the letting agent and asked him to arrange a second visit from the yachtswoman and her husband if they were still interested in leasing the castle. The agent rang back only minutes later,

"I rang the number, Lord Croft, but it seems they were out, so I left a message. I'll call you as soon as I hear anything."

The Irish branch of the Britishe Secret Service Agency were overjoyed when they got the message and relayed the news up to London HQ. It looked as though they would have the opportunity to go over the place with a fine-tooth comb after all. Henry would need to be recalled to go for the second visit, and Marion would be the one to actually stay in the castle whilst they searched the premises. She did actually own a yacht and had volunteered to stay on and use the facilities just in case the IRA smelt a rat during Lord Croft's absence. Things were going according to plan; they would soon know just what it was that the IRA and Lord Croft were up to.

Marion, aka Stella, accompanied by Henry, arrived back at the castle after they had arranged the visit through the letting agency. Roy welcomed them into the house, and they sat and discussed the finer details. Roy informed them that the castle would be fully serviced.

"The gardens will be taken care of by my two gardeners, so there will be no need to concern yourselves over the grounds. I would not expect you to be responsible for that. The grounds of the property are quite extensive. The cook, Bridget, together with two maids, are included in the rental. If you have your own staff, they may stay here, but if you do not intend to use any of mine, I need to know. I will have to make alternative arrangements as we want them to be here when we return."

"That will be fine, Lord Croft. My husband spends quite a lot of his time away, so I shall be here alone most of the time. I would like to bring my yacht over some time before you leave, just to get used to the harbour, if that's all right with you," Stella asked.

To Roy, it appeared that Henry seemed superfluous to requirements as Stella seemed to take all the decisions and ask all the questions. Roy put it down to the fact that it was Stella who would be using the house and put any questions to the back of his mind. He would, however, wonder why he had not queried it, at a date not too distant into the future.

They shook hands on the deal, and Roy promised to have his solicitor contact theirs within a couple of days to finalise matters. Roy watched them drive away, thinking to himself, *Why did I turn her down last time? She is a very attractive woman with a mind of her own. I may get the chance to take up her offer before we leave.*

'Connaught, Connaught and O'Malley', Lord Croft's solicitors, rang two days later and queried the fact that they were being asked to draw up the lease in the name of Mrs Stella Francis. Was that in order? Roy pondered the question. It proved what he had thought all along. They had never seemed like a married couple, but why the pretence? It all seemed too much like a one-act play, and he was determined to get to the bottom of it. He agreed and asked for the papers to be sent to him for signing when she had signed, and not the other way about. She would be coming to the castle with her yacht before he left. He would tackle her about it then.

Roy took Janet together with Morag and the two children to the International airport at Shannon; Elian and Gael followed in the Land Cruiser with the luggage. It was as well they were flying first class. The luggage would have cost a fortune otherwise. It had been arranged that Lord Croft be allowed to go through to the First Class lounge to wait until the flight was ready for take-off, one of the benefits of the titled rank. Janet was concerned about Roy taking the cruiser across the Atlantic.

"Roy," she said softly, "please be careful. I want to see you alive and well. Don't take any chances. I shall not rest until I know you are safely across that stretch of water. I know that Elian and the others will take care of you, in more ways than one, but just remember I love you, and so do the children."

It was all getting a bit tearful for Janet and the children. Roy was glad when the flight was called, and Janet was ushered out of the lounge, on to the electric buggy, to be driven towards the boarding gate. Roy stood and watched the plane climb away westwards, and he drove back to the castle. The place seemed too quiet, and he was glad to go down to the quayside and spend the evening with his crew, something he would be doing every night over the next couple of weeks. He was not surprised when Elian walked back to the castle with him. It seemed only natural when they went upstairs and to bed. It was just as though they were a couple. They made love well into the night before falling into a deep sleep.

Chapter 20

The following morning, Lord Croft stood on the quayside and watched as the yacht tacked across the entrance to the harbour, and as the craft slipped towards the harbour itself, the sail lost the wind as it was sheltered by the cliff. The sail fluttered softly as it struggled to find the breeze; Roy was admiring Stella's obvious ability as, unhurriedly, the mainsail was lowered and the yacht approached slowly under the foresail until that too was lowered and the craft eased alongside the quay and Roy caught the rope and slipped it over through the rings fore and aft. To Roy, Stella had brought the yacht into the harbour as easily as he or Elian would have done with the cruiser. Roy had always considered yachts to be ungainly, compared with the cruiser, but the woman at the helm had made it seem just as easy, if not easier.

Stella waved, her hair held in place by a simple scarf tied at the back. Her auburn hair lacked the neatness he had seen when she had visited before. Her face, ruddy from the breeze and the lack of any make-up, made her more attractive, to Roy, than ever. She moved with grace and tightened the lines securing the craft. The rubbing streaks and fenders had been carefully placed preventing the sides from rubbing against the stone quay. She was dressed in white slacks and a woollen top. She wore deck pumps so that there was no sound as she jumped from the yacht to the quay.

"It's good to see you again, Lord Croft. I'm so glad you did not take offence at anything I said or did."

She put her finger to her lips and took up a coy attitude. Then she deliberately slid her finger into her mouth and pouted her lips as she sucked her finger in a manner that was almost erotic. It may have been innocent to anyone watching, but after what Roy had witnessed on her previous visit, it was confirmation that the offer was still open.

Roy invited her up to the castle, and they sat in the lounge drinking when Roy asked casually,

"Where's Henry today?"

"He's off on one of his travels," Stella said, covering for the fact that he had not been able to accompany her to take up the tenancy.

Roy decided to find out whether she, like Carl, was working on some kind of investigation. He had to get to the bottom of this. He wanted to know what this was all about.

"You mean one of his assignments, don't you?"

Stella stopped dead in her tracks, her mouth half open as if she was frozen, unable to reply. Then, as she recovered her composure quickly, but not quickly enough, she stammered,

"Assignment? What do you mean? I don't understand," she asked, wondering what his Lordship knew.

She motioned him to be quiet as she reached behind her waist and pulled out a small transmitter. Roy stood and watched as she switched the small device off.

"That's better. Now, we can talk. I really don't understand what you mean by assignment," she said.

"What the hell!" Roy asked, looking askance. "Is that some kind of transmitter?" Then in answer to her question he replied, "Oh, I think you understand all too well, Stella. The game is up. If you want a year in this castle, you'd better come clean, or all bets on the lease are off."

Stella was visibly shaken. How could Lord Croft possibly know about the agency? No one knew about them. They were a little known subdivision of MI5 and MI6. What they did was not open to public knowledge. How was she going to handle this? She knew that cutting off the transmission would have alerted someone at HQ. She only hoped someone was listening out for her if things started to go wrong.

She was only too aware that she was taking too long to come to a discussion. Lord Croft suddenly interrupted her thinking,

"Stella, I'm waiting for your explanation. I know all about you and your so-called husband Henry," Roy blagged, feeling he was definitely on to something.

"But how could you? I mean . . ." Stella stammered, feeling exposed and isolated now that she had cut off the transmission.

Roy pressed home his advantage.

"You had better come clean. I could turn nasty. You are in my domain now," Roy said, menacingly.

Stella realised that she was trapped. Whatever she did would expose her more. If she made a break for safety or defended herself, she was virtually admitting that Lord Croft was right in his assumption. If she did nothing, Lord Croft might get nasty. She had not heard that he was violent, but that did not mean she was safe. She was not a field agent in that she did not carry a weapon. She normally did seductions, not violence or killings, which were not in her field. She was supposed to have seduced Lord Croft, but something had alerted him, and now she was way out of her depth. There was no alternative; she would confess.

"Oh, all right, Lord Croft. I'll come clean. They can no longer see or hear me. They will send help as soon as they realise I'm no longer transmitting, so we don't have much time. All I was supposed to do was to seduce you and, on the facts we had, it was not going to be too difficult in your case. I was told you were a man who had slept with many women in your time, often to take advantage of a situation, and you were not known to show any violence to your conquests. I was to get you to sign the lease, and the agency would take this place apart. Apart from your connection with the IRA, nothing is known about you.

The powers that be just want to know why you are involved with a defunct organisation. Knowing your background, it made no sense at all. They have no way of tying you into the IRA before the Good Friday Agreement. Your boat has been spotted off North Africa and the Spanish Coast, but no one knows why. I was to get the lease in place, and the powers that be would send in a team of experts to try and find the connection. That's all I know honestly. Now either let me go, or don't. They know I'm here, and with no transmissions they will, in all probability, have already have despatched my backup."

"Very clever, Stella, or whatever your real name is. If you want to lease this place, you had better contact whoever was listening and tell them you are OK, and you'd better do it now," Roy said, realising he did not want to face more agents, he just wanted to get out of the country for a while.

Marion (Stella) studied the man standing before her and made a decision. He did not really pose a serious threat. Nothing in his file showed that. She walked to the telephone and looked at Roy enquiringly. Roy understood and nodded his head. Agent Marion Stewart dialled the code, followed by the number, and the call was answered almost immediately.

"Marion here," she said. "I'm OK! You can call off the dogs. I stumbled and switched off my set. I've only just realised it. Yes, I'm alone at the moment. I'm in the bathroom, and I'm using the mobile landline. I'll switch it back on when I rejoin Lord Croft. Is that understood? What? Is that really necessary? Oh, all right, "Bluebeard 147". Are you satisfied now? Yes, I'll press the emergency call button if I'm threatened. The man seems perfectly charming. All right, I'll call you later with an update."

"Lord Croft, my name is, as you will have gathered from my phone call, Marion Stewart. I am employed by one of the government security agencies, and I am in the Irish Branch. I am in breach of the Secrets Act just by telling you that, and I could, at best, lose my job, at worst spend time in jail. I am trusting you. I have seen the dossier they have compiled on you from when you were put forward for your knighthood. I have no reason to believe you will do me any harm. Am I right in that assumption?" Marion asked, hoping her assumption was correct.

Roy was keen to see how much she would tell him and, not wishing to alarm her unduly, said,

"No, Marion, or Stella, whichever it is I doubt if either is your real name. I have no intention of harming you whatsoever."

"Good," Marion replied. "Before you ask, I have no idea why they are doing such a deep check on you, other than your involvement with the IRA. I was hoping to be recalled after the Good Friday Agreement, but someone high up wants to be sure that the group no longer presents any threat. The fact that you, a Lord of the realm, are involved seems to have upset someone, I don't know who. I believe if you let things go ahead and, as I suspect, they find nothing, they will let the matter drop. Nothing I have seen or heard has been put on paper, so it may be someone high up, who has a personal grudge against you, or someone in the group of the IRA you are associated with."

"Whoever it is must want me or the other person badly because he sent another couple, who I believe was also sent by your agency," Roy informed her. "What you have told me makes sense, but I have not offended anyone as far as I know. Your theory that it might be someone in our cell is more than possible. I'll warn them."

"Just don't let on who told you," Marion said, smiling. "It may get back. I know how these things work. I believe they had a field agent and a contact that disappeared under mysterious circumstances, in this very area. This may just be a follow-up. I know the IRA smuggled arms into the country during the trouble, and we have confirmation of that. You were not around until after the settlement, but you were suspected of assisting with something, and we were unable to discover just what that was. I don't suppose you have any intention of telling me, have you?" Marion asked cheekily.

Roy shook his head and replied,

"I have a good mind to bring the matter to the House of Lords. You have admitted you have nothing whatsoever to suggest I have committed any crime, and I am the subject of a security check by some unspecified branch of MI5, or was it MI6, or some other bloody organisation funded by the taxpayer, in an attempt to implicate me in the activities of one of my charter clients. It's outrageous. Oh, I know it's not your fault. You are only doing your job. Now that we have got that out of the way, what will you have to drink?"

Roy believed everything was squared away. It was time to put the work to the test.

"Would you like to look around the boathouse? I'm afraid you won't be able to put the yacht in there unless you lower the mast. There is a windlass powered by electricity to recover the hull for the winter. I think there would be ample clearance with the mast down. Let's go and see, shall we?"

Marion was amazed at Lord Croft's audacity. He was aware of what they wanted to do to him. He was very self-assured; she liked that in a man. They need not have asked her to seduce this man in the line of duty. The more she saw of him, the more he turned her on. He seemed to have a raw animal magnitude about him, an attraction she found hard to resist. She would not show her interest. He had turned her down once. The approach must come from him this time, and she knew it would come, but not when. They chatted happily as they walked along the quay. Roy showed her the wicket gate set in the huge doors.

"It's a bit inconvenient having to walk outside to get to the boathouse but it keeps the house and the boating separate. Janet is not a boating person, and the children are too small, so in a way it has its compensations."

"I see your point," replied Marion.

They walked inside, and she was amazed to see how big the place was. But with a seventy-five-foot cruiser to house, Lord Croft would need a huge place. His boat was more than double the length of hers, and the hull of her yacht would look small inside. She looked around. There was no obvious signs that any work had been carried out recently. In fact, the back wall looked mucky and could do with a fresh coat of paint.

"It looks as though this place could do with a fresh coat of paint. Would you object if I did that? I just have that sort of mind. I like nice clean boathouses," Marion said, looking around.

Roy smiled to himself. The job Gordon and the team had done was very convincing. It did indeed look as though the paint had been on the wall since the time the boathouse was built.

"No, I don't mind in the least. I'll order some paint in for you if you like. It's a job I've been meaning to get done, but I just never seemed to get round to it. If you're happy, let's get back to the house. Is there anything you want to see in the main house, or are you OK?"

"If you don't mind, I'll just wander around on my own. I need to get used to the place anyway. You don't really mind if I do it alone, do you?" Marion asked.

"I don't mind in the least. Will you be staying for lunch?" Roy asked.

"If it's no trouble, I'd love to," Marion replied, her senses picking up that there might be an opportunity to redeem her past failure.

Lord Croft watched her climb the stairs. She had taken off the scarf from around her head, and the auburn hair cascaded down over her shoulders. Her slacks emphasised the outline of her trim backside, and the woollen top did little to hide the size of her breasts. He thought, *if only she had not come on to me so hard last time, I might have been able to have had the pleasure of investigating those assets further.* He turned away and walked into the kitchen where Bridget was preparing his lunch.

"Make that lunch for two, Bridget. I have a guest. It will give you a chance to prove your value to the new tenant," Roy informed her.

"Certainly, Lord Croft. It will be ready by about two o'clock, if that's all right with you. What's the new tenant's name, if I may ask?"

"Her name is Stella Francis," Roy replied.

Roy walked down the steps from the kitchen to the newly created wine cellar. The place smelt dusty and was full of cobwebs, thanks to Charlie's team. Roy had not had time to inspect the wine. He had bought it in bulk from the auctioneers, who had advertised a bulk lot of wine from a wine store in liquidation. The cellar certainly looked authentic. The wine racks were covered in a fine film of dust and stacked from floor to ceiling with bottles. Roy selected a bottle and wiped the dust from the label. It was French and was surprisingly a Chateau-bottled claret. He carried it back up into the kitchen and through to the dining room.

Roy uncorked the wine, tested the bouquet, and tasted a small amount in a glass; the wine was not the best but very palatable. Marion came down from her inspection, and from what she could see from her cursory look, the whole project was a complete waste of time and money, but if the agency wanted her to stay in the castle for a whole year, she would treat it as a holiday.

"What's for lunch?" she asked.

"It smelt meaty, so I chose a red. Is that to your taste, Secret Agent Marion? I have told the cook your name is Stella Francis, by the way," Roy added.

"Oh, that's a bit below the belt. I've confessed all, and I need to switch my microphone back on, so can we be friends for a while at least?"

"It would be a pleasure, Mrs Francis, or as you are about to reconnect, should I call you Stella? I shall have to be careful. I'm easily confused."

"Yes," she replied. "I don't believe a word of it. I have a feeling it would take a lot to confuse you, Lord Croft."

She reached behind and under her sweater to try and switch the small box back on.

"You'll have to give me a hand," she said.

Roy went behind her and pulled up her sweater, and he switched the tiny lever to the on position. It was quite simple, and something she could have done without his help. He put his arm around her waist and drew her back against him. The other hand slid up under her sweater and cupped one of her ample breasts. Far from offering any resistance, she snuggled back and tipped her bead. Then, pursing her lips, she invited him to kiss her. Roy refrained, and removed his hand and smiled as she pouted her lips in disappointment.

Lunch was served, and the venison pie was excellent. They drank the wine, and after Cathleen had served cheese and biscuits, they withdrew into the lounge.

"So, Lord Croft, is the offer we made to lease the castle acceptable? If so, will you be signing the document today and when do you plan to leave for the West Indies? I understand from what you said earlier that Lady Croft is already there. It's such a pity she will miss the voyage. I would give my right arm to make that journey, but I must admit I would prefer to use the wind rather than go by power."

"I prefer to use power and not rely on a power that is as fickle as the weather. I could not imagine being becalmed in the middle of the ocean. I told you before that Lady Croft is not fond of the sea. She is looking forward to a break on the beach in the sun and getting her tan. She would not thank me if I had insisted she come with me. She keeps reminding me that the children would have been a nightmare to handle at sea."

"So when is the big day?" she asked, "I'm anxious to move in."

"If that's your problem, Stella, you can move in immediately. I have no objection. When are you expecting Henry to be back?"

"Oh, he won't be around for a few days," she said, anticipating that when the tape was heard, they would hold off until Lord Croft had left.

The two of them sat swapping stories about the benefits of power over sail for the rest of the afternoon. Roy had opened a bottle of white wine for Stella, whereas he had taken to whisky. Roy excused himself to go and have a word with Elian and Gael to see what the weather forecast was for the next few days, leaving the agent to acquaint herself further with the layout of the castle.

Elian and Gael were studying the map and the four-day forecast when Roy opened the door to the main cabin.

"How's it going, and what's the weather going to be like over the next few days?" Roy asked.

"If we take the southerly route, the weather is good, and the long-range forecast seems excellent. When do you plan on leaving?"

"That's a moot point. I think I would like to leave soon but not to really get underway. I want to make it appear that we are leaving but perhaps put in at Cobh to see Fergus. Then come back in, say, a week to see what activity is going on. We could leave Fiona behind to keep in contact with Cathleen and Bridget. I want to make sure my work to hide our stores and munitions have been successful."

"That's a bit of a risk. What if they discover the new work? What then?" asked Gael.

"If that happened, then it's simple we don't come back until the heat has died down. I can spend a couple of years or so in the West Indies, can't you, ladies?"

The question was answered with broad grins.

"Elian, I want you to open the wall in the main cabin and pack it with euros and dollars. If we have to be there for some time, let's do it with panache. I can afford it."

Roy returned to the lounge, and Agent Marion Stewart, alias Stella, had changed. She must have slipped aboard the yacht whilst Roy was aboard the cruiser. She was dressed in a button through blouse and a knee-length

skirt. The blouse showed off her cleavage to perfection, and the shorter
skirt showed off her calves. She sat on the settee with her knees drawn up
under her, showing a portion of her shapely thighs.

"I took the liberty and poured you another drink, Lord Croft. I hope you
don't mind?" she said.

"I appreciate that, Stella." Roy replied "What are you drinking?" he
enquired.

"The bottle was empty, so I poured myself some of your twenty-year-old
Irish. It's luvly stuff, my boyo. Gives a girl oomph," she said, letting the
lilt of the Irish brogue come through.

By the time Roy was ready for bed, they were both in a mellow mood.

"If you want to stay here tonight, you have a choice: the yacht or one of
the guest bedrooms."

"I'll take one of the guest rooms if I may, Lord Croft, and thank you for
the invitation."

Roy showed her to the bedroom next to his own.

"I've signed the documents, and they are on the table in the dining room.
I'll see you in the morning, Stella. Sleep tight."

Roy would have loved to have taken young Stella to bed, but under no
circumstances was he going to let some pervert in HQ listen in to his
lovemaking. That was strictly taboo, as far as he was concerned, and he lay
back wired up but resolved to keep his own company.

He had been in bed for about twenty minutes when he heard the door
open, and a dark shadow slipped into the room. Roy sat up ready for
anything. He snapped on the side lamp, and there before him stood Stella
in her robe.

"Lord Croft, I thought you would be asleep by now. I was going to wake
you slowly. You can call me Marion, for as you can see there's nowhere to
hide my communication device tonight. I'm definitely off duty."

She opened the robe tantalisingly slowly to reveal her nudity. Roy noticed
that she was naturally auburn or she had a matching colour applied by her
hairdresser. There was no sag in her breasts as she pulled back the covers
and slid in beside his Lordship. Her eyes widened as she said,

"I see you sleep as I do nude 'en flagrante'." Then as she looked harder,
"Oh very nice aren't I a lucky girl?"

Roy drew her into his arms and pressed his lips to hers. Marion was in the
mood, and her pouty lips parted, allowing Roy's tongue to explore further.
Marion had decided that she wanted his Lordship on her own terms, and

no one at the agency was going to be any part of her performance. She gave herself wholeheartedly as Roy's hands explored her body. Their passions rose, and Marion felt she was on fire. Her whole body craved satisfaction, and if what she had read and seen with her own eyes, that was what she was going to get. Anyone listening would have known exactly what was going on in the bedroom, the soft moans coming from Marion's open mouth as Roy satisfied her every need. The wild cry gave no doubt to anyone listening that she had achieved her goal, and this was followed shortly afterwards by an animalistic grunt as Roy once again satisfied his own needs, paying little heed to the possible consequences.

The following morning, Marion awoke, her hair tousled, and the bed looked as though a bunch of wrestlers had been enjoying a wild night. She sat up; there was no sign of Lord Croft. She got out of bed and walked into the bathroom. The full-length mirror showed the marks where Lord Croft's lips had raised bites over her whole body. She was covered in hickies. They were clustered most heavily on her thighs and breasts. She gazed in awe at the sight. If satisfaction had been what she was after, Lord Croft had given it to her. She had never had such a night of unrestricted sex in the whole of her life. When she had thought he was finished, he got up and drank, she presumed whisky, from a hip flask and returned to bed with such renewed energy she thought she had been with another man. She walked lazily back to the bed and looked at her watch; it was nine o'clock in the morning. She had not slept that late in years. She wanted to run downstairs and throw her arms around him and begin again, but she knew her tired body would not allow her to do that. She showered and dressed and walked down the wide staircase, expecting to see him around. He was nowhere to be seen. She walked into the kitchen where Bridget and Cathleen were busy.

"Where's Lord Croft?" she asked as casually as she could.

Bridget turned and took one look at the young woman. Her eyes puffy from lack of sleep, her hair still wet from the shower, and the uneasy way with which she moved said it all. She had spent the night with his Lordship. Bridget nudged Cathleen, and they both smiled.

"Oh, I'm sorry, Mrs Francis. He's left," Bridget said.

"Why didn't you wake me?" Marion asked open-mouthed. She had hoped he would be around for a few days.

"Lord Croft told us to let you sleep in as you had a late night, and if you don't mind me saying so, ma'am, you look as though you need a bit more sleep. You look exhausted," Bridget said with a broad smile. "Where would you like breakfast served?"

"In the dining room," Marion said, her voice showing her disappointment. "Are you expecting him back?"

"The boat was packed for a long trip, ma'am. He told us you would be having the run of the castle for the next year, so I guess he's gone on his long trip, miss. We are not privy to everything his Lordship does, Mrs Francis."

The agent had a leisurely breakfast before she telephoned HQ.

"Lord Croft appears to have left. He's signed the lease, and I guess we have possession for a year. Send in the troops as soon as you're ready. The place appears to be ours," she said, unable to hide the satisfaction of a job well done.

Marion could not put the deep disappointment from her mind; Lord Croft had satisfied her more than any man she had been with. His skill in the art of making a woman feel good was beyond anything she had known. He was one of the few men she had come across who seemed to understand a woman's wants and needs, rather than taking the pleasure just for himself. She knew she would let him take her again if and when he ever came back to see her.

Later in the day, vehicles began to arrive, and it was like a military operation as the team began to check around. Dogs sniffed for explosives and drugs, but the aniseed Roy had added to the polish and paint made sure the dogs failed in their attempts. The team tapped and checked everywhere over the next few days and came up empty-handed. They found nothing to give them any clue what Lord Croft had in common with the IRA. They drew a complete blank. The majority of vehicles began to leave one by one, a smaller group was left to check the grounds under the watchful eye of the gardeners, and Agent Marion Stewart was left to sit out the tenancy or until Lord Croft or one of the IRA in the area gave something away, which in Marion's mind did not seem likely in the near future; things had been tidied away too carefully. What she did not know was that the station head had other things planned. The head of their section was determined to get to the bottom of Lord Croft's little game.

Chapter 21

Roy and his crew of two left early. Although he had enjoyed what delights Marion or Stella had to give, he had no intention of facing her that morning. They moved slowly out of the sheltered castle harbour and turned south. The swell was reasonably calm for the time of year, and Roy was tempted to keep going. The cruiser was fully equipped for the journey, but something made him hold back. It was curiosity. He was determined to find out if the so-called experts could find the treasures he had so cunningly concealed. If he were to return, as he had promised Sam, he had to know. He knew it was curiosity that finally killed the cat, but he could not help himself. He put it down to pride. He had to know if he could really outwit the experts, for that was what the agency held itself out to be.

He rang Sam and told him what he had done by letting the castle to the British Secret Service Agency for a whole year. Sam was horrified.

"That's a hell of a risk to take, Roy. What made you do such a crazy thing?" Sam asked.

"I had to know if my carefully designed changes to the castle were effective or not. I could not just come back and be arrested. If my changes pass muster, then I know I'm in the clear. Now, before you say anything more, I want you to keep a watchful eye on the place. Get the gardeners to report to you every week," Roy requested.

"They do that already, so there's no change there," Sam replied.

"You mean you watch me?" Roy said incredulously.

"How do you think we have survived all through the trouble, Roy? We keep a watch on everybody. Even I am not free from surveillance from time to time. Believe me, it's necessary to survive. I recommend you do more of it yourself."

Roy acknowledged that what Sam was saying was the only way the IRA had survived during the trouble when the countryside had been crawling with British spies and undercover agents. Then he told Sam that he was holing up in Cobh for a few days before returning to pick up Fiona, adding that, if the worst came to the worst and the agency discovered his hidden cache of arms, the game would be up for him, and he would have to leave her behind and she would have to rejoin him in Spain or Portugal. Sam listened intently. The thought of the discovery of one of his most trusted men required planning. He would have some of his men in the grounds of the castle and, if necessary, he would wipe out the whole bloody lot of them and dump their bodies where they would never be found as they had done during the trouble. The place was so secret only three people in the world knew where it was, and they would never divulge the location as they would be jailed by the British, where they could easily be got at or disposed of by the hidden IRA sleepers.

"Leave it to me, Roy. I'm sure things will be OK. If I have to, I'll get Fiona down to Cobh by road to meet up with you. Now, Fergus is away doing a collection off the north coast of Africa, so take his berth and await his return. I'm sure you can amuse yourself for a few days, especially with that glamorous crew of yours," and he gave a deep chuckle. "I'll keep in touch, so don't worry yourself about a thing."

Roy felt much better about things, knowing that Sam was fully in charge, and he went ashore at Cobh with his crew for a well-earned meal in one of the local pubs. He was in need of something substantial like a steak and Guinness pie, home baked in the pub's own kitchen. His mouth watered as he savoured the taste. The meal was just as good as he had anticipated and, returning to the cruiser, he was pleasantly surprised when Gael joined him in his cabin, leaving Elian on watch. Elian was taking no chances with all that cash on board; she had been worried when they had left to have a meal and had been constantly on edge throughout the meal, and as a result, she was suffering badly with indigestion.

Over the next few days, Roy was kept informed by Fiona, Cathleen, Bridget, and Sam Delaney. He listened carefully as they told him how a team of people had arrived and had searched, poked, prodded, and drilled but had failed to find anything significant. One of Sam's men had found one man poking around in the rubbish, and when he found a couple of shell casings and a magazine left over from World War II, he had quietly disposed of him. The search for the missing man took the heat away from the house, but after a detailed search in the grounds and the surrounding area over a period of several days, with no sign of the missing man, the manhunt was handed over to the Garda as a missing person file. The last team had finally given up and driven away completely deflated, one man short, and nothing to show for their efforts. Agent Marion Stewart was left in charge of the castle in case anything or anyone turned up to incriminate

Lord Croft. She, of course, was delighted to have the opportunity to sail off the west coast with full pay and a stunning place like Lord Croft's castle to live in.

Roy waited for the safe return of Fergus, but when he had not returned by the scheduled date, he rang Sam. Sam explained that the drop had been delayed due to the sailing from South America being delayed whilst the ship waited for a late cargo. Roy decided to make his trip back to pick up Fiona and bid farewell to the attractive Mrs Francis, or was it Miss Stewart? Her yacht was not in the harbour when Roy pulled alongside the quay. He went ashore, leaving Elian to top off the fuel. He walked up to the kitchen and was welcomed by Bridget and Cathleen, who gave him a complete rundown of where and how the search had gone.

"They spent a long time in the boathouse but discovered nothing. They found a couple of hiding places in the panelling that even we did not know were there. But other than that, they found nothing untoward. Then one of their men mysteriously vanished." Cathleen paused for breath.

"That man going missing caused a stir, I can tell you, sir," Bridget said. "They had men searching everywhere in the grounds and all over the estate, but they never found hide or hair of the man. It was just like during the trouble. A man would just vanish into thin air like magic. None of them were ever found either."

"Where's Mrs Francis?" Roy asked, for that was the name the staff knew her by.

"Oh, she's out sailing her boat, sir. Out most days she is. Usually comes back about tea time hungry as a hunter," said Bridget with a smile. "She seems settled, if you ask me. She's going to be here for the duration of the lease, sir. She's no trouble."

Walking back along the quayside, Roy spotted the sail, and shortly after, Stella's yacht slid silently into the harbour. Gael and Elian tied up the lines, and with a broad smile, the yachtswoman stepped ashore. Her auburn hair windswept, her face ruddy from the breeze, and the roughness of her clothing gave her an appealing appearance. Her face lit up in surprise.

"I saw the cruiser and wondered if it was you. Why didn't you let me know you were still around?" she asked.

"I understood you were busy whilst I was away," Roy responded, giving her a look of disapproval.

"You heard then. I'm sorry, but there was nothing I could do to prevent it. Somebody at the top must have a grudge against you or your local IRA, which by association has targeted you." Then she smiled and asked, "Will you be staying for supper then or are you off on your long trip?"

"I'll stay if you wish. I'm waiting for an extra member of my crew to arrive."

The meal was served by Cathleen in the dining room, and it was strange for Roy to be sitting in his own home and not be the master of the house. The meal, however, was excellent as usual as Bridget had gone out of her way to make it something special as a send-off for his Lordship. They moved into the lounge where Marion, Mrs Stella Francis to the staff, poured Roy his favourite tipple and poured one for herself.

"This must be strange to you, having me wait on you in your own house, Lord Croft."

"I think we know each other well enough to cut out the formalities. I believe Roy would sit better on the tongue. After all, we know each other fairly intimately, don't you think, Marion?" Roy said, smiling.

"Very intimately, Roy. I was devastated when I woke and found you had left already. Why didn't you wake me up before you left? Was I that bad that you could not face me the following morning? Do you realise what it does to a woman to wake up alone after such a night, you wicked man?"

"Sorry, Marion, but needs must. We both had things to do. You had to contact HQ, and I had business to attend to."

It got late, and Marion asked Roy if he cared to stay. His reply was as old as the hills,

"I thought you'd never ask. Of course I'll stay, but I can't promise I'll be here in the morning."

When Marion awoke, he had gone. The bed was cold, but she lay back with the wanton look of a woman who had been up most of the night with a stud of note. She lay there thankful that her team had been unable to find any incriminating evidence. She would have been sorry to see Lord Croft, no it was Roy now, in jail. It would have been such a waste. She was well aware she was just one of the many women he had pleased in his lifetime, but she had enjoyed every minute of it. She would have to ask him about the drink in the hip flask. It had made him recover almost instantly, and they had made love well into the night. She decided to be decadent; she wrapped her gown around her body to hide the hickies Roy had raised, and called down to Bridget to serve breakfast in bed. It was a luxury she did not take often, but today, she was just too tired to go sailing. It would wait until tomorrow. Today she would lie in bed, relax with her memories of Roy, and she only hoped he would visit her again during her tenancy.

Roy had set out before dawn. The three crew members had been woken up when he came aboard; he had showered and had that flush of recent sexual activity in his face. He still had plenty of energy, and whilst they scrambled out of bed and dressed, Roy had cast off and was heading out to sea. Elian was the first to appear.

"My, aren't we bright and bushy-tailed this morning. Dare I ask who got the cream?"

she said, her eyes bright and her smile indicating that she was well aware where he had spent the night and with whom.

"None of your business, Elian. Let's get this show on the road. We have a long journey ahead of us. Has Fiona started breakfast? I could eat a horse this morning."

Elian stood beside him and just let out a hum, drawing the sound out to emphasise that she was familiar with his appetite, especially after a wild night of sex.

Light was beginning to lighten the night sky as Fiona appeared with bacon sandwiches and mugs of hot laced coffee.

"Thanks, Fiona," Roy said with a grin on his face. "You always know your way into a man's heart. These taste wonderful. Just keep them coming. I'm hungry this morning."

Fiona tossed her head, sending her hair in a wave behind her, and with a mischievous smile, she called back jovially,

"I wonder why?" she asked.

"Cheeky monkey!" Roy shouted as she disappeared down to the lower deck.

Roy gave the order to head for Cobh. He wanted to be sure Fergus had got back safely. When they arrived, the berth was empty. Roy called Sam, who confirmed that the drop had taken place, but he had not had confirmation that Fergus had recovered the cargo.

"Don't give me the coordinates over the phone." Roy said, "Send them by SMS on the other phone. I'll check as I am heading south."

Sam was pleased to have Roy checking for him. He was sorry to see him go. He would miss him, and so would Kate. She had been snappy ever since Roy had announced his intention to leave.

They headed south at a fast rate of knots, watching out for Fergus on the way. Roy tried to call him on the short wave, but he would only get the call if he was within range. There was no sign of him as they headed across the Bay of Biscay or at A Coruna, where he would call in for fuel. It was a mystery that needed to be solved before Roy attempted to cross the Atlantic. They were heading out of the Spanish port and turning south when Roy's short wave call was answered by Fergus. He had been held in the port of Cadiz when they had been boarded and searched by the Spanish customs. Roy asked Fergus to meet him back in A Coruna, where they could discuss the matter in private. Roy gave the order, and they swung around in a wide arc and headed back into port to be joined later by Fergus in the other cruiser.

Fergus came alongside and went up to the upper deck with Roy.

"It was very strange," Fergus began. "We were waiting for the last minute coordinates to arrive when this bloody Spanish patrol boat came alongside. The captain was a woman, would you believe? Well, she was determined we were doing something criminal and demanded to search the boat. Christ, we weren't doing anything wrong, but we were in Spanish waters, so I really had no choice but to agree. Two of her men went below, and she demanded to see the ship's log. I showed it to her along with the ship's papers, and she went on to the radio and did some checking with her base. Whatever they told her seemed to work wonders. The two men came up from below, giving us a clean bill of health. She gave me a dazzling smile and, of all things, said, 'I'm sorry to have bothered you. Give my regards to his Lordship. Tell him I miss him'. Then she went back on to her boat, and that was the last I saw of them. Christ, it was uncanny."

"It must have been Captain Cordoba. Catalina Cordoba, an old friend of mine," Roy said.

"No, the first name was correct, but she called herself Captain Mendoza," Fergus replied.

"Oh, she must have married her army officer then. Good for her." Roy commented almost casually

"Bloody hell! I beg your pardon, Lord Croft, but you do seem to know a lot of people," Fergus said surprised at Roy's intimate knowledge of the Spanish Captain.

Roy smiled at the memory of his last meeting with the captain.

"Oh yes, we know each other very well. You could say intimately, although I have to confess I've never met her husband." Roy admitted with a grin.

"Well," Fergus continued, "they had not left five minutes when the coordinates came through. Well, I couldn't leave immediately. It would have looked strange, so I delayed for several hours and then headed for the spot. The buggers could not have made the drop in a worse place. The current was fairly strong, and we had to follow the drift. It took us hours to locate the cargo. It was smack in one of the shipping lanes. We had to wait again for the tide to carry it clear, always listening for the sonar. Finally, we managed to recover the parcels and put them below. On the way back, we spotted the Spanish naval vessel, and would you believe it, she gave us a bloody toot on their fog horn and had the bloody temerity to wave. I almost had a bloody heart attack, but she never came towards us. She let us go undisturbed. I have never had such a close shave in my life. I thought we were goners for sure."

"Fergus, if they did not discover your armaments when they went below, then they would not have found the drugs. You forget they are wrapped up in airtight bags inside an airtight waterproof container that had been in the sea for hours. There would have been nothing to give you away, unless they had boarded you immediately after recovery, and the wet decks would have led them to the hiding place." Roy said with conviction.

"We wipe them dry before taking them below, your Lordship, so they would not have been able to spot the wet trail," Fergus grinned.

"Good one, Fergus. I always knew you were the right man for the job. With all that protection, even if you were boarded by a group with sniffer dogs, unless you opened the parcels to check on the contents, they would not have found any signs of the drugs."

"I never open them until I'm back and safe in the hideout, your Lordship."

"Fergus, how many times do I have to tell you it's Roy. Drop the bloody title, will you? I'll have you bowing and scraping in a minute. Here, have a drink and relax. You've been blooded and survived. Don't worry."

The two men sat down and drank a couple of glasses. They shook hands, and Roy gave the order to head south. They were on their way to Barbados where Janet, his wife, was waiting in the Sand Piper Hotel. Little did he know that the agency had already targeted her for further investigation. He waved as Fergus followed him and turned north, heading for Ireland.

Roy used the satellite phone and left a message for Sam. *Fergus, mission accomplished, am on my way.* There was no reply. Roy did not expect one, but he was on his way to cross one of the most unpredictable stretches of water in a seventy-five-foot boat.

They stopped off in Cadiz to refuel and fill the towable fuel tank, supported by the two inflatable floats that would be towed behind the cruiser to refuel part way across the Atlantic. Roy knew it would slow them down, but with no definite arrival date and three lovely women aboard, he was in no great hurry to get to his destination. If he had known what the agency had in store for Lady Janet, he would not have been so sure that taking his time was the best way forward. He would only get to know that once he had arrived at his destination. They continued in blissful ignorance of what lay ahead.

End of Book One

Lightning Source UK Ltd.
Milton Keynes UK
UKOW040647290313

208378UK00002B/50/P